The Wrath of Charlotte

by Michelle Harvey

Copyright © <2016> <MichelleHarvey>

All rights reserved.

ISBN: 1535328673
ISBN-13:9781535328678

To Daniel and Vienna-Reese who have supported me on this quest.
xxx

Cover Design by Studios East Ltd
www.studioseast.co.uk

Follow Michelle Harvey on Twitter @MichelleHarveyx

Chapter 1

I never understood why the hospital didn't stagger the visiting times rather than attempt to squeeze everyone in at once. A hospital that brags it serves over 230,000 people with forty-seven departments and countless units and clinics, only has enough parking spaces for 250 cars.

I drove around again through the tight spaces of illegally parked cars. Some had parked on the pathway and some on the newly cut grass lawns. I narrowly squeezed past one blocking the bike sheds and headed for the staff car park to try my luck. Though I worked at the hospital, there was a strict 'no work, no parking' rule but it was getting close to my aunt's X-ray appointment and if I was late I would never hear the end of it. The staff carpark was as equally full with an equal amount of stupidly parked cars, many had blocked other cars in hoping for the best. I saw my best friend Amber's silver Mazda blocking in the manager of our departments new black Mercedes. Anyone else would have been given a warning, but not Amber, she had the gift of the gab and could get away with practically anything.

I let out a puff of air and headed out to the only street nearby that wasn't resident only parking. By some miracle I found a parking space by a red mini and pulled in. My car was a ridiculous size considering there was only me and my husband Scott that ever occupied it and since having a miscarriage and no further luck in the conception department, it didn't look like that situation was going to change any time soon. As a result I felt like I was driving a bus when a two seater Smart car would have done. I checked my wheel was within the drop down of the curb and that the mini had enough room to get out, satisfied, I sprinted towards the hospital.

"Charlotte! I thought you would be here an hour ago," my aunt snapped. The lady behind the desk raised an eyebrow and continued with her typing.

"Sorry, I had trouble parking." I took a seat beside her and checked the clock on the wall. I was still early and they had only wheeled her from her ward upstairs which they wouldn't have done too early before her appointment.

"I hate sitting here by myself, you know that," Maureen snapped again. Clearly she had been sitting here long enough to brood.

"Sorry," I apologised again. "I worked last night and have only had three hours sleep. What is your daughter doing today? Couldn't she have sat with you?" I said more to the earwigging receptionist than to my aunt.

"Melissa has two babies to look after." She shook her head keeping her eye on the consultant's door willing it to open faster.

"Babies?" I laughed. "Her youngest is twelve and they're both at school." The receptionist looked up and shot me a sympathetic look.

"She's busy," Maureen spat, signalling the end of that conversation. "Did you write my cards?" She brightened a little at the remembrance of the favour that had taken me all day to complete.

"Yes, and put in the money as you asked, is the money upstairs? I can wheel you up after." Having been in hospital for nearly a month now Maureen had written off Christmas. It had been her eldest, Steven, who had persuaded her to get me to buy (and write) all her cards and put money in them. Now I was £300 down and really needed it back to put diesel in the car.

"I thought I had given that to you already, you can't keep taking advantage of me just because I've had a water infection and am not in my right mind. I can't keep dishing out cash." She stood up as the door opened and snapped that I should stay where I was.

"No! You asked me to do the cards and you would get Steven to withdraw the money out when you saw him next. Have you seen him this week?" I tried to keep it light, she was clearly in one of her moods.

"Yes, and I know this has already been dealt with, don't bring it up again." She pushed past the nurse who called her name nearly knocking her off her feet.

I shook my head in disbelief. She expected to die at any minute and as a result had me eating out of the palm of her hand. Steven could have written her cards for her or even made this appointment, he worked from home, why was I the only one jumping through her hoops? I couldn't just lose £300 especially not now the department were increasing my hours but reducing my pay. I needed every penny I could get, more now than ever.

Her mood hadn't improved after the appointment and she refused my offer to wheel her back to her ward.

I shook it off. She had suffered a stroke as well as several water infections, maybe she had earned her right to be grumpy and after my mum died when I was twelve, it was Maureen who looked after me and my brother, Josh. My dad had worked offshore and was never home, so maybe £300, in her eyes, was the least I could do.

I pushed through the wind back to my car and cursed the hospital's carpark and the English weather. I cursed even more when I saw the neatly placed parking ticket on my windscreen.

I read the notification in disbelief. I had violated code twenty-seven and had parked over a drop down curb. I shook my head again and glanced towards the house behind me and saw the curtain twitch. I huffed and went to open my driver door when I noticed the scratch. A key had been dragged along the driver's side door right across to the rear passengers door. I swung my head back towards the house and saw the floral curtain move again.

Scott was going to kill me.

I cried all the way home some for the car, some for my lost £300 and a lot for the unfair ticket.

It was just going to be one of those days.

I let Scott rant about it while I appealed the ticket. I had taken some photos myself that clearly showed that I had not blocked the drive and that my wheel wasn't over the dropdown. The traffic warden had taken some of his own photos all of which I believed backed up my argument. The driveway was double the size of most of the others down Old School Close, it wasn't as if they couldn't get out if they had needed to. I signed out and went to take a shower to see if I could wash off some of my stress.

Usually I fall asleep as soon as my head hits the pillow but I couldn't sleep. I kept my eyes shut and worried about the ticket. I felt Scott shift beside me but I kept my eyes shut. I didn't want another argument about the scratch or the ticket. I had offered to pay for the damage and I couldn't really do anything else about it.

Scott mumbled something and then got out of bed. He walked past the en-suite and went into the bathroom which usually only I use. I leant over and checked my phone, it was three in the morning! I had another morning shift at seven and really needed to fall asleep. I tried deep breaths to shift the uneasy feeling that had been sitting on my chest all day. I couldn't control it so just needed to think about something else.

I swung my legs out of bed and took a sip of the cordial on Scott's side of the bed, he obviously couldn't sleep either. Words reached my ears and I crept into the hallway. It was three in the morning and Scott was on his mobile phone!

Working late I knew all too well how to sneak about silently. I kept my feet to the outside of the landing and made no sound. I stopped outside the bathroom door and listened carefully. If caught I would simply say I was getting a different drink, we had different tastes so it was a plausible lie.

"After Christmas, for sure," I heard Scott whisper. Why on earth was he on a call at this hour? I leant in closer. "I know I have taken my time but I needed to be sure. I know, I love you too. Be patient," he whispered.

My skin went cold and my legs went numb. Scott was saying 'I love you' to someone other than me! I forced my legs to move to get back to the bed but they didn't want to cooperate. I sank to the floor and sobbed. I could still hear the muffled sound of Scott whispering his sweet nothings but I could no longer make out the words. There was ringing in my ears that physically hurt and a razor sharp lump in my throat. I felt like I was in a dream where your legs get stuck into the floor while the nightmare closes in around you. I used my arms in an army style crawl and made it back to the bed. My skin had developed a sweat but I was freezing. My whole body had been washed with an ice cold feeling that numbed me to my core. Why would he do this to me?

I faked sleep when he returned to the room and reasoned with myself until the sun came up. Scott wouldn't cheat on me, not after everything we had been. Through there was only one way to be sure, I needed to get my hands on his phone.

Chapter 2

My brother Josh is a computer genius. Not every sister can brag that their brother works for the British government but I can. Well, actually I can't, not really, the government frowns upon such careless talk, but still he has impressive credentials. While most of his friends were out getting drunk or stoned or whatever teenage boys do to show they are hip and trendy, Josh was cooped up in his room learning all he could about computers, hacking, programming and all manner of geeky coding that he could absorb into his brain. Maureen's son, Steven, tried to get him interested in the mechanics business to follow in his footsteps to no avail. So on the frequent occasions we stayed at their house Josh stayed in his room with his laptop dreaming of ways to change the world. As a result of his hard work and dedication he had passed two degrees with first class honours, moved to London and earned a small fortune doing a job he was passionate about.

I could have phoned him about the phone cloning device but being the general do-gooder that he was, he would have talked me out of it. He would have said very simply that he never liked Scott anyway and to divorce him and move on. But there was part of me that still doubted what I had heard. I was upset about the parking ticket and was extremely tired, I could have misheard.

I tried to concentrate on plausible explanations and carried on flicking through all of Josh's coursework boxes that he kept at mine from when he lived here during college. One of his papers had been on how monitoring the world, though an invasion of privacy, can and does save the world. His research had been on phone cloning and preventing crime before it happened. I had proofread the document but not having been that interested in it at the time had forgotten the majority of the information.

I started on the second box.

Scott had left earlier than usual this morning and had taken his phone into the ensuite with him so I had been unable to look at it. I wasn't sure if I was overly paranoid but everything he was doing was suspicious. Did he always take his phone in the shower or leave this early for work? It was now eight, he didn't have to be at work until ten, the same as me on a Tuesday and what was all this talking in hushed seductive tones all about? He had never been quiet on my account before.

I shook my head again and pushed down the ice cold feeling that kept spreading inside. Scott could simply be arranging my Christmas present and the call could have been his ill sister Sarah who had just moved over from Canada to spend out her remaining days with her family. I didn't know exactly what the time difference was but she might have been jet lagged. It was a perfectly good explanation, though the chemotherapy had affected her hearing. Scott always shouted when they were on the phone together which is why she much preferred text messages, not such a perfect explanation.

I refocused on the box.

Found it. I flicked through the document and considered putting it back into the box and forgetting about the whole thing. I was happy with Scott, he wasn't violent or difficult to live with. Okay, so the miscarriage had been a low point, he had gotten over it much quicker than I had but he had been loving and patient. I had never been given the impression that he wasn't happy.

I carried the dissertation down stairs and flicked the kettle on. Thinking about the miscarriage had darkened my mood and I was determined now again to know for sure. I searched the index until I found the relevant page which included a picture. The phone cloning machine looked a lot like a debit card payment collection machine that they used in shops and restaurants. It worked by attaching the machine into the charger socket of a phone and all the details were saved onto a memory card and Sim card. There was then a dock which was linked to a computer or if a similar phone was available, the Sim and card could be entered into a second phone and all the information would be available. When the first phone got a text, the cloned phone would get the text, if it got a call, the cloned phone would receive the call too.

I fired up my computer. There were three I could buy, none of which were cheap or the exact one Josh had written his paper on so I ordered the one that looked like the nearest thing. I wasn't Josh when it came to technology, I think mostly because having a techno wiz brother, he always set everything up for me and I never had to think about it for myself. I confirmed the payment before I had the chance to change my mind. I paid the extra ten pounds to have the same day delivery, the idea of waiting one more day seemed unbearable despite the fact that I couldn't really afford it especially now Maureen hadn't paid me back the £300 she owed me and now that I may have an unfair parking ticket to pay for.

I stashed Josh's paper back in the attic and tried to forget about it. I had a shift in an hour which didn't leave me with a lot of time to get ready and find a dreaded parking space.

I found a space in the corner of the staff car park and celebrated my luck with a mini dance in the car that, luckily, no one saw.

"Morning," I yelled to Cassie, the receptionist for our department.

"I didn't realise you were in today, I thought you were at your cabin already," she smiled, walking over to her new coffee making machine. "Got time for a cuppa?"

I nodded and smiled at how easily distracted from her work she was. Any excuse to abandon it and she was off. As a result, I usually nabbed a couple of hours of overtime to help get her paperwork up-to-date, so I never made her crack on. I got coffee, more gossip than I could handle and extra money in my wage packet at the end of the month which, this month, was going to be a God send. I had really needed that promotion and not being successful had been a blow.

Scott's parent's usually paid for the cabin as a Christmas treat for us but this year they had asked us all to chip in so they could concentrate their money on helping Sarah to get better. All in all I was working all the hours that existed just to keep afloat. I wasn't exactly sure where all our money went lately, but somewhere there was a never ending whirlpool that sucked it all up and left me feeling depressed. Amber earned less than me, having never taken the time or trouble to put herself through training, but was still managing to spend New Year in New York. I envied her tremendously. I wasn't sure how she managed to afford her flash new car or endless holidays but I suspected her new finance, David, had something to do with it. He was besotted with her and she knew she had fallen on her feet.

"Amber bought us this for our engagement," Cassie boomed, as if knowing Amber had been on my mind. "I have two and couldn't bare to return it."

"It's a great idea. You do spend most of your time here and this way Amber gets some benefit out of it to," I marvelled. I had put £20 in Cassie's card and considered that ample but Amber had managed a £100 coffee machine for a girl she hardly knew and I knew why. Amber had a gift of getting in the middle of everything and giving a good engagement gift increased the chances of an all day wedding invitation.

I flicked open Cassie's wedding planner that lived on her desk, another reason why her work was never done, and flicked through the all day invite list and sure enough Amber's name had been added to the bottom. I glanced at the evening list and Amber's name had never been on it. She had leap frogged straight on to the A-list and I smiled at her cleverness. I had often wished I had half of her gift for the gab, no one could jump queues in clubs or get served first at bars like Amber. It was like if she expected it then others thought she deserved it and gave it to her. I had tried to be that confident several times but there was just something about me that couldn't quite pull it off. You either had it or you didn't and I just didn't.

"How is all the wedding planning going?" I asked as she presented me with a chocolate topped cappuccino that Costa would have been proud of.

"Ooh, it's very exciting and exhausting. We keep remembering people and then those people are linked to someone else and you feel like you can't invite this person without inviting that person. I'm so worried about offending people but Grant keeps getting cross and telling me to cut back." She blew on her coffee.

"I'm sure you will work it out. Just remember that it is all about the two of you and no one else." I was glad I wasn't doing it all again. My family was tiny and Scott's wasn't that much bigger so who to invite hadn't really been a problem.

"Yes, doing the final invites tonight with Amber over some wine," she smiled.

"Sounds girlie fun." I tried to keep the bitterness of not being invited out of my voice. Cassie had always been *my* friend until I had gotten Amber the job at the hospital, since then I felt like I had been pushed out a bit. Cassie used to do these hilarious girls games nights which were always a monthly highlight but since moving in with Grant these had been scrapped for occasional, smaller gatherings, these gatherings had always included me though. Amber and Cassie were my best friends and I had to admit I was a little hurt.

"Yes, Amber offered to help. She has started coming up here for tea breaks now."

"Well, it is good stuff." I gulped down my coffee and headed with the cup towards the sink when Amber walked in followed by a yelling Grant.

"You are over half an hour late," he yelled.

"I had to feed my uncle's cat then my carpark space was taken. It isn't my fault, it is this hospital's car parking system, it's shocking," she said in her faint American accent.

"Don't do it again or I will regret my decision." Grant said, backing down like I knew he would, no one could resist Amber's charm.

"Don't yell in here sweetie," Cassie purred and blew Grant a kiss. "You know the parking is terrible, just ask Charlotte, she just got a ticket because of this place, didn't she Amber?" Amber nodded.

"Or you could just ask me as I'm still in the room," I raised my eyebrows and turned my cup over to dry.

"And shouldn't you be at work?" Grant yelled at me and looked at his watch. "Oh, you're early," he smiled an apology which was rare enough for me that I was satisfied. "Oh and I haven't received that paperwork from you."

"I'll get it to you soon," I forced a smile. Getting my hours increased and my wages cut was not something I wanted to even fake happiness about. There was something about signing the piece of paperwork acknowledging the fact that it was happening that offended me greatly.

I ignored their banter behind me for a while and concentrated on the lost property boxes. Everything got left here, there were no end to the uncollected purses, teddy bears and gifts but these were not what I was interested in. I glanced at the drawer that was labelled phones and glanced inside, there were all sorts but none like Scott's. I shut the drawer and wondered what he had done with his old one since his last upgrade. No doubt there would be a drawer in the garage somewhere that contained twenty or so of his old models.

I went on with my rounds and tried not to think about anything at all except the people in front of me, but the fact that Christmas was a week away was hard to ignore. Each patient seemed to have decorated their bays in their own little way to try and lift their spirits but all it did was dampen mine. I was supposed to be going to the cabin on Christmas Eve for ten days with a man that may, or may not, be cheating on me.

The parcel was waiting for me when I got home as was Scott.

"It is a new camera lens," I lied. He pulled a face and went back into the kitchen to make himself a coffee. Photography was a passion of mine but it drove him nuts. He said that it made every journey ten times longer because of the constant stopping and he was right. I saw photographic opportunities everywhere and sometimes, if I was in the mood, I could take pictures of a tree silhouetted against the sun all evening if given the chance.

I took the parcel upstairs and unpacked it in the spare room. If caught here I could always use the pretext of wrapping the remainder of the Christmas presents and if he knocked it was a good enough reason to look guilty.

The device was smaller than I expected and actually looked quite simple to use. I had decided to call it Rob. It's very purpose was to rob people of their information and it suited my brain well. I could also think of it as a friend helping me out. Rob would tell the truth and could be relied on better than Scott's words. I knew if I simply asked him what was going on he would deny it and be in a mood with me for bringing it up. I would feel guilty and probably spend the rest of my life feeling rubbish about mentioning it and over compensate with kindness. I plugged the device in to charge and covered it up with wrapping paper. It was unlikely that Scott would set foot in this room but still I wasn't going to take any chances now I had come this far.

"My phone is playing up have you got one of your old ones I could borrow please?"

"Yeah, sure they are in the garage," he smiled, turning back to the stir fry. "No wait, it's okay, I'll get it for you." He switched off the heat and rushed off to the garage. Yesterday my first thought would have been how sweet he was making us tea then dropping everything to get me a phone, but now my paranoia was working overtime. Why didn't he want me in the garage? What didn't he want me to see?

He came back and plugged a phone into the wall. It was the same make as the one he had now and was perfect.

"I had to check as they don't all have chargers," he smiled and returned to our tea.

"Thanks, this is perfect," I said.

I watched him as he bustled in the kitchen. His soft whistle as he stirred in the sauce calmed me and made me question my actions, could this all be in my head? I had never had reason to doubt him before. He was sweet, that was why I had married him. Amber had said he was too safe and I never really knew what she had meant. Could being *too* nice ever be a problem? He looked good, worked hard and earned good money and as a result we lived in a house larger than we needed and were happy.

I had only ever been in one other relationship before hand so didn't have the same amount of men to compare him to as Amber had. I smiled thinking about Miles. He had been an American college student who joined our college for just over a year while his family were over here on business and he was everything that Amber had thought she had wanted. She had dreamed of going back to America for most of our high school life. She had got me in a frenzy about it until a savings jar had been created and the whole trip had been meticulously planned out - until Miles Truman came along. Miles was, in my opinion, a god. He had sandy blonde hair, deep brown eyes, a square jaw and a brooding stare that stunned even the teachers. He was like a young Elvis and James Dean rolled into one and everyone was nuts about him, especially Amber. She made no secret about wanting him in her bed and he wasted no time shutting her down. She had thought being a fellow American, despite the fact that she had moved away from Wisconsin when she was two and actually couldn't remember a thing about it, he would feel some kind of affinity towards her like they were meant to be but he simply waved his hand and announced she wasn't his type. We were all amazed, Amber was in disbelief. I don't think anyone had ever turned her down. She tried several more times until the night of Lloyd Kingston's party. Amber had downed numerous shots of Tequila and made a play for him during an epic beer pong battle. She told him that she was hot, he was hot, think about the hot children they would have. They were both American, they belonged together. He had smiled at her, oblivious to her charms and looked her straight in the eye with one of his smouldering looks. All the girls, including me, practically fainted with the beauty of it all but then what came out of his mouth was blunt and to the point. He told her that he saw her and knew her type. She thought the whole of America must be crying in their sleep over the loss of Amber Mason but it wasn't. Here she was a cute American, but in America she would be nothing, she was exactly the same as every other shallow, self obsessed Barbie doll screaming for attention. If she really wanted to know what every American boy dreamed of, it was charming English girls who respected themselves and others. Amber had fallen a couple of steps back in shock then something registered in her face. Miles had smiled and put his arm around my waist. Then he said to Amber that he liked me and that she needed to stop being weird about it. Amber had stomped away and me and Miles had spent the whole evening kissing and that night he had seduced me completely. Six months later when he had to return to America I had been devastated but keen, more than ever, on mine and Amber's trip to the USA, but Amber had already scrapped the idea. The world was a big place and there were a million and one other places she wanted to visit more. Soon she was excited about Paris and Rome and each week brought a new place that excited her more. America was never mentioned again.

It was through Amber that I met Scott. She was a member at his gym and she had dated his training buddy, Ian, for a couple of months then she had moved on to another member of staff whose name I have already forgotten. She then gave up on the gym and dated Rhys from the hospital before finally meeting David through her dodgy cousin, Thomas.

I had attended a few Aqua-aerobic classes with her before I gave up trying to be thin and learned to love my size fourteen body. She would always drag me over to Scott at the end of a session to ask about how Ian was doing and Scott always joked that he was falling apart without her and pining away without her love. The truth was Ian had never actually left his first girlfriend to date Amber and they were now happily married with two children but Amber knew this now. Ian was best man at our wedding and of course, he brought his wife not realising that me and Amber were such good friends. Not awkward at all!

Scott announced that the stir fry was ready and I busied myself with plates and cutlery, trying to avoid eye contact. I dreaded him looking at me and asking me if something was wrong. I wasn't ready to answer that question yet. We sat and watched a film while we ate. I took the seat furthest from the TV and watched him more than the film he had chosen about boxing. He checked his phone several times and I realised I was counting without even realising it. Guilty or not, the trust had gone. A few texts came through and every smile on his face was a stab through my heart. I rationalised that it could be Sarah or another family member but then again they were not really close or random text kind of people.

I could have just asked him. I didn't know what I was so afraid of. He would either say, 'yes' or 'no' but I then I knew that I wouldn't hear the end of it. There was no point in rocking the boat if there was an easier way. With the device I could know for certain. I wouldn't need his twisted version of the truth or upset him with my crazy paranoia. He needn't ever know I had doubted him.

His phone beeped a couple more times and I knew soon enough he would have to go upstairs and put it on charge. This was usually an every night activity for him but it was always right by his head. I hadn't been able to find out how long the device would take to get all the information off and would it be a silent operation? I really needed him out of the room.

"I think I'm going to go on the treadmill for a while," he announced after the film had finished predictably. Usually he would take his phone and earphones and be gone for at least an hour.

"I'm going to jump in the bath. It's been a stressful week and it's only Tuesday," I forced a smile and jogged up the stairs to run a bath. I filled it with bubbles and grabbed my book from the bedside table. I hadn't read in a while and didn't think I would be able to concentrate on it now but it was just a prop. I slid in the water and watched him get changed into a different pair of joggers.

"Do you want me to lock you in?" He stood at the door with a hand towel around his neck.

"If you are going to be a while," I smiled sweetly. "I will still probably be in here when you're done."

"Okay," he reached over and planted a kiss on my forehead. I listened for the sound of him locking the side door and waited until I heard the rumble of the garage door lift up but the sound never came. I sat up as if I would be able to hear better if I was higher but there was nothing to hear. I craned my neck but couldn't see if he had left his phone behind or not. I reached for the towel just as the side door unlocked and Scott came running back in. I swooped up my book and opened it on a random page.

"Forgot water," he said as he ran back up the stairs. I heard the familiar beep of his phone being plugged in. "Be back soon." He blew me a kiss this time and went back down the stairs and out of the house.

I waited until I heard the garage door go up and back down before I crept out of the bath. I slipped on his towelling dressing gown and dried my legs and feet. I retrieved the Rob device from the charger and hoped Scott's phone was charged enough for it to work. I plugged the small lead into Scott's phone and waited for a signal that it was working while listening carefully for the garage door. A messaged flashed on Rob's screen. I entered Scott's passcode and pressed enter. Another messaged flashed up, did I want all or partial data? I selected all. Did I want the data saved to Sim or card? I selected Sim. Did I want to track this phone? I selected yes and started to panic. How many questions were there going to be? What would I say if Scott caught me?

A progress bar appeared on the screen and after the longest five minutes I had ever experienced, it was complete. I disconnected the device and put Scott's phone back on charge. I put Rob into the depths of my work bag and covered it with an array of old receipts and crept back into the bath to think. I couldn't look tonight, what if I found something and had a total break down? He would know then that something was up and I needed time to process the information. Then there was always the chance that I would find nothing but that would have been disappointing. Part of me had accepted it, I had accepted that he had a secret and that another woman was the only explanation.

I sank under the bubbles and thought about what I was going to find out tomorrow and more importantly what I was going to do about it.

Chapter 3

I got up the second Scott left the house at seven a.m. Scott was on the early shift every day until we left for the cabin, that meant I had until around six-thirty p.m. to get all the information that I needed. Even with this deadline, I couldn't seem to motivate myself to get started. I had managed to put the cloned Sim card into the phone and place it on the kitchen table. I tidied the kitchen, made myself coffee and breakfast until I was running out of excuses not to look at it.

I made another coffee and sat down with a note pad and pen. I entered Scott's passcode and held my breath. The welcome screen popped up and Scott's apps all popped up with the same background photo of him standing proud with his London Marathon medal. There was nothing different about this phone, except that this one was slightly fatter, to give anything away that this wasn't Scott's real phone. I flicked through the photos first and all our pictures were there from our London trip for Valentine's Day, a few vain selfies and some of the lads drinking in the pub, no other women. My heart rested a little.

I switched over to call log and searched for the early morning call. Work was listed. No way was he calling work at three a.m.! I switched to recent messages and an hour later wished that I hadn't.

I had always laughed when people had said to me that they would rather not know. Why wouldn't anyone want to know what was going on right under their nose? To me it had made no sense, but I understood it now. I was now lying under my duvet sobbing into a countless amount of tissues. I had cried so much that I thought my heart was going to break and this is where he would find me dead, curled up in the bed where he had proposed and started a promise that clearly meant nothing to him, the bed where we had made the baby that he had never wanted, and the same bed where, on countless occasions when I was working the night shift, he had welcomed another woman. Ugh! The idea of another woman in our bed turned my stomach. I jumped out of the offending bed and lurched over the toilet until there was nothing left inside me. My food, my organs, my blood - everything, there was nothing left, just a hollow shell that Charlotte Bayfield used to inhabit. I didn't know who Charlotte Bayfield was anymore. She definitely was no longer a good wife. Clearly whatever Scott was looking for in a companion wasn't me.

I slumped by the toilet and ignored the pangs stabbing through my stomach. The girls at Scott's work were all young and stunning. Juliette who taught most of the aerobics was Italian with all the beautiful passion that one would expect and Nadine was blonde and beautiful and never without full make-up and eyelashes long enough to sweep the floors with. Both were under twenty-five, had legs that went on forever and bodies suitable for Vogue Magazine, but I guess that was what you got when you worked at a gym, even the female lifeguards had appeal. His mystery woman could have been any of them and with no name on the phone it would be hard to single one of them out. I read all the messages back in case I could find any clues about who she was but my heart had stopped when I read the messages from when I had my miscarriage, he text;

She finally lost the baby today, don't panic I won't let it happen again.

I read it again and again but it didn't make it anymore real to my brain or my heart.

How was he preventing me from getting pregnant again? Had he had the snip? I got up and started pacing the floor. Why not just be honest and leave rather than live a double life? I grabbed the phone, jogged downstairs and read on. There must be an explanation to why he hadn't left me but countless messages later and I still had nothing to go on. No clues to who the mystery woman was or why he had not just left and been done with me. What did I have that he needed to hang back for? Then it hit me. He hated Aunt Maureen but had taken a special interest once she had had her stroke. He had searched on the internet about recovery times and had encouraged me to be extra helpful. She had money and somehow this was about money.

I had work at ten a.m. which gave me an hour, but I decided not to watch the clock. I grabbed the phone and my marriage certificate and drove to the high street. Most places were winding down for Christmas, some businesses had already closed, so to find somewhere open had been fortunate. I had already contacted a solicitor by phone and told the receptionist more than I had intended through angry sobs. There was something about actually saying it out loud that increased the fury that was burning within me. She had said she would get the forms ready for my arrival and that I should try to remain calm. The poor woman looked sheepish when I burst in. I think she was expecting some kind of emotional breakdown but I had got that out of my system over the phone.

She made me a cup of tea and motioned for me to sit. The solicitor was busy but the first bit was only forms anyway so she offered to talk me through it. I left forty-five minutes later with my head spinning and with a ream of forms for us both to fill in. I hated forms, I hated Scott more and I wasn't overly keen in going into work, but I guessed I had no choice. Our house was bigger than we had needed, I had intended to fill it with children. It was manageable for two of us paying, could I manage with just me?

I found a space beside the bike sheds. It was the staff's least favourite parking spot as the bikes often fell over and scratched the cars, but as it was more Scott's car than mine, I didn't think twice about it.

A fury was taking over me. What I really needed was Cassie or Amber's opinion, but by the time I made it to my desk I decided against telling either of them. Cassie would have cried and Amber would have hit him, neither would have helped me right now.

Cassie had her wedding invitations spread out over my desk so I moved my things over to the staff dining table. She mumbled her apologies but made no attempt to move anything so I blanked her out and concentrated on the forms that lay in my in-tray. I still had to confirm my new contract. The offending form was poking out of my in-tray just under a wedding invitation from Cassie. It would have both our names on it, mine and Scott's, but Scott wouldn't be there and at some point I needed to tell her. I couldn't let her pay for two meals at £75 a head and not take him. I pulled out the invitation and stared in dismay at the reception only invite. At least that solved one problem but didn't improve my mood. I had known Cassie since my first, and very brief, job at the local doctor's surgery. I was a trainee nurse and she was the secretary whose favourite job was giving out the stickers to the children who had been brave during their injections. I was God mother to Cassie's son, Duke, from her previous relationship. I had driven to Scotland to rescue them both from that relationship, a journey that had taken sixteen hours. I had moved her and Duke in with me until her parents prepared rooms for them both which had taken two months and an evening invitation was all I was worth to her. I shoved it back under the mountain of paperwork in the in-tray and rushed to the toilet to cry. What was going on this week? It was if the Universe was out to get me. Had I not spent the week doing good deeds? I sat with Maureen, who didn't appreciate it, got a car park ticket for a minor obstruction, my husband could be having an affair with an eighteen year old fitness instructor and now my friend had down graded me to the same list as Duke's grandparents who she hated with a passion.

I shook it off. It was just one more annoyance in a crappy week. It didn't matter, it didn't mean anything. I faked a sneezing fit to explain the redness around the eyes and sat back down at the dining table to sort out the paperwork from last night's shift.

"Why are you in here?" Grant snapped. "If that paperwork gets sticky, I won't be impressed." He stood by the kettle with his hands on his hips.

"Well, maybe your fiancée could lay out her wedding stuff in here so I can get to my desk," I said, without looking up.

Grant turned and left the room. After a short while he returned. "Ten minutes and it's yours, you can't answer the phone from here." I nodded as he walked off and carried on signing paperwork.

I glanced up to see Amber and Cassie having a conversation. Cassie pointed her thumb my way and I put my head down pretending not to have noticed.

"Morning sunshine," Amber said in a tone that added to my irritation. "Whatcha doing?"

"Same thing I do every morning, sign off yesterday's paperwork." I kept my head down.

"Cassie thinks she has upset you, perhaps you need to apologise," she said in her soft American drawl.

"I am happy to work here all day, it doesn't bother me," I lied. I liked my desk, I liked to be surrounded by my own things. "Grant, however, just hit the roof. He said that I can't answer the phone from here."

"Oh, I see." She walked over to the pigeon holes and flicked her fingers through my paperwork then walked to the lockers to throw her bag in. She bounced back out to speak to Cassie without another word to me. If I wanted to keep my job I needed to keep on the right side of Cassie, she was soon to be the boss's wife and I needed to be careful. Amber hadn't wasted any time getting in the circle, she knew what was best for her.

"Sorry, your desk is clear now," Cassie leant her head through the door. "Coffee is on."

"Thanks, but I have a ton of things to do this morning, can catch up at lunch time if that's okay." I smiled to let her know there were no hard feelings then carried on signing paperwork. I had gotten into the rhythm and was best here until I had finished.

Amber's phone pinged, it wasn't like her to leave it switched on. It pinged again, I sighed and carried on when it pinged again. Must be some kind of group chat. I got up and opened her locker, none of which actually locked. I reached into her bag to switch her phone off. I had done it before when having a meeting in the staff room, the incessant pinging had been a distraction and she had been okay with it. I grabbed the phone and went to switch it off just as a message from Cassie came through.

Grant said he made the decision, did you get the promotion?

Was this my promotion? It couldn't be. I didn't get it and presumed Matthew had got it. Though not as qualified as me he did have a good work ethic and some experience. I strained to think of any other promotions that had been on the table. To be honest if there was anything else I would have gone for it, anything to get some extra money in the bank.

An idea flashed through my mind. Amber wasn't always honest with me and clearly she and Cassie had discussed me during the wedding invite get together. I glanced at my wedding invitation poking out of my tray. Amber checked it, she thought that was why I was in a mood.

I carried her phone to my handbag and plugged it into Rob. *Time to rob your data Amber and see what you have been talking to Cassie about*, I thought to myself. I was already crossing the line with my husband's privacy, might as well push the boat out and enter the mind of my best friend too. I selected yes to everything then waited while it cloned the details. It took about twenty minutes longer than Scott's and every time the staff room door opened, my heart dropped in case it was Amber. It never was, she was on rounds delivering the mail and would probably chat to everyone on the way.

I returned to my desk so Cassie could make me a coffee. After all the years of friendship and all we had been through, the least she could do was make me a coffee. I knew we hadn't been as close lately, I had been distracted with Maureen's care and she with a new house and her wedding, but I still considered her one of my best friends. I only really had her and Amber, Cassie seemed to have loads of friends, a fact that her overflowing wedding planner was testament to.

"Sorry, the wedding has been taking over," Cassie whispered sheepishly. "Doing the invites has been a nightmare."

"I can remember doing mine so no need to tell me about it," I smiled. Cassie and Amber had been my bridesmaids, though they hadn't bonded at the time. Amber thought Cassie was too quiet and lacked personality. I liked Cassie, she had always been sweet though I was struggling right now to ignore the overwhelming desire to reach across the desk and bang her head against the table. I had seen Amber's invite in her bag, Amber had been invited all day. Though they had met at my wedding, they had never spoken. Cassie had spent the whole day flirting with Grant who soon got her the job at the hospital. If it wasn't for me, these two would never have met and no wedding would be taking place.

I breathed in a large lung full of air and let it out. I needed Cassie to get distracted or leave the room so I could search the lost property for a phone like Amber's. I opened my bag and saw that the device had finally finished. I disconnected it and took Amber's phone back to the staff room with the excuse of cleaning the cups. I dropped the phone back into Amber's bag and walked straight to the lost property. Cassie was on the phone talking about the wedding and I knew for at least half an hour, I would be largely ignored.

I sorted through the ridiculous amount of phones and found one that I needed. It was much newer but I hoped it wouldn't matter too much.

I returned to my desk and, as predicted, Cassie hadn't even looked up from her wedding planner book, I could have murdered half the staff and patients and she wouldn't have even noticed.

I slipped the sim card that now contained all of Amber's information into the new phone. I was now betraying the two most important people in my life.

The phone was dead. If I was going to check the data on Scott's clone phone and Amber's regularly, I would probably need one of those universal chargers to keep them both alive. Neither of them were like my prehistoric thing that was only really any good for making calls. I neatened up my paperwork and went to find someone who had one of those universal chargers I could borrow. Half an hour later I had found a tech guy who had one I could borrow as long as I returned it within the hour. I rushed back and plugged it in checking the clock. Grant hated it when staff misused the facilities so, if caught charging a phone in the tea room, I would have been in big trouble. I wondered whether he had ever noticed the lack of work Cassie did and somehow I doubted it.

I made myself a cup of tea while keeping my eye on Cassie through the window. I think she was sulking because Grant made her move her stuff off my desk but I pretended that I didn't notice. I loved her to bits but she got away with murder.

Something beeped and I checked both cloned phones and my own before I realised that it was the charger to signal that it had finished. I quickly unplugged it and threw the phone back into my oversized bag and went about my business.

"Hey chick." Amber bounced in the office about five minutes later.

"Lunch time already?" I smiled. She would have been here since six so on an early lunch at eleven-thirty. Sometimes she would have her lunch at the same time that I was having my tea break and we got to catch up. I had already had one cup of coffee from Cassie's machine and one cup of tea but thought another wouldn't hurt. "Got time for a coffee?"

"No sorry, I have to meet a friend. Catch up with you after the new year though. I probably won't see you now, New York, New York and all that," She smiled broadly.

"Okay my lovely, have a good one, catch up with you soon." I blew her a kiss and watched her bounce out of the door. If she was having lunch with Cassie she could just admit it, I wasn't a child.

I took the charger back to the tech who had leant it to me and took my time returning to my desk. Ordinarily I was the first in and the last out and un-finished work was unheard of, but today I was lacking in my normal work ethic. Clock watching wasn't something I ever did but today was dragging and my curiosity about the Rob device and what it could do was weighing on my mind.

"Have you brought me the sign off sheets from yesterday?" Dr Zusak appeared out of nowhere.

"I'll check if Cassie has logged them and if not, chase them up if you like," I smiled, piqued that he had expected me to do them.

"Oh, I thought that was your job. It is usually you that does it isn't it?" He raised his massive eyebrows. Dr Zusak was a man who prided himself on getting things right and this detail would annoy him. What was wrong with everyone lately?

"I only do it if Cassie hasn't been able to finish her work load. I usually start and finish my day going through her desk. That's what you pay me overtime for." I felt like I was betraying her by blabbing, but if me and Scott *were* to divorce I would need to support a house on my own and I really needed my money to not be cut.

"Oh, I see," he sounded cross. I walked away quickly. I could get them off her desk, finish them and she would never know that he had asked.

Cassie was with Grant at her desk going over wedding details, not with Amber then. They both looked up when I approached the desk. Grant looked embarrassed at being caught not working but Cassie just looked annoyed at being interrupted. "Zusak is asking for the sign offs from yesterday, he asked me to chase them up with you," I smiled and walked away.

"You are supposed to do them before you leave off," Grant snapped at her and her face darkened.

"I've been busy, don't you know," she tapped the wedding planner.

"Well, it isn't good that he has had to chase them, better make that a priority." He walked out and I felt Cassie's mood lower the temperature to zero.

"Getting married is so stressful," she whined. I ignored her, I had taken Amber's cloned phone out of my bag and was setting up the location map app. When we had lunch together, which wasn't often, we always went to Marigold's. It was quiet and quaint and I considered it to be my place. If she had taken someone else there I would have been annoyed.

But she wasn't there. She was down Old School Close which was where I got my parking ticket from. A cold feeling washed over me as I remembered the ticket. They hadn't emailed back yet to confirm that I didn't have to pay it, so close to Christmas too.

I shook it off, I couldn't do anything about it now. Out of curiosity I took Scott's phone out of my bag and clicked the location services on and waited while the map loaded, Old School Close.

A fury raged inside me. I grabbed my keys and stormed out. How I managed to drive through the tears or the heavy rain was a mystery. I couldn't control the water works or the anger. Scott was having an affair which was painful enough but with Amber! My heart couldn't take the crushing realisation. My best friend and my husband, how could they do that to me?

Amber's car was at the front of the driveway and I recognised Scott's colleague Ian's green racer mini parked beside it. As I had our main car, he often borrowed Ian's for random appointments. Maybe Scott left his phone in Ian's car when Ian gave him a lift to work this morning, but it was Scott I saw when I looked up to the window with his shirt off, closing the blinds.

I wailed. The idea of banging on the door occurred to me, but then I remembered the message, **Don't worry she has lost the baby.** Why would Amber want me to go through that pain? I thought she had been happy for me.

I pulled out my phone and turned on the mobile data. An email popped up from the council saying that they had reviewed my case and saw no reason to reverse my ticket.

I cried some more. This was soon becoming the worst week ever.

I viewed the evidence photographs and saw the red mini. I looked up, the red mini was there, opposite to where I was parked. I clicked on the other case pictures the traffic warden had taken to get my bearings and then I was certain. I glanced down the street and no other drive was double the size. This is where I got my parking ticket! It was at this house where my best friend and my husband were fooling around in an upstairs bedroom. Then I remembered Amber saying she was feeding her uncle's cats. I looked down the road again looking for familiarities. She had made me walk over from work once to deliver her shady cousin's Christmas presents because she hadn't wanted to go alone. That had been a double driveway that probably meant that it was Amber's uncle that reported my car and it was probably him who put the deep scratch into the door.

I went to drive off but realised that I was shaking. I switched off the engine and picked up Amber's phone. I entered the number into Scott's cloned phone and sure enough it came up as work. I threw his phone back in the bag and concentrated on Amber's. There were thousands of messages, photos and videos, I concentrated on the ones between her and Scott.

There were plenty of love messages making me feel sick to the stomach but what I really wanted to know was how long it had been going on for. I scrolled to the bottom and was horrified to see that they went back nearly two years. How could I have been so completely unaware for two years! It was madness. How could I have been so stupid?

I ignored the tears and read on. I got down to the bit where Scott had told her that I was pregnant. This would have been the perfect place to end the affair and my heart raised a little when I read Scott suggest it, but Amber was having none of it. She knew a girl who had been date raped and had taken an abortion drug from America. Between them they devised a plan, Amber would order the drug through work and Scott would slip it into my tea.

I read on and on and on until I thought my heart was going to shatter. How could they do this to me? The two people I loved and trusted above everyone.

I heard Amber giggle and I slipped down into my seat. Hopefully with the rain, they wouldn't notice my car sandwiched in-between two others, on the opposite side of the road. But then so what if they did, it was about time they were exposed.

Scott drove off first and I watched Amber as she slipped her uncle's door key under the mat and drove off in the same direction as Scott.

I sat for a while and wondered what to do with myself. I should go back to work, surely I had been missed, but what did it matter? If I never went back it wouldn't have mattered. Without me everyone would be able to lead their perfect lives. Amber could have Scott, Cassie could have my desk all she wanted and Dr Zusak would know exactly who did what job. I knew now that Amber had been given my promotion, I had read the texts. I knew everything now through texts she had sent to Cassie and the ones she had sent to Scott. She had befriended Cassie and convinced her that I was overpaid and over valued myself. Clearly I had more than one thing that Amber wanted.

I remembered what the lady at the solicitors said this morning, there were steps that had to be taken, the papers were just the first step.

I drove to the bank and got a mini statement for our joint bank account. We both put in £600 a month and whatever was left we spent on holidays, but because of my pregnancy we had decided to make whatever was left a bit of a nursery fund. Every year was slightly different but there was usually a couple of thousand left over. This had accumulated over the years and the last time I had checked there had been over five thousand spare and now there was only £900 in it and it didn't look like Scott had put any money into it for at least three months.

I walked in and asked for an adviser. I explained all the details to the attendant who got more details than she needed. I mentioned the miscarriage, the drug that I was poisoned with and the fact that my best friend was running off with my husband. Who else did I have to unload it all on? I had no mother, a father I had not seen or heard from in years and my brother, Josh, wasn't really the sympathetic type. The woman listened, nodding in all the right places. She handed me a box of tissues and left me to make some tea.

She returned with tea, forms and a tub of chocolates. "We need to freeze the account. Unfortunately your direct debit has already gone out but I can reverse that before we freeze it." I nodded as she typed into her computer and printed out some forms. "I also have some news which is pretty bad for you and the bank." The lady slid some copies of paperwork across the desk.

"What is this?" I asked, trying to focus on the small print through my tears.

"It's an application form to mortgage your house but the signatures don't seem to match"

I flicked to the last page and saw where my signature had been carefully filled in. "I didn't sign this," I gasped.

"Luckily we don't need you both here to cancel it. The house is in both of your names so in event of divorce everything gets stopped and this hasn't actually gone through yet."

"So he can't do it," I heaved a sigh of relief. What else could life throw at me?

"No, this will be cancelled." She pulled out a large red stamp, printed it over the paperwork and typed some details into the computer. "I have cancelled your direct debit and if you sign here, I will get you some money. Because you have paid more into this account than he has, the court should award some of that back to you if you mention it." She smiled and handed me some more forms. I pulled out my divorce forms from this morning and placed them on top.

"I can't believe how overwhelming it all is," I said, meaning every word. My world was hanging off its axis and I really didn't know how to move forward.

"I know, I went through it last year. The best thing you can do is work out a Consent Order. Pre-agree everything and the divorce will take half the time," she smiled. "We may need to contact you with reference to the mortgage application. It is the bank's policy to take fraudulent claims like this one very seriously and my manager may want to take it further to prove a point."

I nodded and rose to leave. Could this day get any worse?

She handed me a pouch to keep all my documents in and I slipped in the wallet containing the cash.

£900 was all that was left in the account, that wasn't enough to pay the bills until the divorce was finalised. The house was both of our second homes and had enough money from both of our sales to buy our joint house without a mortgage, but gas, electric, phone and TV all needed to be paid, not to mention the dreaded Council Tax.

Scott had obviously intended to confess soon, the money would not have lasted much longer and I would have found out sooner or later once the bank started issuing withdrawal fines.

I arrived at work two hours later. I didn't go straight back to my desk but went to see my aunt instead. She knew damn well that she hadn't given me that money and I needed it now more than ever.

"Did you get your paperwork?" I smiled at Zusak as I walked in.

"No, not yet," he glanced at his watch. "I did ask for it a couple of hours ago, that should have been plenty of time." He raised his enormous eyebrows.

"I did chase it for you and Grant asked Cassie to make it her first job. It is probably on its way," I smiled and walked off. It was in my nature to offer to get it or to do it but I wasn't feeling partically helpful. That '*Be kind to the Universe and the Universe will be kind to you*' motto that I usually lived by just wasn't holding up its end of the bargain.

"Your aunt is in the toilet." The woman opposite said and went back to reading her book. I nodded and turned to leave but saw Maureen's bag open by the side of her bed. I reached in and opened the zip part that contained her bank card and slipped it into my pocket. I jogged downstairs greeting as many people as I could so if Grant had been looking for me, someone would admit to having seen me. I withdrew the £300 and slipped it into my front pocket.

"Came to check I'm not dead have you?" Maureen joked as I approached her bed. As I bent to take a seat, I dropped the card back into the pocket and pushed the bag back under the bed with my foot.

"You are as tough as old boots and will out live all of us," I smiled. A feeling of relief and balance had washed over me and I no longer felt cross with her. "I just came to wish you a Merry Christmas as I only have a couple of shifts left beforehand and it's going to be manic."

"What! You're not coming to spend time with me Christmas Day? The cabin isn't that far away, I checked," she shuffled against her pillows.

"Melissa and Steven will take good care of you." I planted an unwelcome kiss on her cheek and scuttled away.

Taking my money back from Maureen had left me on a high and I welcomed the feeling of empowerment. Not only did I welcome it, I revelled in it and in the short time it had taken me to walk from Maureen's ward back to my desk I had formulated a plan to right all the wrongs. If the Universe wasn't going to correct the balance, it could sure as hell turn a blind eye while I did.

Chapter 4

Cassie had left Zusak's unfinished paperwork on my desk and was no where to be seen. I ignored the 'urgent' post it note that had been stuck to the top and fished out Amber's cloned phone. She hadn't bothered to disguise Scott's number and use fake an alias like he had. I imagined David trusted her as implicitly as I had Scott. I pushed down the overwhelming feelings of anger and searched through her conversations. An arrangement must have been made about her uncle's cats while she was at her parent's house over Christmas. A message from Cassie pinged up while the phone was in my hand and my screen automatically shifted to that conversation. Cassie was moaning to Amber about the fact that I was complaining about all the wedding stuff being in the way and she was glad Amber had persuaded her to make me an evening guest. She then went on to gush about some table decorations she had fallen in love with down the high street. Amber had replied quickly, I looked around for her but the staffroom was empty. She must have had the phone with her on the floor, another rule Grant would be furious about her breaking. I read the reply from Amber,

Don't think about it. Just know that I just had the most amazing sex with her husband and when you think she is better than you just remind yourself that you know something she doesn't.

So Cassie knew! I took in a deep breath and fought back the tears, surely soon there would be no moisture left.

"I thought you were on lunch," Grant said, entering the office with more paperwork for Cassie. I slid the phone under some paperwork and glanced at the clock. It was now two-forty p.m., my lunch should have started ten minutes ago. "Not had a chance yet. I'm trying to get ahead of myself before I leave for Christmas." Out of the corner of my eye I saw Zusak walk in and felt a stab of annoyance. I picked up Zusak's paperwork and handed it to Grant who hadn't noticed him. "I don't mind helping Cassie out at the end of the day but I can't do her job before I have finished my own. I know the wedding is important but she shouldn't be off picking table decorations in work hours." Zusak was already flicking through Cassie's desk. I continued, "she is getting paid to be here and to do this job. It's not fair to add to my work load just because she can't prioritise." I looked down and continued typing a document that I had started over three hours ago and was in fact, the only piece of actual work I had done all day. "I can't even go to lunch until she gets back and she is already ten minutes late."

"Does that mean Miss Edwards has not finished my paperwork and is currently off the premises?" Dr Zusak snapped.

I acted surprised at his presence and Grant looked crestfallen. "I'm sure she is on a work errand," he mumbled, but his face gave away that even he thought this was doubtful.

"Well, let's call her and find out." Zusak handed Grant the phone and pushed the loud speaker button when the call was connected.

"When are you returning to your desk?" Grant asked. "Zusak is waiting here for his paperwork." Grant looked in my direction as he spoke. I put my head down and carried on typing.

"Oh, I put it on Charlotte's desk to finish. I'm on the high street picking the table cloths. I really like the Mauve pink."

I tried to repress my smile. I felt like another balance had been restored.

"I'm docking this time out of your pay," Zusak snapped. Cassie went silent and Grant went white as a sheet.

"Do you want me to work through my lunch break and get them done for you," I looked up. "If they really are urgent, I don't mind," I smiled, game face on.

"No actually, Miss Edwards can do them and can bring them to me personally when she is done so we can have a chat." He took the sheets out of Grant's hand and dropped them on her keyboard. Zusak banged the door shut and Grant stood motionless like he was about to pass out.

"Sorry, I didn't know he was there, I never meant to get anyone in trouble." I sent my email and stood to signal that I was going to lunch. I didn't care if he *had* noticed that I had been gone all morning. They docked the hour lunch break from my wage whether I worked through it or not.

"No, it's fine. I didn't know she had left. It puts me in an awful position," he said more to himself than to me.

"Well, I am sorry anyway. If she had given them to me last night, I would have done them." I scrolled frantically through the messages until I found what I was looking for. The shady cousins were taking over the cat feeding duties as from tomorrow.

I left Grant standing there without another word. He would moan at Cassie when she got back, she would message Amber and I would know all about it anyway thanks to Rob. A smile crept over my face, it was like having a super power and I felt a small amount of control wash over me.

I drove back to Old school Close and my parking space from before was still vacant. I switched off the engine and thought for a moment about what I wanted to do. Getting my money back from Aunt Maureen had felt good, liberating. I felt like I had to right some of these wrongs and if I didn't I would somehow sink into some pit of despair and this universe, that clearly hated me, would swallow me up, never to be seen again.

I slipped on a pair of hygiene gloves and welcomed the pouring rain. It gave me an excuse to run across the road without looking too shady. I glanced at the white BMW parked neatly in its space down the drive and admired the scratch free doors, they clearly had some money.

I swooped down to collect the key that I had seen Amber slipping under the mat and swiftly let myself in. The smell of cats hit my nose and I paused on the mat, unable to breathe. I was amazed that Scott or Amber could have ignored the horrendous smell but then again I guessed they had other things on their minds.

I locked the door behind me, tucked the key into my pocket and stood a while in the hall, thinking about what item I was going to take. All I need was one thing to the value of £35 to restore the balance. The layout was very similar to our house. The hall was narrow with the stairs set back on the left and a short corridor which led to the lounge. The kitchen was directly to the left so I ventured there first. The smell was worse in here. There was cat mess on the kitchen floor and the food and water bowls were empty. Amber must have forgotten the real reason she was here and not given the cats a second thought. I opened the back door and let them out. There were three cats all similar colours and sizes, two darted out but one stayed and circled around my feet for food. I cleaned the mess up first and threw the soiled kitchen roll into the outside bin now I wouldn't have to worry about where I stood. The cat food was stacked in the utility room. I grabbed an open tin, popped off the plastic lid and filled the cat bowls up with food and water.

The other two cats darted back in and attacked the food like they hadn't eaten for weeks. I grabbed another tin then laughed at my stupidity. I had broken into someone else home to gain some kind of revenge for my parking ticket and had, so far, just succeeded in cleaning up their kitchen and feeding their pets.

I left the tin on the side and explored the lounge. The Christmas tree was still up and there were tiny scraps of paper lying on the floor were they must have opened their presents before they had taken their holiday. They had received a new cordless vacuum cleaner and could have easily have used it to clear up the mess but they must have been in too much of a hurry to begin their holiday. I ignored the mess and started with the dresser which was adorned with random ornaments. There were some pieces of wedgwood and some stylish white figurines of elegant ladies. They were joined by a small collection of little green dragons and tiny teapots which looked odd and out of place. The first cabinet contained books. The top shelf were biographies about boxers and the lower levels contains love stories and mystery novels. This wasn't what I was looking for, I wanted cash if I could find any, like for like. He had cost me £35 and a scratch down my car. I intended to take the value of £35 and leave his car in a similar state. I found what I was looking for in the bottom cabinet. A large glass jar sat on the shelf full of £10 and £20 notes and little pieces of card had been thrown in with them. I lifted the jar and held it up and inspected the writing, they were registration plates. The guy had written down every ticket that had been given because of him and then put the £35 into a jar as some kind of savings scheme. I emptied the jar onto a bean bag and flicked over the scraps until I found my licence number. I separated the handwritten notes then counted them up. There were seven of them. There were six other people out there who this man had made feel as crap as he had to me.

I shook the rage away. To be fair, I didn't realise that the whole car had to be behind the beginning of the drop down of the kerb. I thought as long as the wheel was in, it would be okay. It wasn't this guy's fault that I had broke the law but then I remembered the scratch. I had no proof that it was him that scratched my car but to me it seemed highly likely. I had seen him moving behind the curtains, watching me, waiting for me to discover my scratch, to see my response. Had this man watched me cry and laughed at the pain he had caused me? The rage returned. I thought about Amber and what I knew about her uncle. I didn't know much, but I knew she didn't like admitting that she knew them let alone was related to them. I thought again about the scratch. That was no accident and it hadn't been necessary, he had done it out of spite. I left the money where it was and looked in the other drawers. Take-away menus and old MOT documents, nothing of interest. I didn't know why I was still looking around. I had wanted £35 and I had it, it was there on the bean bag but my eyes were still wandering around the room. Something didn't feel right. There was over £200 sitting right in front of me and I still wasn't satisfied. Getting my money back from Aunt Maureen had felt fair and a relief had washed over me that I had corrected the wrong. This man, who owned this house, went out of his way to deliberately hurt people and the justice needed to be fair.

I moved to the other side of the Christmas tree but there was nothing else in the room. I moved upstairs to the bedroom and waited while my eyes adjusted. It was just past three p.m. and the light was fading which was made duller by the rain clouds covering up the sky. I walked around the bedroom feeling a slight thrill at being somewhere where I shouldn't be. The Christmas presents that had been opened in a hurry had been neatly laid in piles on the bed. The lady of the house's presents consisted of Pandora boxes, mineral make-up and a Mulberry handbag set complete with purse. I flicked the bag over and admired the finish. Amber had a small mulberry bag which had cost over £200, I dreaded to think how much this one had cost. I opened it up and was amazed to see that a matching, smaller handbag was nestled inside. A note was laying inside which read:

Don't think about the money mum, it wasn't our money.

What did that mean?

I moved over to his presents which looked more interesting. For starters he must be a keen photographer. For Christmas he had been bought a new DSLR Nikon, same make as mine, but a much higher model. He also had been given a variety of lens' one of which was the one I had always dreamed of but had never been able to afford. I pulled it out of its box and turned it over in my hands. It was so large it had a grip underneath it to hold on to while using it. I laid it on the bed and emptied the camera out of the other box. I needed something to add to the weight. I took the Mulberry bag downstairs and sat on the kitchen side to reach the higher cupboards. The first row was branded beans but the row behind was the supermarkets own brand. I sniggered, they were just like Amber, all show up front but cheap and nasty behind the surface. I lifted up the front row and placed them on the side ready to be placed back and reached for the cheaper ones at the back. The first tins were heavy but the tins at the back felt empty. I turned the tin over in my hand and saw that like the cat food tin, there was a plastic cap on the bottom. I flipped off the cap and looked inside. Instead of the beans that should have inhabited the tin there was a clear bag full of pills. I felt the weight of the others and the whole back row were the same. I flipped off all the lids, some others contained various drugs but most contained rolled up money. I paused for a moment to think about what was happening. Would Amber's uncle, Ray, have dealt in drugs or would they belonged to Amber's cousin's, the dodgy Flint brothers? They didn't still live here but could have easily have used this house as a base.

I didn't know the answer but I knew I was taking the money. I put the tins that contained drugs back into the cupboard and emptied the money into the Mulberry bag. I walked into the lounge and scooped the car park ticket money up, registration plates included, and placed that into bag along with three genuine tins of beans. I went upstairs and placed the bean tins into the camera lens box and sealed it back up. Now it looked like I had never been here.

I opened the wardrobe and was amazed by how far back it went. Ray's clothes were no where in sight, it was all hers. A large Louis Vuitton weekender bag sat in the corner wrapped in a plastic bag. I opened it up on the bed and suddenly felt something bang down beside me making me jump out of my skin. The cat was oblivious to my intrusion into its home it just wanted fuss. I lifted him up and placed him into the hall. I was about to shut the door when I heard a sound that made my heart stop, someone was unlocking the door and entering the hall. I froze behind the door unsure of which way to turn or what to do. Why hadn't I taken the car park money as planned and left with what I came for?

"We are already late, hurry it up," I heard a male's voice booming from bottom of the stairs.

I backed into the wardrobe and closed the slatted doors as quietly as I could.

"Stop panicking, it won't take two minutes," a guy yelled back and I could hear that he was already upstairs. I heard his heavy feet enter the bedroom and I held my breath. I moved so I could partially see through a wonky slat. A young looking guy was putting an envelope into a bedside table and he slid something into his back pocket.

"Do we need some energy shake from the garage?" The guy from downstairs yelled.

"Nah, there is enough money here. We will come back next week if not." The guy surveyed the presents on the bed and my heart leapt. What if he noticed something was out of place and started searching. I peered through the slat, holding my hands over my mouth. I had left the Louis Vuitton bag on the bed and the camera was lying on the covers out of its box. My stomach twisted and I fought back the urge to be sick. I had left my hand bag downstairs somewhere and inside it were three phones all of which could go off at any minute betraying me as an intruder.

He hovered taking in the contents on the bed. His brow furrowed as if sensing something was wrong but eventually he moved on. I watched him bound out of the room and heard his heavy steps on the stairs. I listened carefully for the front door to be locked before taking another breath.

What was I doing? This was madness.

I had a sudden urge to be sick. I had never been so scared in my life. I slowly opened the wardrobe door and lurched into the en-suite. I heaved three times and sprayed some air freshener to get rid of the vile smell. Now when they investigated, my DNA would be all over the bathroom toilet. I put down some bleach and scooped up the boxed perfume that had been stacked up by the sink. Much of it was the same thing which made me think they were thieves as well as drug dealers. I put my stash onto the bed and went back for the shampoos. No more supermarket's own brand for me anymore. What else did I need? I grabbed a brown leather jacket and a matching pair of UGG boots that were leather, not the regular UGGs that looked like slippers. I had not seen anything like this before so threw them on the bed. I would take a closer look at what I had later on.

I moved to the room at the front of the house and looked out of the window. I could see my car across the street and it dawned on me that this was the room that Scott and Amber were in. I turned and surveyed the surroundings. This spare bedroom had a double bed covered in a disgusting floral bedspread with curtains and a rug to match. It looked out of place with the modern room next door where everything was designer. The bed had been made and if I hadn't of seen them at the window I never would have known they were here.

I ignored the feeling of nausea that was building up inside of me again and opened the wardrobe. This was clearly his things. Rows and rows of trousers were lined up neatly on hangers and several tuxes were hanging in their suits bags. This couple were obviously in high society, everything was designer here too. I opened some drawers and felt around at the backs for anything hidden. Scott always hid his jewellery in the bottom drawer at the back every time we went away.

No jewellery was here but I did feel a thick bulging envelope. I pulled the wad out and saw that it was labelled **Tom's Car.** I flicked through the wad of money, all £20's. I put the envelope on the bed and felt for some more but there was nothing but a porno magazine and some condoms. I threw them on the bed, hopefully the wife would find it and an argument would ensue. Karma Sutra was written in bold letters in the corner of the magazine and I had an idea. I ripped the word in half and took it downstairs to the car park money jar. Now when he got home and looked in the jar he would see the word karma and nothing else. I walked into the kitchen and found the garage door with the key in the keyhole. I unlocked the door and walked in. Really I should have been running for my life but I needed to see the shake containers. My heart was telling me that they contained drugs and I wasn't wrong. The garage looked a lot like ours. There was a treadmill to the left and various weights stacked up between a bench press and a rowing machine. I could see Scott in here, this could have easily been his house and his designer things. That all too familiar fury was building up again. This was Scott's fault, he made me feel this way.

I stormed across the garage and peered into the oversized tubs. The first big yellow tub actually contained energy drink powder but the one underneath was full of bank notes. Two more contained drugs. I had never taken drugs but dispensed them regularly at work, but I was still surprised by all the colours and types. Most were in powder form but there were some that looked like herbs, pills in every colour you could think of and a whole load that looked like sweets. I remembered how close to the high school we were and my heart broke a little. The ones that looked like jelly babies could easily have been taken by accident. The thought of these two sleezeball brothers dealing drugs to the high school children here made my blood boil.

I stormed upstairs satisfied that I had seen and done enough. I filled the Louis Vuitton bag up with all the money, the camera and accessories. I left the boxes so it wouldn't instantly be clear that they had been revenged. I emptied out the large Pandora bag and puffed up the tissue paper back inside so it wasn't instantly recognisable that it was emptied. The Mulberry bags and the Bare Mineral make-up and brushes went on top.

The bag was half full so I re-opened the wardrobe and sifted through the clothes. This lady was a size twelve so her clothes would never have fitted my frame but I had seen a few things that had caught my eye. I threw things into the bag. All her shoes were a size six which was the same as me. I favoured the ones that she had kept in boxes. Some were Gucci, some were Jimmy Choo - all mine now. I kept remembering the note, **Don't think about the money mum, it wasn't our money.** No, it was drug money and it destroyed lives. I fished the note out of the Mulberry and slipped it into the empty Pandora bag.

I opened the drawer to check what the boy had slipped in and was not surprised to see another envelope full of cash, I ignored it. Taking it would have put a time on my arrival and that might go against me later on.

I heaved the Louis Vuitton bag down the stairs and shoved it in the boot of my car as quickly as I could then went back for the vacuum cleaner and did some checks. Three cats in, garage light off, my hand bag not left behind - check.

I turned the key over in my hands and walked over to the nice shiny BMW. I dragged the key gently at first down the passenger side door then along to the rear. Now we were more than even, but this wasn't about getting even, it was about getting closure and teaching a lesson. I dragged the key around the back and squiggled a figure of eight over the boot then continued around to the driver's side. Revenge certainly was sweet.

I slid the paint clogged key back under the mat and returned to my car. I pulled the boot blind over the loot so that no one could see in and drove away.

I still had four hours left of my ten hour shift at work and had so far done nothing.

Cassie had red circles around her eyes and was surrounded by tissues. I felt a stab of guilt as I walked past her and sat at my desk. It wasn't her fault really, Amber had a way of getting you caught up. It was Amber's decision to cut me out of the all day festivities and she was probably too scared to tell me about Scott and Amber's affair, but then again, it wasn't my fault either. I hadn't set her up, she hadn't done her job, she couldn't blame me for that.

I ignored the phones that were vibrating in my bag though I was burning to know what she had told Amber about the paperwork. I glanced up as she blew her nose loudly, normally I would have asked her what was wrong and bent over backwards to offer to help but I just wasn't feeling it. I entered three pieces of paperwork into my computer and ignored her sniffling. How were Cassie and Amber about to be paid more than me? It just wasn't fair.

I should have counted the cash that I just took, it would have been about three months wages at least. I fished out the new job contract out of my tray and ticked all the decline boxes. I don't agree with the new terms that I have been laid out before me and I don't agree with the new pay terms, they suck. I accepted the redundancy now I needed Grant to sign it. "Is Grant about?" I asked the still snivelling Cassie. "I need him to sign off some paperwork."

"He is on ward seven. Could you get him to sign these off too please and are you going anywhere near Zusak's office? If so could you take this please?" She sheepishly handed me some paperwork and I agreed with a large smile. Zusak's office was the exact place I needed to be.

I lined the paperwork up as I walked. Grant had a habit of signing without reading and I hoped today would be no different.

He and Amber were happily chatting by the reception desk and I swallowed a large gulp of air to keep my anger down. "Hi guys," it came out high and squeaky. "Could you sign these off for me please, I need to get them to Zusak." Grant flicked through the top two layers which was Cassie's overdue paperwork but didn't read the rest.

"She was supposed to deliver these to him herself," he grunted as he signed away.

"He's probably doing his rounds, I doubt he will be there anyway, I shouldn't worry." I smiled broadly as he handed back the paperwork and I practically skipped down the hall.

I pulled my redundancy paperwork to the top and checked the date. I had been given it on the first of December so scribbled that into the date box. Like I predicted, Zusak was out of office so I left the paperwork with his receptionist and returned to my desk.

Now I just had to deal with the biggest problem of all... Scott.

Chapter 5

A hire car was parked down the driveway and I guessed it was Sarah's. It was customary for Scott's mum to call over before our cabin stay to give us a never ending list of food and things we needed to take. Either her or Sarah would be sitting in my kitchen and their presence made me feel braver. I needed to get this out in the open now, tonight, it couldn't be put off any longer.

I lifted my haul out of the boot and hid it in the back of an upstairs wardrobe that was reserved for coats that hadn't been worn for at least four years, but we couldn't bear to part with. I could only hear Sarah's voice. I took a couple of deep breaths and I went downstairs. I wondered how to bring up the awful subject up but Sarah kick started the whole thing off for me by asking me if I was okay, to which, I burst into tears.

"Sarah, sorry, could you please give us a minute?" I asked through broken sobs.

"Sarah can stay, she just dropped off the cabin list. Is this about your job?" Scott asked as if emotional outbursts from me happened daily.

Sarah made no move to get up. I had to make a decision, I could either put it off or just get it off my chest.

"This isn't about my job, it is about the fact that you have been having an affair for the past two years and are planning to leave me in the new year."

No one spoke. Scott's features narrowed as if asking me if this was a joke. Something made me doubt myself but then how can everything I have read and seen for myself at the bank been wrong?

"What are you going on about?" Scott finally said. His eyes wide as if I had gone mad.

"I read the messages on your phone. I have been to the bank and seen that you forged my signature to try and mortgage the house. How could you do this to me?"

"You have no right to read through my phone, I'm not that paranoid about you," Scott ranted, his face turning red.

I moved along a couple of steps to lean against the kitchen side for support. Scott had risen to his feet.

"That is because I would have never done this to you and if you hadn't have been so stupid to call her in the middle of the night then I wouldn't have heard you and felt the need to go through your phone." My heart was now beating so hard it was painful and the tears had moved from delicate trickles to Niagara Falls. "That I could have forgiven but the poison. You murdered our baby and that I will never forgive."

"I think I should leave." Sarah rose and handed me the list which I immediately threw at Scott.

"I won't be at the cabin so will not be buying anything." I reached into my bag and took out the divorce papers. "I suggest you use your time at the cabin to fill these in and if I ever find out who helped you get that drug you gave me, there will be hell to pay, do you understand me?"

Sarah hovered, not sure of whether to stay or go.

"I think you have misunderstood some things." Scott's voice was now high pitched and his face had darkened.

"Really! What is the point of denying it now when you were going to leave soon anyway?" My voice was starting to crack with the anger and upset swirling inside of me. "And if you didn't want children you should have just said." I wiped the tears away. I wanted to be strong but it was taking all my strength not to hit him or wrap the iron cord around his neck.

"Okay, fine. I don't want children, I never did," Scott spat.

I ignored Sarah's gasp of surprise as she moved across the room towards the door. "And the other woman?" I whispered, unsure that I really wanted the answer.

"Yes, there is someone else. I don't love you anymore, Sorry," he shrugged, looking anything but sorry.

I turned to Sarah who was looking like a deer caught in the headlights. "I'm sorry that you had to witness this, please take him with you. I'll sort out an estate agents for house viewing some point over Christmas."

"You can't sell the house," he shouted.

"Then I suggest you consult a lawyer about buying me out," I bellowed. There was a screaming banshee inside of me desperate to break out and sucker punch him across the face. I left the room and ran up the stairs. I needed to be alone and cry freely. There was something liberating about getting it all out in the open and there was something safe about Sarah being in the room as well. He hadn't mentioned Amber's name and I wondered which one of them would tell me.

"Are you staying in here? I need to pack," Scott said, without a hint of remorse.

"No, I will leave you to it." I heaved myself off the bed and snatched the car keys. At least this way I knew he couldn't take the car.

I sat and watched the ships enter and leave the busy harbour. Though I had felt hysterical earlier, I felt pretty calm now.

The hard part was done.

A phone buzzed in my bag and I heard the talking before I even had a chance to handle them. This was all part of the automatic answer feature. I recognised Scott's voice straight away. "It's done," he said, sounding pleased with himself.

"Has the money come through already?" Amber asked. I could hear the hope in her voice.

"Doubt she will inherit before the aunt dies," he answered. "But the main thing is that I have ended the relationship and now we can be together. It's your turn now to end things with David like we planned."

Poor David. They were preparing to get married next year and now his life was going to be shook up just like mine was.

"The plan was to make sure we were both financially sound before we made any rash moves." Amber sounded angry and I found myself sniggering. I knew Amber, I knew her well, this wasn't about love. I was now pretty sure now she didn't even have a heart. If she had loved Scott she would have sounded pleased and them being together would have been the only thing that mattered but no, all she had raised an interest in was money.

"We will work through it. Your house sale and mine should come to enough for us to live an okay life," Scott sounded smitten and I let the tears run freely. There was no way I could stay with him now not after the countless betrayals.

"Does she know it's me?" Amber's voice quivered. Maybe she was feeling some regret or remorse.

"No, of course not," he snapped. "You are listed under work, she probably suspects one of the lifeguards."

"I'll tell her when we're ready. I just want to make sure everything is in place first. I don't want to have to rely on anyone once this kicks off and having Charlotte pulling rank on me at work is a huge concern. I can't lose this job."

"Then I hope you have covered your tracks because she knows about the drug."

"How the hell does she know about that?"

"She read through all my messages, don't get cross because there is nothing I can do about it now. Look I have to go, my sister is waiting downstairs to take me to my mother's. Ring me when you get back from your party."

"Will do," Amber hung up without another word. He sounded deeply in love she, on the other hand, just sounded annoyed.

I leant back in my seat and pulled my favourite fluffy blanket over my legs. I had forgotten about the party tonight. I had declined because of getting things ready for the cabin. Amber had an early shift but will still, no doubt, get drunk and disorderly. Maybe I would get a drunk text later on confessing all. I should have guessed it was Amber as soon as Cassie mentioned my parking ticket. I hadn't told anyone but Scott, yet Amber and Cassie knew. Why hadn't I realised that at the time? What other clues had I missed over the years?

The riverside was one of my favourite spots. We used to come here with fish and chips and watch the ships come in. At night all the different coloured lights flash up like fireworks and always set the scene for a romantic make-out session. I suddenly wondered if he had ever parked here with Amber and lost all sense of nostalgia.

I pulled my phone out of my bag and dialled my brother. He answered on the third ring. "Hi Josh, it's Charlotte."

"I know, I have caller display," he laughed. "You okay? You sound quiet." He, however, sounded like he was at a party.

35

"I was wondering if you still had that spare room you needed to fill."

"Yes, Mike moved out over a month ago and I can't find anyone to fill it. You and Scott looking for a fresh start?" I heard a smash behind him and he must have moved to a quieter room as the background noise instantly shut off.

"No, just me, Scott has been having an affair and he gave me an abortion drug to make me lose the baby. I can't forgive him, I need the fresh start."

"Jesus," Josh said. "Well, I'm in Scotland with Meg over Christmas but I can help get some of your stuff up on the way back through on the twenty-seventh and you can follow me down."

"Thanks Josh, not sure how long it will be for. Message me the rent details." I shuddered to think about how much the rent would be in a London apartment, but right now I couldn't think of anywhere else I could go.

"Okay, will do. Speak soon," Josh hung up.

I waited two hours before returning to the house to start my packing. I emailed an estate agent to message me back when they had an available time to come and value the house. I knew the market had gone up considerably so knew we should profit well. I thought about what kind of state Scott would have left the house in. I doubted Sarah would have let him wreck the place, she probably would have been in a hurry too so he probably only took the stuff for the cabin at this time, he would get the rest later no doubt.

I missed several calls from Amber but I ignored them. I wasn't ready to speak to her yet and I needed a bit of time to decide what I was going to say. I also didn't want to sound like I wasn't falling apart. I didn't want her to think she had that kind of power over me. I also needed to decide on a suitable revenge for her. Why should she get away without some kind of punishment? She had breezed through her life with everything being handed to her on a plate and now it was my turn to be in control. I could tell David in advance about her infidelity but it didn't feel strong enough. I had lost my husband, my child, my job, my friends and a hell of a lot of self respect. It was only fair that she lost all those things or something equivalent. If only I could find some proof of her purchasing the drug that should be enough to get her fired then they might offer me the promotion and more money to stay.

I had one shift left before Christmas and if Zusak had already filed my leaving paperwork, I would have no more shifts after that. I hadn't worked out how much redundancy I would get, but it should be enough to tide me over until I got a new job somewhere else.

I considered unpacking the Louis Vuitton case to count the money but resisted the urge. I couldn't even look at it. I was consumed with guilt every time I thought about it. I should really have given the money away, it wasn't really mine to keep but then I might have to confess where I got it.

I got sacks out of the kitchen and bagged almost everything to bin. I had clothes from ten years ago that I had never worn. I had a bad habit of never trying things on and I never returned things. As a result, I had row upon rows of clothes that didn't fit. I was ruthless. I would have to buy new clothes in the sales and my resolution would be to try everything on.

I worked until four in the morning then collapsed on the bed and slept with my clothes on.

Amber's phone went off at six in the morning and I ignored it. My eyes were stinging and I felt like I had a hangover despite the fact that I hadn't been out. I thought it had been a good idea to set the clone phones to alert me when a message was sent and received and with Scott's phone this was fine, but Amber's phone beeped all the time and I couldn't keep up. No wonder she always took so long to reply to anything. I clicked the phone on mute and went back to sleep.

Half an hour later my home phone rang. Amber had called in sick and would I cover her shift. Ordinarily I would have said yes but I was pretty sure that I hadn't been paid for the last time I had covered. With this in mind, I said no unless Grant could sort it out. I was pretty sure that she was leaving this morning to spend Christmas with her parents which would mean that she wouldn't be able to do tomorrow mornings shift either. Why didn't they ever notice these little details? I needed to be firm somewhere down the line and maybe with me covering her arse all the time, they were never really going to realise how often she let them down.

My phone rang again. Grant sounded desperate this time. "I can't find the paperwork on the last time you covered her but if you work her early shift I will get your late shift covered."

I thought about this a moment. I did need to find the drug paperwork ideally before Amber had a chance to destroy it. "Okay, but you better cover my later shift because there is no way that I'm working a double shift."

I huffed and dragged myself to the shower. This was my last official shift at work and I really needed to get all the money I could before I left. I slipped into my baggy uniform and headed out in the rain.

On the way I thought about all the things I had lost and how much Amber had always gained from those losses. I needed closure, I needed revenge. I would find that paperwork even if it meant searching Zusak's office while he was stapled to the wall.

Cassie wasn't in until eight-thirty which gave me an hour to search through the office files. I needed orders approved internally from around thirteen months ago. Luckily filing was something she was actually good at. All medical files had been filed neatly in date order and half an hour later, I had found what I was looking for. Zusak was the authorised signature which pleased me no end. Grant was having a bad enough time covering all these shifts and when I left, he would be stuck with two lazy arse women who talked a lot but did very little. It was his own fault, but I still felt a little bad about it. I photocopied the paperwork and slipped it into my bag and went about doing Amber's rounds starting with the mail.

"Charlotte, can you come into my office for a moment there is a matter we need to urgently discuss," Grant snapped. I glanced at the clock, it was eleven already and I hadn't had a tea break yet. A wave of nausea swept over me, could they have found out about the fact that I was out practically all day yesterday or worse found out what I had been up to?

I tidied up the food trays and stepped into Grant's office. Sitting at a table was Grant, Dr Zusak and our company director.

"I'm afraid there has been a serious complaint raised against you and we must suspend you," Grant said in his mono tonal tone.

"What!" I practically shouted. Okay, I had bunked a little but a suspension was a little harsh.

"It has been reported that a large sum of money has been stolen from a patient and you have been identified as the thief. CCTV has confirmed it there is nothing we can do for you," Zusak said, without looking up.

"I have no idea what you are talking about," I said, confused.

"You can't deny that you took £300 out of a patient's account," Grant shuffled some paperwork.

"My aunt needed £300 to put in to her Christmas cards," I shrugged. I knew this would end badly. "I did not keep a penny of it, it was for her benefit."

"And did her son, who is in charge of her finances, know this?" Zusak asked.

"Of course he did, he asked me to do it because he was too busy."

"He is here, I'll ask him to step in." The Director stood up and returned five minutes later with a furious looking Aunt Maureen being pushed in a wheelchair by an anxious looking Steven.

"Sorry to disturb you madam," Zusak started but Maureen butted in.

"She is a thief, she needs to be fired. How dare she help herself to my money," She practically jumped out of her chair.

"How much money is missing out of her account?" I asked Steven, ignoring Maureen.

"£300! They said you were seen on CCTV taking it out. I must say that I am really surprised." He pulled out a bank statement and laid it out on the desk.

"Grant could you please get my black bag out of the bottom drawer of my desk and bring it through please?"

I watched Grant walk off and I read the bank statement carefully. No other money had been withdrawn during December.

Maureen continued telling the director about how ungrateful I was that she had raised me and this was how I returned the favour. I ignored her and took my bag from Grant when he slid it across the table. Luckily for me I never cleaned out my bag. I pulled out the Christmas card list which Steven had written and handed it to him.

"I'm so sorry," he said, looking drained, "I had forgotten about the Christmas card money. This is a mistake."

"I am missing £300, there is no mistake," Maureen bellowed.

"You asked Charlotte to get that money and put it in your Christmas cards on your behalf," he said to her then turned to me. "I'm so sorry, I forgot all about this. I should have really done it myself but I just thought because you were here already it would be easier."

Maureen hadn't stopped yelling so Steven stood up and wheeled her out of the room and then returned. "This is a simple misunderstanding. I asked Charlotte to get this money out on my mother's behalf, this is the list I wrote and forgot. When she said money was missing I thought she meant on top of this, I really had no idea," Steven looked at my jurors around the table.

"Well, I think you can understand now why I won't be helping you out again. It puts me in a very difficult situation," I said plainly.

"I can vouch that it is a mistake. No complaint needs to be raised." Steven waved his hands out as if brushing the whole misunderstanding aside.

"Thank you for coming in," The director said and ushered Steven out.

"Sorry if this has caused any trouble," Steven half smiled.

"You know that my name wasn't even on that Christmas list, don't you?" I said as they were shutting the door on Steven. That would give him something to think about.

"I'm sorry about that," Zusak said. "In events like these the proper avenues must be taken."

"The complaint has already been filed, it can't be un-filed," Grant said, matter of factly.

"You are joking right?" I shouted.

All three men looked up in surprise at the inner banshee inside of me rearing her ugly head.

"No, it is the company's policy to raise paperwork before a suspension meeting," Grant said, not looking up from his paperwork.

"I have been here since seven this morning covering a shift that you have never paid me for covering for before. You could have asked me about this at any time especially considering my name is down as contact for this woman. And how dare you tell my family that I was on CCTV stealing, that was an outright lie."

"I don't think I have acted out of line," Grant straightened up.

"I think it is amazing considering it takes Cassie over a week to file any other paperwork yet today she managed to file a grievance against me in under half an hour," I snapped.

"This is not personal." Grant pursed his lips together in a stubborn line making me want to lurch over the table and punch him in the face.

"Actually, I think it is a common courtesy to ask me first if I have stolen money from one of my own relatives who just so happens to be on the dementia ward," I started taking deep breaths. "Why on earth would you presume I stole it? Surely you should consider other possibilities before you decide to have me hung, drawn and quartered."

"Considering the fact that we know you and you have worked here so long, I think this could have been handled better. We would not ordinarily take the word of a dementia patient without consulting the suspected member of staff first," The Director spoke. "I was *not* made aware that your name was down on this patient's file."

"I feel like I am being bullied and while you are all in the same room. Here is a list of all the shifts I have covered in the past and not been paid for." I pulled the list I had made earlier out of my bag and slid it across the table.

"Okay, I will make sure this is looked into. The complaint against you will be deleted off the system and I will make sure this is paid into your next pay packet along with your redundancy," Zusak said, rubbing his temples.

"What redundancy?" Grant practically fell off his chair.

"Er, my redundancy." I relaxed into my chair, this bit I was going to enjoy.

"I have not been made aware of you leaving which I must say is extremely unprofessional." If looks could kill Grant would have shot me dead.

"You offered me an appalling new contract which I could either agree to or accept redundancy. I read it over, like you asked, decided against it, ticked the redundancy box and put the paperwork on Cassie's desk for you to sign, like you asked."

"I have not seen it or signed it and you have been put on the rota for New Year's Eve." Grant's face was now turning red.

"Why would you rota me in when I have ten days holiday? I wasn't due back until the second anyway."

"Actually, you have signed off her redundancy paperwork," Zusak said shifting through some paperwork. "It has already been processed. Tonight's shift is her last."

"Actually, I only agreed to cover this shift of Amber's because Grant promised to get my later shift covered. I don't mind helping you out when she rings in sick but I don't want to work a double shift."

Grant leant across the table and looked at the paperwork that bore his signature. "I don't remember signing this." He looked bewildered and for a moment, I felt a tiny thread of remorse.

"What was wrong with your new contract?" Zusak asked.

"It was longer hours for less money. It didn't make sense and I didn't think it was fair considering what other, less qualified people, were offered."

"What other people earn is not really your concern," Grant said without looking up.

I suddenly felt my wave of guilt drain away. "True, but considering I do most of your fiancée's job, I don't see why she should get more money than me, she has no qualifications." He looked up from his paperwork unsure of how to respond. So I continued, "And Amber Mason, she also has no qualifications and has also been offered more money than me. She got the promotion over me and Matthew even though she has barely arrived and only really delivers the mail. You do know she has already left for Christmas at her mother's which means she has no intention of working the tomorrow morning shift either."

"We were told to make cuts and I did my job," Grant huffed. "I don't have to explain myself to you."

"No, but you do have to explain yourself to me," the Director boomed. "Mrs Bayfield, would you please leave the room so that we can discuss this matter further?" The Director asked though it was more of an order than a request.

"Of course, but if it's not too much trouble could I please have a quick word with Dr Zusak outside?"

Zusak waited for the director to nod then ushered me outside to a corresponding office. I threw my bag over my shoulder and followed him through.

"I'm sorry about all this, it's most irregular." He perched himself on a table without bothering to move the files. Looks like his secretary could do with a kick up the backside too. "The problem is if no one like you raises these concerns about hours we just presume everything is running smoothly."

"That is okay as long as the complaint is deleted. I don't want this to ever come up again on any records anywhere."

"It won't," he smiled. "What can I help you with?"

"I don't know where to start so just hear me out," I began, "it is about the miscarriage that I had."

"Yes, I remember. What about it?"

"Well, I have found out that the miscarriage was the result of a drug that I was given." I handed him over the drug order form paperwork.

"This isn't really my area." He turned the document over in his hands. "Are you saying the drug was ordered though us? We don't use this drug it must have been ordered in especially." Zusak scanned the paperwork through.

"Look who approved the order." I watched as his eyes as he darted to the bottom of the document.

"I can assure you that I did not approve this." He jumped up and went over to the other side of the desk and signed into the computer.

"I have found out that Amber Mason ordered the drug because she was having an affair with my husband. I only have text messages as proof."

"This is outrageous," Zusak typed away.

"I can't do anything to get my baby back but I thought I would make you aware that your name has been forged in the hope that it won't happen again," I said.

"Where is the original document?" Zusak snapped.

"I photocopied Miss Edward's copy in our office, I presume the original is in the drug room which is locked."

"I'll have her job for this," he fumed. I wanted no less.

"Makes sense to wait until you have interviewed for my job and replace her then when you have someone already to step into her shoes." I stood up. "Sorry to have brought it up but I couldn't leave with any unfinished business."

"I guess there is no chance you would stay if a better contract was offered," he raised his eyebrows in hope.

"Too much has happened now. I feel like everyone and everything is against me." It felt good to tell the truth. "Maybe after a while I would consider returning but for now I feel like the best thing is to have a break."

He nodded. "Leave this with me, I'll keep you posted."

I nodded and left the room. I didn't need him to keep me posted. I already had Amber's phone. All the information I should ever need was there.

Cassie quickly hung up the phone when I entered but I didn't need to ask who it was. I smiled at her and went about emptying my desk. I didn't want to leave until Grant came back so made myself a coffee and read through Amber's texts.

Cassie had messaged her about the theft of my aunt's money and about me being suspended. More money and overtime for them, or so they thought.

After half an hour I gave up waiting and left. I hadn't even made it out of the door when Cassie picked up the phone and dialled Amber's number.

Chapter 6

I spent all Friday tidying which was a pet hate of mine. Considering there were no children to clean up after it was amazing how dirty everything got.

The estate agent turned up early and he and his assistant took photographs and made positive comments about everything. I nodded and smiled politely but wasn't really feeling it. This had been my home for nearly ten years and I had planned to do so much here. But those plans had included Scott and even if he crawled back on his hands and knees, I would not reinstate any of those plans. He would never father my children or lay again with me in that bed. The idea of even sitting in the same room as him made my skin crawl. I felt an urgency to the whole thing. I couldn't move on until it was all over. I needed to rush everything and finalise all the details before he could make me change my mind.

I let out the estate agent's and slumped on the sofa that wasn't even a year old. Who would get the sofa and everything else for that matter? I couldn't take half of our belongings to London, Josh's apartment, from what I could remember, was too small. I needed to think clearly about what was about to happen. I couldn't live with Josh forever, I needed a plan.

I printed off a 'To Do' list from the internet and made a start. There was so much to do. I cancelled the television package, the internet, home insurance, the phone that no one ever used anyway and then contacted the gas, electric and water companies and gave the twenty-seventh as the last day in the house. If by some miracle Scott could buy me out then he would have to reinstate everything in his own name, I wasn't going to pay for his lifestyle anymore.

I pulled out Amber's phone and was starting to enjoy reading her messages more than watching the soaps. There were twenty-five messages between her and Cassie discussing my meeting with the director. Both seemed to think that my departure would mean extra hours for them and more money. I scrolled down to the end, deleting some as I went to make it more manageable. The last message was Amber asking Cassie to find out why Zusak had called her in for a meeting in the new year. Both decided she was getting an even bigger promotion and had arranged drinks in the new year to celebrate.

I put the phone down. Zusak must have found something, I wondered where she slipped up.

Scott's phone had nothing exciting on it. He must have telephoned his mother to tell her about us splitting up. The only texts that had been sent were a couple to Amber discussing money and the consent form. Amber was swaying him against it saying he would get more by going fifty-fifty, that is how the court would divide it.

I scowled at the phone, interfering wench. If we went through the court the divorce could take ages and I needed closure. I considered my options. I hadn't confessed knowing Amber's involvement for two reasons firstly saying it out loud would have made it real and my heart wasn't ready to accept that I had lost everything, and secondly there was a part of me that thought I might be able to use her to my advantage.

Come four ó clock I had run out of things to do. All my clothes had been tried on and either binned, charity bagged up or put in a laundry bag for London. The house was immaculate and the television was rubbish. On a normal day off I would have watched whatever was on and enjoyed it, or read a book, but I couldn't concentrate and ran out of things to do to busy my brain. I soon felt myself sinking into a depression. I flicked on the heating and sank into bed and cried. I cried for Scott, for the baby, I cried for Amber, the best friend who clearly wasn't the person I thought she had been, I cried for Cassie and the wedding I wasn't welcome to, but mostly I cried for the psycho I had become. Never would I have dreamt of breaking into someones house, stealing things they hold dear and damaging their car. The shame was overwhelming. I pulled the duvet over my head and pretended that I didn't exist.

My private pity party was interrupted by the shrill of my mobile phone. I really needed to change that ring tone to a nice soft pop song instead of the 100 decibel din that made me jump out of my skin every time it rang.

"Hi Charlotte, It's Grant. I'm really sorry about yesterday," he sounded rushed. "You were right about Amber, she cancelled another shift. I know you have officially left already, I should have known about that but that's probably my fault. Your covering money has been sorted out and will go into your next wage packet. Is there any chance in hell you would save my life and do a shift for me tomorrow, two till seven?"

He must have been desperate. I sat up in bed and cleared my throat so he wouldn't guess that he had woken me up. "I am guessing that you are desperate and wouldn't have asked if there was anyone else."

"I know, it sucks. I'm sorry to have to ask," Grant said. "I'm sorry to hear about you and Scott too, I'm really surprised."

"How did you know about that?" I asked, knowing the answer already.

"Cassie mentioned it, I presumed that you had told her," Grant answered innocently.

"No, I never mentioned it. To be honest since she didn't invite me to your wedding day, I presumed I had offended her somehow."

"What do you mean you're not invited? Of course you are invited."

"I know, I was surprised too, I mean you guys met at my wedding, but I suppose someone had to give up their seat for Amber," I added. No point in being polite now.

"I wasn't aware she and Cassie were friends. Sorry, I'll look into it," he said

"Look it doesn't matter, it isn't worth rocking the boat over. I am probably moving away anyway so let's just leave it as a working relationship that is coming to an end. I will work tomorrow because I know you need the help but anything after that is a definite no."

"Okay, thank you so much, I can't tell you enough how much you are saving my arse right now, it's more than I deserve." Grant heaved a massive sigh of relief and hung up.

Now I needed to work out what I was going to say to Cassie. Everything I said would be no doubt repeated to Amber so needed to be carefully thought out. Scott needed to sign that Consent Order and I would need to hard sell.

In the morning I carried on working through the 'To Do' List that I thought I would have finished by now. It had tired me out just hanging on the phone for hours on end. Why couldn't they set up online forms for you to fill in so that you didn't have to wait twenty-five minutes for an operative to take your call, then half the time they transferred you through to someone else? It was not a task I was keen to put off but not one I wanted to do either. Someone was missing a massive money making opportunity here. A scheme needed to be invented where you filed for a divorce and everything in your name automatically cancelled for you. I would have paid big money for it or a divorce planner maybe, they could be the same as a wedding planner but a bit less cheery with equal amounts of alcohol involved.

Usually Saturday mornings were the only time me and Scott always had off work together. His shift never started until five and I always had Saturday's off, now I wished I was at work already. The TV had nothing but sickly family movies on, the radio was depressing me with all it's Christmas songs and messages and a sudden fact washed over me, I was spending Christmas alone.

I did a stock take of the freezer, I couldn't take it with me. I pulled out a chicken to defrost and headed out to the bank and the post office.

Josh had emailed me the rent details for if I wanted to stay but said that I only needed to pay that if I was moving in. If it was only for a couple of months I could stay rent free. I copied out the address and changed all my bank details to Josh's address and at the post office I re-directed all my mail for three months. I didn't know how long it was going to take to set up a completely different life but I knew that I had to leave this one and start a fresh. London seemed as good a place as any to get started though I knew full well I was never going to be able to afford to live there. Josh may have earned a small fortune saving the world from criminal lowlifes but I was never going to earn anything as substantial.

I pulled into the hospital car park and tried not to think about Josh's job. If anything ever came of the fact that I had broke into a house and stole, it could mean major embarrassment for him. I wasn't really the kind of small fry criminal he was employed to foil, but still, the idea of causing him any trouble didn't sit well with me.

Cassie hung up the phone quickly as I entered the office and I pretended not to notice. Had she always been this lazy? I hadn't noticed it before.

"I hear there was a mix up with the wedding invites. I shouldn't have written them while drunk." Cassie smiled and handed me a new invite that only had my name on it.

"Why isn't Scott's name on here?" I asked, testing the waters.

"Oh, I heard…," she stammered, unsure of what to say.

"What did you hear? Considering that me and you haven't spoken about it and Scott is out of town." I leant in so she couldn't avoid looking at me.

"I think Ian from the gym said something to Amber. She must have misheard, I can add his name on." Cassie jumped up with a pen and I stopped her.

"It is okay, we will probably get a divorce, don't worry about it." I walked to the desk that was no longer mine and slumped my bag in-between my feet. I had put Amber's phone on silent in the hope that Cassie would message her while I was here.

"What happened? Do you want to talk about it?" She walked over to the coffee machine and I knew this was my chance.

"I heard him making a love call early hours of the morning, I read his messages and he had someone logged in as work who he has been ringing and texting for nearly two years."

Cassie handed me a coffee. "Do you know who she is?" Her eyes were wide and she didn't blink.

"No, but it really doesn't matter. I have read the texts and whoever she is she is clearly only after his money which is laughable because he doesn't really have any and by the time the divorce has been to court he will have even less."

"He will get half of the house though, won't he?" Cassie blew on her coffee, enjoying her role as Amber's spy.

"No, because I paid more in, I paid the majority of the bills and he had a habit of taking money out of the joint account of which there are records of." I took a sip and decided that machine coffee wasn't as nice as instant. "I gave him forms to fill in to complete a Consent Order, which is where you pre-agree everything, but I am hoping he doesn't fill it in. I have seen a lawyer since who said I would be better off financially if we go through the court, it will just take a bit longer. He will be lucky if he gets thirty percent, I'll get more from him than he will get from me." I didn't really know what I was talking about but she nodded wide eyed, drinking it all in.

"That isn't very much. I thought everything gets split down the middle if no children are involved," Cassie said.

"Well, there is also the fact that he drugged me to make me lose the baby so he could be sued for emotional stress and abuse, it will all come out in court. His parents will be so disappointed but actually it is about time they saw what a lowlife he really is."

"What drug? I thought your miscarriage was just one of those things," Cassie put down her cup.

"Nope, I read the texts. His mistress ordered the drug from America and told him how to administer it so they could continue their affair guilt free. She also tried to get him to mortgage the house to get more money out of him. She's lucky I don't know who she is and I am lucky that I found out before he managed to actually mortgage the house. Which reminds me, he also forged my signature on that document which is fraud, I must remember to tell my lawyer about that and get him to add it onto the list," I really had her attention now. "I feel sorry for his parents really, I mean with Sarah's cancer this is the kind of stress they could do without."

I slumped down into my chair and started on the patient's files that needed logging into the system. I should have really started with my rounds collecting paperwork from other departments but I didn't want Cassie to ring Amber and miss the call. I wanted the whole conversation to be via text so that I could read it later.

I had been hoping for an easy day but they obviously didn't get the late shift covered and now the desk overflowed with charts and paperwork that needed to be entered onto the system. I spent the first hour pulling out all the work that I knew was Cassie's and putting it to the bottom of the pile. I heard Amber's phone vibrate several times but left it so I could bulk read them at break. I also didn't want Cassie to get suspicious at my looking down every two minutes after she sent a text.

I waited until Cassie left the room for her break before I got the phone out and read through the recent texts. In the last hour alone there had been sixty-eight mainly from Amber lying through her teeth. She denied buying the drug and told Cassie I was making it all up to make Scott look bad and make myself look like the victim. She googled the Consent Order though and admitted it was a better idea than dragging everything up through court and had text Scott the details. I fist pumped the air, finally something was about to go my way. I put down the phone and made myself a cup of coffee using the not so bitter instant that had long been ignored since Cassie's engagement party. Of course Amber wouldn't want the details of my miscarriage dragged through the court because that would highlight her involvement.

I scrolled through the remainder of the texts, rolling my eyes as I went. Most of them were dribble going on about how they never meant this to happen, they were in love and I would find out eventually but it would be as if it only just happened. She and Scott had agreed to invent a mystery woman who he would have a brief fling with then they would get together next year. I had to smile at her cleverness, she really had thought of everything. Then Cassie asked the question I had been dying to know the answer to, what about David? Amber and David had been engaged since Valentine's Day and no mention of an actual wedding had been made. I waited for Amber's reply but it didn't come. I tucked the phone away and left to collect the other department's paperwork.

Maureen was sitting in her chair with her arms folded when I approached her bed, her face darkened when she saw me. "I never said you could take that money," she hissed.

"I don't know what you are talking about," I said, playing dumb. "You and Steven both asked me to lend you the money."

"You took my card from my bag," her voice raised in her fury.

"I lent you the money like I was asked to for your Christmas cards and I did that for you because your own children were too busy to do it for you," I smiled and plumped up her cushion while resisting the urge to put it over her miserable moaning face.

"You tricked me." Spit was flying everywhere.

"No, I did exactly what you asked me to do. Anyway It won't happen again, will it." I smiled at a nearby nurse who was checking the charts.

"No, it won't, Melissa is going to try and make my next appointment so you don't have to," Maureen said matter of a factly as if she was injuring me somehow.

"That's good because I am moving away next week and am not going to be able to sit with you anymore. I really came along to thank you for everything that you have ever done for me and to say goodbye. I doubt I'll be coming back down anytime soon."

"Who will take me to my appointments if you're not here?" A few members of staff glanced over as her voice raised several octaves.

"You just said Melissa was going to help you out which is for the best anyway as she is free all day, isn't she." I smiled and walked away before she could reply. It would do Melissa the world of good to help her own mother out for a change.

I felt good when I finally walked out of work. I had finished all the paperwork that was on my pile and then worked on Zusak's secretary's pile leaving a post-it note on top so he knew who had done it. Ordinarily I would have worked through Cassie's without a second thought, after all we were part of a team, but I still hadn't forgiven her. I could forgive her for not telling me about the affair. I guess knowing something like that puts you in a difficult situation, but I couldn't forgive her for taking sides. She had chosen camp Amber and no amount of apologies was going to make me think that the wedding invitation was a mistake.

I fumbled in my bag for my car keys. My bag was still full of paperwork and various other random documents that really should be filed away.

My keys were missing. I flipped over the front flap of the bag and felt for the door key, that was still in the pocket. I was about to turn back and check my locker in case they had fallen out but after a quick scan of the car park, it was quite clear the car was also missing.

I reached into my bag and pulled out Amber's phone. Scott had messaged her eight times since I had last checked and I cursed myself for ignoring it while I worked through Zusak's paperwork like Super girl. Scott had asked Amber if she could get the keys and Amber had enlisted Cassie to get them out of my bag. Now I was really glad I didn't do any of her paperwork.

I walked back into the hospital and borrowed the receptionists internal phone and called Grant's office. "Charlotte, I really wanted a quick chat with you before you left to apologise for a few things, I would hate you to leave with any bad feeling between us," he said.

"Well, it is a little too late for that now seeing as your fiancée stole my car keys out of my bag and now my car is gone," I snapped.

"That is absurd, why would she do that?"

"Good question, I suggest you ask her and check out the CCTV for the last hour. A better question would be how the hell I managed to file all my paperwork and Zusak's while Cassie has done nothing all day. You need to work out how your department is going to survive now the only person who actually did any work has been pushed out." I hung up quickly. It wasn't Grant's fault really. It was in his best interests to make sure Cassie was well paid but he still had to answer to Zusak and the directors.

I stomped out of the building and started the long walk home, reading more of Amber's messages while I walked. Anything that was trivial, I deleted, but anything that I thought might come in handy for later revenge I kept. There must be something on this phone that could be used against her.

I didn't know what I was expecting when I got home. I guessed that with Scott taking the car there was a chance he came home and took some more of his stuff, but I hadn't expected him to take everything.

The first thing I noticed when I entered the hall was the phone missing as well as the small hall table it sat on, this had belonged to my mother. The television, the unit, the sofas, the kitchen appliances were all gone. There was no way he took all that in the car, not by himself anyway. I moved upstairs with a cold frost hardening over my insides. The two junk rooms had been left untouched but the main two had been cleared out. The bed, the spare bed and the wardrobes were all gone.

I hadn't expected this. Most of this stuff I had paid for and now I had nothing. I had expected him to be reasonable about splitting the belongings. He would get the gym equipment but everything else was pretty much all mine.

I went back downstairs and surveyed the lounge, he had even taken the Christmas tree. I ran back upstairs to get the cordless vacuum that I had acquired from twenty-five Old School Close but it was missing. He had obviously opened the spare bedroom door grabbed a couple of things and not bothered with the rest. I moved the black sacks that I had sorted through and behind the coats in the wardrobe, the Louis Vuitton bag was still there. In his haste, he hadn't ventured far in the room.

My stomach churned. How could someone I knew like the back of my hand turn into a completely different person without me noticing?

I moved on. The garage was bare but the garage attic hadn't been touched. I pulled down all the camping stuff and set myself up a camp in the bedroom. Camping had never been my thing so the idea of sleeping on an airbed while my real bed, that I had paid for, was probably sitting somewhere in the back on a truck, didn't sit well with me. Scott wouldn't need it, he was about to go to the cabin where he would get a nice kingsize bed all to himself.

I hated him. I would have to think of something equally as fitting to right this wrong.

"What's up?" Josh asked down the phone.

I took a deep breath. I had practiced this conversation about ninety times and cried with self pity every time. "Scott took the car but it is okay because he also cleared out the entire house so will probably all fit into your car," my voice started to wobble.

"Is he not at the cabin?"

"No, not until tomorrow," I whispered.

"So what are you sleeping on?" Josh's voice started to raise. "Do you want me to come and get you?"

"No," I lied. This was his first Christmas with Meg's parents who were in the military. He had been looking forward to it and dreading it in equal measure since September, the last thing he needed was my miserable face. "I'm okay, I'm sorry, I just needed someone to talk to. He even took mum's hall table." The tears started to fall.

Josh swore quietly which signalled that people were near enough to hear him. "I'll have a think about things then ring you back, okay."

"Don't come back early Josh. I'm a grown woman and I am happy enough knowing that I have somewhere to stay, nothing else matters. I will see you in a couple of days."

"Are you sure?" He asked doubtfully.

"Sure, have a nice Christmas. We will catch up soon." I hung up the phone and walked to the kitchen pantry where all the cabin presents were stored, it was empty. All the presents I had bought for others had been taken, my presents from Amber and everyone else were gone. Even the cheap bottle of wine that had been given to me by a patient had been taken.

I looked at the sink and the chicken I had taken out for Christmas Day was gone.

I ran upstairs and hid under the freezing cold sleeping bag and cried and cried and cried until there was nothing left to cry.

Chapter 7

Christmas morning I popped to the local shop and picked up a few bits that didn't require a fridge or a freezer to keep them fresh. Christmas dinner had consisted of a cheese salad sandwich and a bottle of rosé wine. I could have eaten out. The local restaurant still had places and were not an unreasonable price but the idea of sitting alone surrounded by smiling families depressed me no end.

Everything was now boxed and lined up at the door in priority order. Everything at the back that didn't fit in Josh's car would be left outside for the bin men. My stuff had been folded and boxed nicely, Scott's stuff was thrown in a pile with little regard. It was a small gesture at righting the balance. I gave him the same respect he had given me and my things, though to be fair he had stolen my things so it wasn't really the same thing. The house was bare now to the point were it didn't feel like home. Nothing about it was familiar or inviting and fact that Scott had stolen my mother's hall table was burning a hole into my chest. Maybe I should have just torched his stuff so he could fumble through the ashes.

I checked Scott's phone. I had promised myself not to even think about it on Christmas Day but I wasn't very good at entertaining myself without the Television or the iPad. Scott had left a small selection of my books but I couldn't concentrate and had given up after the first page.

Scott was now at the cabin texting Amber about how he was very much looking forward to the next year they were going to spend together and he was nagging at her to end her engagement with David. Amber had returned all the gooey sentiment and I resisted the urge to bring up my sandwich. She and David were at her mother's house and splitting up would have to wait until after the New York holiday. Mid-January was an ideal time to end it with David as the bills would start to come in and that is when all the arguments would begin. She would simply say she couldn't take it anymore and leave the bills with him and start over. A normal person would have been concerned about how little she felt about her current fiancé but not Scott, the guy was an idiot.

I put down the phone and thought for a moment, Amber had recently transformed her dining room into a mini gym which meant her garage would now be bare. She had always said that when the gym equipment was out of it she would park her car in it but the car was with her in Yorkshire. I pulled out Amber's phone and scrolled through the messages but there was nothing on there regarding where Scott had hidden my belongings.

I went out for a walk and, for the first time ever, wished I had a dog. Families were out trying out their new bikes and these Segways that seemed to cause more accidents than the bikes. And then there was me walking, without a dog, looking as shady as I felt.

It was dark by the time I had made it to Amber's house. I checked all the doors and was not surprised to find them all locked. I tried the garage but that too was locked. She could have given Scott a key before he left and then I remembered Cassie. Cassie had given Scott the keys out of my bag so perhaps she also gave him keys to Amber's garage. The more I thought about it the more it made sense. I lifted the garage door and it rose about an inch before the lock clicked into place. I took some photos on my phone but I couldn't make anything out because there was stuff in the way.

I walked away with a smile on my face, convinced that the stuff in the way was *my* stuff.

I text Amber and Cassie wishing them both a Merry Christmas and didn't mean a word. I actually hoped that the two of them would burn up into ash the next time they told a lie. One of them would slip up eventually. Amber's reply was a basic 'Merry Christmas catch up with you soon,' but Cassie had text back in detail. She denied stealing my keys. She vowed that Grant was looking into it and that I had probably just dropped them somewhere. She then went on to moan that she was being made to work Boxing Day to catch up with paperwork. Her job was on the line and they were going to make me a better offer to return.

Perfect. I offered her two hours Boxing Day morning to help her get on top of it but assured her that I had no intention of going back. I advised her not to tell anyone so that it will look like she did it. She thanked me repeatedly and I formulated a plan. I would only need Cassie to leave the room for a moment so that I could search for Amber's key. I only wanted my table back, Scott could keep the rest. The table was small enough to be carried on a bus and if Josh's car was full to the brim then I would hold it on my lap. This table was the only thing of my mother I had left and there was no way he was going to keep it. The rest of the stuff I could replace with my parking ticket money that I still hadn't counted. I had nearly opened it all up in the morning as a 'Merry Christmas' treat to myself but once I had pulled it out of the wardrobe another sudden wave of guilt had washed over me and had I pushed it back in. The Louis Vuitton bag was the only thing not lined up by the door, I couldn't face it. The shame I felt every time I thought about it was bad enough but seeing it made me nauseous. It was a reminder of how low I had sunk.

"Did you have a nice Christmas?" Cassie boomed, when I walked in Boxing Day morning. Despite it being seven-thirty in the morning and her job being on the line, she was still writing in her wedding planner and going by the array of nail varnishes and toiletries she had brought in, I was guessing that I would be doing the bulk of the work today.

"No, not really considering that Scott cleared the house out. He even took the Christmas tree and the chicken that I had planned to cook for myself Christmas Day." I didn't look up from my desk which had been piled up with the real work she was supposed to be getting through.

"What did you eat then?" Cassie asked quietly, putting down her planner.

"A cheese sandwich," I replied. "He took the cooker, that I had paid for, the microwave, which I had paid for, and also the fridge which I also had paid for, so eating anything hot was out of the question."

"That is awful, you should have text me, you could have joined us." She walked over to my desk and rubbed my arm and for a moment, I remembered the Cassie I used to know and love. "Did you like your Christmas present though?" She suddenly brightened up.

"Scott took everything, Cassie, including all my Christmas presents, I had nothing." I looked back at the computer screen trying to hold the tears in.

"He had no right to do that, I paid for that gift for you. Excuse me, I have to pop out a minute." Cassie grabbed her bag and left the room. I watched her through the window as she looked around and entered the store cupboard. I hadn't bought any phones with me, not even my own, because of the extra weight they added so if she was calling Amber I would never know what was said.

I walked over to her desk and started shifting through the endless supply of hidden paperwork that really should have been filed ages ago. Each drawer was stuffed to the brim, it would have taken hours to go through it all.

"What are you looking for?" Cassie returned.

"Stapler," I lied catching my breath. I grabbed the stapler from the drawer and returned to my desk. This was going to be harder than I thought.

"Oh yeah, sorry, I took some things from your desk." She half smiled and slumped into her seat.

"It is okay, I won't be needing it anymore." I smiled and started on the nearest document. Crazy how she was up to her eyeballs in paperwork yet she chose to use her time raiding my desk!

I studied her features as she typed into her computer. Where would an untidy person keep a key? I asked myself. It could have been in her handbag or even on her chain of keys or it could not even be here at all, this could all be a fantasy solution made up in my head. Scott could have hired a truck and dumped all the stuff off at his mum's bungalow. Though this I doubted.

I worked the first hour and enjoyed Cassie's banter. I had missed human interaction and though I wasn't getting paid to be there, I soon slipped back into the routine of the office and for a while, forgot why I was really there. No further mention had been made about my missing car keys and I wondered if Grant had bothered checking the CCTV at all or had just taken her word for it that it wasn't her. I wasn't supposed to be coming back so maybe he had already forgotten about it and had brushed the whole thing under the carpet, either way, I didn't bring it up. For a couple of hours or so, I needed her on my side.

"Wedding planning is so hard, you are coming, aren't you?" She asked as she poured her third cup of coffee.

"I wouldn't miss it for the world, I bet it is going to be amazing." I smiled and carried on typing while she painted her toe nails. Would I go to this wedding? Was Scott going to be there with Amber? Would she be going to go alone or still be with David by then? Then I wondered what her invite had said. Cassie knew Amber was having an affair with Scott so whose name had she written in the card. Maybe a new invite had been written out now me and Scott had publicly broken up.

I made Cassie three more cups of coffee before she finally left the room to use the toilet. I flicked through the wedding planner until I found the section I was looking for. *To Amber and Guest*, I was slightly disappointed.

I flicked through seeing what else was interesting in there. I hadn't bothered with a planner but my wedding had been low key and hadn't taken over my life the same way as it had dominated Cassie's. As I slumped the planner back on the table several envelopes slipped out of the back. I scooped them up and flicked through them. There were payment envelopes and invoice receipts for the cake, the photographer and the signs, whatever they were, then there was an envelope with Amber's name on it. I opened the envelope and reached inside. Inside there was a flat gold key very much like our garage key. I slipped in into my back pocket and gathered up the remaining paperwork to put back on Cassie's desk when a booming voice made me jump. "What are you doing here?" My heart dropped.

"Helping Cassie with some paperwork," I smiled, but Dr Zusak didn't return it.

"Ah, Dr Zusak." The colour ran from Cassie's cheeks and then a blush erupted over her whole face. "Charlotte was just leaving, she just popped into to give me my Christmas present."

"Why does it smell of nail varnish in here?" He glanced at Cassie's bare feet which answered his question. He looked at my bare finger nails then looked back at Cassie for an answer. She looked at me for back up but I said nothing, I had what I came for and now needed to leave.

"That was from earlier, when I was on a break." She was starting to fluster and I left her to it. I had until tomorrow to get my mum's table. I really wanted to get it now but really should wait until it was dark in case someone saw me.

I paid the bus driver and sat at the back where I could think about where my life was going. Josh couldn't put me up forever. He and Meg would need to make a decision about whether they were going to live in London or Edinburgh and I didn't think an engagement was far away for them either. They had been together for three years and he adored her. The only problem was her heart and job lay in Scotland and his in the heart of London. A long distance relationship was fine in the beginning but if they wanted a family then one of them was going to have to cave.

I needed a plan. Josh had said that I could stay for a couple of months rent free so I really needed a two month plan. Two months to pull myself together and decide on a direction for my life to take.

I thanked the driver and headed toward my house. A removal van was parked up my drive and my heart rose for a second thinking that Scott had, perhaps, had a change of heart and returned some things, but it wasn't Scott standing there. It was an extremely good looking guy in a suit, looking annoyed to be standing out in the cold.

"Can I help you?" I asked as I approached him. He looked like an estate agent but then why would he have a removal van?

"Josh sent me to collect you and your things, I've been calling you for ages." He shoved his phone into his pocket and he moved away from the door so I could let myself in.

"Sorry, I left my phone at home, I wasn't expecting him until tomorrow." I swung the door open and he marched in, so much for ladies first.

"He said his car wasn't big enough and I couldn't get a van for tomorrow. Where is everything?" He asked as he rushed through the empty rooms.

"Scott took it all. I do need to detour though to collect a table," I smiled.

He followed me up the stairs.

"Is this where you have been sleeping?" He pointed to the airbed.

"Yes, and usually gentlemen wait to be invited into a girl's bedroom before insulting it." I pulled the plug out of the airbed and watched it deflate.

"Looks like a squat." He looked around with distaste and a wave of annoyance washed over me.

"Thanks, I did the best with what I was left with after he slept with my best friend and stole my Christmas." I folded up the sleeping bag and shoved it into a black sack. "He took the TV, he took the tree, he even took my presents that were for me and the Christmas dinner I had defrosting in the sink."

"Did he take the crystal glasses set that I bought you for your wedding?"

I turned and took in his features. "Yes, it's Ryan isn't it. You were Josh's date to my wedding. Sorry I didn't recognise you, it was a manic day and seems like a million years ago now."

"Well, I haven't seen you since. Your aunt thought we were gay lovers," he laughed and I was affected by how good looking he was. He looked younger than Josh, I guessed about twenty-five and he had that designer stubble where nothing was out of place. "I'm not gay by the way, I see you wondering."

"I was not even thinking it, I was thinking how surprised I am that you don't have anything better to do on Boxing Day morning."

"I owe Josh a lot so made time for him, but I don't want to spend all day in your hovel so let's hit the road. There is a bed in his spare room so you don't really need to bring this stuff." Ryan grabbed the sack and left the room before I could answer.

It only took twenty minutes to load up the van and put all the stuff that I didn't want into the garage. Scott could decide what he wanted and what he didn't. I was sure I would never camp again so piled it all neatly up. "What about this?" Ryan held up the Louis Vuitton bag and I felt the familiar wave of guilt wash over me.

"Pack it, it is the only decent thing I own and it isn't even mine." He raised his eyebrows but said nothing. He carried it to the van and ushered for me to get in. I put the house keys under a pot and walked away from everything that I had ever known.

"I need to pick up my table. I think it is in my ex-friend's garage." I gave Ryan directions and he pulled into Amber's drive.

"And does this ex-friend know we are here?" He asked.

"Nope," I said, getting the key out of my back pocket. "Nor does she know that I know it's her my husband has been having an affair with for the past two years or that I know she poisoned me forcing me to miscarry in my second trimester." I shoved up the garage door and was welcomed by all my stuff that had been heaped up like trash.

"And all of a sudden I don't feel that guilty about this breaking and entering malarky. These are obviously really shitty people." He smiled and flashed off a row of dazzling teeth that shone bright white against his Italian looking skin. "What are we stealing? It will all fit in."

"It isn't stealing because it all belongs to me anyway. If he wants the crap so badly he can keep it, I just want my hall table, it is irreplaceable. It's mahogany with small flower detail in the corners."

I started shifting boxes and placing stuff into neater piles. The whole contents of my life had just been chucked into a garage without a care. I saw my camera bag shoved underneath the Christmas tree and hoped that he hadn't broken it in his hurry to prove his point.

"I can probably fix it," Ryan said, lifting my table out of a corner.

My heart sank. A leg was hanging off and there was a scratch across the top where he had thrown a game station on top. "My mother died when I was twelve and this was the only thing I have left, except a couple of pictures." The tears flooded down and Ryan just stared, unsure of what to do.

"Why would he take it knowing that it meant so much to you?"

"Good question, lets ask him." I walked out of the garage, threw my camera bag in the back of the van and dialled Scott's number.

"Hello, this is Sarah," his sister answered quietly. "Scott is out for a walk, he left his phone behind."

"Hi Sarah, did you have a nice Christmas?" It wasn't her fault. I took deep breaths to calm myself down. This could be the last time I ever spoke to her and I didn't want her to feel any ill will towards me.

"It was lovely thank you, how was yours?"

"Miserable actually, Scott cleared the house out while I was at work. He took the bed, the TV, the cooker, the Christmas tree, the fridge freezer and all the contents. He even took my Christmas dinner that was defrosting in the sink. I spent the whole of Christmas squatting in my empty house without a single present to open because he stole those too, so please feel free to pass my thanks on to him for that."

Ryan tapped me on the shoulder and held up wrapped presents with my name on them. I nodded and Ryan put them in the van.

"I'm so sorry to hear that, Charlotte. Obviously this is a difficult time and it has put us in an awful position," her response sounded rehearsed.

"It is fine but what is not fine is that Scott has stolen things that I paid for and he even took the hall table that was the only thing I have that belonged to my mother." I forced the tears back and tried to keep my wobbling voice in check. "You can pass on to him that he can forget signing the Consent Order. I have made a list of everything that he has taken, that he didn't pay for, and it will be deducted from what he is awarded. Considering he also stole money out of the joint account and stopped paying into it, I'm doubting very much that he will come out with much at all," I huffed. "I will see him in court." I hung up and walked to the back of the van where Ryan was putting random things in.

"Found the glasses that I bought you and a few other things that may be of use." He held up a packet of tampons. "Not sure what your husband thought he could use these for."

"Honestly, the guy is a dick. Pack them I need them and might not be able to afford anymore."

"Looks like he is trying to hurt you more than he has already." Ryan tucked the tampons in-between some boxes and slammed the van doors shut. "Josh's TV is bigger, the cooker is newer and the spare bed is perfectly comfortable, a fact that I can vouch for. You happy to leave the rest?"

I nodded through the tears. Ryan moved to the passenger side of the van and held the door open for me to get in. I left the garage key in the lock and got in the van. Everything I owed was now in this van and it was pathetic. I felt pathetic.

"When my ex-girlfriend, Alice, left me, she just smashed everything up," Ryan said after about an hour of silence. "Cost one hundred and fifty-two thousand pounds to replace what she broke."

"Did you cheat on her?" I asked, glad of having the chance to think about something else for a moment.

"No, I adored her," he glanced at me briefly then returned his eyes to the road. "She was jealous about the attention I got from other girls when we were out and her paranoia grew until it consumed her. One day she text me saying she couldn't take it anymore. She was leaving me for my friend and hoped me and Daisy would be very happy."

"And who is Daisy?" I asked.

"I have no idea, but when I got home she had trashed the place. She and my friend Alex then emigrated to Australia and I never saw them again."

"Ouch," I said, shifting in my seat.

"No one ever feels sorry for the good looking guys though, do they?" He looked over and gave another perfect smile.

"I guess not," I spoke truthfully. "I guess we normal people already think you have it all and what is one heartbreak when you have fifty more girls lining up to be your next mistake," I laughed.

"Ouch," he gently slapped my leg. "What has Josh told you about me then?"

"You went to college and university together." I racked my brain for Ryan related information that had long been stored into my brain. "You are the good looking socialite who has a very rich family who made your money in property but you choose to work in fashion, probably to liaise with all the good looking models," I smiled.

"Oooh, all true. nWe run our own magazine now. Well, my dad actually owns it, I just smile and make everyone say 'yes' to things."

"It is so depressing, I will have to find a job and a life." I flicked the heating on and relaxed into my chair.

"There are loads of hospitals and medical centres in London, I'm sure something will come up." Ryan negotiated a roundabout and I sensed we were getting close to London. All the fields had given way to high buildings and the traffic was building up, slowing us down.

My stomach growled. It wasn't even lunch time yet, but in my rush to join Cassie at work, I had skipped breakfast. I put my head into my hands and ignored the pangs. The heat in the van was blasting on my face and it wasn't until I felt Ryan's hand on my shoulder that I realised that I had fallen asleep.

"We're here," he said, holding my door open.

"Sorry, I didn't sleep very well on my airbed," I smiled.

"I didn't want to talk to you anyway," he laughed.

He had already carried all my stuff into Josh's apartment and laid it neatly into the small spare room which was now made smaller by everything that I owned in the world, which wasn't much.

"Do you want me to help you unpack?" He lifted up the Louis Vuitton bag. "I am deeply curious to know what it is here that makes you cringe so much." He looked up and my smile fell. "And if it doesn't belong to you, why do you have it?"

"I stole it," I said, deadpan, "and everything in it." I took it out of his hands and shoved it into the corner of the room. "I was angry, suffering with PMT, very emotional and I did something that I am deeply ashamed off." Just saying it made me feel like a massive weight had been lifted off my shoulders.

"Sounds fascinating," he smirked and my heart skipped a beat. This guy was gorgeous, it hurt my eyes just to look at him. "Let's return the van and have some lunch. I doubt Josh will have anything in and your stomach is louder than your voice."

"Thank you so much for your help but don't you have anything else to do? Won't your family be missing you?" It was Boxing Day after all

"Nope, my family are all in Dubai for Christmas and New Year. I stayed behind to close off the magazine. I spent Christmas Day in a soup kitchen with a few of my cousins." He grabbed one of Josh's jackets from the coat rack and held it out for me to put on. "Lets feed that monster in your stomach," he smiled and I followed him out of the door.

Chapter 8

"So the guy that scratched your car was related to your friend who stole your husband and your friend and your promotion?" Ryan took another sip of his wine. We had returned the van and dropped the keys into the letterbox. Ryan had then called us a taxi and found us a table at a quaint little pub set back from the road. We took a low table by a roaring fire and sat and grazed. We started with olives and bread and then ordered several starter courses instead of a main and made our own Tapas meal. People milled in and out after doing their sales shopping and Ryan seemed to know everyone, mainly women.

"I know what we need," he said, jumping up after I had finished my entire life story. "I'll be back in a minute. Order more wine but do *not* order dessert without me," he smiled and left the pub. I watched him as he tried to get across the street without someone stopping him to chat. It was half an hour later when he returned with a bag full of stationery.

"What is all this?" I asked, topping up his glass.

"This is your Christmas present from me." He laid out all the stationery across the table. "Firstly a diary so you can write all about me in it." He slid it across the table and laid a posh looking fountain pen on top. "This is so we can work out all the things we need to do to get your life back on track starting with closure."

"It is a bit early for closure isn't it, I've only just moved out."

"Jesus, Charlotte, you have taken more steps in a week than some do in a year. You found out your husband was having an affair, cloned his phone, burgled a house and moved out in the same week, I've never met anyone who has moved faster," he said. "A plan, let's work on the plan and not waste another minute. This will save you thousands on therapy." He pulled out a pen and notebook and started writing. "We did an article last month about getting closure. We all have that one friend who keeps repeating the same old tale about someone else and they keep repeating it because they don't feel like you have really listened so they can't move past it."

"Okay, so what has that got to do with me? Both my friends turned out to be two faced, back stabbing biatches." I sipped more rosé wine and savoured the feeling it gave me as it slid down my throat.

"We need to work out what causes you anxiety and work through it, then you can move on to a happier stage of your life and forgive those who have wronged you."

"Well, I don't feel annoyed about the parking ticket anymore and the car with the scratch down it is with Scott now anyway," I shrugged. He would have to pay to get the bodywork fixed now.

"Yes, because you committed a felony and restored the balance of justice," he smiled. "I can't really advocate that you do that again. Are you happy to draw a line through that and move on?"

"No," I said, surprising myself. "I don't like the idea that the drugs are still there. Please don't tell Josh," I pleaded. "I don't really know why I told you, it is the worst thing I have ever done in my life, I'm so ashamed." I started to cry and Ryan handed me a napkin. Another girl came over to chat with him but he waved her off and she left in a sulk giving me a death stare as she walked back to her group of friends.

"I don't think Josh would ever believe it so relax about it. The people were scumbags and it wasn't even their money that bought the things, just remind me never to piss you off." He smiled and waved away another girl.

"Thank you. Josh means more to me than anyone else in the world." I sipped the wine which was starting to take effect.

"Well, that is something we have in common, Josh is my rock. Every time I have strayed from my path he has picked me up by the scruff of my neck and steered me right. Though in hindsight I didn't really need the law degree he made me stick to." He held up his wine glass and motioned for me to toast, "To Josh, the best of both of us." I raised my glass and I noticed more women looking our way.

"Am I keeping you from something?" I asked, nodding my head in the direction of the bar.

"No, I hate coming out. Working on the magazine means I work in particular circles," he paused looking for the right words to say. "I have to be nice to everyone, charming and approachable, but sometimes, when I'm out, planning world domination," he held up my notebook, "all the interruptions can get pretty annoying," he breathed deeply. "It doesn't help either that I look like a Greek God."

I burst out laughing at the pained look on his face.

"No really," he defended himself, "when I was a teenager it was a gift, I could have any girl that I wanted and I did." He raised his eyebrows and there was hardly a wrinkle on his brow. "But now I am older and wiser it's a bind." He waved at some girls at the bar and carried on. "When I actually find one I like they are usually put off at my kindness towards the others and the jealousy is unbearable. I think of Alice smashing up my things and it makes me shudder at the idea off going through that again. I am on a women break which makes things worse because they all think that I have a slot open for them or worse that I can get them into the modelling industry."

"What about a date with Beckham?" I laughed again. "I still don't feel sorry for you." I shook my head.

"You will when you're freezing and it takes us five hours to walk you home because of the constant interruptions." He made notes in the notebook.

"Anything to take my mind of my diabolical life is okay with me," I smiled. "How did you get closure from Alice?" I asked and instantly regretted asking, his beautiful features twisted slightly and I could see the pain.

"I haven't. She moved to Australia and deleted me off Facebook well she deleted me from her entire life. She changed her phone number and I have haven't spoken to her since.

I still have her picture beside my bed and am still waiting for the wave of realisation that it has absolutely no right to be there."

He sipped some more wine and chatted to some guys who approached our table and I took the time to watch the way his mouth moved when he spoke. It wasn't hard to see why the world gravitated towards him he really was a thing of beauty. His hair was chocolate brown with no hint of grey and his eyes were a warmer shade of brown than mine. I wondered what Amber would have made of him and what Ryan would have made of her, they certainly would have been well suited.

"Sorry about that," he waved to the guys as they joined some girls at the bar. "There is a party tonight at The Loft if you are interested."

I glanced at the clock on the wall it was now four ò clock. "You don't have to babysit me you know," I smiled. This guy must have a million and one other people he would rather hang out with.

"Josh asked me to look after you until he gets back, now if I left you alone what would you do?"

I thought about this for a moment, I did have some unpacking to do. "Wallow, I would wallow, but I really don't have anything to wear," I smiled.

"That isn't a problem, it's an excuse for some more fun. Lets wrap this up and hit the shops." He smiled and it was hard not to feel uplifted by his mood. He grabbed my list of unfinished business and ushered me out of the pub.

He was right, it took ages to get out through the crowds and make it across the street. He seemed to know everyone and was obviously popular, mainly with beautiful young women.

He handed me a size ten dress and I laughed and handed it back. "I think I was last a size ten when I was aged ten." I laughed and moved toward the size fourteen rail.

"Okay, this is the wrong shop." He grabbed my hand and led me out down a side alley away from the busy shopping street. He keyed in a code and we entered a shabby looking building.

"Okay, this looks like the kind of place you are going to murder me and they will find my body three years later." I waited while my eyes adjusted to the lack of light.

"And who would look for you?" He laughed. "It is only dark because they weren't expecting anyone to use this entrance until the next year. Take off the wedding ring." He ran up the stairs and I followed slowly behind. I slipped the wedding ring into my back pocket and forced the thought of it and what it had once represented, out of my mind.

"Hi Ryan, we weren't expecting you." An immaculately dressed woman lurched toward the door and dragged him into a hug.

I looked away and took in the room. It seemed to be a dressmaker's room. Fabrics and tape measures lined the walls and scissors and post-it notes were all over the place. If Ryan thought they could make me something by tonight, he was crazy.

"I know shopping detour. This is my girlfriend, Charlotte. We have a hot date and she needs to feel special, especially for later on, you know what I mean," he raised his eyebrows and the woman gushed.

"He's drunk," I said flatly.

"But still so handsome, you lucky thing. Let's measure you up." She took my hand and started to undo my blouse buttons.

"I'll wait outside." Ryan practically shouted, clearly seeing the look of panic on my face.

"Nothing you haven't seen before, I'm sure," her eyes twinkled.

"First date, Trish," he yelled from the other side of the panel.

"Ooh, how exciting," she smiled, taking my breasts into her hands. "These clothes are all wrong for her," she shouted over my head.

"I know," Ryan yelled back and I wished he had actually waited outside rather than just ducked behind a screen.

"I am still here, you know." I smiled despite the embarrassment of practically being naked on front of a stranger. I had only ever been measured up once before when I was a bridesmaid, after that I had always guessed my bra size myself. Trish wrote all my measurements down and walked past me and handed the sheet to Ryan.

"Okay, let's see if Marsha is free." He smiled and ushered me out of the room while I was still doing up buttons.

"Who's Marsha?" I asked. The room had opened up into a row of booths all set out like a lavish bedroom. Large crystal chandeliers hung over red and gold velvet chaise lounges and people were milling about drinking champagne. "What is this place?" I asked with amazement.

"Probably your worst nightmare," he said, leading me into a booth full of half naked women. A few ladies had received a spray tan and were walking around in nothing but paper thongs and others were happily being waxed in full view of others. I looked down not sure where to put my eyes but Ryan just walked right in the middle of them like it was an average Tuesday in a board room.

My heart dropped as an overly bubbly blonde said there was a space for me. She took my hand and led me into a back room. She told me to undress then went out to talk to Ryan.

"Oh isn't he adorable, you lucky thing." She gushed, obviously won over by his charm. I thought about telling her that I wasn't his girlfriend but then thought better of it. He obviously lied for a reason so I let it be.

"He is certainly something else," I said, meaning every word but then all Josh's friends were decent. None of them stole his girlfriends or stole all his goods.

"I love him. If I wasn't married and was twenty years younger, I would give him a run for his money," she laughed. She didn't look a day over thirty herself and I was going to tell her this but then she pulled off a wax strip and the searing pain made all ideas of paying her a compliment run out of my mind, it was agony.

"Why do women do this?" I asked after she had finished legs, bikini and armpits.

"You will know later when you don't have to shave for several weeks." She rubbed my cheek as if she was a proud mother. "Ryan has gone for coffee he said to send you to Nathan and Ruby." She reached over and pressed an intercom button and a young girl with purple hair and lots of piercings bounced into the room and grabbed my hand.

"Ruby is so excited to meet you, you're lucky she had a space. Everyone is here spending their Christmas vouchers," she smiled, still holding my hand. "We have been rushed off our feet."

"What time are you open till?" I asked trying to calm my nerves at whatever was going to happen next.

"Ten, but we always run over after Christmas." She checked her watch, "You have plenty of time."

After two hours of having my hair done with a guy called Nathan and an hour having my make-up done with Ruby, I learnt that I was in the back of a massive London department store where your above average Joe public come to be pampered and have a personal shopper. It seemed that everyone was in love with Ryan, including Nathan and it was hard to be aloof when he asked about our fictitious relationship so I stuck with the truth, Ryan was a friend of my brother's and I hadn't seen him for a long time.

"All done, what do you think?" Ruby swivelled the chair so that I was facing the mirror. My hair had been dyed a light brown colour and golden highlights ran through to the ends like strands of glitter and my make-up was amazing, it didn't look like me.

"It is beautiful, thank you." I realised that I didn't have my purse on me and even if I had, my bank balance was abysmal. I would need money out of the Louis Vuitton bag to pay for this lot.

Ruby led me out into the last room which was lined with clothes of all sorts. Each garment was more exquisite than the first. I ran my fingers over the fabric and for a moment got lost in my own world. This was what it was like to be rich and for the first time ever, I wished I was someone else.

"I was thinking this one." Ryan rushed wearing a suit. He held up a champagne coloured dress with a chiffon skirt and sequins all over. He flashed a smile and lifted up underwear in the other hand.

"Nice!" I smiled. "I dread to think how much this costs. My money is back at Josh's"

"We are not thinking about that now. Try these on," he handed me the underwear. "Pria has gone to find some shoes." He stood there smiling until he got the hint and turned around. "Confidence is the one thing I can't buy," he laughed.

"Perhaps that is a good thing. Not everything should be so easily obtained." I slipped into the underwear not taking my eyes off Ryan's back. I didn't expect him to turn around but I wasn't comfortable with him in the room. I slipped in the dress and was amazed by how soft it felt. "Can you do me up please?" The dress flared out at the waistline but the top was tight like a corset the back of which curved out both sides like two C's back to back like the Chanel logo.

He turned and I turned so he could do up the button at the back. He moved my hair slowly off my neck and I shuddered as his fingers traced my bare back up to my neck. "I felt that," he whispered and I shuddered again as his hot breath made contact with my skin.

"Oh sorry, I didn't mean to interrupt." A beautiful brunette with the longest eyelashes I had ever seen breezed in holding up some beige shoes. An army of guys followed her in, carrying a variety of boxes and stacked them up against the wall. She glanced at Ryan with a pained expression before quickly looking away. She forced a smile on her face and walked toward me with the shoes. "These will be perfect." She bent down and lifted my foot of the ground and guided them in. "You look beautiful," she said sheepishly. She looked again at Ryan and I felt a stab of guilt. S he liked him as well and he was misleading all of them into believing we were a couple.

I opened my mouth to speak but Ryan's hands were again on my bare back and I forgot what I was about to say. "I think they are perfect. Let's grab a handbag and then we can be off."

"I'll grab that for you." Pria forced a smile on her face and practically ran out of the room.

"You were going to rat me out, weren't you?" Ryan slipped his arms around me and turned me towards the mirror. "Look what a beautiful couple we are."

"She clearly has feelings for you, how can you be so cold?" I was getting annoyed. Being good looking didn't give anyone the right to treat people like they were toys.

He took his hands away from my waist and took a seat beside the mirror. "Me and Pria have had the talk and I can't help the way she feels," he looked annoyed at having to defend himself.

"What talk?" I asked not talking my eyes of my unfamiliar reflection in the mirror.

"The talk I get bored of giving," he said as Pria waltzed back into the room holding several handbags of similar colour and design. "Thanks Pria," he smiled broadly and I swear I actually saw her heart melt. "Could you please get Grady to drop this all off at my place and charge it to my account." He took a handbag out of her arms and waved her out of the room. I watched him through the mirror as he added my bag of stationery on to the pile. He then reached into several bags, filled up the handbag and placed it onto my arm.

"I'm sorry," I whispered. He had been nothing but kind to me and I had judged him which I had no right to do. I turned to face him and gave him my best smile.

"You have nothing to apologise for. I have a lot of unwelcome attention and I can't help that. The only thing I can do is let them down as gently as I can without hurting their feelings anymore than necessary." He paused as staff entered the room and cleared the clothes off the rails and took the boxes off the floor. "Sometimes it isn't enough. It is like I am talking and they don't hear a single word I say."

"I guess it is a kind of harassment," I said, trying to see it from his point of view which was tough. Whoever thought being beautiful was a curse?

"Well, I have tried everything else but I haven't tried a fake girlfriend so as I have just bought you a room full of clothes, the least you can do is hang on my arm for one night and pretend you like me." He held out his arm for me to grab onto but I was still reeling from what he had just said.

"The room? You paid for everything that was in this room?" I gasped.

"Yes," he replied casually as it was the most obvious thing in the world. "My Christmas gift to you."

"I doubt I will ever be able to repay you." A wave of nausea was washing over me again. I had seen the Jimmy Choo label in my shoes and I knew not one thing in this room had been your ordinary everyday, off the rack stuff.

"Your grateful face is payment enough. Don't cry you will ruin your make-up." He reached over and ran his fingers down the side of my face.

"Okay, but you know this isn't going to work don't you. No one is going to buy this for a second." I shook my head. I was nothing like him. Pria on the other hand was the female version of him. Her skin was flawless and her clothes were tailored to the very millimetre of her skin and she looked a million dollars. I felt overdressed and out of place. Mutton dressed as lamb.

"I'm beautiful, you're beautiful what's not to buy?"

I sniggered.

"What, you don't think I'm good looking? Ah, you're one of those girls are you?" He looked away.

"I think you are stunning," I said. There was no point lying about it. "Which is why I don't match you, people are going to see through us. You look like you have your own personal stylist while I look like a kid playing dress up."

He rose again and stood behind me so we were both in the mirror. "The old you thought like that, but this new, waxed to an inch of your life you, is a stunner who is now going to grab life by the balls and live life to the full."

I smiled at his reflection wishing that it could be true. I had lived a lie up until this point. My husband was a lie, my marriage a sham and my friends not even worth my breath, maybe a new me was just what I needed. "Okay, but just so we don't have to go through the talk later, I feel the need to let you know now that you aren't the man for me," I turned to face him.

"Really! I thought I was the man for everyone." He crossed his arms across his suited chest.

"I like my men confident and I just don't think you are confident enough for me. I'm sorry."

He laughed hard. "I have not heard that before, for sure."

"I would give us two months max," I said, taking his arm.

"Really because I have already picked out an engagement ring." A girl gasped along the corridor and dashed off towards the salons. "I think she bought the idea of us," he smiled.

"This is how rumours start. What will my brother think?"

"Well, he told me to watch out for you and I can't watch you unless you are with me, besides there are marriage rumours about me every week. Let's head off, it's almost eleven, the club will be filling up."

He hailed a cab and we were ushered through a back door of the club.

"Do you queue for anything?" I asked amazed at the size of the queue we just bypassed.

"Not much, we use this club for photoshoots sometimes, they love me here," he laughed and led me to the bar. The previous wine I had drunk at lunch time had evaporated so I gladly excepted the offer of another glass. He purchased a bottle and the staff opened a separate area for us to take a seat in. Other people were let in behind us after Ryan had chosen our seats by the bar.

"How many things have we ticked off my list then?" I asked.

"New image, loss of wedding ring, that's a huge step." I glanced down at my ringless finger. The ring had been a symbol of my marriage and I should have taken it off as soon as I had found out about his unfaithfulness but hadn't really thought about it. "Are you missing it?" Ryan had noticed me eyeing up the bare finger.

"No, just surprised how little I feel about not wearing it," I said, surprising myself.

"The happier you feel inside, the better you will feel about leaving the old life behind. Now lets get drunk and work on step two."

I chinked his glass in a toast. "What's step two?"

"Rebound sex," he winked and I felt my heart melt.

Chapter 9

The club got busy but seemed even more so by the crowds that gathered around us. It was if Ryan was the fountain of youth and every one was drinking it in by just being near him. Several times the crowd got too much and I was moved from his side but every time, he grabbed my hand and pulled me closer to him. He had been right, people did buy us as a couple. A few people mentioned the fact that we were engaged and a few girls even asked to see the ring.

"I think that girl at the salon overheard us and had a few friends to tell," Ryan laughed it off.

"How many times have you been engaged before?" I asked while drinking my third glass of champagne that a group of businessmen had bought us.

"Never," Ryan shouted over the music.

"How many times have you faked an engagement?" I shouted back.

"Never," he laughed.

"Okay, so how many women have you taken into the torture rooms to get pimped up?" I asked.

He stood away from the bar so his face was practically touching mine. "None." He brushed his lips across mine and I felt my legs wobble a bit.

I backed away and he looked disappointed, but I was drunk and he had drunk more than I had. I hadn't seen him get his wallet out since the first wine he bought when we walked in. "We should leave," I said looking at a watch that wasn't actually there, I didn't own a watch.

He laughed at my drunkenness and checked his Rolex. "Blimey, it is two in the morning. Come on then Cinderella, let's get you to bed." He grabbed my hand and led me out of the door. He was also right about the frustrating walk out of the building, he got stopped every two minutes. Some were quick goodbyes, some wanted to talk business and some of the girls blatantly tried to stick their tongues down his throat. He waved them politely away and barged through the crowd onto the street.

"Feels nice to breath some un-perfumed air," I said, enjoying the space.

"Ah, we didn't buy you perfume," he huffed.

"I have some in my stolen bag of sin," I said, wobbling into him.

"I can't wait to open that bag," he smiled a devilish grin. "We need to queue here for a taxi. A queue I can't jump I'm afraid."

"Darn you and your total lack of influence," I laughed, rubbing my bare arms. I didn't have a proper coat. I had tended to go from the car straight into the hospital and had always favoured umbrellas.

"We didn't get you a jacket either," he said, reading my mind. He started taking off his jacket as a fight broke out nearby causing the queue to spread out. I got pushed forward and

Ryan grabbed me by the elbow and guided me towards the side of a bus stop. The crowd started yelling and bashing into us. Ryan put an arm either side of me and pressed his body against mine. With the bus stop behind me I had no way to pull away from him even if I had wanted to. The alcohol in my system was affecting my balance and my heart rate. My shyness from earlier was long gone, it seemed to have drowned three glasses back in the champagne bubbles. I closed my eyes as I felt his hand run over my already goose bumped arms and rest at the back of my neck. His other arm reached around my waist pulling me even closer and I felt his mouth briefly on mine.

"Ryan!" A guy shouted from somewhere, "are you going my way?" Ryan moved his mouth from mine and swung around to find the voice. I let out the breath I hadn't realised I was holding.

"Bobby!" Ryan sounded pleased for the first time tonight to see someone he knew. "Come, he lives around the corner from me." Ryan grabbed my hand and ushered me into the waiting taxi. I dozed off on Ryan's shoulder as him and his friend discussed the magazine and the benefits of men having beards. I wasn't sure how long I had been asleep when Ryan shook me awake.

"Sorry," I said as I stepped out of the taxi. The cold air had woken me up slightly and I was wishing I had asked him to take me back to Josh's, but Ryan hadn't given me the key.

"Are you alright?" Ryan asked pulling me close.

I nodded, unable to lie. He didn't take his eyes off mine the whole time we were in the lift and I tried to look anywhere but at him, he was too intense. The lift finally opened into the biggest lounge I had ever seen and I recognised the boxes stacked up neatly against his wall. Everything from the fitting room had been laid out nicely it looked like a show room. I heard Ryan offering me things but his voice sounded miles away. Everything in the room swallowed up my attention. His whole back wall was a giant window that looked over the Thames. I got lost in the lights for I don't know how long when I felt his arms around my waist. "We didn't get you a nightie either," he whispered and my nerves kicked in. I took a deep breath to speak but didn't know what to say. "I have made up the bed in the spare room," he said, perhaps sensing my awkwardness.

"I'm sorry," I said unsure why.

"Why?" He smiled. "I think tonight was amazing. Goodnight Charlotte." He kissed my cheek and pointed towards a door. I watched him walk into the opposite room leaving me alone in his massive living room.

I put my hand on my heart and slumped down by the window. I had been single for five minutes and had already contemplated having sex with the first guy that had paid me any attention. I glanced back at the room he had just walked though, he was something else. Never had I met someone as powerful or as alluring as he was. He could have asked anything of me and I probably would have done it.

I sat there for about five minutes watching the lights from the boats on the river when I heard Ryan's door open. "Just thought you may not be able to get out of your dress." He walked over and handed me a shirt.

I stood up as elegantly as I could and turned so he could unbutton the dress. I prepared myself for his touch and didn't shudder when his finger brushed my skin.

"Thank you. I probably would have just slept in it," I laughed.

He walked towards me and flipped the dress over my head. His lips brushed my chin and moved swiftly down to my neck. I gasped involuntarily and he took it as a sign. He spun me around, grabbing my head and pulled my mouth onto his. My stomach flipped and I leant into his body without meaning to, it was like my body had a mind of its own and it certainly knew what it wanted. I put my hands into his hair and pulled myself further into him then snapped myself out if it. I didn't know this guy, this wasn't me. I pulled away gently and looked into his face. His eyes were slightly glazed over but other than that he was perfect and he knew it.

"I know what you are going to say," he smiled and flipped the shirt around my back and started to do up the buttons which, somehow, was more erotic than when he had undone the dress. "You are going to say that you are drunk and this isn't something you would ordinarily do. Which is wasting your breath because I already know that," he smiled and kissed me gently on the mouth.

"I was going to say that if this is how you treat all the women you know, then I am surprised you have any money left," I laughed and he joined in. "Thank you for today, I have had the best day ever. You have been too kind and way too generous, I can never thank you enough."

His face changed. "Do you think this is me asking for payment?" He backed away.

"Of course not and to be honest I have had sex with me, if it is payment you're after, I would stick to the Louis Vuitton bag," I smiled, hopefully lightening the mood a little. "We *are* both very drunk and I barely know you, and I don't want to have sex with you." I looked him in the eye, being bold. He looked like I had scolded him and I suddenly felt the need to be over honest. "What I mean is of course I want to have sex with you, my body is screaming for it, but it isn't right *right* now and you know it." I backed even further away afraid that if he kissed me again I would lose all will to fight him.

"All I know is that I have had the best day ever and I have never met anyone quite like you before," he said, walking closer to me and I felt my resolve weakening.

"You don't know me, it's been less than twenty-four hours," I laughed.

"And still I know." He didn't take his eyes off mine and I felt my walls coming down.

"I think that if you kissed me again you would definitely get your own way." He moved closer in triumph. "But then how would you ever know if it was a real feeling or the alcohol taking over and how would you live with the feeling of guilt that you openly seduced a married woman who was on the rebound."

"Ouch," he said moving back. "I would never go against your wishes even though drunk sex really is the best."

"I'm sorry," I laughed. I bent down, scooped up the dress and started walking towards the bedroom that he had motioned as mine.

"Stop being sorry, every choice you make is what makes you perfect." He reached over and kissed my cheek. He turned and went into his room without looking back.

I stared at his closed door for a while and wrestled with myself. If I opened that door I would probably have the most amazing sex of my life but then what would he think of me for being so easily seduced. I turned and entered the spare room which already had a few of the bags from the dressing room in it. I got into bed and stared at the ceiling. What if this opportunity never came again? What if when sober he wasn't interested in me and I just lost the one and only opportunity to have sex with the most beautiful man I had ever met. If it all went wrong in the morning I could have blamed the alcohol and saved face.

A million more 'what if's' swam in and out of my brain until I drifted off to sleep.

The smell of pancakes wafted through the air, but as tempting as they smelt, I couldn't lift my head off the pillow. I mentally tallied up the amount of glasses of wine I had drunk and gave up around eight. The champagne had seemed never ending and I hadn't paid for a single drink.

Loud yelling rang through my ears and I knew I was going to have to get up. I hate sleepovers even when we went to the cabin with Scott's family I hated them. Scott's mother would always get up about five to walk the dogs and by the time the dogs were dry she would have already cleaned the house and already made tea for the week. Me, on the other hand, always seemed to get up at the last minute as if I couldn't never quite get enough hours sleep. But then Scott talked in his sleep constantly and his mother snored like a motorcycle, so no wonder I never slept there.

I ignored the yelling in the hall and drank the glass of water that Ryan must have placed there this morning without me noticing. I felt a knot form in my stomach at the idea of him being in here seeing me drool. He was this picture perfect being and I was this oversized mess of a human who couldn't even focus on the door handle. The more I tried to focus the better I could hear that it was Josh yelling in the hallway. I jumped out and burst through the door nearly knocking him over.

"You're early," I smiled, but his face was like thunder.

"I came back last night ready for work this morning. I waited up."

"Sorry, why didn't you ring me?" I shifted into a bar stool and suddenly remembered that I was wearing Ryan's shirt which was much too short for sitting. I stood back up.

"I did ring you, many times." Josh shot Ryan a deathly stare.

"She stayed in the spare room," he said and returned to the pancakes that he was piling up.

"I did. It was nice not being alone." I smiled wondering how much I could say without giving up how close we actually were to having sex.

"I only have half an hour before I have to be back. Tell me everything but really quickly and only the important bits." Josh made himself a cup of coffee and poured me an orange juice as if he owned the place.

"Where to start?" Already after one day in London, Scott seemed like a long time ago. "Okay, Scott had an affair with my friend Amber…"

"Ooh, the hot American?" Josh interrupted. I raised my eyebrows signalling that that comment was going to be ignored.

"They don't know that I know that it is her. I also found out that she purchased an abortion drug from America which made me miscarry. Amber pushed me out of Cassie's life, got me passed up for a promotion which meant I was the only one who got more hours and less money. I told Scott I knew about the affair and he stole everything out of the house and I meant EVERYTHING."

"It's true," Ryan handed me a plate of pancakes and another orange juice. "When I got there, it looked like she was sleeping rough."

"He even stole my tampons. Shit." I ran from the table, grabbed my bag and went to the toilet. I had completely forgotten about my period. I quickly changed and then put on Ryan's dressing gown that was hanging on a bathroom hook so I could sit properly at the breakfast bar without showing off my bottom.

"And now I know why you slept in the spare room." Josh laughed eating his second pancake.

I shot Ryan a worrying glance but he was sniggering, clearly amused by my forgetfulness.

"So how did you find out?" Josh mumbled.

"I got a parking ticket and the guy that did it also scratched my car…." I started.

"That's awful, give me the address." I put my hand up to wave him quiet.

"This half hour will run better if I speak more and you speak less. I followed the Josh plan of attack, I dealt with it."

"You dealt with it how? I doubt you could have unwritten a ticket," Josh said.

"Oh, I didn't think about that." Why didn't I think of that? Josh could have simply deleted the ticket off the system and all the worry would have been over with.

"What did you do then?" Josh put down his fork.

"We made a list of all the things she wants to achieve." Ryan smiled as if he had been my sidekick the whole time, "I'll grab it." Ryan jumped up and went to the coffee table.

"Anyway, moving on, I couldn't sleep with the worry of it all and I heard Scott making a love call in the bathroom. I read your dissertation paper and ordered one of those phone cloning machines that you always used to go on about."

"You didn't!" Josh was now standing up and I couldn't tell if he was impressed or horrified.

"I did. I discovered the affair, realised Amber was acting shady about me, cloned her phone and found out the rest. I backdated my redundancy paper, no one noticed. Aunt Maureen tried to get me fired but that is another story completely and here I am with a clean slate and not so clean conscience."

"Have you asked for a divorce?" Josh took the notebook from Ryan and looked through.

"It's Christmas and difficult to get seen. I got some consent paperwork which I have given to Scott to fill in but now he has stolen everything there is nothing really, apart from the house, to split."

"I can help you with the divorce, I do have a law degree you know." Ryan defended himself when Josh looked surprised.

"Yes, and you are also helping run your father's magazine and are currently site managing about five property developments." Josh made Ryan sound like a superhero.

"True, but the sooner she is divorced, the sooner I can date your sister." Ryan laughed as Josh nearly spat out his coffee.

"I am still in the room, you know." I liked their mindless banter it felt like it was one of the things missing from the old life I had just left behind.

"There should be a rule about dating sisters, we will talk about that later, though I think her virtue is safe for a couple of days," Josh winked at me. He returned to the notebook and read on while I continued eating my pancakes.

"Oh my God, you stole from someone's house!" Josh burst out and I felt a blush creep over my face.

"Well, yes, that wasn't my finest hour," I whispered.

"But in her defence, the owner did scratch her car and they are drug dealers." Ryan cleared away the plates and stacked them gently in the dishwasher. "And she can always blame a psychotic episode brought on by the stress of her husband's deceit or PMT."

"I see." Josh flipped over the page of the notebook. I cringed as I remembered the sheer amount of alcohol I had consumed when discussing my evil plans of revenge.

"I had only planned to go in there and take back the equivalent of the £35 parking ticket. I wasn't even that bothered about the damage he did to the car. I just felt like there was no justice in the world and it wasn't fair."

"It was really stupid, Charlotte, what if you had been caught?" Josh put down the notebook and rubbed his temples.

"I wore gloves," I said, as if that solved everything. "It was also raining and starting to get dark, I doubt I was seen." I tried to shake the stab of guilt but couldn't. "I can't take the stuff back now can I?"

"I'm going to pretend that I didn't read that bit, they sound like dodgy people. I always knew Amber was dodgy, I never liked her."

"What the hot American?" Ryan laughed.

"Hot yes, but she always made you jump through hoops, it riled me." Josh got up and grabbed his suitcase. "Is the device at home? Can I take a look at it?"

"Knock yourself out." I reached over and gave him a hug. "I missed you so much."

"Behave yourself please. My sister is as precious to me as your hair is to you." Josh waved and left.

"Wow, you must really like your hair," I said as soon as Josh had closed the door.

"Period, huh?" Ryan raised his eyebrows.

"I am stressed and had completely forgotten. I think you did some kind of forgetting wizardry charm that completely changed me for a day." I moved to the window and soaked in the view.

"I had fun for a change. I'll have to take you out for a spin again." Ryan pulled out the notebook and ripped some pages out.

"What are you doing? That is my life list."

"Actually, I don't think it is. I think you are a damn sight stronger than you think and mainly you have accepted your lot in life so easily because it makes sense to you. Well, not anymore." He sat me on the edge of the sofa and he sat on the other end. He swung my legs up so that we were both facing each other and that my legs were resting on his lap. As he spoke he stroked the bottom of my ankle and for the first time I was glad that Marsha had ripped all my skin off, including hairs.

"You think because I was mildly tempted to sleep with you that that means that I have accepted that my old life is better off without me and moved on quicker?" I crossed my arms.

"Mildly, huh?" He smiled. I like the fact that he didn't take himself too seriously. I watched him rub his chin and I wondered how he could possibly look so fresh after all that alcohol, my inside's were churning and I was pretty sure I looked green. He continued, "I just think there might be some part of you that perhaps already knew that Amber wasn't this great friend and maybe you knew Scott didn't tick all your boxes either."

"I think I would have coped differently if I thought I had Amber to lean on, but not only did I lose Scott, but I also lost two best friends, a job and the only family left in Densborough that I had. I think if I had only lost Scott, Amber would have propped me up and guided me through." I thought about this as I said it, would Amber have ever helped me through any kind of crisis? She wasn't really that sort of friend. She dealt with the fun and anything that was tunnel visioned around her, it was more likely to have been Cassie to prop me up with coffee and girlie nights in. "Okay, perhaps my life wasn't the way I thought it was but I'm sitting here and I feel angry about all the wrong things."

"I'll send the table off, it might be fixable." Ryan started jotting down new notes.

"I just think it was a really shitty thing to do considering how shitty he has been already."

"Okay, you need to find something in that room that resembles day time dress we are going out for a walk then lunch. There is a no closure rule in this Penthouse so all air clearing must be done on The Hill." He swung my legs on the floor. "Actually I had better choose your outfit, you shower."

I showered and thought about what had to happen. I felt like Scott had ruined not only our marriage but any friendship that was attached to it. I had spent the last eight days crying myself to sleep and feeling like my insides had been ripped out but now something had shifted and I refused to believe it was the godly figure in the room next door. Love couldn't be switched on and off like a light, maybe deep down, I did know something wasn't quite right with our marriage. I was struggling now to find any recent happy moments to cling on to. I needed to have a clear head, I wouldn't let Scott and Amber's betrayal destroy me and I wasn't going to let Ryan, with his underwear model body, charm his way into my bed just because he could sense my weakness. I didn't need a rebound lover to feel like I was better than Scott. I wanted some kind of revenge but I didn't feel the need to even some kind of sexual score.

I considered Amber. She was always the one who was in control. On a night out she would pick where we went, what time we ate, who was or was not invited. Anytime me or someone else tried to organise something she would change it or pick holes in it. As painful as it was, losing her friendship, I knew, would be a blessing. Just the idea of being able to say I would do something without having to check with her first, was kind of liberating. Being friends with her had been like having a second husband.

I washed my hair with Ryan's shampoo and wobbled out. My stomach was feeling better from the pancakes but not much.

"I have laid you out some things, I'll be out in a minute." Ryan dashed past me to go into the shower.

On the bed he had laid some skinny jeans that looked far too skinny for me and a pretty green top that curved open at the back. I hadn't even remembered this stuff hanging in the room, but I guessed Pria's job had been to find a selection in my size and she would have been eager to please him, who wouldn't. I ran my hands over the rails. It would take me years to get through all these clothes and I wouldn't have to buy anything except sleepwear and some jackets.

"Why are you not dressed?" Ryan appeared at the door wearing nothing but a bright white towel tied around his tanned waist.

"I'm working on it," I smiled. I turned my back on him and opened the box that contained underwear. I knew some of these names from expensive magazines but I had never owned anything so beautiful, even the bra stitching seemed to be woven in gold.

I quickly got dressed and Ryan walked in again, without knocking, while I was searching for the toiletries bag he had packed from Ruby. "I can't find the deodorant," I said as he threw me a towel for my hair.

"Ruby uses industrial strength stuff, you will be good for a couple of days."

"Yuk, I think I would rather overdo it."

"The magazine gets new products in to review all the time, don't get many deodorants though." He moved to the wardrobe and pulled out a box. "I sometimes band the products together to make gift sets for clients." He threw me a deodorant. "Cheap I know."

"I guess you have quite a few people who help the magazine out. What made you choose the magazine instead of law? And where does the property renovating come into your life?"

"I love the profit margins of redesigning and selling on property. I love looking around a shabby house, buying it for peanuts and selling it top whack, but my heart really lies with the magazine. It was originally my mum's dream. She works in the Italian office now, we don't see her much. I love the people and the fact that no two weeks are the same. I love the hustle and bustle and even though it can get really stressful, seeing the end profit is highly rewarding for that too. Law was hardly ever satisfying. It wasn't always about justice, I didn't feel like I was always in control. I did see it through and though divorce wasn't really my area, I do know enough about the procedure to be able to look into it if you trust me."

"I'm sure between the legal talents of you and the undermining tactics of Josh, I'm sure that I have never been in safer hands."

"Well, seeing as it is your time of the month, that couldn't be more true." He winked and threw me the hairdryer.

Chapter 10

I had only ever been to Primrose Hill once when I was in high school on a Geography field trip. The idea had been to see London from the outside looking in. It isn't all high rise buildings and street performers but dog walkers, runners and real people with soul. Our Geography teacher had loved it and pretty much forgot all about us. Amber had spent the whole time trying to drag me away from my camera then had given up to snog Tim Denton instead. I didn't remember it being this hilly.

"You're out of shape." Ryan laughed and started jogging ahead to show off.

"Yes, and extremely hung over. Can you please stop being so bubbly and bright, it's hurting my eyes."

"Worth it though, look at that view." Ryan nabbed a bench and poured coffee out of a flask for us both. "Now, all unloading must be done here to avoid any furniture being smashed to bits in the heat of the moment."

"But I'm not cross with you so wouldn't touch your furniture anyway," I laughed, accepting the coffee. "Though I doubt this would really work anyway. It just took us about fifteen minutes by tube then ten minutes more to walk here. If I was really cross I think I would have killed you before we got here."

"Perhaps," he smiled. He seemed to have completely recovered from the previous nights alcohol intake. "But that's years away so let's begin." He took the notebook out of his pocket and handed it over. "I have shredded the bits that mentioned the actual break in."

"Oh yes, that was great until you handed it to my brother." I sipped my coffee which was divine, Cassie would have been jealous.

"It is okay to be angry here," he laughed. "That was stupid, sorry. I have already broken my first promise." He stretched his feet out and closed his eyes slightly in the sun and I felt a flush wash over my face. He must get this all the time.

"I am not angry, to be honest actually, I feel kind of relieved." I said after I was happy that my blush caused by staring at him had gone.

"You strike me as the do gooder sort." He didn't open his eyes.

"I guess, ordinarily, I am. I hate breaking the rules, I never speed, people ask for help and I'm the first there. I never would have in a millions years committed any type of crime, I don't know what came over me." I crossed my legs over on the bench and watched a man running with his dogs.

"I think if you can accept that it is okay then you can move past it without any psychiatric help needed and only one rebound lover necessary."

I burst out laughing. "Not everyone has a rebound lover."

"Yes, yes they do." He laughed and faced me. "Anyway, if Scott was sitting here instead of me saying he was sorry, how would that conversation go?"

I felt my stomach twinge. "I don't know."

"Be honest. You found out about his affair, he realised he made a mistake and he wants you to take him back. What are you going to do?"

"Firstly, I am going to buy a thicker jacket, this one just isn't cutting it." I flipped up my collar and avoided his gaze.

Ryan stretched out his legs again and closed his eyes, clearly he wasn't going to speak until I had thought about it so I did. "You know part of me would sit here and say I know Scott well, but obviously I don't. If he was standing here now, based on what he knows I know, he would lie about it being Amber. He would say it was a temp from work, it was a one off thing and it meant nothing. That's what he would say."

"Think of all the great things you did together and all the things you could get back if you just smiled and forgave him," Ryan said, eyes still closed. Maybe the alcohol was taking effect after all.

"Like what things?"

Ryan looked up and shrugged.

"He never wanted to go on holiday, he hated the outdoors and my photography. He hated nightclubs and socialising and he always gave me the impression he hated my friends, which was clearly a lie." I looked down at my fingernails that Ruby had beautifully French manicured. "The whole marriage was a lie. I can't think of one thing that I could cling to even if I were desperate. If my life depended on it I would rather trust that old lady pushing the pram." I pointed at a tiny woman pushing an old fashioned pram.

"That's not good, Peggy only cares about her dog in that pram, your life is nothing," Ryan smiled.

"You know her too?" I laughed in disbelief.

"From the soup kitchens." He poured another cup of coffee and I cradled it to warm up my fingers.

"This is where we should say goodbye to Scott," I said sitting up. "To the man who stole my chance of motherhood, my friend, though actually she may have stole him. He stole my mother's hall table and broke it because he actually couldn't have cared less. He also stole my camera that he hates and my tampons that he will clearly will never need, the freak. There is nothing redeemable left," I sighed. "What he did was spiteful. He had the affair, I did nothing to him. If he had any respect for me at all he would have left me when it first started and left the table."

"I heard you mention to Josh about a mortgage?"

"Yes, I think he wants money and I think it is for Amber. Unlike Scott, Amber loves to travel, she loves new handbags, designer sunglasses. If there is someone else who has them then she has moved on to something bigger and better. I think she is a bit like you, very showy."

"Ouch!" He smiled. "If it makes you feel better, I will never sleep with your husband."

"And I promise to never emigrate to Australia with your pal either."

"He wasn't even a good pal to be honest, good riddance. We have the same problem though, we didn't get to say goodbye or wrap it up."

"There is nothing stopping me from driving to Densborough, walking into his work place and saying, 'Scott, you are dead to me.'"

"True, it is a little bit harder for me to drive to Australia though."

"Why can't you call her? Or FaceTime her or use Skype?" His eyes flickered open then shut again and I wondered if I had hit a nerve. "What was it about Alice that made her so special?"

"I don't know what the something was that she had. I guess to put vanity on it I felt like when we were together people were looking at her more than they were looking at me. I never thought I would find anyone more my equal."

"Oh, so she was devishly good-looking," I smiled. I could see it, why would this man settle for anyone else?

"In hindsight I should have seen the alarm bells. We had a few unreasonable bust ups before she chose my friend and trashed my place. I just wanted it to work more than I actually wanted her."

"So you like the idea of romance better that the actually romance?" I laughed.

"Don't we all?" He screwed the lid on the coffee and stood. "Let's relocate this to a warmer place."

I linked my arm into his and we walked down onto a quaint little high street and found cute looking bistro hidden behind a bakery.

"I think I have had a lucky escape from Scott," I said once he had sat down with hot chocolates and cookies. "If I hadn't have gotten the parking ticket, I would have slept like a log and been none the wiser. He would have mortgaged the house and I would have only found out when there was nothing left for him to take. He was like a vampire draining my body of its blood, but he didn't succeed and though I don't feel upset, I just feel really, really angry."

"Because of the drugs that caused you to lose the baby?" Ryan asked.

"Everything, but mostly because if I was so completely wrong for him, why didn't he just leave? Why give me the impression that he wanted a family with me if he really didn't want it? We were on totally different pages. I don't even feel like I know who he was, he could have talked to me. He forged my signature which I can't forgive and he broke my mother's table, which means something else because not only was he happy cheating with someone else, taking all my money, and lying to me, he cleared the entire contents of the house out without any care. If he was so desperate for money he could have sold some of the stuff on which makes me think it wasn't about the money or that he needed it, he just didn't want me to have it. What on earth could I have done to him that would make him behave that way? I can't believe I didn't see it going on right under my nose."

"Some people take years after a divorce to get where you're at."

I looked around. "It is a really nice cafe," I sniggered.

"I mean acceptance. There would be no point in me helping you with your divorce if you turned around and took him back. Your heart needs to be in it. I can be quite ruthless."

"I don't doubt that for a second. Do it, he will expect me to roll over and give him exactly what he wants."

"What about the friend?"

"I think that she is more Scott's type than mine, but then I think she is more everyone's type." Ryan raised an eyebrow to interrupt but I carried on, "I just think they shared interests. She liked to work out and take care of herself and that was his job, she looks good on his arm."

"You think this is about looks?" He looked doubtful.

"He might love her, she might love him, but I just can't get my head around the fact that she wasn't that pleased when he told her we had ended. She seemed annoyed, something wasn't yet in place for her. I would feel much more comfortable if it was about money then I wouldn't feel so cheated out of something I don't think I ever had." I blew on the hot chocolate and waited for the little blush to pass. I didn't think it was selfish for not wanting it to be about love. Scott had never really treated me to anything and looking back he could have worked away for half the year and my daily routine wouldn't have changed. Amber could have had any man and David was far too good for her already. The idea of her actually falling in love with Scott had a romantic edge to it but the very fact that he had tried to mortgage the house had alarm bells ringing. What was he planning to do with that money?

"For what it is worth I think you are right. If they were in love they wouldn't have dragged it on secretly for two years. They wouldn't have been able to wait until their new life together began. I would be interested to read some of these texts, I bet they read like a soap opera."

"Knock yourself out." No doubt Josh would have already inspected the device.

"Let's get your stuff back to yours and catch up with Josh. I would hate him to think I was monopolising his precious sister."

Josh was hammering away at his computer like a man possessed and sheets of paper were firing out of the printer onto the floor. I laid my armful of clothes from Ryan's onto my bed and hurried back to the car to get a second load. The bedroom I had stayed in at Ryan's was massive, Josh's spare room, however, was about three metres square and most of that was taken up by a double bed and the antique wardrobe that matched my mother's broken hall table. There was no way all these new clothes were going to fit in.

"Perhaps we could get you a rail to hang things on," Ryan said, seeing my problem.

"Actually I think I need to find a job and decide where I am going to base myself. London is always going to be far too expensive for me, I need a suburb place." I flicked the kettle on and walked over to Josh.

"I stayed with you through college and I have no problem with returning the favour, you can stay here as long as you like," Josh said without looking up.

"But last week you were moaning that this empty room was causing a hole in your bank balance." I slumped on the sofa leaving Ryan to fuss over the coffee. "What are you doing, anyway?"

"Printing out anything that ever had your name on it." He pointed to the table where neater piles of paperwork sat. "There is Scott and Amber's details and some of their phone messages."

"Are you not supposed to be working?" I sat up and smiled my acceptance of the coffee from Ryan.

"Yes, but I got ahead in Scotland. Meg's family are intense so I hid out for a couple of hours everyday and worked." He sipped his coffee, keeping his eyes glued to the screen. "I had a couple of meetings this morning but don't have to be back in the office until Wednesday." He got up and sorted out some paperwork.

"Did you get the list I emailed?" Ryan asked as Josh numbered sheets.

"Yes, but she has done most of it." Josh shot me a smile.

"What have I done?" I liked having backup but the idea of them both organising my life behind my back was a little annoying.

"Ryan emailed through a divorce list of all the things you needed to cancel and freeze, like bank accounts and TV licence."

"I got a list off the internet. My mail is going to be re-directed here until I can settle, if that's okay?"

"Of course. You work fast considering you have been separated five minutes," Josh said and for a second I wondered if he sensed something between Ryan and Me.

"I think if he hadn't have taken money from the account and tried to mortgage the house perhaps I would have dragged my heels a bit thinking I could fix it. Losing the money made it seem more urgent to sever the ties and did I tell you that he stole mother's hall table? He didn't even like it."

"Once or twice," Josh nodded. "He was probably angry that you found him out too early. I have lots of info but I don't think you are going to like it."

"Give it to me while I am tired and comfortable in this chair." I put my feet on the footstool.

"Amber has bought a plot of land to the south of Densborough and she has applied for planning permission for a three storey mini mansion which she designed with help from Appleby's Architects on the high street."

"Wow, I bet that costs a bit, her wage is smaller than mine, or was smaller than mine was before I left, she was getting my promotion." I tried not to sulk over the unfairness of it all.

"She *couldn't* afford it which is why she got some loans out in other people's names including yours and Scott's." Josh bound some sheets together and sat down opposite me and Ryan.

"That isn't legal, is it?" I sat up. Another debt was the last thing I needed now I was unemployed.

"Luckily, your loan is almost paid off but you need to give these guys a call to let them know not to let it happen again. I would also get the bank to completely change all your numbers or even change bank which might be simpler." He handed me a small file which contained a check list. "These are all the things you need to do in order of importance."

"You really need a hobby," I laughed.

"Are you kidding? I love this. I feel like a highly intelligent superhero helping to right the wrongs of the world," he smirked.

"You are the most intelligent person I know, hands down," Ryan said, looking into his phone.

"Well, I do need to say a few things," Josh warned. "Firstly, breaking into someone's house, I can't get over the fact that you did that. I never in a million years would have even dreamt you capable of a thing."

"I know, can you please look into that address and find something out that might make me feel a little less sick about it?" I thought about the Louis Vuitton weekender bag squashed in my room.

Josh nodded and went back to the computer. I couldn't really change my bank until my redundancy money had been paid in but I might be able to set up a meeting to talk it over. There was a few things that I had forgotten to cancel like a magazine subscription. The Dr's and dentist might as well wait until I get a job and move.

"There are five jobs going at the magazine if you want to come and work for me until you find something else." Ryan handed over his phone.

"I know nothing about fashion," I smiled.

"That is not true, your wardrobe at the moment is pretty impressive," he replied.

I read through the choices. Technology team member was a definite no. Josh obtained all the computer knowhow in our family and all I had been born with was the ability to use Google. Sales team member I decided, was also a no, the hard sell of advertising space was a golden opportunity for those with the gift of the gab and I didn't really have that either. "I guess I could do the secretary job, covering maternity." I handed Ryan back the phone.

"I think they may have covered that, let me check." He walked out into the hall and made a call.

"What is going on?" Josh asked as soon as the apartment door had closed.

"Nothing," I said with a frown. "You asked him to watch me until you got here and he did."

"I didn't ask him to buy you thousands of pounds worth of clothes and invite you to stay over his house for a sleepover." Josh pressed print and swivelled his office chair to face me. "Don't get me wrong, I love him, he is my best friend, but he doesn't need you right now and you sure as hell don't need him, you're not even really single."

"I am not dating Ryan." I put down my cup heavier than I intended, spilling some of its contents. "He saved me from a bad situation and we had a nice night out, that is all."

"Actually I think it was me that saved you, it was me, after all, that sent Ryan to pick you up."

"Okay, well I love you best, thank you." I stood up and gave him a hug. "He is really cute though," I whispered.

"And doesn't he know it," Josh smiled. "Anyway back to topic. Ray Flint lives at twenty-five Old School Close with his second, and much younger wife, Bernadette. They have two sons Marcus and Thomas, cousins to your frenemy, Amber. He also has two older children who he doesn't see. All four have spent time inside. Bernadette's was for shoplifting, Ray's was armed robbery and Marcus and Thomas have been in and out of prison for drug and violence related offences." He turned and gave me a look of concern. "If they had caught you who knows what would have happened."

"I know! I can keep saying I'm sorry but it isn't going to change anything." I slumped back down.

"They get back from their holiday in about ten minutes. Will probably take them two or three hours to get home and realise anything is missing. Did you trash the place?"

"No, I fed their cats and cleared up the cat poop which was all over the kitchen floor." Ryan re-entered the room as Josh was crying with laughter. "What did I miss?"

"Charlotte burgled a house and rather than trash the place in an angry rage, she fed the cats and tidied away their mess. What a criminal mastermind you would make."

"It was an impulse. I won't do it again." I crossed my arms across my chest as Josh wiped away his tears. "Alright that is enough. Where are the clone phones?" Their laughter was annoying me now.

"I consolidated them." Josh opened his top desk drawer and handed me a new iPhone. "Scott's messages come up blue and Amber's are pink. The left are sent and the right are received." He swooped down and collected something he hadn't been expecting from the printer and handed it to me.

"That needs to be filled in now, my dad is interviewing next Friday and wants to shortlist this evening," Ryan said.

I thanked Ryan for everything, gave Josh a kiss on the head and left for my room. They had been chatting about Scott and Amber but I had gone numb on the subject and needed to escape. I had a lot of emotions that I needed to work through and hearing about the fact that Scott has been paying her money and taking her away for romantic weekends away while he told me he was on training courses just made me feel like a fool.

I shook the thought of him out of my head and concentrated on the application form. What did I know about being an editor's secretary? Not a lot but then I learnt fast and if I didn't try, it would be no anyway. I needed to work out what I wanted to do and where I wanted to base myself. This maternity cover would last three or four months max then I would need to find something else. I put Dr Zusak down as a reference then remembered his influence. He could probably get me recommended for any hospital job going. I flicked through Josh's 'To Do' list and found a whole page on job seeking. I wrote in the margins to search for similar jobs to my old one within an hours commute to the city that way Josh wouldn't be too far away but the cost of living might be more manageable.

It was about an hour and a half later when I emerged from the bedroom with the completed application form. "Sorry it has been a while."

"Knowing me is no guarantee of getting this job, you know that don't you?" Ryan pushed the forms into a sleeve and carefully put it in his bag.

"I thought knowing you opened all the doors," I laughed.

"If only. I reckon we should take a field trip Saturday and have a look at this woman's plot. See if it is worth cheating all your friends over."

"I am travelling back up to Scotland to spend New Year with Meg. Could do it on the way though and take two cars," Josh suggested.

"Can I think about it?" I asked, unsure if I actually wanted to see the cause of all my marriage problems.

"Oh sorry, do you have better plans?" Ryan laughed, clearly their minds were made up.

"Actually I can think of a million things I would rather do than re-visit a dead end town that I only just escaped from."

"I guess I could duck in on my way to Scotland and film it for you. Save you having to be nosy," Josh mused.

"Excellent, then I will think of another way for us to spend the weekend. What were you planning to do New Year Eve?" Ryan turned to face me.

"I usually watch the fireworks on the TV with a bottle of wine and junk food." The idea of being at a party in Densborough wasn't really anyone's highlight.

"Oh my God, do not, under any circumstances, agree to going to a party with Ryan, you will hate it," Josh laughed.

"Thanks buddy. Okay so the last couple of New Year parties were all massive failures. I can only apologise," Ryan shrugged.

"What was so bad about them?" I dared to ask.

"Well, lets just say it was really only about who was going to kiss Ryan at midnight. Last year there was actually police and an ambulance crew involved." Josh shook his head.

"Yes, crowd control was terrible, wasn't it?" Ryan conceded.

"Only around you," Josh retorted.

"What is it about relationships that turn normal people into psychos?" I rubbed my temple with my hands. Scott would be watching the fireworks from the cabin this year. I had bought the fireworks for New Year already. No doubt the family would light them and not give me a second thought. Maybe Scott would move straight in with Amber when she got back from New York and live, unashamed, as the couple they had been waiting so long to be, somehow I doubted it. Amber had always dreamed of designing her own home and if she had started putting that dream into motion I guessed she would have calculated to the last pence the money she needed to make it happen. If Scott couldn't provide I guessed she would move on or stay with David who treated her better than I ever imaged Scott would.

"What is it about Ryan that turns women into psychos?" Josh patted him on the leg and returned to his computer.

"Thanks. Shall I book us a table at Gaucho for tonight?" Ryan grabbed his phone and started flicking through the screens.

"You'll be lucky," Josh said.

"Nah, I know a chef there," Ryan smiled.

"By the way, Charlotte, this does get really boring after a while. The rules never apply to him," Josh spun around on his chair then continued typing.

"He loves my connections and so will you. Ah, yes, hi Sampras, it's Ryan Emerson, any tables for tonight?"

"Honestly, you can work at something your whole life and never succeed, Ryan flashes a smile once and voila, all the doors open and people throw themselves at his mercy."

"You didn't complain when I got the Ed Sheeran VIP tickets." Ryan held his hand over the phone while he spoke.

"Hell no, that was awesome. No one has ever questioned why I am your friend."

"I might be busy for dinner anyway, I'll need to check my calendar," I smiled. Amber had always been my most influential friend and even then I had never really benefitted more than the occasional party invite where I was needed to be the driver. I watched Ryan laughing with the guy on the phone. His manner was so easy and unassuming. Amber knew at all times that she was the queen bee. Ryan however, seemed weighed down by his status.

Ryan reached into my handbag and pulled out the diary he had bought me yesterday and flicked through the empty pages. "Oh look, you're free." He walked over and tapped Josh on the shoulder and Josh nodded. "Three people please, any time is fine. Best view possible. Thank you, you're the best." He hung up the phone. "Ten-thirty sit down. Meals are awesome so make sure you are really hungry. Josh wear a suit, Charlotte wear anything from my batch. I'll pick you guys up at nine for pre-dinner drinks." He blew us both kisses and left.

"Gaucho is posh, you might want to pick out something Ryan friendly or he won't invite us again." Josh stood and kissed my head. "I'm going to get showered and press my suit. Help yourself to anything you like."

I watched him leave before I looked through all the files on the table. Everyone in my past life seemed to have an orderly file and it worried me how easy it was to live a secret life. I wouldn't have a clue how to get a loan out in someone else's name and yet Amber, who never had a money worry that I knew of, had managed to secure three. I flicked through Cassie and Grant's file. They knew about Amber and Scott's affair and had manipulated the work bonus scheme to better suit their financial status, but I had expected that anyway. If it had been based on performance, Cassie would have been fired months ago. I wondered what Grant would say if he found out Amber had a loan out in his name. I looked at the loan form, all I would have to do is send him a copy and he would know Amber for the little money grabber she was.

Amber's file was by far the biggest. She had loan information, architect plans, bank payments coming in from all over the place as well as text messages that Josh had printed off. Post-it notes had been attached coding the offence it related to. Scott's affair was in pink, my job and lack of promotion was yellow, her need for money was green and the drugs and my poisoning was in purple.

The new Rob phone vibrated and screeched from across the room. Josh hadn't said whose ring tones were whose but I guessed this was Amber's phone and the call I had been waiting for.

Chapter 11

The call was to Amber from her uncle Ray. I put on the brown leather jacket from the Louis Vuitton bag as I listened in.

"I said, who went to the house with you? We have been burgled," A male voice that I guessed to be Ray's shouted. In the background I could hear other people shouting that things were missing.

"Who...?" Josh interrupted but I waved him quiet. "It is okay, they can't hear us." Josh pulled his dressing gown tight and towel dried his hair.

"Honestly, Ray, I last went in the three days, like you asked me to, fed the cats and left," Amber's voice said in defence. "I put the key back where you told me to and no one saw me do it."

"I saw you do it," I whispered.

"They can't hear us," Josh whispered back.

"Well, they have taken everything. All the Christmas presents, my camera, your aunt's Pandora. They even took her shampoo from the salon." He shouted at someone in the background to pull themselves together. "You need to get over here the police are now on their way."

"I can't, I'm at mum's and I'm about to leave for the airport. Just know that everything was fine when I left. Who fed the cats after me?"

"The boys, but they aren't going to steal stuff they paid for, are they?" I felt a stab of guilt as a woman sobbing could be heard. "I have to go the police are here." The line went dead.

Amber's phone lit up again before the power save mode could kick in. I leant across and read the screen. She was calling Scott. "Hello," he answered after two rings. "Just having dinner, can I call you back?" I heard voices behind him. He must have been at the dinner table and hadn't even bothered to hide the call. I pushed the anger back down and listened.

"Did you know where the key was at my Uncle's Ray's?" She asked.

"Yes, under the mat, you were hardly delicate about it. Why?" Scott sounded bored and for some reason this made me madder.

"Because they have been robbed and now they think we had something to do with it," she snapped.

"Whoa, hang on a minute, I didn't realise anyone knew anything about there being a we." I heard Scott's mother say something close to the phone but couldn't make out what.

"Only four of us knew where the key was and two of them bought the stuff that was stolen." Amber was getting short.

"It was nothing to do with me, floral items aren't really my thing. I have to go I'll call you later." He hung up and Amber cursed.

"Makes me think he doesn't love her, she doesn't love him and they ruined my life for nothing," I said, putting on one of Josh's coats.

"Where are you going?" Josh asked as I scooped the phone into my pocket.

"To make a difference in the world and cross it off my New Year, New Me list." I walked into my room and dragged over the Louis Vuitton bag. There had been no order in how it had been packed. Money was everywhere. Tom's car money was still in the labelled envelope, the car parking money was rolled up in the Mulberry bag and the shake money was shoved in the bottom of the camera case. The bean tin money had fallen out and was everywhere. I scooped out a large handful, left the apartment and headed south. I had forgotten a key but Josh would let me back in. I sent him a quick text reminding him not to put the stereo on full blast and not hear me knocking. The last thing I wanted was Ryan turning up all suited and booted and me still in my jeggings that I had worn all day. I headed towards the tube. At five ò clock it was already dark and homeless people had already appeared out of nowhere and had started slotting into alcoves ready for the rush hour commuters to rush past them and hopefully drop some money into their lap.

The first two I approached couldn't speak English or simply refused to hear me out, the third and forth accused me of being dodgy and didn't want my kind of trouble. The fifth was a man laying out a paper thin sleeping bag and an equally thin jacket as a pillow.

"Do you speak English?" I asked.

"I used to teach it," he said without looking up.

"I need someone to make a call for me in exchange for money." I unfolded my instruction sheet and handed it over.

"And you chose me because?" His eyes darted across the paper.

"Because I can't make the call and if someone else is going to make it for me they might as well benefit from it somehow. If not you, I'll just move down the line." I pointed to the other alcoves that were now filling up with buskers and people settling in for the evening.

"This is the house of a drug dealer and you want me to report it to the police?" He held up the paper with the information on it and turned it over, expecting more.

"They had sweets that looked like jelly babies and they were designed to get them young and ruin their lives forever. If the police asked for your name or details just tell them you are one of their customer's trying to get clean. This stuff needs to be off the street, you will actually be saving lives. I can't risk anyone recognising my voice." I took the Rob phone out from my pocket and switched it to Amber's line.

"You mentioned money." He looked up and smiled, causing his whole face to adapt a lighter, friendlier demeanour. I noticed his perfectly straight, yellow teeth. This man had taken care of himself at some point.

"I did mention money. What do you think would be the value of your time on this occasion?" I sat down in his bed beside him. He could have all the money if he wanted it. I didn't want it, not only was it stolen, but it was drug money.

"You can't put a price on saving lives. I wish this kind of call had been made in my past.

88

This is the kind of intervention I needed after my son died. I took an easy way out and I kept on taking it until there were no other options."

"I'm sorry for the way it turned out for you," I said, not sure of what else to say.

"I made my decisions. My family offered to help me but I was too proud to accept and this is where my pride brought me."

"Okay, so join me and make a difference and I will reward you." I pulled out £40 and handed it to him. He smiled and turned it over as if it wasn't real.

I smiled and handed him the phone. He reported it quickly and efficiently, I couldn't have done it better myself. He refused to give his name saying he was a previous addict and that these guys were pushers of the worst kind. When he had finished he handed me back the phone and the money.

"I can't use your money," he smiled and leant back in his alcove.

"Why not? Surely there is something you would like to buy with it," I said, confused. £40 was £40 there were loads of things I could have bought and I didn't really need anything.

"Nothing here is for keeps. About twenty other people saw you give me money which means by morning I would be penniless and maybe even beaten." He frowned.

"Okay, but I am not leaving until you have accepted something from me or I can't leave feeling like I have done a good deed."

"My life is a circle of ever repeating patterns, I sleep, I pack, I walk, then I return to this spot and do the whole thing over again. You think because my life isn't like yours that I'm not happy?"

"I think because you miss your family and regret not accepting their help means you could be happier. How can I help?"

"Do you have internet?" He asked thoughtfully.

"At my brother's I do, but not on me. What do you need?" I asked pulling out a pen and paper.

"I would like to know whether I still have family."

"Write down all you know and I'll see if I can help or," I looked around, "why don't we check you in to a hotel for a couple of nights and you can negotiate the internet yourself?" I looked at the three hotels that were in my eye line.

"Not sure your £40 is going to cover it," he laughed.

"But now I am doing an extra big good deed so I think I can stretch a little further." I laughed.

"Thanks, but there is no way they are going to let me in there."

"You're kidding right, Beards are all the rage. Stay here and I will sort it out. I'm Charlotte, by the way."

"Nice to meet you Charlotte, I'm Gerald." I stood and left to check out the hotels.

I entered the first hotel. This place was posh. A man opened the door as I entered and tipped his hat. I enquired to the nightly price and nearly fainted on the spot. £265 for a room that had no wifi and measured only three metres by four. I thanked him and left. The second hotel was a similar price but for a slightly larger room. The third was more of a bargain hotel but again the price was extortionate and the rooms tiny but then this was London.

"What kind of place are you looking for?" The young man said behind the desk.

"A nice room, perhaps for the week, with wifi and perhaps a computer there already to use," I mused.

"Why not consider an apartment?" He typed some details into the computer and swung the screen around. £585, seven days, inc wifi, no computer though.

"Oh wow, where is that?" I looked at the screen. This way he would have separate rooms for bedroom, kitchen and lounge. It would feel more like a real house.

"Across the street, my brother owns them and does them cheap for last minute bookings. Better some money than none."

"Okay, I'll take it," I smiled.

He typed some details into the computer and took my cash and Gerald's name and told me to call back in twenty minutes to collect the keys.

I checked the time on my phone, I still had loads of time to get ready. I dashed into the supermarket and filled a trolley full of food and toiletries. Thinking about what someone would want or need for a week was difficult. It would have been better to give him the money and let him buy his own stuff but there was a part of me that thought he wouldn't spent it or spend it on the wrong stuff. I felt a stab of guilt as I selected his razors and shaving foam, shampoo and soap. Who was I to judge him? Just because he had been on drugs once didn't mean that he would do it again as soon as money entered his pocket. I picked up bread, butter, milk, tea, coffee and other essentials. The supermarket did a store card so I put £100 on it. If he chose to spend it on cigarettes and alcohol that would be his choice. I had no right to dictate how he lived his life.

I lugged the bags next door and left them with the hotel man who said it was no problem despite the fact that they took up most of his small reception. I had seen a bag shop on the way to the hotel and had decided this was a good idea. I bought a shopping trolley the kind that had wheels and you dragged your stuff around in it. I bought a super tog sleeping bag and an inflatable pillow and made sure it all fitted into the trolley. Now if Gerald had nothing left at the end of the week at least he would have a warmer bed to sleep in. I walked back to the supermarket and checked out their tablets. Gerald could use it to search for his family and at the end of the week sell it on. I'm sure someone would take it off his hands, either way it saved me having to go back to Josh's to search for his family then having to keep going back to him when I had found out information. I bought the cheapest one and returned to the hotel where the man's twin brother was waiting with a key.

"Wow! That would have confused me," I smiled.

"Yes, we get that a lot, even though I am clearly the better looking." The other brother said.

"Double trouble. I love it."

Both brother's helped me to carry my stuff across the street and I wondered if he would get in trouble for leaving the desk unattended. He didn't seem to rush back either. They both talked me through the rooms and the wifi and I just had to drop the key off at the hotel at the end of the week sometime before noon.

They left and I surveyed the room. It was larger than I had expected. It was basic and there was a damp problem in a corner that had been poorly covered up. The sofa was worn but comfortable and the carpet had a small burn hole in but other than that the place was ideal. I plugged in the tablet to charge and left to think about clothes. Gerald looked the same sort of height as Josh but skinnier so I decided to get Gerald the size smaller.

A nearby sports shop served my purpose. As well as jogging bottoms they had windproof walking trousers and jackets. I couldn't buy the shoes but bought two bags full of clothes and placed £100 on a store card. Again if Gerald didn't want it he could sell it on. I returned to the apartment, dropped off the clothes, then went to find Gerald who had moved from his original spot. A couple were now settling in the alcove with a dog that seemed to be taking up most of the room. They pointed me in the way of the park and I unwillingly set out in the dark to look for his new camp. I found him trying to settle by a statue but struggling to find shelter from the wind.

"I didn't think I would see you again," he smiled as I approached.

"I am a girl of my word. Follow me I have found you a bed."

"A real bed, inside." He raised his eyebrows and I saw that he was making fun of me.

"Yes, a real bed for a real boy, but I have a dinner reservation tonight so I need you to move it, come on already," I laughed.

"Okay, keep your shirt on," he laughed, scooping up his bundle.

"Here we are." I handed him the keys so he could unlock the door himself. "Room twenty-seven, third floor."

"I have never noticed this place before," Gerald said in the lift.

"It was recommended by the guy across the street. You have the place for a week but you must hand the key in Wednesday morning before noon to that hotel across the street."

"A week?" Gerald stumbled as the lift halted.

"Yes, better value and it may take a while to track your family. What size shoe are you, by the way?"

"Nine," he answered, rubbing his beard.

I motioned for him to unlock room twenty-seven then had to gently push him inside. "I have bought you some things for your stay and have some put some money on these store cards. Do you know how these work?" I held up the Tesco card.

"Yes, just like a credit card," he answered slowly, drinking in the room.

"This is mine for the week?" He asked again.

"Cost more than £40 so if I ever need another favour you are totally in my debt," I smiled and started unpacking the bags.

"Indeed!" He had his hands on his hips looking out of the window. To the right his alcove could be seen and to the left in the distance, were the main street lights of the city.

I gave him the tour, the bedroom, the shower, the kitchen. I made sure he knew how everything worked. I talked him through the food and the clothes and he was silent, taking it all in.

I pulled out the tablet and kick started it into life. I showed him how Google worked and how to work the camera. "Anything you do not know how to do but want to know, just type it into Google." I handed him the tablet.

"Can I get a steak delivered to room twenty-seven Risborough Gardens?" He said aloud as he typed and a list of take away companies came up.

"Order one." I handed him my phone and he rang through an order. I pulled out £20 and laid it on the table. "When the delivery guy arrives he will call the intercom. You press here to answer him and here to let him through the front door."

"Got it," he said fiddling with the tablet. "Oh it says there are twenty-three Sheila Morgan's and fifteen Annabel Morgan's," he looked up, bewildered.

"Click on images they might have a Facebook profile," I suggested. "If all else fails, send them all a message." It can't do any harm. "I'm going to get you some weatherproof shoes. I'll take the keys." I left him frantically tapping on the device like his life depended on it.

It was now seven-fifteen. The time was running out fast. The sports shop was open until eight but the young staff looked anything but keen to see me in there. Two guarded the doors and had to be excused so that I could enter. I asked for the walking shoes in a nine and headed back to Risbourough Garden's.

"Is that for twenty- seven?" I asked as the delivery guy stood at the door.

"Yes," the guy turned around looking relieved.

I gave him £20 and rushed inside. Could something have happened to Gerald already?

"Gerald!" I yelled as I entered.

"Just in here," I heard him yell from the toilet.

"Your steak is here." I searched the cupboards for a plate and some cutlery and laid the table. It looked and smelt beautiful and I realised I hadn't eaten since the cookie I ate at about two with Ryan and now my stomach was lurching for food.

"Smells divine," he said entering the room. He had showered and trimmed the beard into a neater mass. He was now wearing a new jogging suit that was a little too big and he looked nothing like a man who had been living on the streets.

"It does. I am going to leave you to it." I handed him the keys. "Everything in here is yours, eat it, wear it, use it. There is money on both cards so use it. I also got you this to say thank you," I pulled out the new sleeping bag and pillow. "This trolley can hide a lot in it so you can take some stuff with you."

"Thank you Charlotte. This is the kindest thing anyone has ever done for me," he said through a mouthful of peas.

"I'm just trying to restore the balance. You have a chance here to make amends with your family. It's just a week of wifi so don't waste it and remember if you get stuck, ask Google." I smiled and left him to his meal.

"Oh my God, I thought you had been kidnapped," Josh said when I returned. "You have less than an hour to get ready before Ryan arrives."

"I have beautified myself in less time." I raised my eyebrows and headed in the shower. The truth was that I didn't have a great deal to do. Marsha had waxed practically every hair off my body already and I don't know how Ruby had applied the line over my eyes, but two showers later and it was still there as thick as ever. The false eyelashes were semi permanent and I could feel them brushing against my lids, I felt made up even before I had started.

I pulled things out of the Louis Vuitton bag no longer feeling guilty, a balance had been restored. I piled all the money out in three stacks and placed it into my bedside cabinet. I would use some of that to pay for tonight's meal and maybe buy Gerald some more time. The week's rent had been cheap and it would make a huge difference to his life. I used the body creams and matching perfume and laid out the Mineral make-up ready for when my face had dried properly from the shower.

"Do you have a hair dryer I can borrow please?" I yelled through to Josh but he said Meg had taken her's with her. He gave me a half an hour warning and continued getting himself ready.

I considered the silver Gucci dress from the Louis Vuitton bag. Some of the clothes Ryan had bought me were a size twelve so I decided it was worth a shot. The zip was a struggle but I felt confident that it wouldn't break. I practiced sitting down until I was satisfied with the choice. I slipped on the matching shoes and by the time I had finished I didn't look or feel like me. I felt like a super hero version of me that had earned the stolen dress and slogged for the matching shoes. It was a risk of course. This very evening these items would have been reported missing, but that just added to the thrill. I brushed my hair into big waves and sprayed it into place. Hair and facially I looked similar to last night, but the dress was something else.

I packed the smaller Mulberry bag with cash, lipgloss and face powder and was satisfied.

"I didn't buy you that dress," Ryan remarked, as I entered the lounge.

"No, but it isn't all about you is it?" I did a little turn in the centre of the room.

"She only got back forty minutes ago," Josh said, typing away at his computer. Both men were wearing dinner suits and smelt divine.

"You went out without me?" Ryan pouted out his lower lip. "Like an independent woman. That's not right," he smiled.

"I know it was dark and everything. I'll tell you all about it over drinks."

We left the apartment and headed towards Tower Bridge. After all the shopping I had done today, I still hadn't picked myself up a proper jacket. There were five days until New Year and the weather had been mild considering but still all the goosebumps on my flesh made an appearance.

"Still haven't got that jacket?" Ryan read my mind and handed me his suit jacket.

"Thank you." I smiled as he helped me into it. His thumb gently brushed both sides of my neck. "But I did only arrive yesterday."

"Seems longer," Josh remarked and I had to agree, it seemed impossible to believe that yesterday morning I had woken up on a dodgy airbed surrounding by nothing of any value to me and yet today I was here in the heart of London with my brother, whom I adored and his friend that had shown me more kindness in twenty-four hours than Scott, Amber and Cassie had in their whole lives put together.

"You really need to start writing in that diary," Ryan said. "How else will you remember how devilishly handsome I looked and how chivalrous I was with my jacket?" He straightened up his thin black tie.

"Perhaps you could remind me every so often so I don't forget," I suggested.

"Nah, no one likes to blow their own trumpet," he laughed.

Josh held open the door and we entered the mighty restaurant's bar area. Low lamp shades decorated in cow print were hung low over the neatly set tables and wide high back chairs greeted the sitter. The most amazing thing about the place by far was the outstanding view of the bridge. I stood in awe of the view while the boys got the drinks in and chatted about a mutual friend who was getting engaged. My concentration drifted in and out as they talked about Meg and lifelong possibilities for marriage but my brain was struggling to find a clear view. Everything seemed out of focus and unreal somehow. Was this really how some people lived? It was such a contrast to Gerald's windy alcove. Had he given it up to the couple with the dog of his own accord? Somehow I doubted it. Imagine every night having to fight to get a sheltered sleeping spot and then having the courage to defend it so nobody took it away from you.

"You're quiet," Josh remarked after we had been seated.

"I'm just thinking about how lucky we are to have been born to the people we were born to, without which we probably wouldn't be where we are now," I said, admiring the window seat Ryan had procured.

"I will drink to that." Ryan held up his wine glass and me and Josh followed suit. "To all of life's fantastic opportunities and here is hoping that your new life opens more doors than the life you have left behind." He held my gaze for longer than I felt comfortable.

I really must write in that diary.

Chapter 12

Ryan had promised to call New Year's Eve for us to see the fireworks and Josh left for Scotland early on the Saturday morning meaning I was left alone. He sent photos back of Amber's field including a selfie of him peeing on it. No building work had been started and it was just a large empty plot. He kindly checked in on my house just to make sure Scott hadn't destroyed it and reported back that all was well.

I ventured out and bought myself a new laptop and an iPad all with the money from the Louis Vuitton bag. It had taken me ages to count it all up. There had been £200 in carpark savings money, over £5000 had been stuffed in the bean tins, £8000 had been Tom's car money. I shredded the envelope with his name on it and counted on. The protein shake containers had been the largest and had contained the most, there had been over £15000! No wonder they had been annoyed about the break in. I had just kept stuffing money in bags it had never occurred to me how much was actually there. I had mentally calculated that I had spent around £1700 on Gerald. I smiled to myself, I had offered him £40 and ended up, hopefully making a bigger difference.

My vengeful streak was lacking. Ray and his sons had all been arrested and Amber had received the blame, she in turn, blamed Scott saying he must have blabbed about the key. I read the texts, detached as if I had no role in it and it no longer mattered to me. I had other things to worry about now, mainly finding a place of my own. Josh would be returning on the third with Meg and she would stay until they both go to Scotland for Burn's night. That was going to be twenty-two days and nights of feeling like a gooseberry in-between the most loved up couple I had ever met.

I had been tempted to call Ryan and make him save me from my boredom but I refrained. What I really wanted was someone to vent to and I didn't want that to be Ryan. I called Amber a couple of times but she never answered the call, not that I really knew what I wanted to say to her anyway. Instead I stalked them all on Facebook. Amber's status said that she was the happiest she had ever been and how everything was finally clicking into place. I felt a storm washing over me, I wasn't happy but I couldn't really pinpoint why. I reasoned after hours of brooding, I was more hurt over the fact that they didn't miss me or really need me in their lives. They had carried on as normal and my absence hadn't made the slightest impact to any of them.

I had tried on every item of clothing to distract myself from my own thoughts, I used my new camera to photograph views from the window, read every last word of my print outs from Josh and I was still restless for something to do. I needed something to fill in my time. The funny thing was if I was still in Densborough I would have been working, watching TV and sleeping, I could do all those things here, but somehow time was dragging and I hated my own company.

I opened my Christmas presents that Ryan had salvaged from the garage. Cassie had bought me a really nice day-a-page diary and calendar set with famous landmarks from all over the world. Cassie was big on travel and always going on about how she never understood why me and Scott hadn't travelled more. Amber had given me a toiletry set that Cassie had given her for her birthday. I knew this because I had helped Cassie pick it out. I threw it in the bin and meditated until the annoyance had worn off. I had bought her a Ted Baker make-up bag that she had had her eye on and she had spent nothing on me and stole my husband!

What if I revealed that Amber had these loans out? I thought about how I could do it. If I didn't reveal her crimes would anybody see her for who she really was? I doubted it and if they did suspect something no doubt she would have an amazing excuse to hide her tracks. Maybe Scott already knew or maybe he would be furious and dump her realising that he had made a massive mistake?

It took me an hour to talk myself into it. I photocopied the loan copies and put them neatly into A4 envelopes. I sent Scott's to his mother's, Cassie's to her parent's address that I got from the wedding invitation, and sent one for myself to the hospital just in case anyone was reading my mail there. I stood by the post box and considered what I had just done. I couldn't change it now. They had been sent first class and at some point in the early part of the new year, Amber would have some explaining to do.

I bought myself two new coats. One a thick parka that would save me from the elements and a black glittery dress jacket that would go with any posh item of clothing. I could have spent a fortune and I considered it. I had the money sitting there and could have treated myself to some great Christmas presents for myself, but I had now ruled returning to Densborough out. I would need to find a job and a place to live and this money might end up being crucial to that plan.

I diverted on the way back and visited Gerald. He didn't know that my husband and my ex-best friend were complete psychos and he wouldn't be asking me if I was okay.

A strange man answered the door and welcomed me fondly with a hug.

"Charlotte, it's so great to see you. Come in, I'll put the kettle on." I stood at the door unable to believe my eyes.

"Who are you?" I laughed.

"I know, good looking under all that facial hair. Going to be cold next week though. I googled the weather prediction." He smiled and laid out two cups.

"I thought I had better leave you my number in case you needed anything else."

"Thank you, but I think you have already done enough." He took both coffees to the table, I followed him over and took a seat. He reached for his tablet and clicked on some buttons and handed it to me. "This is my daughter, Annabel, she is coming to see me on Friday, she thought I was dead." Tears welled up in his eyes. "We are meeting in the park so she doesn't know where I live, or don't live should I say."

"Why don't you want her to know?" I asked flicking through the pictures. "She could help you."

"I don't need help or sympathy. I just need to say all the things I have been holding in for so long and I just need to see her. I have grandchildren, can you believe that?" He reached over and flicked on to some more pictures.

I showed him how to take screen shots so he could compile his own photo album of his family and I had never seen anyone look prouder.

"Look, I'm going to put some more time on this place for you so you can stay here a little longer. I think you have a right to live your life any way you choose but you need to give your family the choice of whether they want to help you or not. You are not alone and don't need to be ever again. They might say they can't help but what if they can?" I sipped my drink. "I would be deeply saddened if my father met me, looked great, then I found out he was too proud to tell me the truth. It is not going to hurt you to be honest."

"I have been a massive disappointment. I don't want to make that any worse," he said.

"Well, what will you say to them if they want to see you again, which they will, oh no wait, they won't even get a reply from you because you will have no internet or phone to reply on. I think that's worse."

"Well, what would you suggest?" He put his arms up in defeat.

"I would message your daughter, right now, and tell her that a charity has given you housing for an extra week so they can come here and stay the night if they want to. You have been living homeless for the last however many years and it will be difficult to get hold of you afterwards so you want to make the most of it. Why not invite them down to stay for the fireworks? They can have your room and you can sleep on the couch."

"I don't know." He rubbed his chin and seemed to surprise himself that the beard had gone.

"Here," I took the tablet from him and compiled an email. "All you have to do is press send."

I stood up to let him think about it and dialled the number of the landlord and booked another week. I put the money into an envelope and put it in my pocket.

"I sent it," he looked terrified.

"If your daughter was on the street and you didn't know about it, how would you feel?" I washed up our cups.

"I would be devastated and would want to help. Maybe it is easier giving help than taking it." He rubbed my hand.

"Maybe, well you have until the tenth here. I wish you the best of luck." I handed him an envelope with £100 in it. If he wanted more takeaways he could. He tried to refuse it but I told him that he could buy his family lunch somewhere and his resolve softened and he gratefully accepted. I gave him a hug and left to drop the money off at the hotel across the street. If he could benefit in any way from the crime I had committed then I could feel a little less guilty and he had a real chance to turn his life around. If nothing came of it he would have had a warm two weeks with warm food and a comfortable bed, but if he went back to life on the streets I would feel like a failure somehow. I crossed my fingers that his family would be able to help him more than I had, something longer term than two weeks out of the cold.

Time dragged until Ryan called at seven New Year's Eve. "Been busy?" He asked.

"No, all has been slack on the world domination front. I need a job and a hobby. I hate my own company," I said honestly. I had spent the last couple of hours sorting out which camera equipment I was going to take with me and which lens I needed. I wasted time charging extra batteries that I knew I wouldn't need and brushing up on night time photography techniques.

"Well, your routine has changed, you will need to adapt. If it makes you feel better, you have an interview at the magazine, ten a.m. Friday, though Dad isn't overly keen on your lack of fashion experience."

"You're kidding! I'm friends with you surely that's all the fashion experience I need," I laughed.

"That's what I told him. Unfortunately my dad doesn't believe in personal favours actually, he may not hire you simply on the basis that I put you forward. He doesn't like complications and he believes pulled favours never end well."

Ryan stood back and surveyed my outfit. "What?" I asked. He said that we were not eating anywhere posh and I needed to wear layers so I had opted for my black, thermal lined leggings, my black and white check skater skirt, a black high neck top with a white opened backed lace top. I only had one pair of flat boots they were high knee but went well. I did prefer the brown ankle boots from the Louis Vuitton bag but brown didn't go and I thought the heels would kill me if we were walking up Primrose Hill again.

"You need a hat and gloves, it's supposed to snow tonight."

"Really!" I started jumping up and down on the spot. It hadn't really snowed here for several years despite regular severe weather warnings.

"The snow is great for one day then it just needs to bugger off so I can get back to work." He took my arm and led me out of the apartment.

We stopped off in a shop and bought a fur lined hat, gloves and shawl set. Walking around the streets and tubes I thought I was going to be sick with the heat but as soon as we reached St John's Wood, the cold hit me.

"Where are we eating?" I asked as we past dozens of decent enough places.

"There is a buffet place down the road. I try to pick quieter places and this has only just opened so should be worth a try."

We sat in a booth down the back and Ryan helped me to take off my coat. While he ordered wine and chatted with the waiter, whom he knew. I found myself comparing him to Scott. Scott had been okay looking. His job required him to be physically fit and his muscles seemed to make him seem better looking than he actually was. He certainly was never a gentleman, though I had never noticed this before. I had never expected him to take my coat off or buy me a gift when it wasn't my birthday or a special occasion, yet to Ryan, this sort of behaviour seemed second nature. Scott always had insisted that we took it in turns to pay for a meal out, not that they ever happened often and he always seemed to use the joint account anyway. What had I seen in him?

"You are not drinking your wine which means I feel the need to slow down," Ryan raised his eyebrows. "Are you okay? You seem somewhere else."

"Sorry, I just keep thinking about the future." I took a large swig of wine.

"Well, in under four hours it will be a completely new year with new worries and new ambitions. Some of the old rubbish will need to be left on the hill." He got up and re-filled his plate.

Leaving my troubles behind was easier said than done. I was having trouble with the closure. Scott and Amber were both dodging all my calls and as a result I had been brooding. The fact that neither of them had answered had been a good thing. One minute I wanted to admit I knew everything and wish them both the best and the next I wanted to yell at them both for being two faced selfish pricks. Perhaps ignoring the whole situation would be the best way of getting past it.

I stood up and re-filled my plate.

"So what have you been doing since I saw you last?" I asked, returning to the table. I hoped his reply would take my mind off the impending doom that was building inside.

"Working on the diet section of the magazine ready for the spring issue. Usually Zoella would help out but she has just been made Editorial assistant so whoever gets the job will be working under her now."

"How many jobs are on offer then?"

"Beth is travelling and Keeley is on maternity, Zoella has stepped up into their place so the job is for a general secretary really." He pushed his cutlery together signalling that he was done. "They just shift us round a lot so when one area is busier than others we all chip in to help out," he topped up my wine, "One minute people want to know about travelling abroad, then they are in to camping, then it's expensive one off creations then it's all about mixing and matching fashions of the past. At the moment it is all about healthy food that the kids will actually eat. We tend to hire experts in rather than over work our staff."

"Sounds like a busy place." I wondered if it was all too different for me.

"There is always something going on. We're now hiring the models for fashion week, the place is like Kings Cross Station."

"Sounds like a whole other world," I said.

"You get used to it. I need to collect a bag before we go." He got up and paid the bill. The side of the restaurant had a bar area for people who were waiting for tables or who had just eaten. Ryan seemed annoyed that the only table available to wait at was a window seat which got me wondering why. Was he trying to hide me or was he really just trying to avoid random acquaintances attention? Several people spotted him and darted in to wish him a happy New Year and within the space of half an hour the place seemed to be entirely filled up with his friends.

His waiter friend barged through the crowd at eleven with a trolley very similar to the one I had bought Gerald and gave it to Ryan.

"What's in the trolley?" I asked putting on my coat and new accessories.

"Can't say, it's a surprise," he smiled.

It took about fifteen minutes to get out of the restaurant. People were all over the place and it seemed that Ryan knew most of them. Most of the women asked where we were going and he said a small party. Some of the girls looked me up and down trying to work out what someone like him was doing with someone like me. I just smiled and said nothing. If it wasn't for Ryan I would be sitting back at the apartment by myself watching the fireworks on TV, probably crying into my ice-cream. If he wanted to lie to his friends about where we were going I wasn't going to call him out.

"Primrose Hill will be busy but it will be dark so I'm hoping it will be quite relaxed." He dragged his trolley down the road.

"You make your life out to be such a burden," I laughed.

"Sometimes, it is. Like when you are in a hurry or when out on a date. The constant interruptions can be tiresome. Sometimes it is hard to stay polite."

"However if you found yourself at a loose end on a random Saturday, you could go out alone and be guaranteed to find someone to adopt you."

"True, but then my calendar is pretty jam packed." He pulled me away from the edge of the road as a car sped dangerously close to a puddle.

"What were you doing tonight before my brother made you adopt me?"

"I was invited to several parties but didn't want to go to any of them. I was going to go up to Scotland with Josh and play gooseberry, but Meg's friend, Laurel, scares the hell out of me."

I laughed. Laurel was a confident girl who grabbed life by the balls. I bet she would tell Ryan exactly what she wanted to do with him.

Primrose Hill was busier than I had expected and the bench areas were jam packed full of people standing around under huge umbrellas. Some people had taken their own camping chairs and a few clever business people had set up hot dog stands and Chestnut trolleys. Ryan led me away from the highest point and set the trolley down a little way down the hill.

"You need to close your eyes," he said and I obliged. "Have you had a thought about what troubles you are going to leave on the hill?" He sounded like he was lifting something heavy.

"Yes, I need to accept that I cannot make Scott love me and rather than think about the things I could do to make him happy, I am going to think about the things that could make me happy."

"Good plan," he rustled some fabric. "What had you been thinking? Were you thinking of ways to win him back?"

"I have done loads of thinking the past couple of days like, what if I had done things differently like worked less and fussed him more, or what if he knew about Amber's loans in his name would he come back to me. Then I asked myself what was it about him that I missed or loved. I then realised that it isn't him at all! What actually hurts the most is the painful truth that I wasn't good enough for him and that this went on for nearly two years and I was so stupidly blind that I didn't notice." I paused as someone offered Ryan a hand.

"Go on." Ryan prompted after he said his thank you's to the kind stranger.

"I thought I wanted him back and that I wanted him to realise he had made a mistake and come back to me this amazing better person but then I remembered my mother's table and the fact that he took the car from my work not caring how I got home, and that he has ignored every call I have tried to make to him this past week."

"Why would you call him?" Ryan butted in sharply.

"Because he ideally needs to sort out the house sale. I need to know if he has filled in the divorce paperwork and I would also really like an apology for his dickness."

"Dickness? I guess that sums it up," he laughed. "You know the estate agents can hold the keys for you, you don't need to rely on Scott for anything. I will make sure he signs the divorce paperwork."

"I just need to be a bit more self sufficient. Living with Josh while Meg is down is going to be awkward. I really need to decide where I want to base myself. Somewhere on the outskirts of London would be ideal. I could get a job at a hospital or a medical centre and see Josh whenever I wanted. There is no point ever going back to Densborough." I felt the first few spits of rain hit my face.

"Just five minutes more," Ryan said. I could hear clicking and the creases in plastic material. "So Scott is a definite no then?"

"I don't see how I could ever forgive him for poisoning me." I had thought about it hard. "Nothing he could do or say would ever make that right. I spent days trying to blame it all on Amber so he could be redeemed but it is impossible." I shifted on my now aching legs and wished we had a seat. "There is no miracle that could save our marriage or make me even like him. I don't know if the fact that I hate him is bigger than the overwhelming feeling of disappointment."

"He does sound like I massive idiot. Just remember that you didn't lose them, you let them go. You moved away and are rebuilding your life without them in it. They have lost you and it won't take them long to realise what they have lost." I heard some clicking and hoped it was a chair of some description. "I don't really remember him or much about your wedding," he continued. "DJ was awesome."

"The DJ was drunk," I laughed. The wedding seemed like decades ago now. "I just feel like Scott has made a massive mistake and I can't wait until he realises what a massive idiot he has been so I can laugh in his face."

"Ideally we need him to sign the consent order first. He could drag his heels about signing and delay your divorce by months even years," Ryan said.

"Oh dear," I said and told him about the fact that I had already sent the loan documents.

"Don't panic, I'll sort it." He turned me around. "You can open your eyes now."

"Wow!" He had erected a small spectator tent that resembled a plastic bird hide. He held open the door for me to step in. Inside he had put up a double camping chair which was covered with a massive white fluffy throw.

"It isn't the ritz," he said, zipping up the door.

"Well, it is going to keep the rain off and protect us from the breeze. Some people never have that luxury," I said, thinking of how different this new year would be for Gerald compared to all his previous years.

"Mulled wine or coffee?" He asked holding up two flasks.

"Wine, please," though I wasn't sure that I had room. "Did the waiter make that for you while we were leaving?"

"Yes, in exchange for two tickets to the magazine's Valentine's Day fashion shoot party, it's quite an event in these parts."

"Really," I remarked, as people started cheering. We both sat up in our seats and looked out of the drop down hole in the plastic. The fireworks erupted in the sky and I started taking pictures. After a while I put the camera down and just watched the spectacle. Though not amazingly close, the view was amazing. You could make out the London Eye which with the array of fireworks that danced around it made it look like an oversized Catherine Wheel.

I felt Ryan's hand slip into mine. "So how are we going to spend this first night of this brand new year?" He moved his fingers up to my cheek then down the edge of my chin. I felt my body move towards him on its own accord like his body had some kind of magnetic pull. Both his hands cupped my face and pulled me in deeper. I didn't know how long we had been kissing for but we were interrupted by a man in an official hi-vis jacket asking us to start clearing up.

"Where did everyone go?" I asked, slightly embarrassed by my unusual forwardness.

"Parties, I Guess. Do you want to gate crash one?" Ryan started to take down the tent and I decided that I could probably fold down the chair without breaking anything. I thought about what I wanted, what did I really want? I didn't doubt for a second that he could get us into any party he liked and we would probably end up kissing some more and perhaps having sex, but did I really want that?

He flashed me a smile so completely unaware of the way he was making me feel. "No," I said to his surprise. "I think it has been a wonderful evening but I think I would like to go home and make a yearly 'To Do' list of all the things I want to achieve this year and wake up tomorrow, well later on, with a clear agenda of where I am going, preferably without a hangover."

A look of disappointment flashed across his face but he quickly covered it up with a smile. He quickly packed the bag and dragged it back to the tube station. "Do you know what would have made this perfect?" He asked as we heaved his trolley on to the packed platform.

I shook my head. "Maybe those chocolate covered marshmallow, strawberry kebab things," I suggested.

"Ooh messy, no I was thinking about the lack of snow, so disappointing."

"The snow you hate?" I leant into him as the tube lurched to a stop and felt his breath on my forehead.

"One day is fine, two days maybe. It should snow Christmas Day." He leant into my body and whispered into my ear "Are you sure you don't want to party some more?" I felt my eyes involuntarily close. I wasn't sure, not sure at all.

"I'm sure," I lied. "Thank you though for a perfectly magical evening. You don't need to walk me home, I can text you when I get there." I smiled as my stop approached.

"The tube is free, it is no trouble." He smiled as a bunch of revellers called his name but he didn't take his eyes away from mine.

"But it is ridiculously busy and you have a stupid trolley. Go party with your friends," I said nervously. The intensity of his stare was weakening my resolve and I felt my inner angel running out of reasons to say no to him. His friends cheered as they drew in closer to us. A woman and her friend wobbled into Ryan and he moved the trolley in-between them as a barrier. "I can take the trolley if you like," I offered.

"Party with us." Ryan grabbed my chin again, ignoring the woman closest to him who was talking to him about how long it had been since she last saw him.

"I can't, I'm tired and I know I would regret it in the morning." I moved my face from his hands and saw the recognition flash across his face. He knew I was talking about sex now.

"She is tired, let her rest," the woman drawled much to my annoyance. I didn't need rest I just needed to slow down and keep my feet somewhere near the ground.

"Okay," he said as if it was anything but, "I'll text you later." He looked crushed and I felt a stab of guilt at my ungrateful attitude towards what he had done for me.

"Thank you and thank you for today. We didn't need snow it was magical anyway." I kissed his cheek and left the tube lugging the trolley behind me.

After a million apologies to everyone that I had bashed, I made it home. Thinking the biggest mistake I had ever made was leaving Ryan on the train.

Chapter 13

I laid in bed with my phone on my pillow in case Ryan text back.

I had sent the standard thank you text and mentioned that I was sorry to have left but was now in bed working on my 'To Do' list. This was a lie. I was in bed, dog tired. I didn't want to sleep in case he called or even better came over, but he didn't, despite my wishing.

I knew I would regret not spending the night with him in the morning, damn I was regretting it already, but then I knew I would have regretting having sex with him too. I was, after all, still a married woman burning from the recent sting of being dumped from an almighty height. How much of my feelings for Ryan were real or was my inner devil trying to even that sexual score?

I woke around seven and no texts had been returned. I had a few from Josh, Meg, Cassie and from my cousin Steven, but nothing from Ryan.

I went back to sleep and woke at various intervals to check my phone. By ten-thirty, I was convinced it was broken, but then other people had text me. By lunch time I started pacing the living room trying to think of reasons that he wouldn't text. I replayed the whole night over and over in my head, refusing to think that it could be down to something as petty as not spending the night with him.

I counted up my texts, twenty-seven. Not bad considering I didn't think that I knew that many people. I switched Amber's phone on, she had over a hundred! I threw her phone into a drawer and showered. Ryan could knock on the door any minute and whisk me off somewhere exciting and romantic and I needed to be ready, just in case.

Thursday came and Ryan still hadn't text me back. I was convinced now that he had shacked up with the semi naked girl from the tube who kept pressing her breasts into his chest. She certainly had eyelashes to die for, maybe Ryan liked that sort of confidence.

A heavy feeling was looming in my stomach and I felt the desperate need to see him. I picked up my phone to dial his number several times but then thought better of it, I would see him tomorrow at my interview anyway. I was to be there for ten, maybe he would invite me out to lunch.

Suddenly my phone burst into song and my heart followed suit. "Don't sound too disappointed to hear from me, blimey." Josh obviously detected the hint of disappointment in my voice.

"Sorry, did you have a great New Year?" I asked knowing he would have.

"Yes, apart from the snow, Edinburgh is freezing. I'm still trying to persuade Meg to move to London."

"Argh, still no luck there then?" I checked my calendar, Josh was coming back today and I really needed to clean up. The state of this place would freak out the cleaning OCD in him.

"No, listen, I'm in Densborough sorting out some things for you. House looks like Scott hasn't been back here, I have given the keys to the estate agent who have said there have been some positive enquiries already and a family are coming to have a look around this afternoon, so hopefully a sale will go through quickly."

Eek! If he was in Densborough already that meant I had less than three hours to get cleaned up. "That's great, thank you for that. Anything else I need to do?" I asked. I found myself wondering he had heard from Ryan and whether he would get suspicious if I asked. I thought better of it, no one knew me like Josh and he would see through me in a second.

"Not yet, the lawyers are sending through some paperwork for you to read over and sign. Do not, under any circumstances, sign and send that off before Ryan has read it over." The mere mention of Ryan's name made my stomach twist. Maybe if Josh asked me how my New Year went then I could ask about Ryan without being suspected of turning into the kind of psycho stalker woman that Josh always jokes about.

"I won't. You know I know nothing about these things anyway. Have you been to see Aunt Maureen?"

"Yes, what an unpleasant trip that was. Meg says she can't come to our wedding, should she ever give me a chance to propose, that is."

"Well, if you move to Edinburgh, you will be out of a job and won't be able to afford a wedding anyway," I laughed.

"Good point, I might have to bring that up. I better go. I'll see you in a couple of hours," he rang off.

I spent the next couple of hours scrubbing. I had spent so long moping and waiting for Ryan to save me from the boredom of myself that everything else had built up.

By the time Josh and Meg arrived the apartment sparkled like a new pin and I was exhausted.

"We are going to have take out, do you want to join us?" Josh asked.

Despite the howling in my stomach, I declined. If they had really wanted me to join them they would have just thrown me the menu and presumed I was in. Instead I hid in my room and listened to their cheerful, loved up banter. What would happen if Meg really refused to move? As a hair dresser and beautician, she could work anywhere. Ryan could probably get her a job anywhere she wanted and she would probably earn more money than she got now.

The thought of Ryan again had me holding my breath. I couldn't shake this uneasy feeling that I had either upset him or worse that I had lost him to a better looking woman who better matched his awesomeness.

Either way I would know tomorrow at the interview. I had laid out a cute dark grey pinafore dress with integral white collar and cuffs. Out of all the outfits that I had tried on, this was my favourite. I teamed it up with a low pair of kitten heels and decided against the tights. I was still tanned from the spray tan that Marsha had given me and it seemed a shame to cover them up.

By nine the next morning, I felt positively sick.

I had looked up the address on street view and knew exactly what I was looking for but was still amazed when I found it. It was bigger and posher than I had thought. The glass fronted walls highlighted the white and gold marble floors and the granite desk stations of the receptionists, were works of art. Every single member of staff was in full contoured make-up looked like a model.

I nervously gave my name and was asked to take a seat.

"Hi, I'm Zoella." A thin strip of a woman floated in and shook my hand. "You can come wait up stairs. You are the last interview and this one is taking its time. You might as well come and see the floor while you wait." She flashed a smile to a man on reception and he blushed slightly then carried on with his call.

"Have there been many interviews?" I asked, thinking only about Ryan.

"Oh, heavens, no, most get let down straight off. Mr Emerson refuses to interview any more than ten, though this time he has interviewed twelve, but best not bring that up, he hates to break rules or traditions." The lift opened and she chatted briefly with a girl at reception giving me a chance to observe her and the floor. Zoella was beautiful. Absolutely everything you would expect about fashion. She stood slightly taller than me, I guessed her to be around 5 foot 9 inches but she looked taller because of the unnaturally high black patent shoes that adorned her feet. She had a Spanish look about her with her thick black curly mass of a mane which fell on her flawless olive skin. She matched Ryan, together they would have been the most aesthetically pleasing couple that I had ever seen, then I remembered the way she had flashed a look at the receptionist. She wasn't interested in Ryan, that was just paranoia dancing around my jealous head.

I looked around searching for Ryan's office. The floor was a symmetrical hall with the lift in the centre. Straight ahead was a small reception area where I was asked to take a seat. I sat, nervously and looked around. From what I could make out there was a canteen to the left and nothing else. I moved my attention back to the two girls on reception who were made up to the nines. They would have been the first faces people saw each morning. Their desk was circular with what I presumed to be the sales team sitting in a row behind them. Every time they ended a call the phone blasted again, it seemed never ending. I wasn't confident about this job, but I was glad I hadn't applied for sales, it looked relentless. Behind the sales desk were lines of doorless offices that ran both sides of the room. Some had meetings going on and I could see Powerpoint presentations going on and flip charts being written on. At the bottom of the hall was a large office that took up the whole back wall which was guarded by two desks either side of the door. Zoella sat on the desk on the left and I guessed the desk on the right would be occupied by whoever was successful at this interview.

I surveyed the rooms again, any one of them could be Ryan's. What if he wasn't even in today?

"Hi, I'm Buddy, head of graphics." A young man with thick blonde curly hair grabbed my hand and shook it ferociously. "Are you nervous? Old Henry has a reputation of being cut throat in interviews, the last two fled, crying." He motioned for me to stand so I did and joined him at the coffee machine. "Help yourself." He swiped a card into the coffee machine and motioned for me to select a drink. "Might make you more alert."

"Thanks," I laughed, making a face. "Is this where I accept the coffee then you grass me up for stealing it?"

"No, I only do that to the ones without a sense of humour." He nudged me playfully and I felt some of the dread leave me. "Oh, look out, is she happy?"

I looked up and smiled at the young girl fleeing the office. She looked anything but happy, she looked on the verge of tears. Her badge was off before she even entered the lift and she was visibly shaking. "Oh dear, is he really that bad?" I was unable to believe I was about to meet Ryan's father and that he wasn't going to be this nice friendly fatherly figure I had been expecting.

"To be honest, I have been here for five years and haven't actually had a conversation with him since the interview, we deal much more with Ryan."

My heart leapt. "And where's his office?" I asked, my voice a little higher pitched than I had intended.

"Behind you," Buddy grabbed my waist and swung me around. "Don't ever think you can get away with sneaking out early, he see's everything."

I smiled a nervous smile. Ryan was looking straight at me and looked anything but pleased to see me. I wanted to wave but didn't know whether I was supposed to be letting on that we knew each other or not. His phone rang and he turned to take his call. I checked my phone. I had been sitting here for over twenty minutes and his office had been behind me the whole time. He would have seen me sitting there and could have come out to speak if he had wanted to but he hadn't.

"He looks happy this morning," I joked. Maybe Buddy already knew he knew me.

"He's lovely. Just don't spill coffee on him like the last girl did. He made her nervous, he fired her," Buddy said, smiling at Ryan's office. "Looks like you are up." I glanced up, ignoring the feeling of dread that was fast taking over my insides. Zoella was walking towards me, beckoning me to join her.

"Can I run the other way?" I whispered. I wasn't ready for this.

"They do free cake here every Friday, it's worth fighting for." Buddy patted me on the back and gently pushed me forward. I turned back and glanced into Ryan's office hoping for a smile of encouragement but he just glared at me while he chatted on the phone and I felt my pathetic lip wobble. Clearly I had offended him somehow or he had regretted his decision of bringing me in here into his domain.

"You okay?" Zoella asked, guiding me down the hall.

"A little nervous, the last girl looked in bits," I remarked.

"Yes, she argued with Mr Emerson about something, not a good move really." Zoella pursed her lips and knocked on Mr Emerson's door. I took in a large intake of air and walked in. I stood up straight as he rose to greet me and was disappointed to see that Zoella wouldn't be sitting in.

Mr Emerson looked a lot like Ryan but an older and crosser looking version. The Italian looking skin must have come from the mother but he definitely got his eyes from his father.

He stepped forward and shook my hand. "I see you have never worked in fashion." He waved my application form in the air then threw it back on to the pile in front of him. No wasting time here then.

"No, sir, I haven't, this would be a first." This was going to be a fast interview. I had never been speed dating but I felt like this was going to be as close to the experience as I was going to get.

"Ordinarily you would have gone straight on the 'No' pile but Ryan doesn't put names forward often, actually I don't think he has ever put a name forward, which is why I thought I had better honour you with an interview, but I do need to be frank." He pressed his hands together like he was praying and rested his chin on his fingers. "You have no experience or qualifications for this job. This is a high pressure job, it isn't for the faint hearted. I just don't think you have what we are looking for, I need someone who can make life and death decisions daily and who isn't going to crumble under pressure," he paused as I had burst out laughing, mainly through nerves. "Is something I'm saying amusing?" He asked, looking anything but amused.

"My previous job was in a hospital. I don't think you can really get any more life and death than *actual* life and death." I felt my nerves disappear. He had already decided I wasn't suitable so what did I have to lose. "I thought this position was for a secretary for which I thought I would be good at. When I worked for Dr Zusak my office skills were exemplary." I smiled and relaxed in my chair.

"I met him a couple of times." Mr Emerson leant back in his chair, his features had softened.

"Who, the Dr?"

"Yes, he treated my mother a couple of times, nice bloke." Mr Emerson lifted up my application form and read the reference section. "Okay, if he vouches for you, I will consider your application," he said.

"Really?" I asked surprised.

"Yes, it is only for a couple of months to cover maternity and I guess you are right, there are dead lines then there are *deadlines*," he laughed. "Zoella will be in touch."

"Thank you for your time." I rose out of my chair, a little shell shocked, and shook his hand.

Walking out of the office was the easy part but now I had to walk down the centre aisle with Ryan's office right in from of me.

I glanced to the left and saw girls lined up in a variety of beach hats, clearly working now on a summer holiday issue.

"Hey, no tears, good sign." Buddy appeared from somewhere on the right and was grinning from ear to ear.

"If by him telling me I had nothing to offer the publication is a good sign then, yay, Go Team Charlotte." Not sure why I felt the need to say my own name, it sounded weird and the fist pump was definitely over the top.

"You must be a strong character, he likes that, he needs it." Buddy started walking backwards in front of me.

I saw a shadow move in Ryan's office and I wasn't sure whether to remain professional, make a run for it or just look up and issue him with a massive wave.

"We will see, anyway thanks for the coffee. If I get another interview, I will make sure it is on a Friday to get the free cake," I laughed.

"Buddy!" Ryan's voice boomed from the other side of the sales desk. "How is the cover coming on?"

"Great boss," Buddy smiled, quickly retreating back towards his office. "Nearly finished."

"Excellent," Ryan handed some paperwork to the blushing girl on the sales desk and for a moment I froze. Was I supposed to say something?

"Did you have a nice New Year?" I asked then wished I hadn't. His face darkened and he ushered me into his office.

A cold fear spread over me and I wasn't sure what I had done wrong I just knew that I had done something that had upset him greatly.

"Sorry, I didn't know whether you were busy or not or whether people knew that you had put me forward for the interview." He shot me a look which should have shut me up but he was making me nervous and I couldn't control my mouth so I blurted on, "I wasn't very professional, sorry."

"Stop!" He raised his hand as if my voice was giving him a headache.

I glanced around out of his window and could see the sales girl keep swinging her head round every now and then to glance in.

"Are you okay?" I didn't really want an answer, I just wanted to escape. I hated confrontation and was much braver over text. I needed time to think about my answers and face-to-face exchanges always made me nervous.

"You and Buddy were a bit friendly considering that you have only just met," he said, straightening his tie.

"Er, I guess." What was he implying?

"You guess? His hands were all over you. Maybe I don't know you as well as I thought." He looked away from the point left of my shoulder and stared at me straight in the eyes.

"I think he was just trying to put me at ease over the interview. Thanks for setting that up by the way, it was worth a shot." I moved closer to him so the desk girl wouldn't be able to see us. "What's wrong? I text you loads."

"I realised what kind of girl you are and what kind of fool I am," he snapped.

"I don't understand."

"I travelled, God knows, how many hours to collect you from your hell hole life, I gave you my money, my time. Everyone's asking about you and I don't know how to answer. I spent hours setting up New Year Eve and you can't even give me the time of day." He started pacing the floor. I could see every step he took was building friction that he was using against me.

I felt a fury build inside of me. What had he expected from me? "I never asked you for anything."

"Do you know how many parties I refused to spend New Year with you?" He rubbed his cheeks with his palms, perhaps to try to calm himself down.

"So what are you saying, that *I owe you*?" I walked closer. "I have known you a week!" I shook my head. "I am still a married woman. I need to know exactly what I am doing and running around town with a playboy who is calculating my worth just doesn't do anything for me. I'm sorry."

I was fuming now and so was he.

"Playboy, is that what you think I am? You think I buy thousands of pounds worth of clothes for every girl I meet?"

"You had known me for like… five hours and half of those I was asleep for. I have no idea what kind of guy you are." I shook my head. "I don't understand it."

"Forget it, just leave," he snapped, but my feet wouldn't move.

"You can have the clothes back, I never expected them. And I'm sorry you expected more from me but I have been going through a lot and I don't want to confuse things."

"I am not confused," he loosened his tie, "just disappointed."

I was about to demand a better explanation when Buddy burst in with his front cover mock up. I waited for Ryan to say that I was just leaving but he didn't so I stayed put. I just watched his beautiful features grimace at everything Buddy was saying. Buddy left the office and Ryan glared at me.

"What is this really about?" I asked moving closer.

"I told you, it was just a mistake," he looked away.

Did he mean a mistake for getting me the job interview or with giving me his precious time? I guessed there were loads of women that would be lining up to spend time with him. Maybe he had realised what an unattractive bore I was, not to mention the fact that I had only been split up from Scott less than two weeks.

"Is this about the job? I can withdraw the application if you are regretting putting me forward."

He suddenly lurched at me and pinned me against the wall that was the back of the lift. "I'm not talking about the job, I'm talking about the fact that I like you more than you like me." I gasped, his hands were now either side of my head and anyone could have walked in at any minute. "And you dismiss me like I am nothing and are overly friendly to everyone else." He moved away from me. "You were all over Buddy like a prostitute. I feel like you used me as a distraction."

I gasped again for a completely different reason. "I have known you a week! Two weeks ago I lived a different life with a husband, best friends a secure job and someone pulled the rug from under my feet, and since I met you my feet haven't touched the ground, it doesn't even feel real." I shrugged my shoulders and ignored his pacing which was getting faster and faster. "I'm confused, like I'm missing the joke."

He turned to shout at me again, no doubt another put down on my overly protected virtue or maybe something about my past life being a joke but no words left his mouth. As he fast approached me I spun round and pinned him against the wall. My mouth found his on auto pilot and he didn't push me away. All the anger he had been channelling into hurtful comments had now been converted into passion. His hands groped my ears and chin. I couldn't get him close enough to me.

He must have been thinking the same thing. He lifted me off the floor, draping my legs around his waist and carried me through a door to the left of the lift. He rested me on top of a small sideboard next to a wash basin. Between frantic kisses and him pulling off my underwear, a thought danced through my mind, had he had sex here before? The thought made way for deeper feelings of lust and I pulled my legs tighter around his back.

"We should argue more often," he said as we rearranged our clothing.

"No, we shouldn't, though perhaps we should talk more."

I viewed my guilty looking reflection in the mirror. I now had to walk past the girls on the sales desk and look innocent.

Ryan came up behind me and started kissing my neck. "Sorry implied that you behaved like a prostitute, I wasn't thinking straight."

"Well, if I do get the job then this can never happen again or that is exactly what I would be." I was still struggling to regain my breath.

"How so?"

"Well, you would be paying me to be here and anything done in work hours would be, in theory, because you were paying me."

"Maybe I'll have a few extra demands written into your contract." He turned me around and pulled my mouth into his. "I don't want you to leave this room."

"Your staff saw me in here and every second I stay, the more uncomfortable I am going to feel sneaking out," I smiled.

He nodded and unlocked the door.

"Thanks for thinking of me for the interview," I added, reaching for the office door.

"I haven't stopped thinking about you, Miss Temple, since I picked you up from your squat."

I smiled and left the office completely forgetting to look at whether the office staff had noticed me leave or not. I just kept thinking of the way he had said my name. I could have stayed Mrs Bayfield or Ms as some people prefer after a divorce, but I had changed all my details back with the bank now. It would save me having to change it at a later date or even have to explain that I once lived another life. That life seemed a million years ago with Scott and Amber being distant memories and for the first time since it all happened, I wasn't bothered about the way my marriage had ended, it was a blessing. My marriage fell apart so something even better could enter my life in the beautiful form of Ryan.

I sat on the tube with a massive smirk on my face. I knew people around me had noticed me grinning like the Cheshire Cat but I didn't care. I could still feel him inside me. I could still feel the ripple effect of the climax and I knew my life had just changed forever for the better.

Chapter 14

Perhaps I had swapped one obsession with another.

I no longer checked Amber or Scott's phones or actually cared about where they were or what they were doing. It was like they had done me a favour and I was over it.

I had a new hobby now, Ryan.

Ryan had text me before I had made it home to say he was sorry again and that we should do dinner the following evening.

The following day he text to cancel, something had come up and he was sorry. I tried to tone down my disappointment. I had already picked out an outfit, a figure hugging black beauty with a standup collar. More importantly I had picked out the underwear to go with it, also black and covered with lace.

Zoella raised my spirits by calling and offering me the job and asking if I could start on Monday. I was delighted especially now me and Ryan had moved on in our relationship.

I told Josh and Meg that I had to prepare and retreated to my room where I could fantasise about lunches and secret kisses without the other staff knowing.

Ryan text on the Sunday to apologise for cancelling dinner but congratulated me on the job. I text him back trying to sound aloof, like it was no big deal but inside I was cartwheeling and planning our next rendezvous.

Tomorrow I would see him and maybe I could find an excuse to go into his office and maybe into his dressing room which could really do with a bed or a chaise longue.

Monday morning took ages to arrive. I got up an hour earlier than needed and showered and dressed with extra care. It was only work but I chose the extra lacy underwear anyway, just in case.

I entered the office with a small packed lunch and a few essentials. I wasn't sure what I needed and thought it best to be prepared. I packed a black and blue pen, a notepad, my purse, phone and key. What else could I need?

I posed for a photo taken by a member of the floor team called Brooke. She issued me with my own keycard that would open all the doors and operate the lift. It also told Ryan when I was in and out of the building. I tried to keep my features as neutral as possible when she mentioned his name but my insides were churning. I needed to see his face. More than that I need to feel his fingers sweep across my jaw bone, creep to the back of my head and pull my face to his.

It was all I could think about. I wondered, while I was in the lift, if this was how Scott and Amber had felt at some point. Scott had never made me feel this way. He had grown on me slowly, I knew he was a decent enough guy, I just knew now that I had settled. Lust had never came into the equation, not once in our whole relationship had I hungered for his touch. I remembered being happy but now I had met Ryan I knew this was something else, something stronger.

I smiled at the sales girl's as I entered the room and stole a glance behind them. I couldn't see Ryan in his office but then most of it was obscured by the lift. He could be sitting at his desk or out of the office doing some important job. I smiled at the thought of him in his suit. There was nothing sexier than a man in a suit.

I walked down to Zoella's desk like she had asked me to and waved at Buddy on my way past who was displaying large sections of the magazine on a screen that covered the whole side wall. He raised two thumbs ups and the other people in his office turned to see was getting his attention. I smiled and kept on walking.

"You're early," Zoella remarked.

"First day, good impressions and all that," I laughed. "It probably won't last."

"Okay, let me walk you round." Zoella rose and straightened her pencil skirt which she had paired with a beige and white stripe shirt. "Mr Emerson's office, as you know, is behind us." She turned and pointed behind our desks that were side by side. "We never go in there unless summoned. We deal with Persia whose office is in here." She pointed to a corner office that linked with Mr Emerson's. "She is the manager, she deals with the day to day running of things and makes sure we pull our weight. We O.K. everything with her or Ryan," Zoella moved in closer. "Persia always leaves at four so for the last hour we get to use her toilet." She said, as if it was the best perk in the world.

She continued walking out of the office and walked down the left hand side of the massive hall. "This door is for the accountants. They don't bother us much though you will need to learn quickly their names and extensions as they get a lot of calls." She waved her hands at the various desks dotted around in front of the offices. "These belong to the writers and other various contributors. They change each issue and most work from home, but you will get to know some of the same faces." She opened the door which clearly stated it was the toilets, I thought this room would be self explanatory. "This is where all the drama happens," she whispered. I could hear gossiping voices coming from the end cubicle. "Emma also went for your job so she might be a little bitter." Zoella whispered and led me to the next room. "This is a general meeting room. They tend to have us all in here on a Friday to throw ideas around then again on a Monday to see what ideas anyone has had. This is also where they sometimes put the models to have their make-up done on fashion shoot days. Not often though because most of the exciting bits are done upstairs, it's a versatile room though."

"Another floor, wow, this place is huge," I remarked.

"We don't really go upstairs, that's Ryan's department, he is really the front of house guy, we are more admin," she smiled and carried on with the tour. "This is a store room of fashion collectables that actually belong to us. We don't usually keep things but this is where the permanent stuff is stored. Ryan and the fashion department hold the keys though you should ways ask Lorena before approaching Ryan, should anyone send you for keys."

I tried to ignore the soaring feeling in the pit of my stomach at the mere mention of his name.

"This is Lorena and her fashion department, they work on both floors so have their own set of stairs." She pointed to the corner office which sided on to Ryan's office. I glanced his way and saw him sitting at his desk talking on the phone.

We went into Lorena's office and she smiled welcomingly. "This is really where all the magic happens," Zoella smiled.

"I agree," Lorena laughed. She reminded me of an older, glamorous version of Cassie. Both had thick blonde curls and naturally tanned looking skin that I, and many others, would have paid thousands for. I wondered if Cassie would have fitted better in here than I would, she certainly would have had the wedding issue down.

"This months trend is all about black and white stripes making us all appear thinner than we really are." Zoella held up some black and white dresses all containing stripes in various directions.

"Ah, real magic," I laughed.

Ryan's office would be next. I wondered if Zoella would bypass going in like she had with Mr Emerson and Persia. I watched Lorena show Zoella some designs and couldn't decide if I wanted them to hurry up and finish or to take their time to delay the inevitable. We hadn't discussed how the office dynamics were going to work. Were we hiding the fact that we were an item and keeping a professional front or just going to be ourselves? I was, after all, only there for a couple of months.

"Okay, let's move on." I was about to find out.

Zoella knocked on the door and I heard Ryan's sweet voice beckon us in.

"This is Ryan's office, he gets most of the mail."

I glanced up and his eyes were averted towards the window as he waited to be connected on a call.

"Do I deliver the mail?" I asked trying to drag my eyes away from the side of Ryan's head.

"Yes, every morning when you arrive, before you even come to your desk, call in here and take everything out of Ryan's out tray." Zoella walked to Ryan's desk and handed me all the paperwork that was in there.

He finally glanced up and gave me an awkward smile. Okay, so now I knew how it was going to be played, a secret romance. He was a professional that did not sleep with members of his staff. I had expected this option more than the holding hands in the staff room scenario.

"Okay," I smiled at Zoella.

"Ryan actually gets the most calls, but we never put calls through to him directly unless he has messaged us that he is waiting for someone to call him back. All staff here have his direct line, sales calls should go to sales regardless of who they have asked for. Always take a number and bring Ryan the memo. This job will keep you well fit," she smiled. I glanced again at Ryan, his eyes met mine briefly then darted away. Any more secret rendezvous in his private bathroom and I would be well exercised enough. I glanced at the closed door and wondered if he thought about it every time he washed his hands in there or whether he was too busy to think about me on the job.

"This is the seating area where people are seated before meetings. There is a canteen next door, mainly for visitors, this is where most of the floor get their tea and coffee. Interviewees are usually are seated here, sometimes you will be asked to meet them from the lift, offer tea or coffee then lead them to however they are meeting, usually Ryan or photography," she said, spinning around. "This is the sales team. No point trying to get a conversation out of them they are always busy." The girl I recognised as the Ryan admirer looked up and smiled. We were now facing the way we had come and were walking down the opposite side. Ryan was now sitting somewhere out of view and I felt disappointed that I had not had a chance to linger longer in his presence. But then again, I had made the comment about having sex while I was under his payroll being close to prostitution. I smiled to myself, I would need to make it clear that I was actually okay with that.

"This is the graphics office and tech team." Zoella opened the room and Buddy faked looking busy. "Ha ha, wrong boss." Zoella playfully punched him in the arm.

"We actually work the hardest." Buddy rose from his seat and gave me and Zoella a hug.

"Does he do that daily?" I asked, as if Buddy wasn't still attached to her.

"Er, no, only after near death experiences which occur on a monthly basis," Zoella grinned.

"That's not true," Buddy looked offended.

A plain looking girl rose from her desk and added, "Over Christmas he had a car accident which left him in hospital over night, the month before he was in a skiing accident..."

"And the month before that he got knocked off his bike in central," a tech guy added with laughter.

"Okay, so you are accident prone and lucky to be alive," I laughed.

I shook the hands of the guys and girl and introduced myself simply as Charlotte. I didn't want to use Bayfield but I didn't feel ready to revert back to Temple. It was as if Bayfield was a fictitious lie and Temple felt like admitting I was a failure in marriage and back to square one, but then again, square one meant freedom to explore other avenues. I mock glanced around the office and noticed Ryan looking in from his office. I didn't hesitate and carried on turning as if I hadn't seen him. Maybe he and Buddy had some kind of history with a shared interest.

"That's odd," I heard Buddy trying to whisper to Zoella.

I turned and they both smiled, obviously talking about me.

"Leave it with me," he nudged her playfully, "I will find out." Buddy grinned at me not realising or caring that I had overheard.

Maybe they already knew, offices often had initiation tests. Maybe Ryan told them I was his girlfriend but they were all to play dumb, loser was whoever gave the game away first.

"Let's move on or they will talk to us all day and we will never get any work done." Zoella held open the door and I noticed her glance at Ryan as she let me through.

Okay, so they knew something, I could play dumb. It was no big deal to me not now I knew I would have to go into his office twice daily to collect his mail, maybe more if I had mail to drop off. It didn't matter if he pretended not to know me that well during the day, we would always have the evenings.

I shook hands with the one photographer who was not on the shoot today and tried to not think about Ryan's tongue on my neck.

"And this is the copier room. This is where the comb binding happens, laminating and printing." She grabbed me by the shoulders "Please for the love of God tell me that you know what a comb binder is."

I laughed at her sense of urgency. "Yes, I found my love of comb binding in college."

"Thank God." She heaved a huge sigh of relief. "The last temp made a pig's ear of it every time, in the end we had to ask that she didn't touch it."

"Phew, I feel slightly received to actually have a quality that this job requires." I smiled.

Zoella looked me up and down seriously. "Mr Emerson always hires the right person. I have long given up trying to pinpoint what he looks for in staff but it always works. Ryan will come round."

Ryan will come round? What did that mean? I considered ignoring the comment but it was too much of a bombshell to just leave hanging there.

"Ah, you need to do the mail," Zoella said before I could raise my query. Now it was going to bother me all day. "There is a letter opener in your pen tidy. Not everything addressed to Ryan needs to go to Ryan, if it is a general sales query send it to sales. Invoices you input, then hand them over to accounts to check over once on the system. I get all the mail addressed to Mr Emerson senior and for Persia, anything you're not sure of, put on my desk. If it says private and confidential, it comes to me, Okay?" She started laughing. "Any marriage proposals for Ryan go in recycle unless they are hilarious then they get pinned to the tea room wall. I'll help you get through the mountain of Valentine's Day cards." She shook her head as if it was hilarious.

"Is he popular?" Was the only thing I could think of to ask.

"He is a millionaire who happens to be single and has a face as smooth as marble." She sat at her desk and clicked her computer on. "Most are from countries where they have read an article about him and have never actually met him. It wastes our time and their money."

I nodded. I couldn't tell if she liked him or not, either way I was desperate to get started and make my first visit to Ryan's office. Zoella got started on her tasks which seemed to be processing paperwork directly from Mr Emerson and Persia. Every now and then she would be called into their office to draft a letter or they would call through and place paperwork onto her keyboard all containing coloured post-it notes denoting its level's of urgency.

I opened the never ending pile of mail and applied my own common sense. The amount of junk mail was immense but I soon learnt what was classed as interesting and what would probably be straight for recycling. I put these in separate piles for sales to decide. It seemed to take hours to open all the letters and the freebies but finally, I was done. If it was my job to input all the invoices then I was going to be rushed off my feet, the pile was massive. There were separate piles for Ryan, some were replies to his correspondence but most were generic sales enquiries which I piled up for the sales team. I printed off a department sheet and studied the names. Buddy and his team, Kyle, Louisa and Morten, I had met already. Three tech guys shared Buddy's room but I had already forgotten their names. Lorena tended to get all the glossy magazines and samples which I found hard not to look at when sorting. I supposed she needed to know what else was going on in the industry to keep up to date.

I was never going to be able to carry all this stuff. "Is there a mail trolley?" I asked Zoella as I handed her a pile of Private and Confidential and VIP mail.

"In the stock room," she said, without looking up.

I hovered, thinking about the *Ryan coming round* comment. It was unsettling and I didn't like it. Her phone blasted out and she answered it promptly with efficient politeness. I had missed my chance.

I piled up the trolley and headed out using the same route that Zoella had taken me when showing me round.

Persia could be heard yelling at someone down the phone for letting her down and she was pacing like a caged lion. I imagined her sinking her razor sharp nails into someones face to teach them a lesson. She made me uneasy and I hadn't even spoken to her yet. Maybe that was what was putting me on edge. Everyone else had made an effort and been super friendly but she had ignored me even though a smile on first contact wouldn't have killed her.

Maybe it was an age thing. The older accountants were equally as standoffish. On delivering their mail I was given the run down of how they expected things to be done and that just because I was new that didn't mean mistakes would be allowed. There would be things I was holding that they would be relying on somewhere down the line.

I could see there was a clear divide of them and us. The older generation which consisted of Persia and the accountants were not going to be my friends. I was there to serve their purpose and nothing else. I guessed these guys did not show up much for the drink get togethers after work.

I nodded in all the right places and clarified that I understood my place in the pyramid scheme of authority.

I was relieved to move on down past the writers. They all had name plaques on their desks which made them easy to pin point. They were much too absorbed to chat but all smiled their thanks when handed their mail.

"Ooh, check this out," Lorena yelled when I entered the room. I glanced round in case she was talking to someone else but there was only me in the room. "Max says this is a bit touch and go but I have decided that as less people wear gold wedding rings nowadays, white metal is going to be the next incorporated metal. What do you think?"

She held up a beautiful blue skater style dress with a white metal trim that draped diagonally from the left shoulder to the hem.

"Did you make this?" I asked, admiring the fabric.

"Yes, I have to submit three designs into the fashion show in February. It's hard because everyone is trying to outdo everyone else and we need to get some press this year."

"Impressive," I said feeling the silky fabric. "The white colour makes sense as long as it washes okay, I guess."

"Well, this is just a prototype really. If it gets the go-ahead, it will be mass produced by proper companies, they might even name it after me," she giggled and returned to her work.

I handed her the mail and moved on.

I knocked on Ryan's door before entering even though Zoella had told me not to bother. He didn't look up from his computer screen so I just tip-toed over to put the mail in his in tray and retrieved the documents that had accumulated in his out tray in the short while since I had been in here last.

"Are you okay?" I asked nervously as he still hadn't look up.

"It shouldn't take you over an hour to deliver the mail," he said without looking up.

I glanced up at the clock. I wasn't entirely sure where the time had gone but it was almost one ò clock.

"I know, but Zoella had to give me instructions on what went where and the accountants wanted to discuss their expectations of me. I doubt it will take so long tomorrow." I said cheerfully hoping that my mood was infectious.

"It had better not or nothing will ever get done. We are trying to run a business here." He looked up but past me, over my shoulder. "Yes?"

I turned around to see Louisa had been standing their for goodness how long. Had she heard him having a go at me?

"I just need the graphics approval for the back page." She hovered at the doorway, afraid to come in.

"Miss Temple is on her way with it now." He looked back down at his computer signalling the end of the conversation.

I turned and followed Louisa to the sales desk. I handed them the three piles I had sorted out for them, the stuff that was addressed to the sales team, the stuff that was addressed to Ryan, but was a sales enquiry, and the third pile was stuff that I considered junk but hadn't been told what to do with. Then I turned and gave Louisa the file from Ryan that had 'Graphics' written on a pink post-it note stuck to the front.

There was a post-it note order. Pink was urgent, orange was by the end of the day and yellow was anything else. Green seemed to indicate that the sender wanted a reply either by email, telephone or good old fashion post.

"Thanks for this." A sales girl called Lynsey held up the junk mail. "This usually takes me hours to sort through."

"You're welcome," I smiled. At least I had one happy customer.

I walked into the graphics office and Louisa was in the middle of telling Buddy something deeply fascinating and private. They hushed when I entered the room, indicating that their conversation was about me.

"Who wants the mail?" I asked, holding up their pile. "Sorry it took me a while to get round to you, everyone is real chatty," I said. Yes, Ryan had been rude but I was choosing to ignore it. Perhaps we needed to hurry that office rules chat.

Louisa stood up to get the mail and shot Buddy and sly look.

"What?" I asked.

"Nothing it's just Lou got the impression that Ryan doesn't like you much." Buddy shrugged as if it was no big deal.

"Oh," I said feeling a stab of pain despite knowing that it wasn't true. "Is he not like that with everyone? I just presumed he was being professional." I glanced back at his office but couldn't see his desk from this angle. "I mean the accountants didn't shake my hands or compliment my shoes either."

The guy called Kyle laughed. "You need about fifty more letters after your name before the accountants even bother to learn your name."

"Well, I will chat more about this with you later. I had better get a move on before I'm fired on my first day." I smiled and legged it out of the room. I probably would have got plenty of gossip from that room but I figured that I would have gained nothing from hearing what they had to say. I had to keep some self-esteem.

I handed Zoella her pile from Ryan and sat down to work through the invoices as quickly as I could. I needed to get ahead. I needed at some point for Ryan to come through our archway and say that I was doing something right.

Zoella got up and left for lunch without mentioning my break. I looked around and half the office seemed to be here and half were out. I strained my eyes to see into Ryan's office but his desk was shielded behind the lift, all I could see were the empty chairs sitting at the other side of his desk.

I sighed and stuffed my sandwich at my desk and continued with the invoices.

After about an hour an angry accountant came in demanding some invoices, I was supposed to hand them over to him after I had completed ten. I apologised and handed him the thirty that I had done. Zoella hadn't mentioned it and nor had they when I had delivered their mail so I shrugged it off. It was my first day after all and being psychic hadn't been in the job description. I would hold it all together despite the rising panic in my chest. This wasn't the hospital, the system wasn't the same and I was out of my comfort zone.

I kept one eye on the lift as I typed. Ryan would either arrive or leave at some point but Zoella was the only member of staff I saw return. Just as she past the sales office, Ryan appeared at his door and called her into his office. I raised my head while reading a document so it wasn't obvious that I was staring. I saw him glance at me as he waited for her to pass him into his office.

I put my head down and worked on. Every phone call received while Zoella was gone was a painful interruption. It took me ages to look up who was on what extension and I had eleven messages to take through to Ryan but decided to wait until Zoella came back. She popped into Buddy's office before returning to her desk. I decided Buddy must have been the office hub for all the gossip. Maybe Ryan had confessed that we were a couple, either way I had a feeling I was about to find out.

"How's it been?" Zoella asked upon her return.

"Fine." I smiled and carried on typing without looking up. "There are three messages for you and five for Persia. When am I supposed to go to lunch?"

"Oh, twelve, I think you were still delivering the mail. Ryan said it took you ages, I have to report it to Persia."

I looked up horrified. "Report it, what does that mean?" It wasn't as if I skived off for a whole day like I had in my previous job, not that they ever found out but at least they had a reason to be cross.

"It's just standard procedure. At the end of the day Persia has to address these issues, it is part of her job. It happens to all of us, don't worry about it."

Easy for her to say.

"I have some messages for Ryan," I said, trying not to sound sulky. "Does he want them as they come or in one heap at the end of the day? I thought he was at lunch too."

"I'll take those." She jumped up a little too quickly and snatched them out of my hand.

Now a dark feeling was really dwelling in my stomach. Something had changed.

Chapter 15

Persia was too busy to fit me in that evening but left me a message asking if I would call into her office at nine-thirty the next morning with a notepad and pen.

I had knuckled down for the rest of the afternoon and left at five like I was supposed to. Zoella glanced up in surprise when was I putting my coat on making me think it was customary practice to work late. As this was another thing that had not been specified, I just said my goodbyes and left. I could see Ryan out of the corner of my eye as I waited for Lynsey, who asked me to hold the lift for her, but I didn't look up. He had the whole time it took Lynsey to get her coat on to call me into his office but he didn't so I just carried on like he was a stranger.

"So how was your first day?" The blushing sales team member called Emma asked, while we travelled down in the lift.

"Busy, but then I guess it is always harder in your first week as you have to find your feet and learn how everyone likes things done." I forced myself to smile.

"Yesterday," Lynsey scoffed and Emma burst into laughter.

"My contract said eight-thirty til five but Zoella looked surprised when I put my coat on," I said, testing the waters.

"Well, let's just say when Keeley gets back Zoella is hoping they don't rush to give her the job back. Here brown nosing always gets you noticed." Lynsey raised her immaculate eyebrows and there was not a wrinkle in sight.

"I hear you didn't make Ryan's fan list either." Emma remarked and for a second I felt like telling her about the hot sex we had had in his back room but decided against it.

"He remarked on the time it took me to sort and deliver the mail," I shrugged. It was the only thing I could think of.

"Zoella never sorted the mail as well as you did, she used to just throw it all together in a heap for us to sort," Lynsey said. "You saved us about thirty minutes each."

"Well, I have a meeting tomorrow morning with Persia to discuss my first day, no doubt it will come up."

"Don't worry, it is just for a couple of months until Keeley returns. My day was better because you were in it anyway." Lynsey beamed.

At least someone had been happy with something I had done.

I had expected Ryan to call that evening but he hadn't and I painfully resisted the urge to call him.

It was a long night.

The next morning I dressed with equal care.

I was going to have to sit in a meeting with Persia and the idea terrified me. Maybe it was because she hadn't bothered to introduce herself to me yet, or that her hair was pitch black and pulled so tightly on her head that it made her permanently look like a stern school teacher. Either way, I wasn't looking forward to going into work.

I packed into the tube and wished the time away.

My phone rang an unrecognised number and I hoped it was Ryan, but it wasn't, it was Gerald. "Great news," he said between sobs. "I'm going to live with Annabel." I could hear him crying.

"That's wonderful, listen Gerald, I'm on the tube if we get cut off I'll ring you straight back." I lowered my voice slightly as half of the carriage turned to glare at the shrieking woman that was me. "Tell me about it," I said in a calmer, more ladylike fashion.

"It was wonderful, She was wonderful, the children were wonderful. The whole meeting was magical. Thank you so much. I don't know how I'll ever thank you."

I rushed off the tube and headed towards the office. "Listen, you don't ever need to. You did me a good deed and I simply returned the favour."

I swiped into the building and entered the lift still not losing signal.

"That was one expensive phone call," Gerald scoffed, "hardly seems fair."

"You don't know how many lives you may have saved by making that call," I said. "I'm at work now Gerald, I need to go, but I do honestly wish you all the luck in the world. You deserve it."

He asked some pleasantries about where I worked and I filled him in while I hung up my coat. Zoella gave me a disapproving glance but I was early so I ignored her glare. I wished him luck and said my farewells.

"I am early," I said in my defence after I had hung up.

Zoella looked at her watch but said nothing.

I had over an hour before my meeting with Persia so I ploughed on through my in-tray that seemed never ending. As soon as I thought I was getting ahead someone would walk through from one of the departments and dump new invoices in my tray.

I jumped up in surprise, making Zoella jump. "I forgot to pick up the stuff from Ryan's office."

"Oh, I'll get that from now on. Don't worry about that any more." She got up and practically sprinted to Ryan's office. Had he asked for me not to go into his office? Surely I was thinking too much into it.

I shook the negativity out of my head and rushed through he invoices. I had gotten myself into a routine that seemed to be working well.

At about nine, Persia breezed past and started wandering in and out of the offices. I took a deep breath. I was hoping she would be so busy that she would forget about me, but at nine-thirty on the dot she called me through at the same time as the mail arrived. I heaped the piles on my desk and shrugged at Zoella leaving her looking horrified at the prospect of the mail being ignored.

"Sit." Persia extended her arm out and I shook it.

"Thanks," I said nervously. "Should I come back after I have done the mail? I'm not really sure yet what my priorities should be." I dreaded her reply.

"The mail can wait," she said, placing a pair of rimless glasses onto her face that just added to the sternness of her facial features.

I smiled nervously and tried to get comfy in the rock hard seat.

"How did you find your first day?" she asked, without looking up from her notes.

"Good, people were very kind and to the point about what they expected of me, which I appreciate. It may take up time to go over things but I have a good memory and am a quick learner so don't need to be told twice."

I felt like I was at another interview, a scarier one.

"I see. I heard that the mail wasn't delivered before twelve." She looked up over her glasses and placed her notes done in disgust. "Zoella usually has it done and dusted by eleven."

She looked up waiting for my long list of excuses which I had lost a lot of sleep preparing.

"I don't think that can really be judged by the first day." I crossed my legs to hide the fact that they were shaking. "By the time Zoella had shown me my desk and discussed the office responsibilities an hour had past. She then introduced me to nearly every member of the staff and explained to me the role they undertook in the office. I doubt it was anywhere near eleven when I returned to my desk to even start on the mail," I said a little quicker than I had rehearsed in my head.

"I see," She pursed her lips.

"Were there any other complaints?" I asked with a smile as if hearing people list all my faults was one of my favourite pastimes. "I know it will take time to do everything the exact way Keeley or Zoella does, but I am all up for feedback to improve."

Persia smiled and it made a huge difference to her features. "Actually the accounts team said that you produced an impressive output and the sales team were largely impressed with your mail sorting, so all in all, I would say your first day was a huge success." She leant back in her chair.

"Thank you." I wasn't sure what else there was to say.

"We will have another meeting in a week's time and see how you are getting on. Do you have any questions for me?" She leant forward and her body language opened up.

"Em no, I don't think so though I am a little unsure what my responsibilities are with Ryan."

"In what way?"

"Only that I was told to collect and deliver his mail and now I have been told not to. If I have offended him already I would hate for that to add to Zoella's already heavy load."

Persia rolled her eyes. "Relax, Ryan is a sweetie. We have a meeting every evening before I leave so I will get a complete and definitive job description compiled for you."

"Thank you, that may save me asking any more questions. I like to plough on."

She stood so I followed suit, guessing that it was the end of the meeting.

"Nice meeting you Charlotte," She said. And I left letting out a huge sigh of relief.

"Alright?" Zoella asked with extra interest.

"Yes." I smiled and took the accountants some invoices I had been working on before I started on the massive pile of mail.

I set a timer to see how long it would take. It took forty-five minutes to open everything and sort into departments. I made notes then piled the trolley. I paused to ask Zoella about Ryan but then decided against it.

The accountants ignored me as usual, the writers were all absent. I had to drag myself out from under a hat that Lorena threw on my head and had to promise to pop back in to see her around lunch time.

I knocked at Ryan's door and he looked genuinely surprised to see me there.

"Mail," I announced as cheerfully as I could manage.

I walked it over to his desk and scooped the contents of his out tray and quickly sorted it out into piles.

"Did Zoella have a chance to have a word with you?" He asked, a bit too formal for my liking.

"About how long it took me to deliver the mail?" I turned and faced him.

"Yes, and about her coming to collect my paperwork instead of you," he shifted in his seat.

"Is everything alright?" I asked. Once again the feeling I was getting was freezing all of my organs.

"Yes, just trying to keep things professional," he snapped.

"She hasn't made it clear what is expected of me where you are concerned but Persia is going to talk to you this evening and present me with an outline of my job description." I turned and pushed my trolley out towards the door.

"Charlotte," he called me back but I kept walking. I had no clue what I had done this time but if I was going to survive in this job then I needed to separate my feelings for Ryan the amazing super hero hunk from Ryan the stone cold ice lolly sitting in his office.

"Morning," I forced a smile for Lynsey and Emma and handed them their mail. "I do hope this mail delivery is arriving at a more acceptable time that yesterday." I put my head on the side in a playful manner.

"It just means extra work for us. Any time is torture." Lynsey laughed. "How did your meeting go?" She whispered.

"Not too bad. I think some lovely sales people put in a kind word for me." I smiled and walked in Buddy's office.

"How did it go?" Buddy was on his feet and sitting on the corner of his desk before I had chance to get his mail off the trolley. There was something about him that reminded me of my old History teacher who taught most of his lessons on the edge of a table with an empty pipe resting in his mouth. He never lit it, he just needed to feel it there.

"Fine," I smiled. "I worried for nothing, she was really nice."

Louisa put down her pencil and swung her chair around. "So she didn't say anything negative at all?"

"Only that the mail is usually delivered by eleven." I glanced at the clock on the wall, it was ten forty-five. "Not easy with you chatterboxes around."

"What did you say?" Louisa shifted her chair further forward.

"Only that for my first day most of the morning was taken up by me being introduced to everyone and getting in-depth details on what they all did. It took ages for me to learn who was getting what mail. You can't judge someone by their first day."

"You never said that?" Kyle seemed shocked.

"Well, it's true. I don't think I even started the mail until gone eleven yesterday. I didn't even know it was my job to do until Zoella told me." I mock checked my bare wrist in an exaggerated manner. "Must dash."

They all waved their goodbyes and I smiled to myself as Kyle whispered something about me having balls as I left.

The photographers were all in the office after a successful shoot and were working on all their photos. I tried not to touch any of their gear as I weaved through their desks. I spotted a lens a lot like my new lens that I had acquired from twenty-five Old School Close and I wondered for the first time how much it must have cost.

I handed Zoella her pile of paperwork from Ryan's office and returned the trolley to the printer room. She took a breath as if to say something but obviously thought better of it and carried on with her work.

At twelve I got up to go to lunch and Zoella seemed shocked again to see me rise.

"Is my lunch time still twelve?" I asked, feeling confused.

"Oh, yes, yes it is." She smiled and carried on with her work.

I grabbed my bag and headed out of the door. I had packed lunch but I didn't want Zoella to think I would work for free. Brown nosing wasn't really something I could be bothered with and I was a firm believer that if you need someone to work more then you needed to pay them more to work longer or employ someone else. Working through lunch would be a rarity if I ever did it.

"Charlotte," Emma ran over to the lift and grabbed my arm. "We are going to lunch at Sylvia's Bistro around the corner. Are you free to join us?"

I nodded and followed the sales team into the trendy cafe that was literally on the corner of our building.

"You've caused quite a stir," a sales guy called Aiden said. He sat down and handed out the drinks.

"Really?" How intriguing. "In what way?"

"Well, for a start you haven't been found in the toilet yet crying," a guy called Matt laughed.

"No one's stolen my pen yet," I joked.

I ordered a tuna salad and listened while they cheerfully chatted about their customers and the Valentine's Day fashion show that was coming up.

"You will love it Charlotte, it's one of the highlights of the year. All inclusive food and champagne. We all get our hair and make-up done and wear ball gowns," Lynsey gushed.

"No, we don't all do that," Aiden added seriously.

"I do," Matt shrugged seriously.

"If you ever get a chance to look in old Emerson's office have a look at the photos on the wall, they are epic," Emma smiled. "I can't wait. Ryan wore a tuxedo last year and I swear he was mistaken for a model more times than the actual models."

Lynsey nudged her and my heart sank. She clearly liked him and by not telling her about me and Ryan I felt like I was lying.

"I guess I had better go back," I suggested, trying not to think about the enigma that was Ryan. I would really need to suss his moods out.

"You're new and trying to give a good impression but you time the others. Zoella will have a good hour and a half, Persia often doesn't even bother coming back." Emma frowned.

"I'm only here for three months. Maybe I'll turn into a rebel in my last week." I smiled, grabbed my bag and headed back to the office.

As I approached the desk Zoella checked her watch, grabbed her bag and headed out for lunch.

I ploughed on filling out invoices, connecting calls and keeping an eye on Ryan's office. He didn't approach me. I must have checked my emails a thousand times but nothing was from him so I placed all messages concerning him onto Zoella's table. If he wanted to remain neutral then so could I.

For the next week Ryan treated me like a stranger. I had text him the once and asked if he wanted to meet up after work but he never replied. To say I had cried would have been an understatement. I kept it together at work which was otherwise going great.

Zoella had started to loosen up a little and Persia had started chatting to me in the mornings. Even the accountants seemed to be more pleased to see me than Ryan was.

I swiped myself in and headed up in the lift. Another day of wishing Ryan would at least say good morning to me but not holding my breath.

As the doors opened I could tell something was different. Emma looked so excited that I thought she was going to combust. "Charlotte, oh my God," she gushed, "They…"

"Charlotte, in here please," Ryan interrupted her mini celebration.

Emma shrank back to her desk and pretended to be busy with some paperwork.

I looked back for support but finding none, edged slowly into Ryan's office.

My heart lifted. On his desk was the biggest bouquet of luscious red roses that I had ever seen. I looked at Ryan with a short-lived affection. I had thought for a stupid moment that he had bought them for me to apologise for ignoring me but I could see by his face that he hadn't.

I blushed slightly and tried to neutralise my features. I could feel the tears welling up. Hope had erupted in every fibre of my being but how quickly that hope had drowned in its own stupidity.

"Who is Gerald?" He demanded thrusting the card into my hand.

I ignored him and read the card.

Dearest Charlotte.
You have changed my life forever and I will never forget the day you found me or the countless deeds you did for me.
We are far from even.
Much love
Gerald
XXX

A smile spread across my face and even seeing Ryan's scowl couldn't change it.

"Wow!" Buddy said after bursting in without knocking. "Why do you always get the flowers Ryan, it's not fair?"

"Actually they are mine," I beamed.

"Woo," Buddy whooped excitedly. "Well, who has been a good girl?" He reached over and snatched the card out of my hand. "Gerald, hey?" He grinned. "Countless deeds, sounds naughty." He raised his eyebrows and dropped some paperwork on Ryan's desk. "No doubt someones allergic." Buddy handed me back the card and headed out towards his office.

"Sorry, I'll get these out of your way." I went to take the flowers but he blocked my path with a face like thunder.

I stopped, shocked at his obstruction. "What is your problem?" I asked unable to hold it in anymore. "One minute you like me, the next minute you can't even look at me. Why are you so happy for everyone here to think you hate me?"

Ryan took the card out of my hands and slowly placed it back into its slot in the bouquet. He moved back to his side of the desk but I didn't move an inch nor was I going to until I knew what was going on. "Look, we had sex once. I never asked you out, you never asked me out. It was hardly a *Pride and Prejudice* or *Romeo and Juliet* epic love affair was it?"

I stood still, numb and unable to breathe. "Do you want me to take the flowers off your desk?" Was the only thing my mouth could manage to say.

"You can collect them at the end of the day. Pretty sure Persia is allergic," he said, not looking up.

I nodded feebly and about turned. My legs felt like lead and every step out of his airspace felt heavy and un-natural.

Emma smiled as I closed his office door behind me and I tried my best to look upbeat.

"Persia is allergic," I pouted out my lips, fake-sulking. "I have to collect them at the end of the day. It's like being at school when they confiscate your stickers." I forced a smile and raced back to my desk.

For the rest of the day I laid low. To anyone that asked me if I was alright, I answered that I had a headache but was pretty sure I would survive the day.

I had sobbed uncontrollably three times before the end of the day. Early on I faked a sneezing fit and rushed off to the toilets, relieved to find them empty, I blew off lunch with the others and sat in the park and cried and when Zoella left for lunch, I crept into Persia's office, wept on her toilet floor until there was nothing left.

He had used me. He had been interested before the sex and now he had got what he wanted the interest had waned.

I returned to my desk and tried to ignore the gaping hole in my chest. He was just a man, a man I hardly knew. I kept telling myself that I was being silly but I couldn't get my head around the disappointment that consumed me.

I did a couple of invoices after five hoping that Ryan would leave first but he didn't. At quarter past I bit the bullet and gathered up my things. I felt sick.

I ducked into the toilets and applied some face powder which dulled the redness a little around my eyes.

I took a deep breath and headed to his office to retrieve my flowers. I knocked then walked straight in and was greeted by a familiar looking blonde.

"Hi, I just came for my flowers, sorry to interrupt." Maybe she was one of the models from the magazine.

"Oh they're yours, you lucky thing," The blonde gushed in an Australian accent.

Alice! I didn't think my heart could have dropped further but it plummeted down through the basement and I felt the room start to spin. "I had hoped they were mine." She rubbed Ryan's arm and I forced back some bile.

"I helped a homeless guy." I swooped in and grabbed the flowers. "Thanks for holding them for me."

I ran out of the room and took the stairs. The lift wouldn't have come soon enough and the tears couldn't wait.

I cried on the walk, sobbed on the tube and bawled all the way home. Luckily Josh and Meg were at the theatre and didn't see the horror that was my face.

Alice, that was what or who, had changed Ryan's mind about me. She had flown in from Australia to pick up where they left off and all of a sudden I was dropped like an anvil.

I ran to the toilet and threw up. I had skipped lunch in favour of crying like a baby. I entered the kitchen to make some toast but decided against it.

I spent the weekend in bed and crying some more.

I slept badly, I kept waking in a sweaty mess, unable to breathe. I kept having a recurring dream where I was walking into work naked and having the whole staff erupt with laughter. Sometimes it was just Ryan and Alice standing there, but sometimes it was Amber and Cassie and the entire high school football team. I need to get a grip.

I decided avoidance was going to be the key. The days would be easy because I could ignored him and my mind would be busy. It would be the nights that killed me because all I would do was think and I hated my own company.

Ryan had text me a couple of times Friday evening. He had had sex with Alice twice it had been a mistake, he was sorry to have hurt me. I re-read the text over and over. Twice? That was 50% more than he had with me. I wondered what exactly he meant by mistake? Once with me or twice with Alice? I didn't ask. I just sent him one text wishing him all the best and asking him not to speak to me at work and to not text me again. Enough was enough, a line needed to be drawn.

"What is going on with you and Ryan?" Josh asked, Sunday night after I had been sick from a bug.

"Nothing," I said defensively. He and Meg were off to a party again and I had got myself into a bad habit of skipping tea or settling for soup, a diet my body wasn't happy about.

"Don't lie to me," Josh said, joining me at the sink while Meg curled her hair. "Ryan never comes over while you are here and you turn away at the mere mention of his name."

"I'm sorry if I have made things awkward between you both. I'm sorry, I shouldn't have had sex with him. He's back with his ex-Alice and now things are just awkward."

"You had sex with him? When?" Josh's eyes widened.

"The day of my interview, it was an accident." I shrugged and walked away. The last thing I wanted to do was discuss my non-existent sex life with my brother, especially when the guy in question was his best friend.

Chapter 16

Monday Ryan was out all day and my heart rested a little at work but Tuesday, I considered calling in sick.

"You need to get yourself checked out," Josh said at the bathroom door as I threw up the non-existent contents of my stomach.

"I just need some proper food." I forced down a banana and brushed my teeth.

Josh left before me, leaving Meg in bed.

I put on my brave face and left for work. I had decided not to crumble. Scott had split from Amber since it had become common knowledge about her illegal loans. David had also called off their engagement after finding out about Amber and Scott. I should have been pleased about the karma of it all but I wasn't. Scott didn't want me and neither did Ryan. What was ridiculous was the fact that Ryan had hurt me more and he had taken less from me. I think the reason for the sheer amount of pain was that he had lifted me higher, with him I had felt like anything was possible and this was stupid because I barely knew him. I felt like I loved him more than I had ever loved anything.

I shook the self pity out of my head. Self pity and tears were for evenings only. During the day I needed to be the super receptionist always with a professional smile on my face.

I swiped in the office and had to take the stairs as the lift was being repaired all week. Okay for the way down but exhausting for the way up. People had actually started to use the staff canteen to avoid the extra footwork.

I had just sat in my seat when Ryan called my intercom and asked me to go see him. If Zoella hadn't have been sitting beside me and heard his request, I think I would have made an excuse and refused. That wouldn't have been vey professional though and I was trying to convince myself and all around me that I was this super efficient receptionist that excelled at everything. I grabbed a notepad and pen and took some deep short breaths until I reached his door, knocked and walked it.

He was pacing the floor and my stomach lurched. He looked upset and I wondered if Alice had left him again.

He nudged his head toward his dressing room and I felt my insides twist. The last time we had been in that room we had been semi naked on his unit.

"Do it," he spat shoving a box in my hand.

"What's this?" I asked looking at the box.

"It will tell exactly how far you are so you know whether to congratulate me or Scott."

Impossible, how could I be pregnant? I turned the test over in my hands.

"What are you waiting for?" He shouted. His face contorted into an angry rage and I just stared at him, horrified.

He pushed me in the room and slammed the door shut behind me leaving me alone with the pregnancy test.

Why would he even think that I was pregnant? I calculated the dates in my head. I had started bleeding before Christmas and it was now the twenty-third. I wasn't necessarily late.

I took the lid off his shaving gel and urinated. I didn't need to read the instructions, it wasn't my first time.

I leant on the unit then quickly moved my hands from the scene of the crime. I rinsed out the lid and dried it with toilet roll. Not very hygienic but I'm sure it wouldn't kill him. Ovulation was usually fourteen days after the first day of the period. I did the mental math and it all tied in with the day of my interview.

I saw the lines appear on the test and my legs gave way. I leant my head over the toilet and sobbed.

This had been all I had ever wanted and now here I was an unwanted woman, carrying an unwanted baby.

I sobbed louder, unable to control myself. I leant against the door with both hands over my mouth, trying to keep the sobs in but it was no use.

"Charlotte, open the door." Ryan sounded frantic but I couldn't even muster the strength to stand.

Josh must have called him and told him that I had been sick. Why hadn't Josh messaged me?

I pulled myself together. I could do this. I unlocked the door as quietly as I could.

"I'm sorry." I said to Ryan who looked horrified at the sight of my face.

I darted for the door, then the stairs, then the street. I cried and ran. I ran past the tube. I didn't have my Oyster card or my door key, my bag was back at the office.

I knocked, hoping Meg would be home but no one answered. I climbed to the roof unsure of where else to go and sank behind a metal vent. I curled into the foetal position and cried until I fell asleep.

When Josh found me it was after dark. He led me downstairs without saying a word and led me into the living room where Ryan and Meg where looking worried.

I turned towards my bedroom, slammed the door and hid under the covers. I didn't want this conversation, not even with myself.

"Charlotte, please talk to me." Ryan had let himself in and was running his fingers through my hair. I turned away from him. "Charlotte, we need to talk."

I sat bolt up in bed causing him to fall back slightly. "There is nothing to talk about. I am surprised and a little upset. I think I have a right to be a little broken at this time."

"I never said…" Ryan started but I cut him off.

"You never said a lot of things but let's concentrate on the things you did say." My voice rose and I was aware of the venom in its tone. "It was a one off mistake, no big deal, nothing special, certainly not anything epic like that of a great novel."

Ryan raised his arms to interrupt but I dashed off the bed and held open my door.

"You can tell Scott what a lucky man he is, be my guest. Josh will give you his number for sure." I waved my arm signalling that I wanted him to leave.

"I saw the test, Charlotte, I know its mine." He joined me at the door, looking crestfallen.

"But you doubted it, you doubted me, and your wrong, this baby is mine." I shoved him out of the door and slammed it behind him. I threw myself on the bed then cursed my roughness. I had a life inside me now and I needed to protect it.

I laid in bed for hours rubbing my stomach. I couldn't believe it, I cursed my stupidity. I should have gone on the pill as soon as I had been tempted by Ryan the first night but everything had escalated so fast that I hadn't even registered with a doctor yet.

Meg came in with soup sometime around ten and it was hard to be mad at her face.

"How are you doing?" She asked, handing me the tray.

"Fine," I lied and she laughed at my futile attempt at normal.

"Did Josh tell him he thought I was pregnant?" I asked and Meg nodded. "Why didn't he tell me? I had no idea."

"He thought Ryan was being a shite and needed a friend to kick him up the arse."

I smiled at her accent. Swear words always sounded sweeter from her mouth.

"Can you please ask Josh to text Ryan and tell him I won't be going in tomorrow, but I will go in Thursday. I just need one day to get my head around it."

"Of course." She kissed my head and left.

"I'm sorry Charlotte, I wasn't thinking," Josh came in and took away my tray.

"It's okay," I lied, deep down I was furious. As his sister he should have thought about me and my feelings first but he didn't, his first call was to his best friend.

I slept most of Wednesday but not really soundly. Meg checked on me regularly and I heard her phone ring several times with enquiries about my mental and physical state. I wasn't sure what they were expecting but a breakdown wasn't on my agenda, I just needed to mentally prepare myself for what was going to happen.

Thursday I dragged myself out of bed and forced breakfast down my throat.

I felt sick but I didn't know whether that was because of the pregnancy or the fact that I was now going to work and was going to have to face Ryan.

I felt like I was walking to my execution. Ryan would call me into his office and either fire me or give me the 'let's behave like adults' talk. Neither one appealed to me, I would rather be ignored like I was before.

I swiped into the building and started the long climb up the stairs.

Brooke had smiled at me the same way as she always had which settled my mind a little bit, at least it wasn't common knowledge.

"It was all about me you know." A shrill voice boomed from above me.

I clambered up the next set of stairs, already struggling for breath and came face to face with Alice.

"Tricia, who measured you up in Stanley's is my aunt." She blocked my path, her face was contorted with rage.

Maybe Ryan had called off their affair.

"I don't know what you mean," I said, taking a few steps back down.

"Ryan told her that you were his girlfriend to get me all jealous and back in the country." She looked me up and down with disgust.

"We had sex you know, I could be pregnant now too." She looked at my stomach.

So Ryan had told her. I shook my head not sure of what to say.

"I knew there was something wrong when he told me I had been a mistake, I knew something must have changed his mind." She took a step toward me. "No one changes their mind that quickly."

So he had already dumped her. I didn't know how I felt about it.

"He is mine. He was always mine and will always be mine and no dirty little lying tramp, who can't keep her legs closed is going to take him away from me." She lurched towards me and swiped me to the right. I felt my legs wobble on the step and she rushed towards me lifting me by the groin area until I toppled over the banister.

I let out a small shriek of fear as my head hit the railing. The fall onto the stairs below wasn't a particularly large one but I felt my head bounce twice.

The last thing I remembered before I blacked out was the searing pain in my stomach and the hysterical screaming.

The sound got further and further away until there was nothing.

I woke three days later in a hospital room surrounded by cards and flowers.

Josh was curled up asleep on a chair beside the bed but I couldn't reach him due to the cables holding me in place.

I tried to sit up but I couldn't move. I gasped. I couldn't feel my legs.

I tried to call for Josh but my voice was tiny and barely any sound came out.

A buzzer was strapped to my finger so I pressed it, trying not to panic. A group of nurses bust in knocking Josh out of his chair. He rubbed his hands over his face and chuckled.

"You know how to keep us all on edge," he said, kissing my head.

"You look like shit," I said, trying to sound normal.

"Thanks. I have been here, sleeping in that crappy chair, for three nights." He ran his fingers through his hair.

"I can't feel my legs." My voice rose with panic.

"Someone is on their way to talk to you." He pressed his lips into a thin line which might have been his feeble attempt at a smile but I could see the worry on his face.

"Charlotte." Dr Zusak whooshed into the room like a breath of fresh air and shook my hand.

"What are you doing here?" I asked, glad of the friendly face. I didn't actually need to ask. I was pretty sure one of the Emerson's had paid for my private room and probably Zusak too.

"You have had quite an ordeal and I need to go over a few things, would you like your brother to leave?"

I shook my head. Josh stood up and took my hand.

"What do you remember?" Zusak asked while checking my vitals.

"I remember Alice pushing me over the staircase. I can't feel my legs," I added. Why wasn't he bothered by this?

"While you have been recovering we have numbed everything so your body didn't have to work so hard. Now you are conscious and no longer critical we will get you off all these drips and your feeling will return."

I nodded.

"Unfortunately, Charlotte, you have lost the baby, I'm sorry." Zusak squeezed one hand and Josh squeezed the other.

I nodded. I had suspected as much. I mentally closed the door of the whole pregnancy situation, I would deal with that bombshell later when I was alone.

"You have sustained several injuries, none permanent, apart from the miscarriage, you have been very lucky."

"Lucky that guy Matt was late for work, everyone else was already in the office." Josh added.

"What happened?" I asked, needing to know.

"Let me get these away from you then I'll leave you two to talk." Zusak smiled. He disconnected a variety of wires from my cannula and left the room.

"From what I can gather, Alice heard about you and Ryan and was so overwhelmed with jealously, she got on a plane back to England and surprised him. According to Ryan it was the evening of your interview, she turned up at the office just as he was leaving."

"That was the day we had sex." I added as if Josh really needed to know.

He nodded and continued, "Ryan said he was confused, told her he had moved on but agreed to talk it through, he said he needed closure. They had too much to drink, one thing led to another and she spent the night."

"They had sex twice." I wasn't sure why I felt the need to add this extra piece of information. The fact that he said Alice had stayed the night was enough to explain that he knew the details.

"Yes, same night though," he added then shook his head as if it didn't really make a difference how many times on how many nights. What mattered is those events led us here.

I shrugged. It didn't matter to me how long they had stretched it out. Me and Ryan had been over before we ever really began. He hadn't chosen me and that was all that mattered.

"Apparently he told her the morning after that he didn't want to see her again, that he had met someone new and had moved on. She freaked out and turned up at his work."

"I saw her." I remembered her admiring my flowers from Gerald.

"He says he never told her who you were. He doesn't know how she put two and two together." He ran his hand through his hair and I tried to imagine Josh having this rational conversation with Ryan, somehow the image wouldn't come.

"When did you speak to him?" I had to know.

"When I got here. I wasn't allowed in, well no one was allowed in. Scott is still down as your next of kin you know." He shook his head, wondering how I could have missed such an important change.

"Sorry, ending up in hospital wasn't high up on my list of possible outcomes when sorting out my divorce."

"I didn't mean it like that. I just didn't like being the last to know."

"Didn't Ryan call you?"

"No, he freaked out, I think he is still freaking out. Scott called me. We were half way to Edinburgh for the Burns night party. I practically threw Meg on a train."

"I'm so sorry," I mumbled. I wriggled uncomfortably in the bed. My arms operated fine but my legs had to be dragged. "I'll get that changed. What did Scott say?" Was he bothered?

"He sounded quite upset actually but I told him not to come down. I told him you were trying to put your old life behind you."

"Did you mention Ryan or the baby?" I asked a little too sharply.

"No, of course not, I had just been told my sister was in critical condition after being brutally attacked, giving him the complicated ins and outs of your new love triangle wasn't really on my mind."

I laughed, despite myself.

"Glad you find this amusing," he smiled too.

"It isn't funny. If you think about it is terribly tragic, my life is a ruin. As soon as I think I have steered my ship in a nice sunny direction, I hit an iceberg."

"It could be worse, at least you're okay."

"Has Ryan been in?"

Josh's features darkened. "I told him he wasn't welcome here." He crossed his arms across his chest.

"I'm sorry, I never meant to come between you. I should have given it more thought."

"It's your call. If you want him here then I will respect your decision but this is hard to forgive." Josh looked as close to tears as I had ever seen him. "I never would have expected this from Ryan." He shook his head as if the movement would make all the puzzle pieces fall into place. "I guess because he has never dated anyone I know before."

"It wasn't really his fault, Alice is unstable. Where is she now?" A moment of terror grabbed me.

"Detained. I'm not really sure what is happening to her. She might get sent back to Australia or made to stay here. I haven't really followed the story, it has been on the news, though you've not been named."

"Oooh celebrity."

"I should go get showered, then I'll come back." He stood to leave.

"Why don't you have a rest or go out to see a film or just have a stress free night in? I'm going to be fine."

"Are you sure? I am in need of a shower and a real bed," he rotated his neck.

"I'm fine, honest." Because the word 'honest' made it so.

After I had said goodbye to Josh I fell asleep which was crazy because it was, apparently, all I had been doing for the last three days.

I woke early hours of Tuesday morning hurting everywhere. I rang the bell and a pair of nurses came and gave me some morphine to ease the pain. I smiled at them gratefully and fell back into a long sleep where I dreamt I was sitting at my own trial except I was the villain of the piece. I had stolen Ryan from Alice's shelf where he was supposed to sit untouched, gathering dust, until she chose to return for him. The nightmare ended with the guilty verdict and me being thrown into a never-ending well where the bottom never came. I woke in a cold sweat.

"Morning Sunshine." The door opened and a mass of curls entered the room.

"Hi Buddy, what are you doing here?" I tried to sit up but the pain was excruciating. Buddy called a nurse and she operated my bed until I was in the sitting position.

"You look like shit," he patted my hand.

"You too, Jesus what have been doing with yourself?" I laughed.

"I know, I need a hair cut. If one more person asks me if I am related to Will Ferrell, I think I'll scream."

"Now you mention it," I grabbed his hand. "Aren't you going to be late for work?"

"I am spying for the boss so have a pass."

"I hear my brother has barred him from the property."

Buddy checked where my body was and sat on the edge of the bed. "You can't blame him really though, can you? I mean Alice was unhinged."

"I hope they sort it out, they have been friends forever." I had decided to intervene if I had to.

"Your brother was pretty clear, I thought Ryan was going to get punched in his pretty face." Buddy's eyes widened with the horror of such a thing.

"You saw them together?" I asked, still unsure of events.

"Yes, we were here when your brother arrived. It wasn't pretty, your brother was furious with him for mentioning to Alice about the baby, he didn't see what good Ryan thought he was doing."

I shrugged. The mind of Ryan was clearly something I hadn't understood.

"Ryan had said he was just trying to be clear to her that it was over. We in the office had no idea." He playfully tapped me on the arm like I was some secret minx.

"I never really knew where I stood so I didn't know what to say," I sighed.

"Well, what done is done, you can't change it now. What happens next?"

"I will be in here for a while." I shrugged again. "Not sure how long that will be. I guess Mr Emerson will need to find someone else to do my job. I bet Angus and the other accountants are missing me terribly," I laughed.

"Everyone is missing you." Buddy leant over and kissed my forehead. "I had better run I suppose."

"I might join you," I joked.

Buddy grimaced, "Sorry that was tactless."

"It's okay, the doctor said all feeling should return, no major damage done."

"I'm sorry anyway. Anything I can do for you before I leave?" He looked around the room. "Do you need a drink?"

"No thanks. Could you please pass me all my cards, I'd like to see who loves me."

"They're all from me," he joked, gathering up all the cards from the back wall and the windowsill. "Wow! Nice view."

"Tell me about it," I mumbled.

"Oh my God sorry, again tactless." He piled the cards into my lap and I felt my body underneath them.

"It's fine, stop worrying."

He kissed my head again and left.

I hadn't asked him who else was at the hospital. Buddy had said *we were here*. Did he mean him and Ryan or were there others?

I started thinking all sorts of questions like; when Matt saved me from Alice, did she try to run or was she proud of what she had done? What was she thinking now? I bet she wishes she had stayed in Australia with Ryan's friend.

I shook the idea of Alice out of my head and started reading my cards.

I had one from every individual in the office. This made me smile. At the hospital we had always bought one card and got everyone to sign it. I mentally put faces to the names on the cards. Zoella, Persia, Mr Emerson, Ryan, Buddy, Kyle, Louisa, Emma, Lynsey, Angus, Morten, Lorena, Matt, Aiden, Max, and Brooke were all the names that I recognised, but there were many that I didn't. I guessed some were photographers as some of the cards had amazing scenery on the front. I couldn't remember the name of the other accountants or most of the writers either though whoever Steve was he must have been a writer because his card came together with a novel bearing his name. I put it on the side to read later.

I wondered how long I would be in here until. Would I miss Valentine's Day? Not that it mattered. Ryan had been quite clear about the insignificance of our relationship. Nothing had really changed. I pushed all thoughts of him to the back of my find and tried to focus on how I felt physically. A dull ache had washed over my entire body, even my legs now felt like I had run a marathon and my back was in agony. I wiggled my toes and was pleased when they wiggled back.

"How's the patient?" Zusak walked in with a clipboard.

"Okay and ready for the straight truth, give it to me," I braced myself.

"Vitals seem good," he grinned.

"How long do you think I need to be in here for?"

"How are your legs?"

"I can feel the weight of them," I smiled. I could also feel a sharp shooting pain running down my right side, but I kept that to myself.

Zusak put down his clip board and started running tests. I answered all his questions and lied a little about the pain.

"Okay, all seems well. What we will do is come back after tea and see how much movement your legs can do. Could be a quick recovery but you have twisted your hip on the right side which may make walking painful for a while." He pursed his lips as if holding something back. "Blood pressure and blood tests have all come back well, I would guess a couple of weeks."

He said nothing more but left me with exercises for me to do, stretching and sitting up a little more each time. I was determined but the pain was still excruciating.

I did them while I read the rest of my cards.

I could feel the pain medication wearing off and wondered whether I should ask for more. I could play the pain down and perhaps get out quicker but then what? Josh would be at work and I would be left alone in my room which was darker than this one.

"Mr Emerson Senior to see you if that's okay?" A nurse popped her head in.

I nodded. To be honest if Ryan had turned up I wouldn't have turned him away though I hadn't really thought yet about the things I wanted to say.

"Hey Charlotte." Mr Emerson walked in carrying a huge bouquet of synthetically coloured roses. "How are you feeling?"

"Good thanks," though I wasn't sure how true this was.

He looked me up and down and I saw him take a sharp inhale of breath.

"Worse than you thought?" I asked.

"Sorry, I didn't mean to stare. Nothing like this has ever happened to a member of our staff before, it seems a little surreal." He looked down at his hands. "This isn't the first time I have been in to be honest. I'm relieved to see all the wires and tubes gone but I didn't expect you to still look so colourful." He leant over and patted my hand.

"The drugs have affected my legs so I haven't looked in the mirror yet."

"Perhaps best put that off for a couple of days." He took another deep intake of breath.

"I'm sorry about the work load."

"Oh, don't worry about that, Ryan has stepped in, though he isn't really doing well either."

I knew I should be angry with him and the way he treated me but my heart strings were plucking. For a moment, at least, he would have dealt with the fact that he was going to be a father. I suppose Alice hurt both of us.

"I hope he is okay, I never meant to cause any trouble." A tear fell and in a flash I felt silly.

Mr Emerson dragged the chair over to the side of the bed and grabbed my hand. "None of this was your fault and you don't need to worry about anything except getting yourself better. Ryan will be fine, the job will be fine. Relax and concentrate on yourself."

I took a deep breath. Emotions were building up inside me that I hadn't yet categorised yet. If I cried I like to be clear on what exactly the tears were for. Was I sad at that moment for the baby, for losing Ryan, self pity or just for the fact that I hadn't seen it coming? Yet again a man had hoodwinked me into thinking I was happy and safe then they had pulled the rug from under my feet. *Fooled you.*

I tried to speak but couldn't.

"It's okay, the doctor said that you are doing really well." He stood to leave. "These are from Ryan, am I okay to leave them here?" For a moment he looked terrified that I was going to say no. He left the flowers on the chair he had just vacated and left me alone.

Chapter 17

The recovery had been quicker than Zusak said he'd dreamt possible but for me it dragged on.

It was a month later when Josh picked me up and drove me to my new apartment. I had considered my options carefully over the course of my recovery. My first option was a central London apartment paid for by the Emerson's and I would return to my job at the magazine where my position had been held open for me, despite the letter I had sent outlining that I would not be going back.

The second option had been set up by Zusak. I had told him that I wanted a new job and another fresh start. He had rolled his eyes and told me with my qualifications I could do anything and printed me a list of available jobs in the surrounding area. I chose the one that was not the best paid but it did come with a tiny flat nearby.

Josh needed his life back and I needed some time to work out what I wanted to do with myself. I had loved the magazine but for all the wrong reasons. I didn't know if I actually was any good at it. I felt like I had got carried away without doing any kind of thinking for myself. I needed to take back control of my life and that was never going to happen surrounded by people looking at me like some kind of precious china doll.

Josh had argued of course but he knew it made sense. I needed some distance and Josh said that Ryan had honoured all of my decisions. I didn't know whether he was that cut up about it. Surely his office days were easier without having to look at me all day.

"Ah smell that fresh air." Josh laughed when he came to pick me up from the hospital with his car rammed full of my stuff.

"I know it is great to be free, I could kiss the ground." I kissed him on the cheek instead and headed toward his car.

"I've taken the day off to help you settle in. Thought we could slog it out for what's left of the morning then head out to lunch." He raised his eyebrows and waited for me to approve or disapprove.

"How can we possibly decide what and where to eat? I want everything."

I climbed into his car seat and was dangerously close to the sun visor.

"Sorry, I had to move your seat forward to fit all your stuff in and am going to have to do a second trip."

"I didn't think I had that much stuff," I remarked as he pulled away.

"I couldn't fit the rails in and the shoes boxes took up loads of room."

I had forgotten about all of Ryan gifts.

"This is it," he said, pulling up outside a high rise set of flats. "The hospital is behind, a short walk away apparently. The building belongs to the hospital so I think they deduct the rent straight from your salary."

I nodded Zusak had outlined the details before he had left to continue his real job back in Densborough.

"It's fine with me, at least it is mine." I looked up at the dull grey building with its white metal balconies. It was to be my new start but it looked like a prison.

"You are always welcome to come back and stay at mine at any time," Josh said, grabbing a box.

He and Ryan were texting again, about me mostly, and hopefully would soon get back to where they were before I bulldozed my way into their lives. Ryan had used the divorce as an excuse and Josh had bit the bullet and met up with him on the understanding that I wasn't to be discussed. I gave Josh a good old fashioned letter to give to Ryan saying that I would message him when I was settled and catch up. I had kept it light. I didn't know where we would go from here but I had asked for space and not once did he try to come and see me or send me a message.

I took the keys out of my pocket and grabbed some bags. I was on the ninth floor so hoped this lift was never out. I had to swipe a fob over a sensor to open the front door, then swipe it again to open the lift. At least I would be safe.

Despite the no smoking warnings the whole building had the smell of stale cigarettes. A few cigarette butts lined the floor of the lift and I laughed at the fact that people working in the health profession would have spent all their work life preaching good health habits then as soon as they were out of sight had done the complete opposite.

Josh wriggled his nose with distaste but said nothing.

Number 184 was left out of the lift and at the very end of the corridor meaning I had a corner apartment.

"Wow!" Josh plunked some boxes on the table. "This place is smaller than mine and that's saying something."

"Yes, but yours has two bedrooms, it's designed for more than one." I ran my fingers through the dust and wondered what my job would be like. Would I find a new best friend and forget about all about Amber? I still hadn't been honest with her but then again she hadn't contacted me either. Scott had rung a couple of times to try and arrange a meeting about how things were going but I knew he was trying to stall the final stages of the divorce. Ryan had professional looking letters sent to the hospital to keep me updated.

"I'll bring up the boxes and you can make the tea and sort them," Josh said, grabbing the keys. "No, you have been told not to lift and to take it easy," he protested when I went to follow him out. "You can't lie to me, I was there."

I nodded. Yes, Zusak had said those things but I had guessed he simply meant no weightlifting or skiing.

I surveyed the rooms of which there were three. The front door opened up into a small open corridor with a small bathroom directly on the left and the bedroom along side it. The whole right side was taken up by the open plan lounge /dinner and a small airing cupboard and storage space. It was small but then I didn't have a lot so it wouldn't take long to make it feel like my own. For me it was perfect.

It was already furnished with the large essential items like a bed, wardrobe, washing machine and small fridge freezer. The other items seemed to have been covered by my colleagues at the magazine who had clubbed together and bought me a kettle and matching toaster as a house warming present.

I missed them but was glad not to be going back. The idea of seeing the stairs or thinking about Alice made me sick and the idea of Ryan was completely bitter sweet. On one hand I knew I still had feelings for him but I didn't know to what extent and was in no rush to over analyse the situation, and on the other hand I hadn't forgiven him for having sex with Alice straight after convincing me that I was the luckiest girl in the world for having his undivided attention.

"Haven't you made that coffee yet woman?" Josh joked, piling up the lounge with another set of boxes.

"Still looking for the coffee," I lied. I was still to open a box.

He walked to a box and handed me the tea, coffee and sugar pot and spread his arms out like he was some sort of magician.

"Incredible," I laughed as he left again to get another load.

I made the coffees and started moving the boxes into their appropriate rooms. It pained me to say it but I was going to have to send some of the clothes back to Ryan. My wardrobe would now house two sets of uniform and my two jackets, after that there wasn't much room left for anything else.

"This is the last of it," Josh shouted through.

"Really!" I said in surprise. I thought there would have been ten trips at least.

"I had help." I turned with a sinking feeling in my stomach. I wasn't ready to see Ryan and it would have been just like him to arrive with flowers to welcome me in on my first day.

But it wasn't Ryan and I was surprised to feel a wave of disappointment.

"Hi, I'm Ben from upstairs and this is Meela. I think you two will be working together, you're Dr Zusak's golden child, right?"

I chuckled. "He did put me forward for the job but that is only because I worked with him back in Densborough."

My two intruders started walking around the flat.

"Wow! You have an extra window that makes a huge difference." Meela said, looking out of the window.

"It's huge," Ben remarked, looking in the bedroom.

I laughed, thinking of my old house back in Densborough. "I have just come from a four bedroom house with a garden bigger than this."

"Oh trust me this is huge, come and see mine." Ben's face was all seriousness.

Me and Josh followed them up one floor to his flat that was opposite the lift doors. He opened the door and waved us in.

"Oh my God, you are so tidy," I said. His place was the tidiest man pad that I had ever seen.

"My brother is a carpenter so occasionally he takes pity on me and builds me storage solutions," Ben shrugged.

He led me into the bedroom. "You can't take me into your bedroom on my first day, people will talk," I said, dead pan.

Meela burst into laughter.

"Gossip is currency around here. The more you are talked about the more popular you are." He turned and gave Meela a wink. "Look no second window." He presented his back wall like it was some art presentation. "This is where my other window should be." He led me out to his toilet. "Look, this room, total darkness." He flicked on the light.

"Sorry," I said meaning it. "I feel like I have stolen your dream place."

"Ignore him," Meela said. "There is no way he would leave this shelving unit behind."

"True, and they don't offer us different rooms anyway unless we have a decent excuse for needing to be lower down." Ben shrugged again. Shrugging seemed to be his thing.

"Hey, why don't you have a welcome party tonight?" Meela started clapping her hands together and jumping up and down.

"I only just arrived, the place is a mess!" I laughed.

"Perfect because you don't have to tidy up, everyone will expect it. Probably the only time the fridge will be empty for beer too," Ben smirked.

"I'll arrange everything just expect everyone at seven." Meela's face was so hopeful I didn't have the heart to say no.

"Okay, I guess it will be a good way to meet everyone," I smiled.

Ben shrugged so I shrugged back. Maybe it was contagious.

Me and Josh went back to drink our coffees and unpack.

"What are you going to do with all this stuff?" Josh pointed at all the clothes that had come from Ryan.

"I daren't ask for a bigger place," I joked.

"It's huge," Josh imitated Ben adding a shrug at the end.

"I don't really feel like I should give them to charity. I bet they were expensive and most of them I have never worn." I ran my hands down the pretty fabrics. There was no question of their beauty but where was I going to wear them?

I folded all the ball gown style dresses up and placed them into a large box that had housed my new kitchen appliances. I kept the champagne dress that I had worn on my first night in London and a few other items that were practical in my new life. I kept the jeans and the day tops. I kept a few of the subtler dresses but anything too posh or designer, I boxed up and my heart felt heavy doing it. It was like I was giving away a part of myself.

"Don't worry, he will understand." His furrowed brow betraying the fact that he thought otherwise.

I nodded. The all too familiar knot, that occurred every time I thought of Ryan, was forming in my stomach. Would he understand or would he be offended? I had heard nothing but then the ball had been left in my court. I wanted to see him so badly my insides were aching but I knew now wasn't the right time. I shook the thought of Ryan away, I needed to get into the party mood and thinking about his lips on my neck would only send me into a depression and ruin everyone's first impressions of me.

"That's the last box, are you sure you can't come back to my party?" I pleaded again even though he had declined already five times.

"I can't, I have some loose ends to tie up before I move to Scotland." He pursed his lips together and I said nothing. It was his choice to quit his job and move to be with the woman he loved. On one hand I thought it was the ultimate romantic sacrifice and then on the other I thought she was selfish, but I kept those thoughts to myself. It was his life and these were his mistakes to make.

"Should I text Ryan to let him know you are coming?" I said, suddenly worried about his reaction to the unexpected delivery.

"No, I'll handle it." Josh leant forward and kissed my cheek. "You'll be good here Charlotte, have some fun."

I stood at the window and waved Josh off down the street and started to prepare for my party.

Ben and Meela arrived earlier than everyone else with snacks and alcohol. 'Tradition' they had said as they filled up my fridge and piled up bowls with crisps and crudités. When someone new came into the building, the others chipped in for the food and drink. "One less thing for you to think about." Meela had smiled, Ben had probably shrugged.

The party went well and the people seemed nice. I would be working closely with Meela, Evie and Lydia. Ben worked in the fracture clinic with Freya and Dolly and though I would not see them often at work, our hours were the same so these would be my hard fast drinking buddies.

I didn't tell them about my accident only that I was on antibiotics and couldn't drink. If I was going to have a new start then I needed to not dwell on the past.

My first real drinking session didn't happen until Dolly's twenty-first birthday party a month later on the twenty-third of March.

Our shift had finished at seven and we had all dashed home to change into our cheerleading costumes, Dolly's choice.

I had a bit of reputation of being a bit of a goody goody. The fact that I had come into the job highly recommended hadn't been lost on other members of the staff nor had the fact that I had one of the few, sought after corner flats. My work ethic hadn't changed and the fact that I was trying to keep myself busy so I didn't think of Ryan just meant that I had kept my head down and worked harder.

This party was my chance to win over the odd few that still regarded me as the mole.

My new best friends were Meela and Freya. Both were younger than me, me thirty next year and they were both twenty-seven, but the ages were close enough for us still to have plenty in common and still have a laugh on the job.

Both came back to mine to get ready. Freya lived in Brixton and Meela in Streatham, and Dolly had made it clear that everyone needed to be in the first pub by nine so it saved time.

I showered first while they started the wine and pumped up the music. I had the day before been to be waxed, something I had only ever had done the one time I was with Ryan, a fact that made the whole experience more painful that it should have been.

Though I had promised to call him, time had past and I still hadn't come up with the right words to say and a text just seemed inadequate now.

Josh had already moved to Edinburgh so I couldn't pump him for information and though I was friends on Facebook with Buddy, Emma and Lynsey, it seemed childish to ask them details when it should have been Ryan directly that I should be talking to.

I was sure he would have moved on. I had expected a 'New Home' card but it never came. I had spent Valentine's Day in hospital but no cards came then either. I knew Josh had told him not to visit and I had never lifted that rule but I had still hoped every day that he would break it, but he hadn't. I didn't text him and he never contacted me. There was a vacuum inside of me where all the un-said words were and I was hoping the alcohol tonight would fill it.

I flicked off the shower and shook all thoughts of Ryan from my head. Tonight was about being a girl and though I had dreaded the idea of wearing the skimpy costume when Dolly presented me with it, since trying it on, excitement had built inside me. Being in hospital had helped me shed some pounds and for that much I was grateful.

I slipped into my costume as Freya jumped into the shower. My legs were smooth and tanned which detracted a little of the shame away from the fact that the skirt was so short. Meela had tried to soothe my concerns by reminding me that it wasn't a skirt but a skort. The built in shorts made it okay because even if you flash nobody would see anything.

I smiled and gave her a hug. She had recently been outcasted by her whole family for turning her back on her religion and an arranged marriage which made this harder for her. I expected her to pull out at any minute but half an hour later she appeared out of the bedroom in her tiny outfit just like the rest of us and started on the wine.

Ben banged on the door shortly afterwards telling us we had to leave. "Everybody ready? Got your chip and pins? Okay then, let's hit the road." He was the cheerleading coach all set with whistle that he had already used far too much.

"Where are we going?" I asked, as I ignored all the stares from the commuters.

"The Loft. You will love it, plenty of people, plenty of room." Ben started dancing in the aisle and a lady looked up from her book and started to laugh.

"He isn't gay," Meela added with a smile.

"Really!" Freya couldn't hide her astonishment. "And you would know this how?" Eyebrows raised high.

Meela shrugged. A guilty look spread right across her face.

The Loft was busy. Though we were on the guest list we still had to queue just in a slightly smaller one. Luckily the weather was pretty mild for March. The day had been in the late teens and everyone felt that summer was around the corner.

Plans for summer were made in the queue. Meela wanted to do everything at once, especially swimming as she had never been.

"You have never been swimming?" Ben was amazed. "What never? Not even as a kid?"

"No, it's not something we do, it's a flesh on show thing." She shrugged. Now we knew they were a couple it was hard to see how we had missed these little mannerisms that had been adopted.

"Let's make a list." I suggested thinking of all the things I always said I would get around to doing but never getting done. "I want to go Ice skating and go on the Boris Bikes."

"I want to have a picnic in Holland park." Dolly cheered, shaking her pom-poms. "On a sunny day of course." She added quietly as the bouncers frowned in her direction.

"Oh that will be the one day in August we are all working." Ben shrugged and turned to face the front of the queue, willing it to go faster.

We held our breath as a bouncer neared our group, we had been a bit rowdy.

"You guys better have your id's ready." He frowned looking at our heeled trainers.

"I'll go last," Meela announced. "I look the youngest, that way some of you might get away with not having to produce any."

"I want to be asked," I laughed. "I'm nearly thirty, my days of being humiliated by under age style questions have long since past."

I started shifting from one foot to the other to warm up. It may have been mild but I was still nearly naked and the alcohol in my system wasn't quite having the warming effect Freya had vowed it would.

We finally got inside and Meela was the only one stopped. The joys of being five foot nothing with a face of an angel.

We went up to the bar and I felt an enormous sense of deja-vous.

"I've been here before," I yelled over the music.

"You said you hadn't been anywhere, you little liar," Ben yelled too close to my ear.

"This is familiar." Though I couldn't place it.

"Dolly is trying to get us on the VIP floor." A pretty blonde girl called Lydia announced.

"No chance if we are no longer on the list." Ben whispered so Meela couldn't hear.

VIP area? I wandered to the stairs that led up and recognised the doorman guarding the precious red rope.

I had been here with Ryan. Upstairs there would be a door that led to a secret balcony locked to the masses as a health and safety risk.

"Can I help you?" The bouncer asked perhaps frightened that I would make a run for it.

"No just seeing if the air smells the same up there." I smiled and walked away.

Dolly was being consoled by Lydia. She had been denied access to the upper floor and was now in fits of tears.

"This is all my fault," Meela whispered by my side.

"How so?" I asked confused.

"We were on the guest list. But my fall from grace also got us chopped from the list," she sobbed loudly.

"I don't understand." Yes, she had just refused her arranged marriage causing her family to be a little disgruntled but to completely disown her had seemed a little extreme. How could a religion be more precious than your own child? "Do you want to talk about it?"

She nodded and we followed the smoker signs to an outside bench area. I ducked into the toilets to grab some tissue and followed her to a picnic bench.

"I'm being silly," she panted.

"No, you're not." I stroked her arm.

"Ben won't listen, he just says, this is for the best. He isn't even that close to his family," she held her stomach. "My mum won't even return my calls."

"I thought it was your mum's suggestion not to marry him."

"It was. She is miserable. My father hates her, she hates him. I don't want that life. I want Ben."

I handed her another tissue.

"And now my father has kicked me out and my brother is trying to get me fired. It was him that got us on the list, then crossed us off it, and now even Dolly hates me."

"She doesn't hate you, don't be silly."

"She does, she is sobbing. This is all she has been talking about since she was eighteen and I have ruined everything."

"She is disappointed but not with you." I rubbed her back. "You are the bravest girl I know. So lets pull out our pom-poms and show the VIP area what they are missing."

I gave her a hug and led her to the bar. I felt my phone vibrate in my bum bag but ignored it while I got us both a drink.

"How is she?" Evie asked, wobbling slightly as he leant over.

"Trying to put on a brave face. How is Dolly?" I could see from where I was standing that she was being calmed down by Lydia who looked like she was starting to lose her patience.

"I'll go check." Evie disappeared to join Lydia at Dolly's side. I saw Evie raise her arms and usher Meela outside. The bar man started asking for orders and I was trapped. I really needed to make sure Meela was okay but I had waited ages for the barman to come my way so I gave him my order, defeated. "Two large wines please." I kept my eyes on the door.

My phone rang again. I answered it thinking it might have been Freya who I hadn't seen for a while.

"Hello," I yelled. There was no way I was going to hear a thing in here.

I gave the waiter my money and made my apologies. "I'm sorry I can't hear you, I'll call you back," I bellowed. I hadn't even heard a voice on the other end.

I accepted my change and left to find Meela.

Meela was sitting on the same seat getting an ear bashing from Evie about letting Dolly down.

I handed Meela the wine and gave Evie a look that said back off.

"What? I'm just passing on a message." She shrugged, as if it was no big deal.

"Well, she has just lost everything, her family, her home, some friends, I don't think she really needs to lose any respect here do you?" I placed the wine down a bit heavy and some spilled over.

"I'm not disrespecting her." Evie looked horrified at the very idea. "I love you, I do. And I said you can move in with me, didn't I?" She looked at me rather than Meela while she spoke. "Dolly was just wondering if there was anything you could do like a pretend it all never happened over ride."

I burst out laughing and Meela joined in.

"What?" Evie looked offended.

"She is not wearing very much, her hair isn't covered and she is drinking wine, I think your chances are pretty slim." I sat beside Meela and draped my arm around her. "If there is anything I can do let me know."

My phone rang again, "Ah this will be Freya."

I grabbed the phone, but it wasn't Freya.

"I have put you gorgeous lot on the list."

"Ryan?" My heart momentarily stopped and all of a sudden I felt very sober.

"You look well."

I searched around for his face but couldn't see it.

"Thank you, I am well." I put my hand over the receiver. "I think we might now be on the list. Why don't you go check and then you can let Dolly know."

"I like the pigtails." His voice was calm and smooth.

I smiled. I had hated them when I was sober but now I was tipsy I felt every bit the girlie girl.

"Where are you?" I asked still not finding him.

"Waiting for you in the VIP area." He hung up.

I took several steps back then looked up. The off limits smoking area was directly above us and Ryan was standing looking gorgeous above my head.

I smiled and waved coyly. I grabbed mine and Meela's drink and headed through the busy bar.

"We're on the list," Meela said in disbelief. "I asked and look! they're letting us up." She grabbed both my shoulders and spilt more wine. "I can't believe it."

I handed her what was left of her drink and said I would meet her up there. I just needed the loo.

Her smile reached from ear to ear and Dolly gave her a massive hug on the way up.

I turned back the way I had come and ducked into the toilets.

I was about to speak to Ryan in the first time in months and I didn't know if I was ready.

Chapter 18

I stared at my reflection and analysed my appearance.

The curly pig tails made me look five years younger and Freya had done my make-up for me so I could have looked worse.

I had just been to the toilet but needed to go again. My stomach was in knots and I inhaled slow and deep to calm myself down. Why was I so nervous?

I nodded at my reflection and headed towards the door. As I got nearer Ben and Freya walked in together and shared a knowing smile.

"Hi." I yelled as the music volume dipped and several people turned around.

Freya blushed scarlet and Ben moved several inches away from her. *Too late now guys, you're busted*, I thought to myself. I could only think of Meela who had already put her heart firmly in Ben's hands and here he was fooling with her best friend. Freya must have known how Meela felt about him.

"Where is everybody?" Ben asked, looking around the room.

"Everyone's looking for you two," I said. Freya's eyes shot in horror. "I'm kidding, no one even noticed you were gone. We're in the VIP area."

I headed up the stairs wondering what I should say, if anything to Meela. If she was changing for herself then I supported her all the way but if this was for Ben then she was making a mistake, a huge mistake.

The volume dropped immensely as I reached the next floor. It was as if being a VIP earned you the right to be able to hear each other talking without the loud thud of the drum and bass.

Ben ran past us and I steered Freya into the upstairs bathroom.

"What are you doing?" I asked.

"It isn't what it looks like." She put her hands out like she was dissuading a dog from jumping up.

"Then why do you look so guilty?" I folded my arms across my chest which wasn't easy with pom-poms in the way.

"I didn't know he liked me," she said. She shrugged her shoulders as if that was the most logical answer in the world. "I like him."

"And so does Meela, remember, your best friend." Flashes of Amber crossed my mind and for the first time I wondered which one of them had instigated the affair. Had either of them felt an ounce of guilt for the way they had made me feel? Freya clearly hadn't given much thought to Meela.

"They haven't had sex, they're not even really dating." Freya shook her pom-poms in the air.

"What if she has only changed for him, Freya? Her family have disowned her."

"She did it for herself, not him."

"I hope you're right and I hope you know what you are doing." I turned and left her in the bathroom. Now I knew how Cassie felt being in the middle. On one hand Meela had a right to know the man she put all her hope in just wasn't that interested, then on the other hand I didn't want to be the one to tell her. If it was no big deal, Freya could do that herself.

"Charlotte!" Ben yelled, handing out the shots.

I smiled and accepted. I knew his game, I was starting to think I knew his type, he would get blinding drunk and blame the alcohol for all his misdeeds if called out.

At least Ryan admitted that he screwed up. He hadn't looked for excuses or blamed anything other than his own lack of judgement.

I suddenly felt sorry for him and needed to feel his touch. I looked around and saw him talking to Lydia and Meela at the bar just behind Ben.

He smiled at me as I walked over and ordered us a bottle of wine without asking. "You never called," he said, passing the glasses around.

"You know Ryan?" Lydia squealed causing Ben and a few others to turn round.

"Yes," I paused, unsure of what to say. Did I say we had been lovers, colleagues, or that he saved me from my old life back home? Instead I settled for "Yes, Ryan is a friend of my brother, Josh."

The pause hadn't gone un-noticed and Ben had now turned around giving us his full attention.

"Charlotte?" Ben said, pointing at Ryan.

I looked at Ryan and he looked white as a sheet.

"Charlotte," Ben repeated slower. "This is *the* Charlotte?" He took in a sharp intake of breath and looked at me. "I'm sorry, I didn't know." He frowned and I wondered what he knew.

"Oh my God," Meela shouted out surprising the room with her sudden outburst. "You dated him and ended up in a coma?" She put her hand over her mouth. "That was you?"

"It wasn't really a coma," I laughed, sipping my drink. I glanced up at Ryan who was now looking at the floor as if wishing a hole would appear and swallow him up.

"Small world," Lydia smiled, not taking her eyes of Ryan. "Single again now though." She fell into him slightly and made it look like Ben had knocked her in his surge for another round of shots from the bar. She turned and smiled at me, her intentions clear. Thousands of emotions shot through my body and my brain started sifting through ideas to remove Lydia from Ryan's side. Ryan sidestepped out of her way and it was enough to calm my inner diva.

"Are you still able to get the keys." I nodded toward the smoking balcony and he got the barman's attention.

I felt all eyes on us as we slid through the door and locked it up behind us.

"I thought you would have told them," Ryan said sheepishly. He sat on the same table top as we sat last time.

"I should have known you would know everybody," I smiled. I rested my pom-poms on a nearby bench and sat on the table top beside him.

Ryan shrugged out of his jacket and placed it on my shoulders.

"Thanks, but I'm not cold," I lied but didn't return it.

"Not wearing much," He looked at my bare thighs.

"They are shorts, not my knickers," I laughed.

"I saw," he raised his eyebrows. "Let's go sit over there," He pointed to a corner seat that had low wooden bench style seats. "Here give me a hand," I followed him to a locker that contained soft seat pads and helped him drag them to the bench.

He sat down and patted the seat beside him.

I hesitated. This was cosy, intimate even and the nerves began to build up.

"It is okay to still be angry with me," he looked pained as he spoke. "I just need to hear you say it, well, say anything."

"I'm not angry with you. I was just disappointed that it meant nothing," I shrugged, Ben would have been proud.

"You never meant nothing, Charlotte," His rubbed his face with his hands. "You meant the world to me, you still do."

"I had very little else to go on, all things considered. It is okay now, we don't need to go over everything, I get the gist of what happened." I heard the words come out of my mouth but knew that I didn't mean them. I wasn't okay but I wasn't exactly falling apart. Maybe what I was feeling was a compromise.

"If it was okay then why did you never call? It has been torture."

I relented and sat beside him. The soft cushion slopped down under my weight and leant his way. I straightened myself up with my foot then curled both feet underneath me. "I just presumed that I had left it too late and perhaps it didn't matter any more." Another shrug, I was getting good at these.

"Of course it mattered, I did this to you, it was my fault." He ran his hand through his hair.

"No, you didn't, you were right. We only had sex once, you never asked me to be your girlfriend and it wasn't the epic romance that you find in the novels. I guessed that, maybe I had created a romance in my head that didn't exist."

"I never meant that." Ryan looked desperate. His eyes searched mine perhaps looking for any shred of evidence that I hadn't actually believed it.

I didn't know what to say so I shrugged and looked away.

"Charlotte," he whispered.

"What do you want me to say that I forgive you? I do, I never really blamed you, I blamed myself."

"Why would you blame yourself? You did nothing wrong." He took my hand and I felt a thrill run through my body.

"Because I wasn't really single. I had left Scott days before you came into my life and I jumped straight in. I never really considered what I was doing or whether you were actually in to me or not, I was confused."

"You think I do this all the time?"

"How would I know?" I shifted to face him. "I just felt so stupid. I should have been on the pill, especially after the first night and I am responsible for myself, I am a grown woman."

"I didn't mean the pregnancy, I meant Alice, but to be fair I had a condom in my wallet and didn't even give it a second thought, we were both to blame for the pregnancy." He rubbed my hand and looked past me to the door and I wondered what he was thinking.

"Did you tell Alice that I was pregnant?" Suddenly I needed to know.

"I told her that I had a girlfriend, that I didn't love her and that I didn't think I ever did. She tried on the charm that had worked when she first arrived, but I hadn't been thinking clearly then, her arrival had taken me completely by surprise and I guess part of me wanted her to still want me. When she tried it on again I had to be firmer so I told her that I was in love with someone else and we were going to get married and start a family."

I looked at him amazed. Married? This is news to me.

"I know I jumped a few steps ahead but I thought I was doing the right thing by being crystal clear."

"Yes, because nothing says *we're through* like two rolls in the hay."

"I'm sorry," he mumbled. "I never told her who it was but I think she had gone through my phone already and then she asked Brooke loads of questions about you, she had said she was an old school friend."

"You knew she was unstable," I added.

"I thought that she was only that way because of me, I didn't know she was generally unstable." He suddenly stood and started pacing. "I didn't think how much I hurt you or how much I had hurt her or myself. And Josh! Josh is only just speaking to me again and there is a no Charlotte rule when we talk."

"He's your best friend, he'll come round."

I stood. Ryan had started to water at the eyes and I didn't know how to help. I felt like there was nothing else to say.

"How about we meet up somewhere next week. I finish Friday at seven and then have the whole week off. We could go somewhere low key and quiet and just hang out. What do you say?"

"Sounds like more than I deserve." He didn't lift his eyes up from the floor and I got a sudden urge to shake him.

"Look, let me be clear."

His eyes shot up in fear.

"I like you, you took my mind off my failed marriage and broken life and I think I needed it. I'm divorced now and feel in a much better place, but there is no way I'm going to start seeing you again if you are going to be carrying around that face."

He smiled despite himself. "What face? I'll have you know people are quite fond of this face."

"I just mean you can't keep apologising. You can't change it. If we move on then we have to move on and leave all this other crap behind us."

"And never talk about it again?" I couldn't tell if he was pleased or horrified at the notion.

"I can't look at you looking guilty all the time because I don't want to be reminded of all that sadness."

"Have you seen someone?"

"What like a therapist?" I laughed. "I wasn't that traumatised. The baby hadn't sunk in and part of me hadn't even accepted that it was real. Alice is locked up, that was more of a shock."

"You were in hospital for four weeks, Charlotte." He looked unsure of how to process my new positive attitude that I had been working on. Yes, it all sounded a bit too sunny but after being hurt by Scott, then Amber then Cassie, I guess I had just got used to departmentalising the pain into varying degrees.

"I think I was more hurt by the fact that you had been ignoring me and you were happy to let the staff believe that I was the only person in the world that you didn't like. I was with Scott since I was nineteen and he never hurt me the way you did and I barely know you. It doesn't make sense, none of it makes sense, so don't tell me how I should be feeling." My voice rose and he took some steps back. "I just thought you made things too easy for me. I never called because I knew you would hand me anything I needed on a plate. I didn't want that. I don't want that. I like the fact that I have supported myself and I have pulled myself through."

Ryan flinched but I saw a small smile dance on his lips. "I have never bought anyone's affection in my life." Stubbornness set across his face.

"Okay, so if I called you and said that my flat is the size of your bathroom you wouldn't have found me something bigger?" I put my arms across my chest daring him to argue.

He snorted. "If it meant I would have seen you again, probably, yes."

"I rest my case. You set yourself up to be used. I don't want to be that woman and I sure as hell don't want you to be that man who constantly feels like he owes me something."

I pulled the pads off the benches signalling the end of our discussion. "Let's meet up in a week and see where we go from there. I'm paying so don't pick somewhere ridiculous."

"You can trust me, Charlotte," he whispered.

"I will make that decision for myself, thanks," I smiled trying to be strong. His lips curled up at the sides and I wanted to kiss them so badly but I knew this wasn't the time. I couldn't date him until he had forgiven himself.

"Okay, I will send you details of where to meet." He threw in the last of the seat pads and shut up the locker.

"Perfect," I smiled and he leant in to kiss me. I held my breath wanting him to go for the lips but he didn't he pecked my cheek.

"Thank you for speaking with me," he rubbed my cheek.

"Thank you for getting us on the VIP list." I smiled and followed him through the door.

I watched him jog down the steps and wondered why he hadn't hung around, he was obviously friends with Ben and some of the others. I turned towards the others who looked nervous as I rejoined the group.

"I didn't know you knew him." Lydia pulled me towards her. "You still have his jacket."

I ran my hands over the sleeve. Ryan had already left but now I had an excuse to keep up the contact. "I'm seeing him next week, he'll get it back." I shrugged.

"Have you known him long?" She asked. This was the most we had ever spoken and I realised she was fishing.

I knew at this point that I wanted him back. I had moved past Alice and the deceit, I wasn't sure when and all of a sudden I was feeling territorial. Ryan was mine and I always wanted it to be that way. Yes, we had a bumpy start but I was in love with him. I strained my brain to work out exactly when it had happened and shook my head with surprise. Could it have been as early on as when he fastened me up in the champagne coloured dress? A wave of emotion flooded over me.

"Charlotte?" Lydia was still talking to me but I couldn't remember what she had asked. The blood thundering around my head had affecting my hearing. "You and Ryan? Have you known him long?"

"Yes, for years," I said. It wasn't a lie, he had been at my wedding after all. I couldn't really define it until I had sorted it out in my head. I held up my empty glass and headed towards the bar.

I ordered a wine and listened as Evie told stories of when she and Ryan were at school together. I scooped out my phone and my heart fluttered as his face popped onto the screen. I had lost count of the amount of times I had looked at it or how many times I had considered deleting it. I was glad I hadn't. I sent him a quick message saying that I had forgotten to return his jacket and that I could drop it off if he really needed it back by next week. I ended with a kiss which was how I ended all messages, even the ones to Josh, but something about this one seemed loaded with extra meaning.

He messaged back after an hour saying he was waiting for me outside. My heart leapt, this was my chance to tell him how I really felt. There was no point dragging it out or over analysing every last detail. It was what it was.

He was standing outside on the other side of the street leaning against Grady's black Jaguar. He hadn't changed, but there was something about his confidence that made him look better looking than he had the hour before and I realised as I approached him that I was holding my breath.

"Here this is for you," he handed me a brown leather bound book. "Then there will be nothing left unsaid."

I opened the front cover and looked at the neat handwritten pages.

"Is this a diary?" I asked in disbelief. "I thought you said that you didn't keep one."

"I lied," he said looking down. "It is unabridged so I can only apologise for the cringeworthy bits."

"You don't need to give me this, honestly." I passed the book back to him but he refused to take it.

"You don't think what I felt for you was real and I can see now that I did nothing to give you any impression that it was. This way you know what was going through my head and if you read it then I will never have to say it."

"Oh I see, so when we meet next week I will have your apology already." I held up the book.

"You will have my whole life and then some," he raised his eyebrows. "Just please skip the New Year bit, promise me you will."

Now he had asked me to skip it there was no way I was going to so I changed the subject.

"Is it okay to get a lift home with you?" I pointed towards his car. "If you're going that way that is. Everyone is moving on to another club and I'm beat."

"Sure, though you know I live nowhere near you." He held the door open for me and I threw my pom-poms in the back. "I like red, it's your colour." I heard him chuckle as I tried to pull down the skirt to a reasonable level.

"Thanks," I smiled and gave Grady my address.

"I have something for you, will you come up and get it?" I said when we arrived at mine. I saw Grady check his watch. "It's just a hand over. He will be ten minutes max," I smiled.

"Which floor?" Ryan asked, as we got in the lift.

"Nine," I smiled, getting my key ready.

"Wow! That's a lot of stairs."

I let him in and went straight to my bedside table. I slipped Ryan's diary in and took out my own. His theory made sense and I had a bad habit of forgetting all the important things I wanted to say. When I was at the magazine I would go to sleep and dream of the conversations I wanted to have with him and rehearse them until they were perfectly constructed, then I would see him and forget the lot. Being articulate wasn't one of my gifts.

He was washing up drinking glasses when I returned.

"You're right, I would have found you a bigger place," he smiled.

"It is fine for me, but you can see why I had to return your clothes."

"I can now, I was devastated at the time. You can't swing a cat in here."

"I don't really like cats," I laughed and handed him my book.

"Your diary?" His eyes expanded full width.

"Yes, now we will be on a level playing field. I will know you and you will know me."

"I don't need this." He handed it back.

"Then I'm not taking yours. Think quick, Grady's waiting."

"Okay. I will see you Friday night, you are paying and it will be somewhere casual." He smiled and kissed my cheek. "I have missed you." He whispered into my ear and I shuddered. "I felt that." He smiled and rubbed my cheek.

"At least you know you still have it," I said. This wine was making me brave.

His smile widened and he nodded happily. "See you next week."

I smiled and shut the door. If I had to look at his face any longer I think I would have caved and invited him to stay the night. I couldn't lie and say that he hadn't moved me. His whole presence had set me on edge and I realised, after seeing him, that I wasn't feeling as flippant about the whole thing as I thought I had. Yes, I had my own place and my own job, but I wasn't complete.

I shrugged off his jacket that I hadn't returned and took it into the bedroom. The collar still smelt of his aftershave and I inhaled it in. I could text him to come back and get it and I didn't doubt for a second that he would and where it would lead, but I needed to be stronger. It was one week and I would see him. What was seven days when I hadn't seen him for over two months?

I showered and got into my pyjamas. I put his jacket around my shoulders and imagined his arms around me. I text Meela and Freya and told them I had gone home and would catch up with them later.

I didn't have to be in work until four which gave me plenty of time to get stuck into Ryan's diary.

I ran my fingers over the cover. His fingers would have been exactly where mine were now and his fingerprints were now mingled with mine. I flipped the cover over gently as if it was some precious heirloom and was greeted by a plastic sleeve full of receipts and keepsakes.

I crawled into bed and emptied the contents into my lap. There were receipts for the New Year meal and the diary he had bought me and now had. There was a small plastic pocket that had a few strands of my hair in them and I wondered where he had got them from. I guessed from his spare room pillow from when I had stayed the night. Behind the plastic sleeve was my staff photo which he probably had printed off the system.

I put the book down and looked up. Where on earth did a guy as busy as Ryan manage to find the time to keep a journal?

My eyes were getting heavy with sleep and the wine in my system was making the handwriting blur. I closed the book and decided to read it with a clear head.

The next morning I prepared myself before I opened the diary. I got breakfast and made a coffee and built a fort in the bedroom.

I opened the book and skipped to Boxing Day. It wasn't that I wasn't interested in his life before I had entered into it, it was just that there was a lot to get through and I had loads of shifts this week that would interfere with the reading time.

It was time learn everything there was to know about Ryan Emerson and I didn't need to wait any longer.

Chapter 19

Ryan's Diary

26th December

I've offered to pick up Josh's sister whose husband has just left her. Not my idea of Boxing Day heaven but I owe Josh a lot. It is that or Buddy's usual Boxing day party and Emma keeps being weird. What is it about Christmas time that doubles women's weirdness? If I liked her she would know about it regardless of holiday season.

I have driven for three and a half hours in an awful hire van with a broken radio to collect a woman who isn't even here. The house looks deserted and she isn't answering her phone.

I'm giving her ten minutes then I'm leaving.

She arrived. I got fed up of ringing her number that Josh had given me and was banging on her door. I had completely lost my patience when she turned the corner looking annoyed that I should be on her property. I quickly explained who I was and why I was there and she was not impressed. She was expecting her brother tomorrow but it made no real difference as there was nothing to pack and I mean NOTHING. She had an airbed in her bedroom with a thin sleeping bag that had a hole in the bottom.

We detoured to an address to pick up some bits that her husband had taken from her friend's garage. Charlotte made it quite clear that she had stolen the key and we were not supposed to be there. It was her things and I could plead ignorance if it came to it, so I helped root through her things.

There were some decent things but she was only interested in her mother's table. Josh never talks about his mother so it was nice to get some info. From what I can gather her mother died when she was young and the table was the only thing she owned of hers. The husband knew this and took it anyway. I found it broken in a heap in a corner with the crystal glasses I had bought them for their wedding. Weird that I can remember what I bought them as a gift but actually couldn't remember what either of them looked like. Charlotte is quite pretty. Her clothes are oversized with elasticated waist so it is hard to see her figure but then again she wasn't expecting me and actually hasn't paid me a blind bit of notice at all.

Quite refreshing.

In the van home I decided to take a risk and bare all about Alice, something that still stings. I got to the end of my story and turned for her honest input but she was asleep! I had just poured my heart out and she wasn't even remotely interested.

I pulled up outside Josh's apartment and watched her sleep. There is something about her that I can't quite put my finger on but as I touched her cheek to wake her I felt a stirring and a desperate need to kiss her. I dismissed it and shook her instead. She left her shitty husband three hours ago the last thing she needs in her already complicated life is me.

She told me about breaking in to someones house and a realisation hit me. Never in my life have I met someone as brutally honest. Nothing about this woman is fake. She isn't trying to impress me or sell me a glorified version of her life - she is just normal.

Okay, so I have taken a risk and decided to pursue Charlotte. I haven't had a girlfriend since Alice and nor have a wanted one but after lunch and some wine I can't keep my eyes of her. My hands keep operating on their own and trying to touch her, I can't seem to control them.

I have bought her a diary in the hope that she will keep it up and have just bought her to Stanley's to be pampered. Trish will probably blab to Alice but Alice is engaged so shouldn't be bothered about me moving on even if she was told.

Charlotte is now having her hair done. I have told the staff that she is my girlfriend and to my surprise she didn't argue. Maybe deep down she is attracted to me though she is giving nothing away which is driving me crazy.

I had better go select her some clothes. I'm thinking of something short and sexy that screams 'look at me'. This woman needs some confidence.

Okay so I'm slightly drunk after the best night ever. I chose her a champagne coloured dress decorated in Swarovski crystals. It cost nine thousand pounds and then there were the shoes and the underwear to go with it. I couldn't keep my eyes off her, she looked incredible while completely unaware at how much money she was wearing. I did up the back and imagined that she held her breath as I did. I wasn't sure if she did or not but after I mentioned it she seemed unfazed so I guess it was in my head.

This is what I love about this woman, she is totally unaffected by me, which to be honest, is also driving me a little nuts. Usually I go out and I hate the attention. I can't even have one conversation without some giggling girl butting in trying to get my number. I smile politely then try to get to the end of my conversation before the next interruption.

Anyway, Charlotte was ignoring me. The interruptions didn't bother her at all she seemed to welcome the third party conversation. I used the loudness of The Loft as an excuse to lean in and get closer. No idea why I crave her attention so much, I just needed her to look at me a little longer than she should have. She did say I was stunning but in a way like it was a fact rather than a shared feeling. Still it stirred some buried deep feelings in me and all I could think of all night was how I was going to kiss her.

Nearly kissed her at the bus stop when a fight broke out but was interrupted by a taxi. Bobby kept talking in the cab about the Valentine's fashion shoot but I drowned out his voice the sexual tension between me and Charlotte was immense.

I took her back to mine thinking it was nearer than Josh's and she wouldn't be alone. I had no intention of having sex with her but as soon as she slipped her heels off that was all I could think about. We kissed and that was explosive enough. I need to slow down before I ruin my chances.

27^h December

Josh went nuts. He arrived home early and expected to find his sister at his place. Luckily she was in the spare room unconscious. She later revealed she was on her period but before this revelation he thought I had seduced his sister.

This annoys me for two reasons; the first is that I have never really seduced anyone so why he presumed I had done this is beyond me. It is not as if I am this massive Casanova that goes after every woman that I see. She was in the spare room exactly where a gentleman would put her;

And secondly I am annoyed because I *want* to seduce her, badly. I don't know why I want her so much I can't even rationalise it, I just can't wait to be near her again.

Josh knows me better than anyone. Surely he knows worse people that his sister could end up with. But then I guess she only left her husband's house yesterday and I have't really given her any room to just deal with that. Perhaps I need to back off and give her some space.

But not today.

Today I have planned lunch and a walk around Primrose Hill. I need to talk to her and get to know her. Mainly I want to know how she feels about her husband. I have just spent thousands on a woman who could potentially go back to her husband tomorrow and never grace my life again.

I caught her selecting her underwear while I only had a towel on. Not my finest moment but Jesus this woman is hot.

We walked and talked for hours. Charlotte is so easy to talk to and I feel like I have known her years. I have suggested she go for a job at the magazine. Dad was going to suggest Emma went for it but it is bad enough having her opposite my office everyday without giving her an excuse to keep calling in. Nice girl but seriously needs to find a boyfriend.

When Charlotte left to fill in the application form Josh had another go at me for seducing his sister?? All I have done so far is take her for lunch. Okay the clothes were a bit extravagant and I am having trouble keeping my eyes off her. I need to back off. I can't upset Josh.

I booked a table at Gaucho and included Josh. I would hate to think I was leaving him out. Ha! I googled Charlotte's soon-to-be ex husband. This guy has some serious muscles going on and infuriatingly isn't a bad looking guy. I need Charlotte to adapt to London life so she will want to stay. Not really sure how to pull all the stops out without Josh getting suspicious.

Charlotte wore a silver dress that I'm convinced was Gucci. I didn't buy her this but she looked amazing. Josh kicked me under the table for staring at her but I can't help it.

Im now not going to see her until New Year's Eve which is four days away. I've told Josh that I'm falling for his sister and am going to give her space. I expected him to be annoyed but actually he was quite calm about it.

31st December

New Year Eve FINALLY.

Last few days have been dull. Work, work and more work just to take my mind of Charlotte. I keep thinking she will text and cancel tonight and go back to her squat to make out with her ex.

I have done a couple of gym sessions but my muscles just aren't cooperating. Hopefully she isn't all about the body. A six pack I can manage, biceps not so much.

I have got loads done since I saw Charlotte last. Most importantly I have filled in her divorce paperwork.

I have packed a trolley full of things for tonight. It can only be packed one way to fit everything in so I either need to bin some stuff or remain relatively sober to get it back in. I have a thin spectator shelter to watch the fireworks in, a two seater love seat and a blanket. The forecast is snow this could be really romantic.

I can't wait to see her and make an excuse to touch her. I hope she feels the same.

Night didn't go as planned.

I should have practiced putting the tent up. It was impossible in the dark. Some guy took pity on me and helped me out. I felt like a right idiot. Luckily Charlotte's eyes were closed so she couldn't see what an arse I was making of myself.

Charlotte was impressed with the effort and we kissed at midnight. It was the best kiss, I think, I have ever had. I felt like she felt the same but she refused to spend any more time with me. I tried every trick in the book to keep her with me but she stood firm.

Kate from finance was drooling all over me on the tube and Charlotte wasn't even remotely jealous. Maybe I have this all wrong.

I'm now sitting at home, alone, New Years morning, brooding.

4th January

Charlotte has text a couple of times and I have ignored her. I don't know what to say. How can you fall in love with someone so quickly? It doesn't make any sense. I need to brood some more and get my head around it. I feel like if I tell her how I really feel about her she won't believe me. Maybe she will think that I do this sort of thing all the time and yet I can't keep ignoring her messages. I think about her all the time and feel sick thinking that I might have hurt her feelings.

Alice has emailed me out of the blue several times and I have barred her email address so they bounce back undelivered. Odd how when she was all I wanted she couldn't wait to show me how insignificant I was and now I have moved on she can't leave me alone.

5th January

Back to work. Charlotte has her interview and I have butterflies in my stomach. Dad has already said that he isn't going to hire her and I know I should have told her, but I need to see her and find out if she has any feelings for me at all.

Emma keeps grinning at me I would fire her but she is less annoying than the last girl and the next could be a million times worse.

Charlotte arrived and didn't even look my way. She and Buddy keep touching and it is annoying the hell out of me. I'm supposed to be proofreading an article on skin cancer but I can't keep my eyes of them.

Charlotte came out of the interview smiling but I didn't really expect her to be any other way. This woman is so aloof, maybe she is a robot without feelings. She is now talking to Buddy again and I'm thinking of excuses to fire him. He isn't like this with anyone else.

I dragged Charlotte in the office and practically called her a whore. A massive argument broke out, I'm surprised the whole office didn't hear us. It got quite nasty, I didn't really know why I was so upset but then suddenly we were kissing. Not entirely sure how it happened but we ended up having really hot anger sex in my dressing room. Several times I heard the ping of the lift next door and somehow being that close to people just made the whole thing hotter. Though I don't want to get that angry again, the sex was unbelievable. I am taking her out tomorrow and going to discuss our relationship properly.

Dad has just said Charlotte is getting the job. Ha! After all that hooha about her being the least qualified. She won him over just like she bewitched me.

I'm now trying to get work done but can't keep my eyes of my dressing room door and thinking of Charlotte with her dress pulled up to her waist.

Work output for today = Shockingly low. :)

I have made a HUGE mistake.

Alice was waiting at my door when I got home holding two bottles of French wine. Not sure when we had ever discussed my favourite wine but here she was wearing a skin tight black shift dress with bare tanned legs.

I don't know why I let her in, I guess it was the shock of seeing her there in the flesh. I had waited months for her to even call or email and here she was, at my door, with a huge grin on her face. She looked good - a little fuller but she had always been too skinny before like she would snap if you hugged her too hard.

We chatted about our relationship and why it hadn't worked. To begin with I felt like she was getting closure too and part of me thought she was apologising for trashing my place but that never came.

After two bottles of wine and no food we were having sex on the couch. Inside my head was screaming 'no' but she knew what buttons to push and we fell into an old routine which was comfortable. I should have asked her to leave but we fell into easy conversation about old times and fun times we had and before I knew what was happening we were naked again. It was like my body craved the sudden renewal of human interaction and clouded my judgement.

I felt awful. Alice stayed the night, I didn't know how to kick her out without being more of a shit than I had been already. In the morning I told her I liked someone else. She asked if I was in a relationship and I didn't lie. I hadn't asked Charlotte out but that wasn't the point. I may have just ruined the most exciting thing that has happened to me in years before it has even started.

I had to practically throw Alice out.

I apologised for giving her the wrong impression. I offered to pay for the wine but she freaked out. She hasn't changed despite all that she said, I can see the psycho woman still in there waiting to smash my life up. I shouldn't have let her in and should have kicked her out the second I felt her leaning in on me. The alcohol was no excuse. I'm a shit and my head is killing me.

I have cancelled my date with Charlotte. I feel awful and it's not the alcohol. How can I look at her knowing what I have done?

8th January

Charlotte has started the job and has noticed that something is wrong.
I can't even look at her.
She came into the office several times and I was rude and it wasn't even on purpose. I need to get a grip.
Alice rang the work phone as I had ignored her texts. I asked her never to call me again. I told her I am not interested in the slightest, she needs to go back to Australia and leave me alone.
She ranted down the phone and called me all the names under the sun. Her flight back to Australia is over two weeks away. I just need her gone.

I have asked Zoella to bring me my messages instead of Charlotte. She gave me this look which makes me regret not having the talk with her about not being interested. I watched her go straight into Buddy's office. I regret this decision already.

Zoella keeps flirting with me and it's annoying the hell out of me. She is fast becoming worse than Emma and that is saying something.

19th January

Charlotte is ignoring me, she knows something is up. I need to tell her and be honest but I'm not sure how or where to begin. It doesn't help that I can see her laughing with Zoella from my desk or that when I go down to her desk while she is on lunch I can still smell her perfume. This is driving me nuts.

Charlotte just got the most beautiful bouquet of flowers delivered and I have taken them away from the sales staff so I can read the message.
Gerald! Who the hell is Gerald? I feel sick. If she is with another man, I can't blame her, I have treated her terribly. But I can't bare it. The idea of her with someone else is filling me with a rage that I can't control.
I called Charlotte in and the sheer joy at the card and the flowers was clear upon her face. She looked so happy and I feel shit. I said some really hurtful things and wouldn't let her take the flowers. So childish. Now I am going to have to apologise and make it up some how but everything I say is going to make things worse.

I have called Charlotte and she won't pick up. I have now text her and confessed all about Alice. I just wish I had told her before she caught Alice saying goodbye in my office. Now she thinks I have been cold because of an affair with Alice rather than the weight of the guilt. I don't know how to make this better, I think I have just made things worse.

I had to get Security Steve to escort Alice out of the building and make sure she isn't allowed back in. She just doesn't take no for an answer.

I remember Gerald now. He was the homeless guy she gave a room to. Now I feel even worse.

Charlotte finally text back wishing me and Alice all the best for the future. I tried to call her back but the phone just goes dead, I think she has blocked me. I deserve this so am not going to moan about the injustice of it all. You reap what you sew.

22nd January

Josh called me to ask what is going on with me and Charlotte. It's funny, he doesn't want me with her but he doesn't want me not with her either. I'm so confused. I told him that I was in love with Charlotte but had sex with Alice. It meant nothing and was a mistake, but I didn't know how to get over the guilt. I told him that I hadn't asked Charlotte out yet so wasn't in a relationship with her. Not sure I even believe that. I felt very much in a relationship with Charlotte after we had sex and I know the reason why I felt so guilty about Alice was because I felt like a cheat.

Charlotte is still ignoring me. Emma bought me my mail today. WTF.

On a plus point Alice's plane should have taken off two hours ago. One problem solved.

23rd January

Josh just rang, he thinks Charlotte is pregnant. I have never heard him so angry. He called me a liar and all manner of slime bag things. He doesn't think she knows.

I went out and bought a pregnancy test. I felt a little humiliated because I recognised the girl across the counter as one of my friend Ben's ex girlfriends. I don't really need this rumour spreading around town so I tell her it is for a member of staff. She bought it despite the fact that most rational women can buy their own tests in more private settings.

Charlotte is late for work and I'm working myself up into a frenzy. Zoella has been in twice for no reason whatsoever and I'm struggling to hold it all together.

Charlotte has done the test and she is pregnant. The test shows clearly that its mine but I knew that anyway. I don't know why I even mentioned Scott's name. She was on a period the night I met her. We argued. She did the test then she ran out howling and now I realise how insensitive I have been. I should have given her the test to do at home or not been so harsh about it. I should have used a condom, I keep one in my wallet, I just didn't think and now no one knows where she is. Her bag is at work so she has no keys, no phone, no money, no tube pass. Where would she go?

Charlotte was found sleeping on the roof. She looked awful when Josh brought her in. I tried to speak to her but she told me to leave.

I have really screwed up this time. Not sure things could get any worse.

24th January

I have booked me and Charlotte a long weekend away in Venice. Just me and her, hopefully we can be honest and work things out.

I need to get things back on track and also we need to talk about the baby and where we are going to live. (Presuming that she will consider moving in with me after everything I've done.)

Josh rang Charlotte in sick but she will be back on Thursday.

The cleaner found the pregnancy test in my office bin and has very unprofessionally told Buddy about it. I'm now processing her P45 as I write and considering his.

28th January

Josh left for Hogmanay on the 25th but sent me a warning text before he left. *Charlotte deserves better.*

Charlotte was late for work and I remember worrying that she wouldn't make it in. The lift has been out for several days and it should have been fixed yesterday but wasn't. Matt was late for work and he was heard screaming for help on the stairwell. We all dropped everything and rushed down the flights of stairs to find him pinning Alice to the ground whilst trying to call an ambulance. I couldn't see at first who the ambulance was for. Alice had scratched his head and was screaming like a banshee but both looked fine. It wasn't until Buddy ran to help him pin Alice down and stood in shock to the sight around the corner. I heard him whisper Charlotte's name and my legs gave way.

167

There was blood everywhere and I couldn't even see where it was coming from. I tried talking to her but she was unconscious, lying in a heap. Emma felt for a pulse and started checking for wounds while I just cried in disbelief. I was useless.

The police and ambulance arrived and Matt started telling them what had happened. Alice was still screaming but I can't remember what she was saying.

The scene keeps replaying in my head in my head but the volume won't come. It is like my ears burst with the shock of the situation and I still don't know what she said. Why didn't I pick Charlotte up for work?

I haven't gone back into work.

Charlotte is conscious, after three days but she has lost the baby and I'm not allowed in.

In my distress I forgot to ring Josh and tell him his sister had been attacked. Scott told him as he is still Charlotte's next of kin. Josh told Scott that he couldn't come down and I was ordered to leave. I have never seen him so upset.

How could something so perfect go so horribly wrong?

She does deserve better and I deserve to feel this awful. This is all my fault.

14th February

Everyone at work is buzzing about the fashion shoot except when they are around me. Most people are avoiding me and I can't blame them, my company is rubbish. The only people being nice to me are Buddy and Emma who have been to see Charlotte and are happy to report back to me. Zoella is furious but I think it is because I actually liked someone for a change and it wasn't her. That or the extra work load she is now struggling with.

I messaged Josh for a Charlotte update but he won't reply to my messages and neither will Charlotte. I visited while I knew Josh was at work but there were strict instructions not to let me in. I sat in the car and cried like a baby. I want to fix this and make it better but don't know how. I had to get updates from the others, Buddy said she couldn't walk, Dad said her face was still yellow from all the bruises. Now he knows all the details about us Dad has this new found love for Charlotte. He keeps telling me how lovely she is and out of all of his employees she was his favourite. Not sure what has bought all this on but my mum is probably giving him grief down the phone about the fact that I'm not married yet.

Alice had to go to court but I didn't go. Matt and Emma went to give statements but my dad pulled strings so that I didn't have to face her. She is being detained somewhere up north and her fiancé has refused to fly over. I bet she is fuming about the lack of attention she is getting. Weird that this is the woman who had me in a knot all this time.

As I haven't been allowed to see Charlotte I have been pouring my time into all things concerned with Charlotte. I now work on her desk helping Zoella with the mail and other Charlotte related tasks. I touch her things when Zoella leaves. I stole the pink pen that advertises a stationery company. It has slight indentations where she has chewed the end. I collected up the post-it notes that have her handwriting on them, these were the last things she touched. I'm pretty sure now that she will never come back to work here. She sent dad an email telling him not to hold her job open. He waited until every member of staff had left before he told me.

I have also poured my time into Charlotte's divorce and rebuilding my relationship with Josh. He has decided that he is moving to Scotland but I think this is a mistake. I like Megan, I think she is sweet but my God is she selfish. Josh has given up his job to be with her and she has just quit her job. She could work anywhere. Josh is talking to me again like normal which can only mean that charlotte is much better and he is holding less of a grudge against me.

Fingers crossed.

I met Scott. I went down to Densborough really to feel close to Charlotte but used the divorce papers as an excuse. Josh had got Charlotte to agree to some things and even though I could have mailed the paperwork I chose to set up a meeting instead. This guy clearly regrets treating Charlotte so badly. He confessed to still loving her and wanting her back and nearly didn't sign the papers. I used my powers of persuasion to tell him that if there was any chance for them they would be better to start a fresh and put all the other stuff behind them including their failed marriage. He finally agreed and signed.

I saw the girl Amber sitting in a cafe having coffee with a friend. I recognised her face from Charlotte's Facebook pictures. I suppose I can see what the appeal is but just seeing her sitting there her arrogance was clear. Her eyes were too narrow and her constant pout made it look like she was looking down on her friend. No wonder Charlotte didn't want to return.

Walking past an estate agents I saw a plot of land for sale. I popped in and asked a few questions and am certain it was the plot Amber had bought to build her house on. I bought it. Charlotte was sure that Amber had used Scott for his money to build this dream house of hers and it looked like that had all fallen through. Charlotte could have the land. Turn it into a car park or a car boot plot, either way this land would be a gift from me to do with what she wanted.

I left Densborough with a huge sense of triumph but arrived back in London with a sick feeling in my stomach. Charlotte had gotten over Scott, whom she had known for years, in less than a week. If my maths was correct, that meant she would have gotten over me in minutes.

27th February

I drove to the hospital today and watched Josh pick Charlotte up.

I offered her a large apartment in the city but she turned it down in favour of a small apartment close to a dingy hospital on the outskirts. I asked my dad if he could pull any kind of favours to get her a decent room but he said it wasn't that kind of place and that I was to let it go, I couldn't control everything.

I had considered getting out of the car to help her with all her stuff but she looked so happy that I couldn't intrude.

This is killing me. I can't breathe.

1st March

Charlotte has returned nearly all of the clothes I bought her. Alice trashed my house but Charlotte is killing me with kindness. None of it had been worn so it didn't smell of her. I noticed a few things missing including the champagne coloured Swarovski dress and shoe set. My heart hopes a little bit that she kept them out of sentimentality but that would be more than I deserve.

Charlotte sent me a letter asking me to stop texting her and give her time to process. I must have read it twenty times and can't squeeze an ounce of affection from it. There are no kisses, no love from, nothing. It's fair but hurts like hell. I am clinging to a thin strand of hope that she still feels something towards me but the more I think about our strange relationship the less likely that seems. We didn't share enough moments or go on enough dates. Would I give me a second chance? The truth is I definitely wouldn't.

I can only wait now until she contacts me. This is excruciating. I hate my own company and hate other people's company more.

If Zoella asks me to go out for coffee one more time I'm going to explode.

21st March

Charlotte's divorce is now finalised. I wrestled with the idea of texting her to congratulate her but I kept talking myself out of it. My old college friends are going to The Loft on Friday and have asked if I am going. I have declined the last three and am running out of excuses. I don't want to be around people but I don't want to be on my own all I do is check Charlotte's Facebook, which she hasn't been updating. I think she works at the same hospital as my friend Ben but I can't bring myself to ask him about her. His Facebook says he is going out to The Loft on Friday for a birthday. I have just messaged my college pals and accepted the invite. If there is any chance that Charlotte may be there I need to take it.

I had better shave.

Chapter 20

I kept Ryan's diary in my bedside drawer and started writing in it like I would have my own.

He would have read mine by now and know how much I was in love with him despite everything that happened. It wasn't something I could control I didn't even know exactly when it had happened. I just knew that I wanted to spend the rest of my life with him and I couldn't wait for the that chapter to start.

I spent the week fantasying about how our long weekend in Venice would have been then I slowly phased it out of my head. The 'what ifs' had to go and a more positive me had to take over.

Work dragged on, it was like Friday wouldn't come. It felt like waiting for my tenth birthday all over again. I swear that was the longest year ever.

I took a detour after work, despite my rush to get ready and see Ryan's face, I needed to speak to Ben about Meela.

"Hello. I wasn't expecting you to throw yourself at my door," he laughed letting me in. "Especially not when you have Ryan Emerson at your feet." He pulled a face. "The amount of girls that would kill to get a look from him."

I raised my eyebrows and watched the blood drain from his face.

"Sorry, I just meant, figuratively, obviously you did nearly die for him. Harsh stuff, Sorry."

"That isn't why I'm here, Ben. I feel awful about Meela and Freya."

His face dropped. He might say this was none of my business but Meela had spent the last couple of days going on about how much she loved him and I couldn't advice her properly based on what I know.

"It isn't really your business is it?" He slumped down on his sofa.

"I know and you don't have to tell me anything. I just feel awful listening to Meela rave about what an excellent boyfriend you are when I know that you're not."

"Thanks."

"You know what I mean. Tell me how I can help." I slumped down beside him.

"Can you make Meela latch onto someone else?" He rubbed his hands through his hair.

"Can you try to be less of a dick?" I suggested.

He laughed. "I guess I had that coming. The thing is I like Meela. I really wanted her when I knew I couldn't have her and now I'm not sure whether I craved her or the idea of her. Freya was a mistake. I have told her that." He ran his hands through his hair. "The enormity of what Meela went through and the pressure that I am now all she has, it is suffocating."

"Okay, this is what I suggest. You tell Meela that you need a break and use that time to sort your head out."

"How am I supposed to do that, she gave up everything for me?" He looked desperate and for the first time I felt a bit sorry for him.

"Tell her that you are feeling the pressure and you just need the both of you to take a few steps back to make sure that she is doing, she is doing for all the right reasons. She can't focus everything on you or your relationship will suffocate."

He nodded. "So, she won't think I am breaking up with her rather that we need to slow it down. Yes!" He stood up and started pacing the floor. "Then if she does find out about Freya, I can say it was when we were on a break."

"I didn't come up here to give you ideas on how to be a bigger dick." I shook my head and stood up to leave.

"I adore Meela, I do. I just think I have had a little cold feet which will pass. She is really clingy."

I left Ben dialling Meela's phone number. It hadn't quite gone as expected but at least I wouldn't have to feel like I was a part of Ben's lie. If he liked Freya then he really should be honest to Meela about his lack of commitment to her.

I shook off the bad feeling I had and stepped into the shower. In less than two hours Ryan would pick me up and we would go to dinner.

Smart casual what does that even mean? I put on a trouser suit and matching jacket. One of the new purchases I had made with my redundancy money. Emerson's had continued to pay me even though I had barely worked there and I think there had been a mistake on my rent. That or Ryan was paying most of it. It was far too cheap.

My phone beeped as I dried my hair, it was Meela surprisingly happy. She took Ben's let down as a positive sign that he wanted to take the next step. Having this break meant they would both see how much they missed each other.

I shook my head. Either way I wouldn't feel so rotten every time I looked at her.

I text her back telling her to totally ignore him until he comes running. Hopefully that would be exactly what would happen.

I was ready too early but then Ryan turned up early too. I had expected him to have flowers or something corny but he didn't and I found myself a little disappointed.

"You look beautiful." He planted a kiss on my cheek and opened the taxi door.

"You too," I smiled. He was wearing dark jeans and a bright white shirt that looked brand new.

I handed him his diary and he handed me mine. We hadn't spoken since the diary swap, not even by text, the weight of which had been unbearable. The urge to text him had been so strong all week.

I told him this.

"I know, I felt the same but I thought it was important to let you set the pace." He locked his fingers around mine and kissed my knuckles.

"Why are we at The Loft? I didn't know they do food here." I frowned as the taxi pulled up. It was early for a Friday night but the place was already starting to fill up.

"They don't," he said. A man on a moped pulled up with a take-away bag. "You're paying, don't forget," he smirked and nodded to the scooter man.

I pulled out my purse and paid the bill.

"Chinese takeaway isn't exactly what I had in mind," I said. He grabbed my hand and led me up the stairs and out onto the forgotten smoking patio.

The scene was breathtaking. He had decorated the whole patio with fairy lights and candles which were arranged around a centre round table set with a red glitter table cloth.

"Wow! You could charge for this service. They are really missing a trick here." I smiled as he led me to my chair.

"Sadly they have someone coming in next week to install a perspex barrier so they can open it up again. I feel like I will be losing my only sanctuary."

He moved around me and slid off my jacket. His fingers lingered slightly on my shoulders then he quickly moved them away.

"You will always have the shelter at Primrose Hill," I smiled.

"Ah yes," he started laughing. "Now you know how long it took me to erect the stupid thing."

"I do," I looked at him fondly. I didn't want to talk about the diaries. He knew how I felt and I knew what he had been through too. The idea of picking over it embarrassed me for some reason and I just wanted to move past it.

I helped dish up the Chinese while he poured the wine.

"What is it?" Ryan asked when we were seated.

"Is there anything that you want to talk about?" *Please say no, please say no*

"I don't know what else is there is to say. I screwed up." He looked down at his plate.

"I don't want to go over it, any of it," I shook my head. "What happened *happened*. It is in the past."

He looked momentarily crushed then quickly regained his composure. "Friends then?" *Friends?*

This isn't what I wanted. After reading his diary this isn't what I thought he wanted.

"Is that what you want?" I was afraid of the answer but needed to ask the question.

"I want you in my life, Charlotte. I will take whatever you give me." He reached over and laid his hand on top of mine. A thrill swept through my body.

"I am happy to start again from scratch, as if nothing ever happened." I took a leap of faith.

"How can you forget it all?" He leant back in his chair, looking doubtful.

"I want to be with you, I want to trust you but most importantly I don't want to be with you if you constantly feel the need to apologise or feel that you have to make up for something."

"I see," he frowned. He sat up and started digging into his dinner, deep in thought.

"Have you heard from Josh?" I asked after we had finished and had moved to the padded corner seat.

"Yes, he asked me to be best man which totally surprised me. I still can't get over it."

"Well, who else would he pick?" I smiled.

"Someone who wasn't responsible for the near death of his sister."

"Do we need another visit to Primrose Hill?" I pulled my jacket over my shoulders.

"Maybe, I do have a lot of issues." He put his arm around me and I was surprised how natural it felt.

"What would you like to do now?" I asked.

"It's your date," he smiled. "Though I do have to be at work early tomorrow as the issue is about to go to print and we are so behind." He rubbed his temples.

"Anything I can do to help?" I offered.

"Ha ha, yes you can take your old job back and reset the balance of the universe."

"Argh, you guys falling apart without me?"

"Kind of, somehow several bits of last months magazine got duplicated by mistake so what we thought was a full issue is now seriously lacking and we were behind anyway. Dad hired a temp to cover your position but she bailed after two days and there was no one to replace her. Keeley has announced she isn't returning and wouldn't even come in for a few days to tide us over. Now we have to cram a months worth of work into a week."

"I do have some time off now, I could help." I touched his hand. "I do know how to use the printer and sort the mail at least."

"That is really all that is needed. It is mainly running things from one department to another. Honestly you haven't seen anything like it, it's chaos." He frowned and looked down. "Most of it is my fault. I was good for nothing for at least a month and I'm surprised my father didn't kill me."

"Okay, but no touching," I announced.

"Okay to what? And why no touching?" He leant in and ran his thumb over my jaw line.

"Okay, I will arrive at Emerson's at half eight tomorrow morning, even though it is a Saturday and there should be a law against it." I leant in so my breasts were touching his chest and whispered in his ear. "But we must have a no touching at work rule."

"And out of work?" He raised his eyebrows.

"We will be far too tired for the first week anyway," I leant back in my chair and put my feet up on the low table.

"My father will think I have guilt tripped into you coming back."

"Tell him that it will be good therapy for both of us. I have the week free but I have to be back in the hospital Saturday evening then I'm on mornings for four in a row, so can't really offer more than a week. I have to be in Densborough next Thursday so I can't offer anything after that I'm afraid. Scott's sister Sarah has died." I shifted uncomfortably in my seat. "I have refused the invitation to go to the funeral on the Friday but I do want to pop down there and give my card and condolence in person."

"Do you want me to drive you?"

"No, thanks. My train ticket is all booked. Scott is taking me out to lunch. I have decided to confess all."

"Not the robbery?" Ryan looked horrified but I wasn't sure whether it was the idea of a full confession or that Scott was taking me out to lunch.

"No," I laughed at his outrage. "But I am going to admit that I knew it was Amber and I might even tell him that I cloned his phone."

"Ouch, let me know how that goes."

"It's weird but I feel like that life is so far away from me now, like it happened, but to someone else like in a movie." I drank more wine.

"I know it seems weird knowing how I felt about you so early on and how you felt about me, it's crazy to think that you were happy with him two weeks before," Ryan shifted in his seat.

"I wasn't happy. I just didn't know it," I shrugged. "I wasn't even really living. You wrote a bit in your diary about my clothes and I think it kind of summed up my life. It fitted so I didn't care. Elastic is all well and good but tailored is definitely better."

He burst out laughing. "Elastic, one size fits all." He leant in and kissed me gently on the mouth. "Does that mean that I am the better fit?"

"Without a doubt," I smiled.

We stayed until midnight talking like we had known each other forever. I declined the offer of the second bottle of wine. We both had an early start in the morning and I was really looking forward to it.

He went to kiss me as the taxi pulled up outside my flat but I playfully pulled away.

"I want to be in your life but I want to go so slowly that when you finally do kiss me again it's because you can't stand to not do it any longer. I want the sexual tension to be so unbearable that you think you are going to pop." I leant in and kissed his cheek.

"Does that mean you would consider us becoming a couple?" He grabbed my hand his face full of hope.

"Yes, it was a really good date."

I smiled and headed back to my little box of an apartment. Somehow it seemed smaller and drabber than before.

I couldn't believe how excited I was to be returning to the magazine, it was ridiculous.

Slightly drunk, I laid out my clothes, shoes and make-up. I showered and set my hair in a bun maker so it would be curly in the morning. It was like a first date.

I had a little further to travel and googled tube times so I wouldn't be late. I was giddy and I couldn't suppress the silly smile on my face.

In hospital I had decided that I would never return. I had thought that the sight of the stairs or just seeing the old staff would have broken me but when Ryan had stressed their need of me, my insides had performed a mini celebration and I couldn't wait to see those faces.

Brooke handed me my badge which had been in Ryan's office and called the lift for me, I declined and took the stairs. I felt her eyes on my back as I turned the corner but I didn't mind the gossip. I needed to face the demons and the scene of the crime wasn't going to break my good mood today.

I hovered on the second set of stairs. There was no sign that anything had taken place here. No memorial, no spot of blood, nothing. The new security camera was the only new addition.

I walked on. I was fine. I was going to be fine.

I don't know what I had expected when I arrived but Ryan hadn't down played the chaos. The sales team were barely visible under piles of paperwork, shouting was coming from Lorena's room and Buddy was running through to the photographer's room leaving a trail of images that were too numerous for him to carry.

I smiled at Emma and Lynsey and ran behind Buddy to collect what he had dropped. Everyone stopped when I entered the room.

"Well, aren't you a sight for sore eyes," Buddy smiled and gave me a squeeze.

I handed over the stray pictures and left to find my desk which was somewhere under three weeks of un-opened mail.

"Don't ask," Zoella shook her head as I cleared the parcels from my chair. "We had a few temps, it…" She trailed off and her voice went quiet.

"Are you alright?" I hoped she wasn't going to cry.

She nodded but looked far from convinced.

I decided not to look up. If I avoided eye contact she might be okay. I pulled several empty boxes out of the printer room and started separating the mail. Anything that looked like junk got piled in the back, anything for Ryan went into another and VIP I piled up for Zoella though she didn't look well enough to be given it so I put it into a separate box.

"Charlotte, how good is it to see you?" Angus from accounts swung in and waved a box of chocolates in my face.

"Ooh, Thank you," I selected a green triangle chocolate. "Anything in this heap that is urgent?" I waved my hand across the desk that was still buried.

"Did Zoella not give you the list?" He shot Zoella a deadly stare and she just shrugged.

"No, was it hand written or typed? If it was typed just email it to me," I smiled, hoping to relieve the tension.

"Have you lost it?" Angus walked to Zoella's desk and I noticed Persia lingering at the doorway.

"It is on her desk," Zoella didn't look up. Clearly too busy to deal with Angus.

Angus shook his head and retreated back into his room and I heard Zoella let out her breath.

"Would you like a cup of tea?" I offered.

"You kidding right?" Zoella nodded at the paperwork drowning my desk.

"I'm not supposed to be here, I'm an extra. If you could benefit from a cup of tea, I'm quite happy to go get you one." I reasoned they weren't going to sack me for slacking when technically I wasn't even hired.

"Sure," Zoella raised her eyebrows and gave a look that said, 'On your head be it.'

I took the largest of the parcels down to Lorena who was on the phone to a supplier. She gave me a massive hug and squeezed my chin as if I was her grandchild.

She placed her palm over the mouth piece. "That lot was supposed to be signed off last week." She nodded to a pile of invoices.

I piled them into my trolley and entered Ryan's office. He was attached to a phone, on hold. His suit was new and tailored, paired with a bright white shirt. I also had opted for a white shirt, that was relatively new but it didn't look as white as his and I wondered if he wore them once then binned them.

"What no mail?" He looked up surprised.

"You're kidding, right?" I collected his paperwork that he had started piling on the floor. "There is going to be so much mail that you are going to need a week to read it all. I'm trying to prioritise. Is there anything that is urgent?" I straightened the paperwork and tried to keep my eye off the top button that had come undone on his shirt.

"Not from me, concentrate on the finance department. All this issues invoices need to be filed within a fortnight and I suspect half of them are still in people's out trays." He pulled a box out of his drawer and placed it on the table.

"What's this?" I asked.

"A thank you for saving us gift," he smiled.

I walked over and unwrapped the neatly wrapped box. Inside was a beautiful silver coloured watch. I held out my wrist so he could help me fasten it.

"Thank you, I love it." I rotated my wrist and admired the way it caught the light.

"Now every time you look at it you will think of me."

"Thanks." I leant over and kissed his forehead.

"What happened to the no kissing game?" He smirked.

"It only counts if tongues are involved."

"No, sorry Mr Greenson, I wasn't talking to you." Ryan cringed as his call had finally been connected.

I sniggered and left the room before I thought about the dressing room and all the time we could waste in there.

I made Zoella's tea while Emma piled up my trolley.

"You know this trolley is supposed to be empty by the time I get to my desk not the other way round," I joked.

"The temp was useless, she didn't even make it to the end of her second day," Aiden remarked before taking the next call.

"It has been crazy," Lynsey hung up the phone and ignored the immediate buzz of the next. "Three people should be there in the office, Keeley is gone, Zoella is doing Keeley's job but no one is doing Zoella's and I bet they are regretting not replacing Beth."

"Zoella has been buckling under the pressure. We have all took bets on when she is going to run out crying," Matt smirked.

"Not on my watch," I held up the tea and carried on with my rounds.

"You will need to drink it now, I didn't realise how much paperwork was to be collected from Buddy's room. He was so busy he didn't even have time to gossip." I laughed to Zoella.

"And neither do you." She nodded at the paperwork still on my desk.

"Rome wasn't built in a day." I refused to feel her pressure. "Who was Beth?" I asked.

"Beth was Persia's personal assistant. I stupidly said I could do both jobs but with Keeley gone it has been awful," her voice wobbled.

"Well, concentrate on doing your job and I will help out whenever I can. Think of me as your PA. I'm sure in a week we can get back to some sort of normality."

"You're here all week! Oh my God, I thought you were only here today" her relief was evident.

"Relax a little," I smiled and started slicing through the paperwork.

Zoella left for lunch at one without a word and at half one I really needed her advice. I had opened an advertising letter that should have been dealt with over a month ago.

I stood up and looked around. Persia and Mr Emerson were on a conference call and Ryan wasn't answering his phone.

I re- read the official looking letter. Two major companies paid us for advertising space on the premise that the back cover was alternated. Chanel one month, Dior, the other but for some reason we had put the same one on the cover for three months in a row, one more slip up and they were threatening to pull out.

I checked my watch. I could wait for Zoella but somehow this seemed pivotal and Ryan was nowhere to be seen.

I waved trying to get Persia's attention but her eyes were glued to the large screen. Interrupting a conference call was no mean feat.

I took a deep breath and entered Mr Emerson's forbidden office.

All eyes on me.

I apologised for the interruption. Mr Emerson's and Persia's faces were darkened at the interruption. I slipped the paper to Persia, whispered my apologies and walked out. Now the ball would be in her court.

A bang on the glass called me back through. The screen had been paused.

"Holy shit," Persia yelled. "When did this come through?" She started pacing.

"No idea, sorry, I only just opened it," I crossed my hands and started rubbing them nervously. "I'm really sorry to interrupt, Zoella is out and I didn't think it could wait."

I held my breath waiting for Mr Emerson to speak.

"It can't. Take this to Ryan, he should be in the graphics room. Jesus, now is not the time to lose our main advertiser." He handed me back the letter. "I'll check in after this call and make sure we are still on track."

Persia nodded at me and sat back down at the desk to resume the call.

Okay good call. I was worried then, I hate taking risks. The idea of getting into trouble fills me with dread.

I entered Buddy's office where Ryan and the graphics team were on a conference call. As I entered and Kyle looked sympathetic as once again all eyes were on me.

"Please forgive the interruption, there is an urgent call for Mr Emerson," I smiled wondering if Ryan would challenge my announcement.

He didn't. He frowned and followed me outside. I saw Buddy stand up to take over the call but his eyes kept darting on the window at us. "Did we not have a chat about lying?" Ryan smiled.

"Small lie," I handed him over the letter. "Urgent though."

"Shit!" He flipped over the letter. "How the hell did we miss this?"

"Is there time to fix it?" I asked.

"Let's find out." He ran to the graphics room and grabbed the magazine mock up. "Can you please go to the store room and bring me the last twelve months of magazines? And from Persia's office I need Chanel and Dior's contracts."

I nodded and headed to Persia's office. I had no clue where to start looking hopefully her files were filed alphabetically.

"What do you need?" Persia asked after I had been searching for ten minutes.

I told her and she pulled the first one out at once.

"Sorry, I didn't want to interrupt you again."

"It's fine," She smiled and handed me the remaining contract. I noticed her look at Zoella's empty desk and then the clock. Not a good time for Zoella to be late. No doubt she would hear about it later on.

"Thanks," I smiled and headed to the store.

"You took your time." Ryan stressed when I re-entered the room.

"Sorry, I didn't know where they were kept," I shrugged. "Zoella is out for lunch and Persia was on a conference call in Mr Emerson's office." I handed him the paperwork and back issues and he and Buddy poured over them.

"Zoella's at lunch, Now?" Buddy shook his head. "I haven't even stopped for breakfast yet."

"Got it," Louisa yelled bringing up an image on her screen.

"Okay, cancelled the print job," Kyle yelled, hanging up the phone.

"Fab, Buddy, I trust you to sort this. I'm going to beg for mercy." He winked at me as he walked past to leave. "Always a sight to behold."

"Glad he is calm in a crisis," Kyle sniggered. "Flying by the seat of our pants here."

"We could have done with you last week," Buddy smiled and grabbed the phone.

I smiled and shrugged.

I was glad that I had offered to lend a hand.

Chapter 21

My hospital shift dragged.

After a week of the hustle and bustle of the magazine, going back to the hospital had seemed like a punishment of sorts.

Gone were my feelings of fierce independence and smugness that I had made all my own choices. I didn't want any of now. Even the smell of the hospital was making me feel sick. The only thing that cheered me up was Meela.

"We are going out on Friday, are you free?" She bounced beside me helping me with my medication rounds.

"I can't," I sighed. A night out was exactly what I needed. "I have to go to my old home town and sort some things out, then Ryan is taking me away for a surprise weekend away somewhere."

I had refused the funeral. I felt bad about it when Scott had ranted down the phone but I needed to deal with Sarah's death in my own way and standing along side a family that I didn't feel like I knew anymore just didn't feel right.

Thursday I would visit, deliver flowers to Scott's mum and dad, say my piece, then leave.

Ryan had the weekend off. The drama at the magazine was over for another month and the weekend was going to the first time that I was going to properly see him since we had made up.

We had agreed to not catch up during the week so he could straighten things out at the magazine so things didn't get that crazy again and it meant a lot of late nights.

"Your divorce is done, isn't it?" She asked.

"Yes, but I'm seeing my ex-husband for the first time since," I cringed. Scott had hinted at a reconciliation and I had been blunt on the phone but I still felt that this needed to be handled face to face. I would travel down by train and Ryan would pick me up in the afternoon and I would leave the stress of the past behind.

"Sounds awful," She paused. "I don't think Ben really likes me," she said out of nowhere.

"What makes you think that?" I asked, pleading ignorance.

"Just a few things Freya has said. Has he said anything to you?" She whispered as we approached a patient.

I used small talking with the patient as an excuse to think for a moment. I didn't want to lie but didn't want to give her false hope either.

"Only that what you have done is an enormous thing. I guess he feels the pressure," I smiled. "You're young and beautiful and could have any man that you want. Relax, now is the not the time to be thinking that your life needs to be pre-written and signed off."

She smiled and headed out in the opposite direction.

I saw Freya's worried face watching us from down the hall and wondered why I felt like I was a part of some dishonest conspiracy.

I waved as if nothing was said and went about the boring routine of my job.

Thursday morning couldn't come soon enough. I needed the change of scenery. The job was depressing me and my flat was making me claustrophobic. I had been tempted to ask Ryan if I could stay at his for a couple of nights but had decided against it. How could we take things slowly if I was in his house? And besides I knew that I would never want to come back to my shoebox after living in his luxurious penthouse for a week.

I put on my blue skinny jeans with the zips up the side and wore my black Converse that had been a gift from Max from the magazine. He had laughed at me running through the offices in my heels and insisted I took the running shoes instead of the kitten heels. It had been a good trade, I loved them. They looked good with the cream camisole top and the backless jumper. It wasn't particularly cold but I slipped on my new fake leather jacket courtesy of Lorena. That was the good thing about the magazine, there were a lot of freebies.

I tubed to the magazine and used my id card, that I hadn't returned, to get upstairs. Mr Emerson had asked to see me before I caught my train. He hadn't said why but I guessed it was to thank me for helping out in their crisis week. He still hadn't stopped paying me from before, despite my protests, so it couldn't be about pay.

I took a deep breath as I exited the lift. I could smell the hairspray and the ink from the photocopier. I liked it, it smelt like home.

I smiled at Emma and co on the sales desk and they blew me kisses while chatting away on the phones.

Buddy waved despite being on a conference call. Everybody was more relaxed, a stark contrast to last week.

"Hey beautiful," Ryan grabbed my hand as I walked down the centre aisle of the office. "All ready for later?"

"You make it sound like surgery." I laughed enjoying the feel of his warm fingers in mine.

"Well, it is Scott, and I hear that he is going to offer you a second chance, you lucky girl."

"Are you and Josh still reading their phone messages?" I stopped him as we reached what had been desk.

"Maybe," he shrugged innocently, "every now and then." He gave some paperwork to Zoella and walked back to his office.

"Hey Charlotte," Zoella laughed, "missing us all already?"

"Mr Emerson asked to see me," I checked my new watch. I had an hour and a half before my train arrived.

"I'll let him know that you are here." She got up and called through the office door. "Go through, he's expecting you."

"Charlotte," Mr Emerson stood and took my hand in both of his.

"Hello Mr Emerson, things seem calmer this week." I smiled and took the seat he offered opposite his.

"Henry, please, you are dating my son. I can't be doing with all these formalities," he slid the magazine across the table. "Gets released on Friday. The week after final submission is always the quietest before we go mad and do it all over again," he laughed.

"Do you have time for coffee?"

I nodded.

He called through Zoella and she arrived a while later with coffee.

"You know the accountants have their own coffee machine in their offices, why don't you?" I laughed.

"I don't drink much to be fair, besides it makes Zoella feel important."

A door to the right opened and Persia walked in.

"You may know why we have asked you here," Mr Emerson said smiling at Persia.

I shook my head.

"Keeley isn't coming back which leaves us with one, possibly two, jobs available," Mr Emerson said.

"We would like to offer you the job of my PA," she smiled.

I took a deep breath. "Isn't that Zoella's job?"

"Well, actually it was Beth's job. Beth left to go to New York and was supposed to come back in the new year, but we have heard nothing. Keeley stepped up and did Beth's job and Zoella stepped into Keeley's position. This hasn't really worked out," Persia said.

"Oh" I looked from face to face. Did they want a decision now? "What would happen to Zoella?" A dread formed in my stomach. Could I work beside her knowing that I had taken her job?

"She would go back into her old job," Mr Emerson looked nervously at Persia.

"Zoella was never given or guaranteed Beth or Keeley's job so it isn't as if you would be stepping on her toes," Persia added.

"I have loved working here…," I started.

"And we have loved having you here which is why we are offering you the full time position," Mr Emerson smiled.

I thought about it. This week at the hospital had been dull in comparison. I had been inadvertently seduced by the gloss and the glamour and I wasn't going to lie, I wanted the job.

"Okay, the thing is," I sipped my coffee and leant back in my chair, "I want to work here. The hospital just seems mundane and I have loved the challenges here but I would feel awful pushing Zoella out. The guys seem to be happy with the job I have been doing, they like the way I do the mail. Would I not be better sticking the role you know that I am good at?"

"How about a trial to see how you go?" Mr Emerson said.

I thought for a moment, "If you are employing two people to do three people's jobs, why don't you scrap all the jobs and re-create them as two. That way you can give me the responsibilities you think I would do better and Zoella wouldn't feel pushed out," I suggested.

"Yes, I guess we could have a word with her. Last week really stressed her out so I could find out what she liked and what she didn't," Persia mused.

"I would rather Charlotte did the mail," Mr Emerson added as if I wasn't there.

"Agreed. The advertising debacle was a close call. Zoella had already opened a warning letter about it and ignored it, she can't be trusted with the mail. I'm also not happy about the lunch breaks," Persia nodded.

"You can set out new contracts with new guidelines in them. We clock in and out of the building so perhaps lunch breaks could be more closely monitored," I said, feeling a bit of traitor for suggesting it.

"And you will take the second job?" Mr Emerson pressed his hands together.

"As long as you don't have a no staff dating rule," I laughed.

"You two work very well together, no one here had a clue," he smiled.

"I like to keep my work and private life separate," I said though wasn't entirely sure this was true. It wasn't really something I had thought about but I was pretty sure that if Ryan asked me to join him in his dressing room, I wouldn't refuse.

"Excellent, leave it with us and we will be in touch. How much notice do you need to give at the hospital?" Persia asked.

"Three weeks," I couldn't remember if it was two or three so better safe than sorry.

Zoella looked down as I left the office. I guessed she had an inkling to what the meeting was about and sure enough Buddy collared me on my way past and asked me if I was getting Zoella's job.

"Not Zoella's job but they have offered me a job." I made an excuse and left his office. It wasn't my place to tell them anything.   Ryan called me into Lorena's room where Ruby and Marsha were working on some models.

"I hear you are going to see the ex," Ruby smirked as she finished a model's French Manicure. She pointed toward the empty chair.

I nodded. "I don't really need to be pimped up, it's just Densborough."

"And a weekend away with me!" Ryan smiled. I raised my eyebrows but he disappeared before I could question him about his plans.

"It will take two minutes." Ruby's voice went up at the end.

"Okay, if it will make you happy." I conceded. I was meeting up with Cassie and Amber and part of me wanted to look my best if only to show how far I had come.

I left forty minutes later and had to run for my train.

Densborough hadn't changed. It was as if someone had pressed pause on a remote control and the whole place had held its breath until I returned. It was ghostly and seemed incredibly small. I don't really know why I thought it should be different, it wasn't as if I was coming back years later, it was less than four months since I had been here last.

Picking up a funeral bouquet was a drama. The lady in the shop stressed that I should of ordered and that there was no way I would be able to have anything done by tomorrow. Because I had opted out of attending the funeral I decided on a bouquet for Scott and Sarah's mum instead. I ordered a second bouquet for Aunt Maureen, who had been released from hospital and said I would pick them up later. The woman was still moaning about how everybody knows they should order when I walked out.

I played a game on the walk to Scott's parents house to see if I could remember what was around the corner, longing for a surprise. It never came. The same shops still had the same 'Help Wanted' signs up and the same members of staff still worked in the same shops like a stagnate pool, no one had moved on or even changed tills. I looked at them and some smiled back. Maybe some had noticed my absence but I doubted it. In a town this small everyone should have known everyone but it just wasn't that sort of place. Most kept day dreaming out of the window longing to be anywhere other than there without doing a single thing about it.

That wasn't going to be me. I didn't want to work at the hospital anymore, I had lost the love for it. Maybe I never had any love for it in the first place, either way I had composed and sent my resignation via email from the train and would now count down the days until I was back at the magazine. My life had finally begun and there was an excitement inside of me that was because of so many things. I just needed to tie up a few lose ends then I would never need to look back.

I knocked at Scott's mother's door with a heavy heart. I didn't know why I was so nervous I think it was because I didn't want to be here. I had only met Sarah a handful of times, the last time I had seen her had been another lifetime ago in my kitchen when I told Scott that I knew of his affair.

It would have felt wrong going to her funeral feeling everything that I felt now and even though I hadn't really forgiven Scott or his parents for the way they had treated me over Christmas, I still felt guilty enough to have to travel this far to explain.

"Charlotte." Janice pulled a face as if surprised to see me knocking at her front door. She drew me into a hug and kissed both cheeks. I couldn't remember the last time she had welcomed me this fondly.

I forced a smile on my face, I needed to get out of here as quickly as possible. "Hello,

I'm so sorry for your loss." I handed her the card and flowers and followed her into the kitchen.

A large picture of Sarah and her dogs was beautifully framed ready for the service. I remarked how beautiful the picture was and how lovely Sarah was despite the fact that I didn't know her well.

"Shame you can't come tomorrow. It's times like these that family should stick together." She pursed her lips together into a thin line.

I noticed Scott enter the room with his trainers in his hands and do a double take at the sight of me.

"Well, we aren't family anymore, are we?" I smiled at Scott to show it wasn't an insult.

"We will always be family." She tapped my hand in what was supposed to be a reassuring gesture. "You were a large part of my son's life for a long time, we will never forget that."

I just stared at her and wondered if now was really the time to lay it straight.

"She only just got here Mum." Scott perched on a bar stool and struggled with his shoes.

"I know but it seems such a shame not to say that I hope you two work it out." She turned to me with a wistful look on her face, "You always meant the world to us Charlotte."

"Really? Because I didn't get a Christmas card or a present, or any kind of message." It fell out of my mouth before I could stop it.

"Well, it was a tricky time and we didn't really know how to behave." She fussed with teas and I looked at Scott for support but he just stared at me as if seeing me for the first time.

"That's in the past now," Scott's dad, Greg, appeared out of nowhere and gave Janice a kiss on the cheek.

"Indeed. I hope tomorrow goes well for you all anyway and I am truly sorry for your loss," I repeated. I turned to Scott. "Are you ready?"

"Are you not eating here?" Janice looked startled.

"I thought we were eating at Headly's on the high street." I kept my fingers crossed for Scott to confirm this.

He shrugged. "We need to talk Mum."

Her features brightened and I wondered what she thought we would be discussing.

Scott grabbed his coat and headed towards the door. Janice swooped me to one side, grabbing my hand as she spoke. "I hope you two can get back together, we all make mistakes you know." She started rubbing my hand. "If Sarah has taught us nothing else it is that life is too short to hold grudges."

"I am never getting back together with Scott." Might as well be honest.

She jolted back as if I had slapped her.

"Scott slept with my best friend behind my back for two years. He poisoned me to make sure that I miscarried our baby." Her face contorted in shock but I needed to be clear. "He stole money from me to give to Amber and he forged my signature to mortgage our house to give her even more money. And if that wasn't enough he took everything from the house, even things that weren't his. My mum's hall table which was all I had left of her, he threw it in Amber's garage and smashed it without a second thought to how I would feel about it. He did it to hurt me and I never want to go back to that kind of life." Greg was lurking in the background but I just carried on as if I was a pre-recorded message that couldn't be stopped. "I came to pay my respects to a family that have given me no respect. Once I leave here today I will not ever have any reason to return." I forced a smile and left her standing in the hallway. She must have known half of the details at least. I remembered listening in to the conversation over Christmas between Scott and Amber, she had been sitting next to him while they spoke. He hadn't even tried to hide it. Maybe she had known all along. I shook the annoyance off. It didn't matter now, the past was gone, never to be revisited again.

Scott was already sitting in the car warming up the engine of what had once been my main mode of transport. Nothing had changed there either. The same Jellybean air freshener still hung on the mirror, the scent long gone. My fluffy white blanket was strewn over the backseat where I had thrown it after sitting by the river last. I put on my seat belt and opened the glove box. Three Now CDs sat exactly where I had left them.

"Do you want some music on?" He leant across me to grab the CD at the top. His arm un-necessarily brushed my leg in the process but he didn't apologise.

"Whatever is fine with me. Why are we driving?" The high street was within walking distance.

"Because I need to go to work straight after. I told them I had a dentist appointment," he smirked, lying came so easily to him.

We got out and headed towards the cafe. Later I would meet Cassie and Amber several doors down the road and I wondered if we would bump into them while I was with Scott and if so, how would Amber act?

I shook the idea out of my head. They had split up, Josh had confirmed it and if they got back together what did I care? For the first time in my life I felt entirely comfortable where I was. Ryan had made mistakes and I had forgiven them because deep down I knew that I was in love with him.

"What are you smiling for?" Scott asked as he held the door open to the cafe, a gesture that I don't think he had ever done before. Scott was an advocate for equal opportunities not realising that holding the door open for whoever happened to be behind was actually good manners and nothing to do with gender expectations.

I shrugged off my jacket and took a seat in the dark booth at the back of the cafe. We were the only customers yet it still took the waitress five minutes to approach our table to offer drinks.

We ordered and Scott got straight to business. "You look really good Charlotte, have you missed me?"

Something about his cockiness annoyed me but also amused me. He clearly had the wrong impression as to why we were here.

"I have been really busy," I smiled. "I can't believe how fast the time has gone."

"I know," Scott frowned. "I collected the mail from the new people in our house yesterday, they seem there for the long haul. There was nothing for you though."

"I re-directed it, didn't you do the same?"

He shook his head. "Mum keeps telling me to sort myself out but I've been busy. The Decree Nisi came through really fast. I didn't feel ready,"

"I had a good lawyer," I smiled. Ryan wasn't going to let anyone drag their heels.

"I know, I met him," he said. "Did you meet him, he was super aggressive."

"I know Ryan well, he is a friend of Josh's." An un-controllable smile crept on my face. "He was actually at our wedding."

"Really!" Scott raised his eyebrows in disbelief.

The food came and we were silent while we ate. Every now and then I would catch Scott staring at me but he didn't look away. I shifted uncomfortably in my seat, why did this feel like a date all of a sudden?

"I just thought while I was passing through we might as well meet and clear a few things up," I said, no point in delaying the inevitable. "Is there anything you wanted to say?" Like *sorry.* I thought to myself.

"There is a party Saturday night at The Crypt, did you want to come?" He smiled and rather than find him charming I just found him annoying. "For old times sake. Maybe we could talk about starting again."

"Starting what again?" I asked. Surely he didn't mean what I thought he meant.

"You know, us?" He waved his hand between us.

"I think you have behaved like a dick. Why on earth would you think that you have anything that I want?" No point in beating around the bush.

"Look, you got the wrong end of the stick…," he started but I butted in.

"So you didn't have sex with my best friend behind my back?"

He looked struck and felt in his pocket for his mobile that he must have left at home.

"And you didn't forge my signature to mortgage the house?"

His eyes grew wider but I didn't stop.

"You didn't slip a drug into my tea forcing me to miscarry?"

He put down his cutlery and cleared his throat to speak but I wasn't finished.

"You cleared out the house not caring what was yours and what was mine. You had no respect for me at all and you deserve none of my time."

"There is no need to be cruel," he raised his voice.

"I'm not being cruel, I'm being kind. Which is a damn sight more than you were to me. I just want to be clear here as to which end of the stick I think I'm holding. I'm also a little curious in what makes you think you are such a good idea for me." I spooned in some of the jacket potato that seemed reheated.

"I signed all your paperwork." He didn't blink.

"How did you spend your Christmas?"

"You know how I spent my Christmas." His voice was turning sulky.

"Yes, in a cabin that I paid for watching fireworks paid for by me. Now think about how

I spent my Christmas."

"How would I know how you spent your Christmas?" He snapped.

"Well, have a little think of what you left behind in the house. I had a chicken defrosting in the sink but you took it, I had a bed, that I had paid for but you took it. So what do you think I ate? Where do you think I slept?"

He shrugged, "At Josh's mansion in London."

"Josh was in Scotland. The point is you acted the way you did because you couldn't have given a shit about me. You took the bed not caring at all where I would sleep. You didn't need the bed you were going to the cabin. You took the food, just because you could. You took the car not even giving a second thought as to whether I had bus money or not and worse you enlisted the help of my only friends which are also now lost to me."

"The car was mine," he retorted as if that righted all of his wrongs.

I tried a different tack. "Okay, all things considered, tell me one redeeming quality that you think you have. What do you think I should be thinking and feeling right now?"

"I just thought that time apart would have softened you a little."

"What do you mean? Like I would forget all the shitty things you have done and want you back." I couldn't believe what I was hearing. Sitting here opposite him I felt nothing. No sense of nostalgia no sense of loss or remorse. "So what have you done that makes you the kind of person I would want to spend my life with? I'm confused. You ruined everything and expect so much from me when you have given me nothing. Explain it to me."

"Where did you get the idea from that I was seeing Amber?" He sat up straight, ready to defend himself.

"I read the texts on her phone," not a total lie. "Yours said work but hers wasn't so cloak and dagger."

"It was a mistake, I got swept away." He looked crestfallen and for a second I felt a little sorry for him. Amber did have something about her that got everyone running around her and eating out of the palm of her hand. But marriage is a life choice that shouldn't be taken lightly. If you can't be honest then perhaps it was never right in the first place.

"Then you should have said two years ago or however many years ago it started, that you wanted out of our marriage. You could have set up house with Amber and I could have moved on and had children with someone who actually wanted them."

"I do want them now," he leant over and took my hand.

My words were falling on deaf ears. What was this guy thinking?

"Look, I feel a little bad about not coming to Sarah's funeral but your family didn't even wish me a Merry Christmas or give me a second thought. I owe you guys nothing." I took my hand away and placed it in my lap.

"Perhaps you're more like Amber than you think," he scoffed.

"In what way? Did I sleep with her fella? Er no. Did I try and cheat her friend out of money so I could build a pipe dream house? Er no. Did I help poison my best friend and sit by and watch while her life fell apart when she lost a baby? Er no. If that is the kind of woman you thought for one second that you could be happy with, then I wish you the best of luck because she is one of a kind. There is no-one else quite like Amber."

I checked my watch and instantly thought of Ryan. I had to meet Amber and Cassie in less than half an hour, I really needed to wrap this up. I needed a clear head to work out what I was going to say to them.

"I just meant your bluntness. Amber knows what she wants and she takes it." I couldn't tell if he meant this as a positive or a negative.

"I don't see the point in beating around the bush. I needed to meet with you so I knew that everything that was left unsaid had been said and that there was nothing hanging over us. I want nothing more to do with you or your family, or Densborough for that matter. I'm done." I replaced my cutlery though not finished. My appetite had gone not helped by the fact that the jacket potato was rock solid at the bottom and some of the cheese was rock solid. London may have been busier but the quality was certainly better.

"I just thought you would feel differently after time," he shrugged.

"Maybe if you had apologised at any point or at least pretended to acknowledge what a hideous person you have been to me but have heard nothing. I really don't understand what aspect of us you think was that great that I would move back here and re-live it."

I waved for the bill.

"I thought you loved me."

"And I thought the same of you and look how you treated me."

I paid the bill and stood up.

"Loads of people make mistakes, Charlotte. I can do better."

"Well, I don't think you could have do any worse. I am with someone else now and it feels more real to me in the short time that we have been together than our whole marriage felt. I'm sorry but we had a crappy past and certainly don't have future."

"You didn't waste anytime," he spat. "Perhaps you *are* more like Amber than you think." He crossed his arms across his chest and blocked the door, demanding an explanation.

"At least I waited until we were separated unlike yourself. But like you say, it is all in the past and not worth going over again and again so this really is goodbye."

He moved to let another couple in and I ducked out behind them.

"Anything else you feel the need to say before I go?" I asked he might as well get closure as well.

He joined me outside and I closed my eyes briefly letting the sun warm my face. I felt like a huge weight, I didn't even know was there, had been lifted off my shoulders.

"No, I think you have covered it all. I am a shit and our marriage was a joke."

I softened a little. "It wasn't a joke, I just feel like it was a lie. How long would you have carried on with Amber for behind my back? When would you have told me? How many more miscarriages would you have let me endure before you set me free? Would you have taken every penny out of the bank account and dragged me through debt for the love of her?" I turned to face him. "You chose her which is why you can never have me. Everything you gave her, you stole from me. Every step you took towards her was a step away from me, that's just how it is."

He shook his head but didn't say anything.

"I wish you good luck." I said, ignoring his moody expression. He had ruined his marriage over the false love of Amber and look where that had gotten him. I felt like a balance had been restored and I hadn't even had to enact any kind of revenge myself. Karma had done the deed all by itself.

I smiled my goodbye and headed down the high street towards the job centre. This way he wouldn't know what cafe I was heading to and wouldn't be able to pre-warn Amber that I knew about the two of them. Behind the job centre I could double back and still be at the cafe before they arrived, ready for the showdown.

Chapter 22

Amber and Cassie surprised me by arriving together. I thought the idea of Amber taking a loan out in her name would have been enough to split them up but I guessed with Densborough being such a small town, it would have been hard to ignore her.

I smiled at them both as they walked in. Amber looked as confident as always but Cassie looked nervous. Both smiled back and gave me hugs and I just rolled with it. No point starting as soon as they had arrived.

"Oh my God look at you," Cassie gushed. "You look like a super model." She ran her hand down my waist and I led them to the window seat that I had chosen earlier.

"The lift was out at work I have been using the stairs," I smiled.

"Did you hear about me and Grant getting back together?" Cassie beamed.

"No, but then I hadn't heard that you had split up." I smiled as her beautiful features fell. Of course I did know but that was because I was nothing short of a stalker and had kept myself in the know.

"Oh, well it has been a hectic couple of months," she mumbled.

I smiled at Amber as the lady bought over my pot of tea. I would usually be the conversation instigator. Amber liked to feel as if people were dying to hear all about her adventures, but today I was going to be aloof and ask very little.

I moved my attention back to Cassie knowing the avoidance would drive Amber nuts. "So is the wedding back on as planed?"

Cassie's featured lit up. "Well, yes but postponed. Didn't you get the second invite?"

I shook my head and she magically produced an invitation out of her bag and handed it across.

I thanked her and sipped my tea. There was no way I was going to attend this wedding.

Amber said nothing and I wondered if Scott had got to her after all.

"So are you here for the funeral?" Cassie asked looking uncomfortable at having to force the conversation.

"No, I have just seen the family. I'm just passing through."

"Have you seen Scott?" Amber finally spoke.

I nodded but said nothing.

"Shame about his sister. I'm sure it must have been a shock," Cassie frowned.

The lady came to bring them their lunches and I took the opportunity to look at them both properly. Cassie looked the same as she always did and I imagined her wedding day she would look exactly the same. Blonde hair in tight curls, full make-up on and tanned to an inch of her life. Amber, on the other hand, had made a bit too much of an effort. She was wearing a floral skater dress and shiny black tights. Her make-up was full and streaky around the edges and for the first time I was entirely grateful that Ruby had done mine.

"She was ill for a long time, they knew it was coming. I didn't know her that well as she lived in Canada."

"And were they okay about you not going?" Cassie's eyes widened.

"Why wouldn't they be? I had only met her a couple of times." I sipped my tea. I knew what I was saying made sense but I still felt a mixture of anger for having to defend my decision not to go and guilt because part of me did believe I would have been expected to be there.

"I said I would go," Amber stared boldly into my eyes. "It's a community thing."

Ah a community that I was no longer a part of.

"I didn't realise that you knew her." I stared back with equal force.

"I don't, but I thought in your absence Scott might need the support." she shifted uncomfortably and I enjoyed the view.

"Oh, Scott told you that I wasn't going did he?" I put down my cup to give her my full attention.

"I have seen him a couple of times at the gym," she shrugged. "I thought you might come down and reconcile now he has inherited some money," she said.

Clever girl, this was her fishing to see if he had money or not. I thought for a moment. I didn't want Scott, I knew that for a fact but did I want him to be happy with Amber? The truth was no matter how far I had come or how grown up I thought I was, I didn't want Amber to be happy at all. I had toyed with the notion of just sitting here listening to the two of them go on about their exciting non-stop lives but something had shifted inside of me. Now all I wanted to do was brag. I wanted Amber to know how much I learnt, how wonderful Ryan was and more importantly how little I had thought of them since I had left but I reeled it in. One step at a time.

"I think he had inherited some but not very much. Knowing Scott, it certainly won't last long." He could have inherited Buckingham Palace for all I care, nothing would make me want him back.

"Not enough to quit work and buy several Ferrari's then?" Cassie looked at Amber with a smirk on her face, clearly this had been discussed.

"I didn't ask. What are you two doing now? Zusak gave me the impression that you both quit." A little white lie.

They shared a look. "Well, I got fired actually." At least Cassie was honest. I wouldn't expect the same from Amber, I was sure of it.

"What for? I got the impression they were well short staffed." I put my best surprised face on.

"I think after you left they realised how much you actually did and how little I did." Cassie shrugged like it was no big deal.

Amber shot her an annoyed look. "Well, they should have known what was in your job description and what was in hers," she said, nodding towards me as she spoke.

"I work in the bookies now," Cassie shrugged. "The money isn't as good but I think it has given me and Grant the space we needed for our relationship."

"What have you been doing?" Amber tried to change the subject so she wouldn't have to answer. No way was I going to let her control this conversation.

"I have been really lucky, so why are you not at the hospital anymore?" I kept eye contact despite her fiddling with her phone in her bag.

"I got stitched up. I did nothing wrong and am in the process of seeking legal action." She didn't look up from her bag.

"Sounds intense," I smirked. "But if you have done nothing wrong then you have nothing to worry about have you?"

"They said she ordered in drugs which isn't even her job," Cassie said without thinking and Amber shot her another look.

"Oh I think Dr Zusak mentioned something about that. He didn't say who it involved but that the staff in question didn't realise about the CCTV camera's and some fingerprint evidence left on documents." I shook my head as if my memory was cloudy. "Didn't realise it was about you," I shrugged. "Nothing to worry about though, if you didn't do it. The document is not going to have your fingerprints on it if you never touched it." I smiled my best reassuring smile and relished the worried look on her face.

"Exactly," Cassie concurred. "So enough about our sorrowful, depressing lives, what have you been doing with yourself? I expected Grant to say you were going back to the hospital, they were going to offer you a huge pay rise."

"No, I did work for a bit at a hospital near Primrose Hill for a while but I have just been offered a full time position as a PA at Emerson's magazine. I worked there when I first arrived in London, I love it."

Amber's eyes lit up like a Christmas tree and I mentally high fived myself. "You totally have to get me a job." She practically leapt over the table.

Half a year ago this would have been the most amazing idea in the world to me but now I could think of nothing worse. "It's a cut throat industry." I remarked not knowing what else to say other than 'Hell no.'

"What?" She looked offended. "I would totally fit in, look at me."

I did look at her. Her blues eyes widened to their maximum capacity and her contoured face was glowing with the idea of a glamorous lifestyle.

"What do you do there?" Cassie asked, clearly not noticing that this was an 'All about Amber' moment.

"Mail, phone calls, run messages through the departments. I love the photography section, it is an amazing experience and the pay is surreal."

"Oh my God," Amber pulled up Emerson's on her phone. "I need this job, you must get me an interview," she grabbed my hand. "I could live with you for a while, it would be a fab girly time."

Cassie hunched her shoulders as if this was a dream that she could play no part in but Amber was clearly arranging the whole thing in her head at lightning speed.

"There are no jobs going." I said bluntly, wondering how to confess all my sins. "And I don't want to live with you. I'm really happy with my life exactly the way it is."

"What! We had an amazing time when we lived together in college," Amber frowned.

"Yes, but that was back when we were friends." I looked her straight in the face. "I haven't heard from you in ages. You didn't return any of my calls or messages."

"Well, it has been hectic here, I am being dragged through court." Her lip quivered.

"Well, I have been in a coma." Okay so it was only three days but that wasn't the point. She had every opportunity to make contact and she didn't.

"I did wish you well on Facebook," she sulked as if that solved everything.

"Hello, who is that?" Cassie was distracted by someone out of the window.

I looked up and saw the perfection that was Ryan walking towards us.

"I recognise him from that eligible bachelor list we looked at the other week." Amber straightened up and started combing her hair with her fingers. "How do I look?" She turned to Cassie who just shrugged.

"That is Ryan Emerson," I said as casually as I could manage. "He is a friend of Josh's. He was at my wedding, remember?"

"You know him?" Amber's eyes widened in disbelief. "Is he single?" She asked not talking her eyes off him as he entered the cafe.

"No!" I chuckled as he sauntered over and planted a kiss on my lips.

"How long are you going to be?" He asked totally ignoring Amber and Cassie.

"I can be ready whenever," I smiled.

"I just have to drop off some paperwork to the solicitors around the corner so how about we leave in fifteen?" He glanced at his watch. I didn't know what he had planned but I did know it involved a tight schedule.

"Perfect," I smiled and watched him walk out.

Amber's eyes followed him down the street then turned on me in disbelief. "Really?" She asked in a manner that wasn't obvious if she was impressed or disgusted.

"He's gorgeous," Cassie smiled. "How did you nab him?"

"I thought you would get back with Scott. You didn't waste any time did you?" Amber sulked.

"Like I told Scott, at least I waited until we split before I moved on." I looked at Amber whose featured had darkened into a brooding storm. "I really don't understand what made Scott think I would ever take him back. He was so deluded at lunch."

"Maybe you should have taken your hunk with you that would have soon got the 'no' message across," Cassie laughed, but Amber was dwelling on something. I knew this face, she would go over the conversation in her head before she let it out so her attack would be maximum effect.

"I didn't realise Scott would want you back. I thought that was the point of the divorce." She placed her hands into her lap and straightened her back, she was regaining control.

"I thought it was clear too but apparently not. He said he thought that the time apart would have made me fonder and forgiving." I raised my eyebrows in disbelief.

"I would never forgive an affair," Cassie blurted out.

"I have moved on. I have never been happier and I hope he can accept what he did and if he has any regrets then that's all his fault not mine."

"Last time I saw him he said he had never been happier," Amber cut in.

"I hope so," I shrugged. "Either way it means very little to me as long as he knows we are never getting back together. I don't want anything to do with his smug treacherous face."

"That's a bit harsh, his sister has just died." Amber shook her head unable to believe my insensitivity.

"I can't bear it when people don't take responsibility for their own actions. If you act in a certain way then it affects things around you. It's the butterfly effect."

Amber shook her head.

"Oh, you think this is rubbish?" She nodded so I continued. "Okay, so why did Cassie lose her job?" I pointed to Cassie and she straightened up.

"Because her boss didn't appreciate her," Amber said.

"Wrong, no offence, Cassie lost her job because she did sod all *all* day. She planned a wedding, she took an extra hour at lunch and she painted her nails when she was supposed to be working." I shrugged at Cassie. It wasn't personal. "Being engaged to the boss gave her a certain amount of leeway but at the end of the day someone needed to do that work."

"You shouldn't have left then, maybe it is all your fault," Amber said triumphantly.

"Why should I be paid peanuts to do two people's jobs? Besides I was made redundant, I didn't quit," I waved my hands to present my case.

"You could have stayed," Cassie whispered.

"I was treated badly and I did something about it. I accepted my payout and got a better job, a much *better* job," I smiled. "I was given the impression that I wasn't needed."

"I think they regretted that decision," Cassie laughed. "I am surprised they kept me for so long really."

"You shouldn't put yourself down." Amber rubbed her arm. "They have missed us both, I'm sure. That will teach them."

"And let's look at the fact that you are being dragged through court." I turned to Amber and she looked defiant. "If you hadn't have taken loans out illegally in other people's names they wouldn't have arrested you." Her eyes grew wide and she went to butt in but I waved her silent. "Then let's look at why you were fired, as if the fraud against you wasn't enough, you forged your boss' signature." I pursed my lips together. "Your life is the way it is now because of the choices you have made, no one is to blame but yourself."

"You've changed," Amber huffed as if I was the villain.

I saw Ryan's car pull up in a space opposite. My fifteen minutes must have been up.

"I *have* changed but then I had my entire life swept from under my feet." I slowly put on my jacket. "I discovered my husband was having an affair and I was heart broken. I thought it couldn't get any worse but I read his messages, well actually I cloned both of your phones."

I nodded toward Amber so it was perfectly clear. "I then learnt that not only was he shagging my best friend behind my back but together they had forced me to miscarry."

Cassie gasped but Amber just looked defiant as if this was all common knowledge, no big deal.

"I told Dr Zusak that you had forged his signature and I also sent out your loan documents to all the people you tried to steal from."

"You bitch," Amber spat, rising to her feet.

"*I'm the bitch?* You took everything away from me and lied to my face the whole time. I never did anything to you and you have made it quite clear that you never even liked him."

"I did like him. I do," she flustered.

"Good because he is all yours," I glanced at Ryan and the girls followed my gaze.

"I see." Amber's face was now red with fury. "You have moved on. You're much too good for this town. Well, I'm not sorry for any of it."

"Good, well if I am asked to bear witness at your court case then that is the statement I will pass on."

I handed Cassie my regret card for her wedding that I had written on the train. "I'm sorry I won't be attending your wedding because I no longer consider us friends." Cassie looked crestfallen but I didn't back down. "You knew she was sleeping with my husband and you laughed at me behind my back." She shook her head. "You went in my bag and gave Scott my keys so he could take the car, no thought at all about how I was getting home. Don't shake your head because I read all the txt messages about it. I don't call that friendship and that is not the kind of person I want to associate with anymore, though I do wish you the best of luck."

I grabbed my bag and turned to Amber. "Sorry I can't stay and chat more about what awesome friends you are as I have just bought a plot of land really cheap and need to go have a look at it." Her face fell. "It's just on the edge of town, you might know it." I saw the onset of tears building in her eyes. She wasn't sad that I knew about her treachery or that our friendship was over. She was sad because I had bought her land and that despite her best efforts she hadn't been able to afford to keep. I turned to face her for a final blow, "Oh and by the way, that's what it feels like when someone swoops in out of nowhere and steals your dreams. Have a nice life."

I swept my bag onto my shoulder and left towards Ryan. He held open my car door and kissed my cheek as I settled into my seat.

"How was it?" Ryan asked, pulling away.

"More or less how I thought it would be. Scott had left his phone at home so hadn't been able to warn Amber about my knowledge. I think I had a bit too much fun."

We picked up the flowers for Aunt Maureen and drove to her cottage. Just driving away from the high street was exhilarating. I knew it was a cliche but I did feel too good for this backstabbing town, I had found something better. A better man in my life, a better job and better friends, not that any of these things were that hard to do. I couldn't even understand how I had ever been happy here. It was mind boggling.

I smiled at Ryan who was still in his suit and he flashed a bright smile back and my stomach flipped. I was exactly where I wanted to be.

There was a note on Aunt Maureen's door saying she had gone to bingo, could I call back in a couple of hours.

Ryan shrugged. He was happy either way. I however, was itching to leave, every second I remained in Densborough the heavier I felt.

I left the flowers on the doorstep with the 'Glad you are feeling better' card and didn't look back. I hadn't been particularly looking forward to the visit anyway it was more something that I felt like I had been expected to do but I needed to let that go. My dad should have been the one looking after me and Josh if she had a problem with the responsibility that had been forced upon her then it was his fault not ours.

I pulled my phone out and text Josh. I hadn't heard from our dad in years but no doubt Josh would have contacted him about the engagement.

"Are you alright?" Ryan's hand crept across to give my knee a squeeze and I nodded. "I worry when you are quiet," he smiled, keeping his eyes on the road.

"I feel great. Like there is no unfinished business," I breathed deeply. "I feel really refreshed."

"Do you want the roof down?"

"No thanks," I laughed. "It's a bit too fresh."

We drove an hour out before I realised we were not heading back to London. "Where are we going?" I interrupted his ideas for the job sharing at the magazine.

"Another hour away. I told you it's a surprise weekend away with me. What more could you want?" He smiled.

"An idea for a plot of land you have just bought out of spite."

"What would restore the balance?"

"A weekly bonfire containing nothing but Scott and Amber's photographs," I suggested.

The money from the Louis Vuitton bag had made me uncomfortable. I needed to direct the rest of the money somewhere good to help alleviate some of the guilt and to some extent, helping Gerald had done that. I hadn't needed him to make the call really. Josh's or Ryan's voices wouldn't have been recognised by Amber, should she have listened to who made the call. The point was to make myself feel less guilty about what I had done. I had committed a crime and stole from some scumbags but it was just a coincidence that they were unsavoury. They could have just as easily been an old couple annoyed at hospital parkers continuously blocking their drive to save a couple of quid on car parking.

I could just sell the land on. I'm sure there were developers around that wanted land. The only problem with Densborough was that there were not enough people to buy the houses. 'Help Wanted' signs were up all through town. Business' were trying to thrive but the majority of people were gaining their qualifications and escaping.

I closed my eyes and started thinking up some ideas.

I wasn't sure when I had nodded off but Ryan shook me awake a while later. "We're here," he smiled broadly, helping me out of the car.

I put on my sunglasses until my eyes had adjusted to the sun. We were at a large farm house. Chickens ducked under the gate trying to escape a little girl wearing a pretty party dress and bright red wellingtons boots.

"Charlotte!" I turned to see Gerald striding towards us. He opened his arms and pulled me into a hug. "And this lucky man must be Ryan," he let me go and shook Ryan's hand. The little girl gave up on chasing the chickens and came to investigate us.

"This is my granddaughter, Marie," Gerald smiled. "There are two more mulling about. Believe it or not, this is the shy one," he laughed as Marie latched on to Ryan's leg.

A young woman came out of the house wiping her hands on her jeans. I guessed her to be a similar age to myself and yet here she was with three children already and I noticed that I felt glad. Before if I had seen young mothers I had been saddened remembering the loss of my own, but for the first time ever I knew that I hadn't been ready before. If Scott had been unfaithful and left me with children I don't think I could have been as strong.

She introduced herself as Annabel and did the customary double take at the sight of Ryan, even happily married mothers were struck by his handsome face. My insides danced. This guy was all mine. He stood proudly beside me, holding my hand and it seemed surreal. This was the first time we had presented ourselves as a couple and I liked the way it felt.

"This house is amazing," Ryan remarked as Annabel led us inside for coffee and cake.

"Thanks. I needed the space for my cake making business and Pete needed the barn for his sculpting. It was a ruin when we bought it, the work is never ending."

The kitchen was quaint with red gingham touches on the seat covers and jam pots giving it the quintessential country cottage feel.

I flicked through her cake design books as she set out the tea things and admired the sheer artistry that went into a cake. "These are amazing," I said lingering on a five tiered cake that had a sugar paste peacock draped down the left hand side. "These must take forever."

She chuckled. "It is a labour of love. Are you two married?"

"Not yet," Ryan answered before I had even digested the question.

Not yet? Did that mean it was something he had thought about? He could have simply said *no* we hadn't been together that long it really didn't need explaining.

I downplayed my smile and moved my attention to Gerald. "Tell me everything that I don't already know."

"Well, my daughter insisted that I move in with them until I find my feet." He rubbed her back as he spoke.

"As long as you like Dad, there's plenty of room." Annabel swooped down and rescued Ryan's leg from Marie's grip.

"I like that man," Marie sulked as she was taken through to the other room.

"You don't even know that man," Annabel said sternly. "He could hate Disney for all you know."

Annabel returned shaking her head.

"I have been working as a teaching assistant for a school down the road and doing some courses to brush up a little," he said.

"They couldn't believe it when he said he was homeless only a few months ago. They did a bit about him in the paper." Annabel handed over the paper.

"I didn't give your full name as didn't know if you would approve," Gerald smiled.

I read the article and out of the corner of my eye saw Marie sneak back in. "Do you like Frozen?" She whispered to Ryan.

"I've not seen it," he confessed.

Marie frowned.

"I have seen The Little Mermaid though and Beauty and the Beast," he offered.

She seemed visibly received. "So you do like Disney." She shot her mum a triumphant look and skipped out into the back garden to play.

"Phew, it was touch and go there for a minute." I playfully tapped Ryan's leg.

"I know, I'm so behind with the times," he laughed.

"This is really good Gerald. I'm so happy for you." I handed back the article and wiped away a tear.

"And it's all thanks to you, Charlotte. I couldn't have done it without you and there is no way I could have ever had these opportunities in London. There just doesn't seem as many bottom of the ladder jobs available for people like me."

"You are not bottom of the ladder, dad. You have qualifications you just hit hard times." Annabel leant over and tapped his hand.

"I know, I have been lucky but millions aren't," he mused.

"I hope you don't mind Charlotte but the kids have put something together for you." Annabel led us to the living where a small stage had been set.

"I am Monty," a boy of about nine declared in a loud clear voice.

"And I am Autumn," a girl of about seven said.

"I am Marie," Marie presented herself, mainly to Ryan.

"And we would like you to enjoy our show," Monty announced as the girls ran behind a screen.

Marie came back out wearing a long brown coat with holes in it. "I'm Granddad," she cried.

"Gerald!" Monty screeched.

"I'm Gerald," Marie said as if she hadn't slipped up. "I sleep outside and I'm cold."

"Hi, I'm Charlotte, would you like a place to stay?" Autumn came out in a pair of her mother's heels and a long beaded necklace.

"Yes please," Marie squealed and gave Autumn a huge hug.

"I know we could find your family," Autumn did a little dance and Marie hugged her again.

"I am Annabel," Monty appeared with a long brown wig on. "Come live with us."

Marie did a dance and gave Monty a hug.

Monty shoved Marie until she spoke. "I am so happy, all thanks to Charlotte. You are my hero."

The children all ran behind the screen and re-appeared carrying gifts. Monty had a massive bouquet of flowers, Autumn had a tub of chocolates and Marie had a wad of drawings re-telling the story.

We left after an hour of hugs, best wishes and floods of tears from Marie.

Chapter 23

"A nice surprise?" Ryan asked as we settled back into the car and continued driving, further away from London.

"It was a wonderful surprise, thank you." I rested my hand onto his leg. "Anymore secrets? I noticed we seemed to be heading towards Scotland rather than London."

"Well, I thought seeing as your brother is holding an engagement party tonight and is going to be surrounded by all Meg's friends and none of his own, we could make an appearance."

I squeezed his leg to show my approval. I couldn't think of a better way to spend a weekend.

Ryan pulled over after two hours of driving by a quaint little bridge with a warning about otters on it. I sat up in my seat and wondered if I would see one. I had seen an otter once in the zoo but never in the wild. I had never really thought of them as a wild animal.

I didn't get a chance to see much. Ryan grabbed my face and pulled my mouth to his.

"What was that for?" I asked when he finally released me from his grasp.

"You have belonged to everyone else all day and I have been itching to kiss you for hours." His breath was heavy and his voice patchy.

"Well, I have had to compete with the likes of Marie," I laughed. "I think she liked you a lot."

"I know, who knew huh?" He leant over and kissed me again.

"Do you want to stretch your legs? Maybe we will see an otter," I said hopefully.

Ryan looked around and shook his head. "No, I just wanted some Charlotte moments before Josh steals you from me to talk about revenge type stuff and Meg bombards you with wedding talk. It has been crazy all day and I thought I would never get the chance to say all the things I need to."

"Like what?" My heart was pounding so loud I could almost hear it thudding through my ears.

"Normal things like how happy you make me, how thrilled I am that you gave me a second chance, though I actually don't think I deserved it." He looked down at his fingers sheepishly. "I booked us a double room without thinking then felt bad because I should have discussed it with you first." He screwed his face up in a playful manner as if waiting for a punch.

"I can't think of anywhere else I would rather be," I smiled and leant back in my chair. I moved my hand and rested it back on his knee. A double room probably meant he was thinking of a sex filled weekend, but I was pretty certain tonight would be out. I was so tired it was ridiculous. I felt like I hadn't slept for a month and my mind was still working every time to process the events of the morning, let alone everything else on top. I had crammed so much into one day it hardly seemed possible. Aunt Maureen being out was a God send as it probably saved us a couple of hours, yet it was still pitch black. We had to check in before ten and then go have drinks with Josh and Meg to celebrate their engagement.

I stifled a yawn. If I fell asleep now I probably wouldn't wake up. "We should get moving. Do you want me to drive?" I felt like I should offer but really wanted him to say no. I was struggling to keep my eyes open and I hated driving in the dark, especially on unfamiliar roads.

"No, have a nap. We have over an hour to go yet and I'm sure Meg is going to be intense so you better get mentally prepared." He leant over and gave me a quick peck on the cheek then continued the journey to our double room booked hotel.

Hotel was the wrong word for the place where we were staying. It was a castle! Ryan had stayed here once before on a family holiday before his mother had started favouring holidays abroad and he had never forgotten about it.

"I'll drop the bags then come back, you can stay in the car," Ryan said, opening his door.

"What!" My seat belt was already off. I could see candles alight on the dining room tables and I was pretty sure there was a roaring fire.

"If you promise that you won't be distracted every two minutes by the interior then fine, come in," he frowned. "Otherwise we have the whole of tomorrow."

Fair point. "Okay, I'll wait in the car." I refastened the seat belt. I would be distracted, I was easily distracted. Knowing me I would sit in front of the fire and we would never get to see Josh and Meg.

Ten minutes later he was back in the car and we were following the Sat Nav to Meg's house.

Josh had messaged that they had been house hunting and that the Edinburgh area was still much cheaper than London so this was a good thing. My heart had sank a little at the text. I didn't agree with his move to Scotland but I had never voiced it and never would. I was pretty sure he would land on his feet and find a better than decent job, he always had before. He had this amazing ability to turn his hand to anything and shine, a trait I wished I had inherited. The message seemed loaded with Josh's doubts. Was he trying to convince himself that Edinburgh was better was London? It was certainly colder. Ice warnings kept lighting up the car dashboard as we drove and the journey ended up taking half an hour longer than the Sat Nav predicted.

The party was in full swing when we arrived at ten minutes past the ten ó clock schedule. Even without the Maureen stop we hadn't managed to be early.

We entered the living room and saw Meg first. She was wearing a black, figure hugging dress that had two strips of fabric barely covering her breasts and a split up the left side covering very little else. She had clearly been drinking already. Her face was pink from the wine being handed out and she was leaning over a couple showing them her beautiful ring.

Her eyes lit up when she saw us and she left the baffled couple while they were still talking. "So glad you guys made it," she smiled and pulled us both separately into big hugs, Ryan's lasting longer than mine.

"Where's Josh?" I accepted the glass of wine thrust into my hand and followed her gaze. Josh was sitting at the side of the room looking awkward with an older couple who I guessed were Meg's parents or aunt and uncle.

"Oh my God I thought you two would never get here," Josh pulled us both into a hug, mine lasting longer than Ryan's, and ushered us into a side room containing a table and chairs.

"It was a bit of a drive mate." Ryan accepted a coke and sat at the table. "How are the plans going?"

Josh shrugged. "I think I just have to turn up on the date she picks and wear what she has laid out. Though I have caused a bit of an upset by refusing to wear the kilt."

"I thought only Scottish men wore kilts, you would be an imposter," I laughed.

"I know but they have lied to some aunt Mary that I am Scottish and wanted me to keep up the charade. She is ill," he added looking sorry for himself.

"Sounds very organised and a bit stressful," I said, ignoring the wine. I was tired, dog tired and wine wasn't going to help.

"Well, we are supposed to be house hunting but it seems Meg had already set her heart on a place before I arrived and as for the wedding, I don't think men really have much of an input on the matter."

"What would you want if you did?" I asked.

"Trousers and more people I knew there." he gulped his beer. "I don't remember you being a Bridezilla when you married Scott."

"I guess we knew the same people. I had already met most of his family and he had met mine. Have you told dad?" I asked with bated breath, not wanting to get annoyed thinking about Scott. Our dad was an elusive creature. He couldn't make it to my wedding for a variety of reasons. He had injured his leg, couldn't get a flight and was ill, none of which was ever proved. He had a new wife a new family and we were almost forgotten about, getting a reply from him was a miracle in itself.

"No, I messaged him but got no reply. We are now going over the guest list so if I don't hear anything by June then he won't be getting an invitation."

"I have never met him," Meg burst into the room with Laurel by her side. "You guys are missing all the fun." She leant over and filled up my glass that only had three sips at most missing. "I don't even know why you bothered contacting him at all." She looked at Laurel and raised her eyebrows.

"Because my family is tiny and a wedding is a big deal," Josh said in monotone, like he had answered this question several times already.

"Still we really should be surrounded by only the people who matter," Meg retorted.

"My dad *does* matter," Josh snapped. "Besides you want to invite cousins of cousins that you have never met, how's that different?"

"You don't understand because you have no family. I have expectations to please everyone. You should be pleased that you don't have that pressure," she looked at Ryan for support but he just looked away. It wasn't like Josh to snap, he had the patience of a saint, especially where Meg was concerned.

"Have you had the tour?" Laurel said brightly to Ryan. She swayed her hips across the room and sat on the arm of his chair.

"No, we haven't," Ryan said, looking at me. I knew from his diary that Laurel liked him and I smiled. A good looking guy like Ryan should be used to unwanted attention and though I should have offered some kind of support, I just found the terrified look in his eye amusing.

"Come," Laurel grabbed his hand and pulled him off the chair. He looked at me again for backup so I stood. Laurel gave me a warning look and for a moment I didn't know what to do, should I sit back down or follow them out?

Ryan must have sensed my hesitation because he leant over and grabbed my hand. "Let's leave these two love birds alone to discuss their wedding matters." He flashed Josh a huge grin and practically dragged me out of the room.

"How are the wedding plans going?" I asked Laurel, who was looking miffed at my continued presence.

"Fabulous. I'm matron of honour, of course," her eyes lit up. "You're the best man Ryan so you will have to walk me back down the aisle," she smiled broadly.

He squirmed. This woman seemed to frighten him more than most.

I raised my eyebrows, "They seem a little tense."

"Well, Megs has great taste and vision. Josh would have a small wedding at a registry office and honeymoon in Skegness if he had his way."

"Sounds peaceful and stress free," Ryan said, looking around. The living room was packed with young people kissing. It seemed anyone over the age of twenty-five had taken off.

"What! With all your money I would have thought you would have got married in some palace somewhere with whole streets closed down."

"It isn't really about the money, is it?" Ryan walked over to a table and poured himself another coke.

"It was kind of Ryan to bring you," Laurel remarked when he was out of earshot.

"Yes, he is all kindness." She either knew we were a couple but didn't believe it or she suspected and was testing the waters, either way, I wasn't telling her anything.

"Are you ready to go back to the hotel?" Ryan rejoined us.

"Already! You only just arrived," Laurel was appalled at the idea.

"It was a really long drive and an even longer day." He turned his back on Laurel and spoke to me, "Shall we say goodbye to your brother and meet up with them tomorrow? I'm whacked."

I nodded and followed him back towards the dinning room. Raised voices could be heard before we approached the door. Clearly these two had some issues to work through. This argument seemed to be about money and the fact that Josh hadn't found a job despite Meg's uncle offering him work on a fishing boat.

I knocked on the door and walked in. "We're going to head off, it was a really long drive." I walked over and gave him a hug. "Are we meeting somewhere tomorrow for lunch?"

Josh nodded and whispered something to Ryan. Josh stood and led me out past Laurel who was animatedly texting into her phone.

"Is everything alright?" I asked rubbing his arm.

"Overwhelming, but I guess that is to be expected. Can you hand in the keys to my apartment to the estate agents please." He placed his keys into my palm and his fingers lingered there for a moment.

"You could have just rented it out, you know, it would have been good extra income."

"I know but Meg said that selling the apartment showed that I was committed to her and the relationship," he frowned.

"There is no rush to prove anything," I tried to smile but the annoyance was taking over. "Just because you can afford a massive wedding doesn't mean you should and your money is still your money until you are married, she has no right to spend it yet."

"She has a planner, you should see it. Our unbuilt house is designed, our children have already been named. It is like I'm a robot that has already been programmed. I can see the path laid out before me and while it isn't unpleasant, I would still rather I had some say in something about the way it all pans out."

"Perhaps you should talk a little more before anything is booked. Make sure you are both on the same page." Or even reading from the same book.

"We need to leave," Ryan sounded urgent. He took my arm and nodded towards the door.

"See you tomorrow," I hugged Josh again. "I'll message you in the morning."

Ryan patted his arm and frogmarched me outside and into the car.

"Where's the fire?" I laughed as the engine started before I even had the chance to buckle up.

"Meg just kissed me," Ryan said, matter of factly.

"What?"

"You need to tell Josh. There is no way I can bring something like that up," he looked white as a sheet.

"What happened?"

"She started talking about vision and how we had the same mindset and how much of a better couple we would be if things were different. She mentioned the fact that Laurel had a boyfriend but was still going to go after me just because she always wanted what Meg wanted," he shot me a look. "I don't know if she means generally as in happiness or marriage or me," he shrugged. "I should have expected it, she was being weird, but I didn't. She just leant in and tried to put her tongue down my throat," he juddered.

Laurel, I had expected to come on to Ryan and for some reason I was okay with that, perhaps because I knew Ryan didn't like her and I knew how forward Laurel could be, but Meg was a different story.

I was angry. It wasn't because she had kissed Ryan. I was pretty certain he was mine now through and through, but it was because she had tried to cheat on Josh and he deserved better.

"Okay I'll deal with it." I gritted my teeth trying to remain calm. I thought about ringing Josh but decided a text might be easier for him to digest.

I wrote

Josh, Meg just kissed Ryan. You need to have a word with her. If she isn't happy now she isn't going to be happy later. Sorry. See you tomorrow.

What else could I say?

A text came back about twenty minutes later.

I know. I just walked in on her and Laurel arguing about it. I also have your Rob machine, don't forget. Text you tomorrow x

Cracks were appearing but at least they could call it off or iron things out before things really got out of hand.

"How hard do you think it would be to get Josh's place back?" I asked as we pulled in to the castle grounds.

"He can always stay at mine or yours if you would rather move in with me," he smiled and parked up.

"I just feel so helpless," I checked my phone incase he had text again.

"Some relationships are better long distance." He grabbed my hand and led me into the foyer. "Close your eyes, this tour needs to wait until tomorrow. You look ready to drop."

I closed my eyes despite the urgency to take it all in. "I hope it is better than the Laurel tour," I snickered.

"Ha ha, yes, that was the worst tour ever. She knew we were together, Josh told her. That woman has no scruples."

I felt the lift surge upwards causing my stomach to flip. I opened my eyes to avoid the sick feeling that was building up.

"Ooh pretty," I said, admiring the walnut finish in the lift.

"The whole place is pretty awesome, you will see. Let's get an early night and make an early start." He reached over and kissed my cheek.

I was dog tired and had worried that he would hint for sex. I had mixed feelings about being let off the hook. On one hand having sex with him again was all I had thought about since the one and only time in his office, but on the other hand I could barely open my eyes and knew that anything we did with me in this state would be sub standard. When it happened again, it needed to be epic.

The bedroom was amazing. The carpet was a thick cream pile that swallowed your feet up when you walked on it. I quickly took off my shoes and savoured the luxurious feeling under my feet. The bed was a dark wood four poster with a matching chaise longue at the bottom. I walked around the room, taking it all in. By the window there were two tub chairs around a dark wood table. Ryan had already placed a laptop and a notebook by the table and it made me wonder whether he had some work to do over the weekend, I hoped not. There was a sheepskin rug in front of the fireplace and I would happily spend the next two days laying there with him, doing nothing until it was time to leave.

"Bathroom is all yours," Ryan said as I was running my fingers over the intricate wood detailing around the fireplace. "This is the best room that they have," he stepped up behind me and wrapped his arms around my waist. I felt his lips create a wet trace across my neck and even though I was dog tired I would have quite happily let him undress me and have his wicked way. But he pushed me gently toward the bathroom and started removing the army of pillows that were invading our bed.

I quickly washed and brushed my teeth. I could have undressed in the bedroom, but I was suddenly conscious of my body and used the privacy of the bathroom to whip on my pyjamas.

I yawned my way back into the bedroom.

"That says it all," Ryan laughed and held open the covers for me to get in.

"I'm sorry. Tomorrow I'm going to be the Energiser Bunny and you won't know what to do with me," I smiled.

"Well, I think we should start with a lie in and a Ryan tour."

"What time are we meeting Josh?" I nestled my head to his chest and inhaled his citrus smelling aftershave.

"One, but perhaps we will play that by ear."

"On one hand I hope they sort it out but on the other I hope he dumps her ass and finds someone better. I love Meg but all of a sudden she seems to be changing everything about him."

"I changed a lot about you," Ryan laughed.

"Like what?" I tried to lift my head up but it was heavy with impending sleep.

"Clothes, shoes, underwear," he said slowly.

"Yes, but you gave me things. You created opportunities for me to have a better life, you didn't take anything away."

"Yes, but your life could have been happier without me in it. I sometimes think that with all that happened between us, maybe you would have been happier if I hadn't have fallen in love with you and made your life hell."

I moved my head to my own pillow so I could see his face. "My life is exactly what I want it to be. We had a blip but I feel like we are stronger now. You love me and I love you, what more could we want or need?"

He reached over and kissed my mouth. "I could have been faithful," his voice was small, barely a whisper.

"Well, actually, you never asked me to be your girlfriend so perhaps we will write it off," I laughed, moving my head back onto his chest.

"I didn't know if seeing Scott again would have stirred up any old feelings. I expected you to be a bit thoughtful and perhaps a little more challenging."

"Challenging? I'm not challenging."

"You know what I mean. We have moved at lightning speed and part of me is just waiting for the fall."

I leant up and kissed his mouth. "I know what I want and it's you. Seeing Scott only confirmed to me how happy I am with my life at the moment. Densborough seemed so grey compared to the life I have in London. Scott's cocky attitude just annoyed me, and Amber's, both of them are so alike it's frightening. They both expect so much but give nothing. He expected me to forgive him and he didn't apologise. He talked to me as if I was the one who did something wrong and he doesn't even realise how badly he treated me. I think he thought that by getting a divorce it was if all the old stuff was dead and buried and I had no right to ever talk about it again. I honestly believe he had forgotten all about it already. No way was I ever going to beg for him back. It is laughable that he even expected me to still have feelings for him. Arrogant idiot."

"So what's next for you?"

"I have an idea." I smirked. "I told Amber we had bought her land. She was furious. It was immensely satisfying."

"I can imagine. Had you told her about me? She looked like she recognised me."

"She said you were in a list of eligible bachelors." I moved to face him and smiled.

"Yes, about that…" He pulled me over to him and started kissing me deeply. "Was thinking you could marry me and then I wouldn't make the list next year," he said in between breaths.

"I could do that but you would need to find a palace and close off some streets for my carriage," I laughed and moved away from him. Things were hotting up but my eyes were struggling more than ever.

"Yes, I'm sure you would be needy as hell," he joked, settling back into his pillow.

"I hadn't thought about it," I laughed and rested my head on his chest. Nothing would make me happier than being Mrs Emerson. But I couldn't think about it, I was too tired. I heard his breathing fall into a hypnotising rhythm until I too fell into a deep satisfying sleep.

Chapter 24

We woke up just in time for breakfast and I couldn't remember a time when I had slept so well.

Ryan let me have the shower first. In his mind all women took longer to shower and get ready so it made sense for him to go second. I would have argued the point but despite my rushing to be dried, dressed with make-up on before he appeared out of the shower was an epic failure. I hadn't even finished drying my hair.

Breakfast was more of a feast designed to feed a small army. It was encouraged to start with cereal and coffee, then a full English, then fruit and yogurt. By the time we had finished I felt like I could have quite happily gone back to sleep for the rest of the day and skipped seeing Josh.

I thought he would have messaged one of us this morning but he hadn't and it made me wonder how his evening had panned out. He had mentioned the Rob device which could only mean that he hadn't told Meg about them or about me using them against Scott. Maybe he hadn't trusted her this whole time.

"I like Meg," Ryan said when asked. "Don't think that I don't, I just think she is the type of girl that will never be happy. I think she will always be looking for the next bigger, better thing."

Meg had always seemed sweet and non-demanding to me and it made me wonder what side to Meg he had seen that I hadn't. "I know she likes designer clothes but I never really thought of her as a gold digger, if that is what you are implying."

"No, I don't think it is really about the money." Ryan raised his hands in defence. "I just think she always wants proof of how important she is and words and simple gestures aren't enough for her anymore. I think she likes London but she needed Josh to take risks to prove his love for her. It made no sense to sell his London place but he did it for her. I feel like he has lost a bit of himself to make this relationship work."

"I guess," I agreed. Josh had never really been a push over. I had presumed the move this far away from everything he knew was a well thought out plan that would come up trumps somewhere along the line.

"Let's explore." We abandoned the half drunk coffee and set off to explore, my camera in hand.

Every room was grander than the last but the library was my favourite. The furniture was green leather with walnut wood trim all situated around a grand fireplace with two candelabras resting on the mantlepiece. Every time I lingered on an item Ryan would ask me what I liked about it. The interior design part of him seemed to never switch off. It turned out that we liked similar things. We both liked the old fashioned wood details like the dado rails and window shutters. We both adored fireplaces and the heavy mantlepieces that surrounded them and this castle had it all in abundance.

"What about books?" Ryan asked as I was photographing the long tree lined drive way.

"What about them?" I replied.

"Hard back or paperback?"

"Hard back with old fashioned covers with gold font titles," I smiled and packed up my camera.

"Nice, good answer," He swung me around to face him and kissed me.

"How long do we have before meeting Josh?" I asked as my fingers untucked his shirt, searching for skin.

"Hours." We kissed again only stopping when a family came out of the castle making more noise than humanly possible.

"Hours?" I frowned.

"Okay about one hour to be precise," he smirked and led me back inside to our bedroom.

"For the record," I said an hour later after we had made love. "I would like the love you have for me proven that way every time."

"Deal," he leant over and kissed my head while putting on his socks.

"We are going to be so late now." I quickly text Josh blaming the photography. We were supposed to meeting him and Meg to discuss wedding arrangements but I wondered if that was still on. Would he forgive her?

The cafe was empty when we arrived. I rang Josh but he didn't answer. "Don't worry about it," Ryan said, ordering cakes that I wasn't hungry for.

"They are probably talking it through," I said, checking the time on my watch. "Do you think I should ring Meg? I could pretend that I don't know anything."

"They're here." Ryan nodded towards the door.

Josh and Meg entered holding hands as if nothing ever happened. I noticed Ryan frown and I had to admit his disapproval was starting to wear off on me. If Meg did need constant reassurance, when would she stop testing my brother? It would have to end somewhere.

Nothing was mentioned about the kiss. It was really as if nothing had happened. Wedding dates were discussed and Ryan's role as best man was laid out, all by Meg. Josh smiled and said nothing.

"You two would love Edinburgh, you should move here," Meg smiled as we finished our coffees.

"But my job is in London. It would make no sense whatsoever to move here," Ryan snapped.

"But don't you want to be closer to your friend?" Meg shot Josh a strange glance. "Josh has nobody up here."

"He should move back to London then," Ryan raised his eyebrows. "I certainly wouldn't quit my jobs, leave all my family and friends to live with anyone less than amazing."

Meg beamed. Somehow she had taken Ryan's retort as a compliment. I squeezed Ryan's leg as a warning. In two days we would be back in London away from the drama surrounding this wedding and their strange relationship.

"Oh, sorry, excuse me," Meg smiled as her phone blasted out. She rose from the table and took the call outside.

"Josh," Ryan started but Josh waved him silent. He pulled out a small phone out of his pocket and pressed some buttons until Meg's voice could be heard clearly on loud speaker.

"It was a mistake," Meg blurted out.

"You knew I liked him," Laurel snapped.

"She told me she was so drunk, she can't remember last night," Josh said. "I didn't bring up Ryan at all. I thought I would get Rob to find out the truth for me."

"He is here with his girlfriend anyway," Meg said in her soft calming tones.

"What happened anyway?" Laurel asked.

"We were both drunk and we kissed. I can't really remember how it happened." You could hear the smile in Meg's voice.

"I never kissed her," Ryan snapped.

I touched his leg in support and listened in.

"I don't believe you," Laurel snapped again. "Josh is great and you have already cheated on him with Charles and now his best man. Jesus woman, make a decision."

I glanced at Josh. Who was Charles?

Josh shook his head as if he heard the thoughts in my head. He silenced Meg's call and searched through her phone for texts to Charles. I knew he had found something when his features darkened.

"You two might as well head off," Josh whispered. It was all going to kick off now.

Ryan patted him on the shoulder and I kissed his head and we headed out of the cafe door.

"Bye, Ryan, yes it was lovely to see you again," Meg trilled as we waved our goodbyes. No mention of me, I noticed.

We had only taken a few steps when Ryan about turned and marched towards Meg. He snatched the phone out of her hand and shouted down the phone to Laurel, "Let me make it clear that Meg kissed me. At no point did I ever make a pass at her nor would I ever. I have never been even the slightest bit interested in her or you for that matter and I think it is about time that you both appreciated the men you have in your lives before you both end up alone and miserable." He shoved the phone back into a shocked looking Meg's hand. "You owe Josh a huge apology and perhaps stop being so selfish before you lose him."

Meg started to speak in her defence but Ryan waved her quiet. He turned, grabbed my hand and marched me back to the car.

"I am pretty sure that she has already lost him," I frowned. "And remind me never to get on the bad side of you."

"I know women like her. It doesn't matter how many times you say no, they always think you are secretly in love with them. I'm sorry, but your brother deserves better."

"Okay, well there is nothing else we can do. Where now?"

"John Ò Groats."

"Why?" John Ò Groats was hours away.

"You will see," He shot me a smile and I relaxed into the seat. "Sleep, you will need some energy for later."

I was tired which wasn't really a surprise. I had only gotten six hours sleep last night and though I had woken up feeling refreshed, the love making had caught up on me. I closed my eyes with the intention of a short snooze but three hours later, Ryan was shaking me awake.

"Where are we?" I asked looking around. It seemed to be some kind of sleepy seaside town overrun with cyclists and well wishers.

"John Ò Groats. The end of the Earth, well kind of," he smiled and helped me out of the car.

"What no car park to pay for?" I exaggerated my statement. "Maybe it *is* worth moving here for."

"Blinking windy though," Ryan grabbed a stray bit of my hair and tucked it back behind my ear.

I watched the cyclists take off down the hill and wondered how the hell they had managed to bike up it. There were some crazy people in this world. Once they had gone the whole place seemed deserted and eerie, like a forgotten town.

"This is what we are here for." Ryan tapped the sign. "The furthest north you can go, on the main land anyway."

"I wonder where the furthest west is?" I asked thoughtfully. Land's End was furthest south and Lowestoft was furthest East, but I had never really given much thought to what was furthest west.

"Well, we have the rest of our lives to find out." Ryan said bending to one knee.

I gasped, "Ryan!"

"I know it's too soon. I know you have been divorced for two minutes and there is probably a million things we don't know about each other. But I love you more than I have ever loved anything in my life, including my limited edition fountain pen that my father bought me from Italy for my eighteenth birthday," he smiled and continued. "I have never felt this way before and I am pretty sure that you feel the same so here, at the end of the Earth, sort of, I want to ask you, Charlotte Temple, to be my wife." He reached into his pocket and pulled out a beautiful diamond ring.

My stomach flipped. I could hear my heart pounding in my ears and for a moment I wondered if I was going to pass out.

I don't know why I was crying but tears flooded down my cheeks. So many emotions flooded through me at once, dominated by an overpowering sense of love that I had for this man that in reality, I had only just met, but felt like I had known a lifetime.

I nodded and he slipped the ring on my finger.

A round of applause erupted from somewhere and I turned to see a whole new set of cyclists waiting to have their photo taken with the sign we were hogging.

I smiled nervously and dragged Ryan off his knees into a hug. This man meant everything to me. So much more than Scott ever had. Ryan knew me, he understood me and it had taken him no time to fall into step with me. This to me, was a sign that we were meant to be.

We walked back to the car not saying a word. The ring felt heavy on my finger and I couldn't help glancing at it every opportunity I got.

"Thank you, it's beautiful," I said as we reached the car.

"As are you." he stopped me at my door and kissed me slowly. Each probe of his tongue was an erotic hint at what was to come later when we got back to our room.

"Did you tell anyone you were going to do this?" I asked in between breaths.

"I discussed it in length with my dad, who thinks you are perfect, by the way. I was going to tell Josh last night but things kind of went wrong."

I thought for a moment who I would tell. My best friends from home had fallen from grace and my new friends I hardly knew.

For a second my heart sank. Who would be my bridesmaids?

I could have asked Meg but she did just try and kiss my boyfriend or Fiancé as he was now.

An uneasy feeling crept in to my stomach.

"Are you alright?" Ryan pulled the car over.

I nodded weakly but he wasn't fooled.

"Have I rushed this? Is this too soon?" A terrified look on his face.

"No, it isn't that. It isn't you or us. We are exactly as I want us. It just dawned on me how alone I am. Who am I going to tell?" I quickly totted through the family. Aunt Maureen couldn't care less, Steven hadn't been forgiven yet about his speediness to get me fired over the money and Melissa was always too busy with her children to communicate with me.

"If Amber and Cassie meant that much to you, perhaps you could just forgive them." A smile crept across his face and I knew he was joking.

"And perhaps Scott could give me away." I leant back in my seat and closed my eyes.

"It doesn't have to be a big wedding," he added. He started up the car again.

"When were you thinking?" I asked and he pulled over again in the next lay-by. "We are never going to get home at this rate," I laughed.

"I love you, you know that don't you?"

I nodded.

"I really want to start a life with you, a house with a garden, the children, perhaps a dog. I want it all with you," he ran his fingers over my cheek bone causing me to shudder. "I would be happy if we got married here, in some Scottish castle, today."

"Wearing jeans!" I mocked outrage at what he was wearing.

"There should be a notepad and pen in the glove box." He leant over and grabbed it out. "Start a list of the things you want and the things you don't and we will start from there."

"I don't need any streets closed down," I smiled, trying to lift the mood.

"Glad to hear it. I can pull off most things but I wasn't too sure about that."

"Do you need me to drive?" I hadn't driven the whole way and it had been non stop driving since we had left London.

"No, we will drive for two hours then stop for a coffee somewhere." He started up the engine and set off again down the hilly road.

"How the heck do the cyclists make it up here?" I watched in wonder as a row of cyclists were forcing themselves up the hill.

"What is more amazing is that they usually have biked for seven days from Land's End," he flashed me a smile. "I think John Ò Groats to Land's End would be better. Down hill."

"It's incredible." Not one of them had gotten off to walk.

"You are digressing." Ryan reached across and tapped the empty note pad. "Start with the venue. This country or abroad?"

I liked the idea of Hawaii but a girl from Densborough had said getting married abroad had worked out dearer in the long run. Another party had to be arranged when she got home and all the same people had to be fed again. Though thinking about it cost probably wasn't going to be an issue. Not like when I married Scott. The guest list was whittled down ruthlessly, I'm surprised Josh had been allowed to bring Ryan.

We stopped for coffee.

Josh had messaged to say things were back on track with Meg and we decided not to mention our engagement until later. I had a feeling Meg wouldn't like the idea of being upstaged though Josh would be fine.

Taking the ring off when we had set out to meet them for dinner had been tough.

"Do I have to take it off?" I asked Ryan as I admired the way the diamond caught the light and made fleeting patterns on the bedroom wall.

"It was your idea to keep it quiet." His arms reached around me from behind and he kissed my neck.

"I don't think Meg will take it well."

"This isn't about Meg." He spun me around and cupped my chin. "We have to tell Josh some time."

"Perhaps you could tell him quietly, at dinner," I mused. "And I think their wedding should be first."

"Why are you always thinking about others first?"

"I just don't want her to think I am stepping on her toes."

"We will tell them tonight. Put the ring in your bag." He kissed my forehead and crossed the room to put on his shoes.

We got in a taxi and the idea of the ring in my handbag weighed heavy on my mind. It didn't belong there. I looked at my bare finger and Ryan smiled when he caught me doing it.

"I'm glad you like the ring." He linked my hand into his. "Some women like to choose it themselves. The sales assistant was most appalled that I hadn't brought you in."

"Really! I would have thought most men chose the ring to surprise the love of their lives."

"It was the only ring that I could see you wearing. It is bold and simple at the same time, like you," he smiled.

"Thanks, I think." I slipped it back on my finger and admired it again. It was just a symbol and I knew I should have given my reply a bit more thought but the truth was I felt like I had wasted my life prior to meeting Ryan. Everything before Ryan made no sense and yes, we had had some low points but the feeling in the pit of my stomach was in no doubt due to the strength of the love I was feeling.

I slipped the ring back into my bag and rested my head on Ryan's shoulder. Soon we would be back in London arranging our life and I couldn't wait. The only uneasy feeling I had now was for Josh.

Josh and Meg seemed to be having a heated discussion when we arrived which they played down on seeing us walk down the path.

Meg swooped over and planted us both with a kiss on each cheek and I wondered whether she would apologise for the other night but she didn't. She acted like it had never happened but every now and then I caught her looking at Ryan.

Josh noticed too. He shifted uncomfortably in his seat. "Charlotte can I have a quick word outside please?" Josh asked.

Ryan looked up startled. The idea of being left alone with Meg terrified him. I patted him on the back in support and followed Josh out of the restaurant with a smile on my face.

"How are things?" I asked as he started to pace.

"Not good. I have read all her messages. She implies to Laurel that she has feelings for Ryan stemming from the day you went missing from work and we were all searching for you," he paused and shook his head. "Nothing happened, but I can tell something is different. I think Ryan is right she is testing me, seeing how far she can push me before I break."

"You're not the breaking kind," I added thoughtfully. He had already quit his job, sold his apartment and moved hundreds of miles to a different country. What else could she ask him to sacrifice.

"She is now mentioning things like she wants kids, then she doesn't want kids it is like she is waiting for my opinion so she can contradict it."

"Are you happy?"

"I was when I was clueless to how little I meant," he patted my shoulder. "I don't mean to talk to you about this but I have no one else."

"You have Ryan."

"Yes, but he would just protest his innocence and couldn't advise me without bias." Josh looked into the window of the restaurant.

"I can't advise you without bias either. You are my brother. The only real family I have left. If Meg is looking for something that you can't give her then end the relationship before there are children involved."

Josh nodded his head. "I want to end it. I tried last night but she somehow talked me out of it like I had made the mistake, which is ridiculous because I used the Rob device to read her messages. She had an affair with an estate agent about two months ago."

"So why don't you just say someone told you about it?"

"I could do. I need something big something that brings out the worst in her so I can back off a bit and not be manipulated."

"Ryan proposed to me this morning," I smiled and pulled out the engagement ring. "That might make her a bit high maintenance." I remembered the conversation we had had over the importance of the invitations. I knew another bride on the scene, potentially stealing her attention, would drive her crazy.

Josh pulled me into a hug. "Congratulations." He pulled my hand towards him and inspected the ring. "Wow! It's blinding."

"We were going to tell you both but we thought your wedding should be first so decided to wait a while. We didn't want either of you to feel like we were stealing your thunder."

"Okay, I'm ready," Josh said taking my arm and leading me back into the restaurant.

"For what exactly?"

"For you to steal my thunder."

The evening for me and Ryan was an awkward nightmare but Josh seemed to thrive. Meg, as planned, was clearly piqued at the idea of having to share her wedding planning. The more she drank the more unreasonable she got. By the time we left she had planned a horse drawn carriage and twenty bridesmaids. She had asked for an extra napkin and frantically scribbled down ideas as if having them in writing secured her ownership of them. Luckily I didn't want a horse drawn carriage and God knows were I would have found twenty friends to be bridesmaids.

We couldn't leave soon enough.

"Now you have a choice. We can go back to the castle and leave early in the morning or leave now and wake up in our own bed."

"Haven't you driven enough?" John Ò Groats had been an epic trip.

"Yes, but it has been a really long weekend already. Don't you feel a little overwhelmed?"

"Yes, but my camera doesn't," I smiled. "I would like to pack up and spend tomorrow looking around for inspiring things of beauty."

"I'm looking forward to seeing all these pictures."

"I wouldn't get too excited about it. My strategy is to take loads of pictures of the same thing and delete the rubbish ones. One is bound to come out well," I laughed.

"Maybe you should do a course," he offered. "You could probably do an evening course or maybe something online."

"I might just do that," I smiled as we drove down the long tree lined driveway of the castle. Only the bits with Meg and Josh had been stressful. The rest of the trip had been a joy. The scenery was amazing, and the weather had been pretty good considering it had been forecasted to rain.

"I'm glad you are in a good mood because I have something to tell you that might not go down well." Ryan held open my car door.

"Really!" My mind searched for something really bad and Alice was the worst thing that sprang to mind. I had told him that I didn't want to know anything about her or her whereabouts and so far he had honoured that request.

He took a deep breath. "I bought a house, I thought we could move in together," he said, squinting as if waiting for a slap.

"A house?" It didn't sink in.

"A real house with stairs and a garden. I have been renovating it for a couple of years and was supposed to sell it on, but someone has just made me a ridiculous offer to rent out my penthouse but needs to know straightaway so I had to make an on the spot decision."

"When?" Was this before or after the ring I wondered?

"After our first date, there is something else."

I prepared myself now for the bad news. The house was a surprise but not totally unpleasant.

"I knew you would say yes." He motioned to the ring and pulled me into a deep kiss right outside the front doors of the hotel in full view of the diners.

Chapter 25

"You can see now why I couldn't sell it on," Ryan said, walking me around our new home.

I tried to nod in agreement but everything was so overwhelming. I had given my notice in on my apartment and we had agreed not to move in until it had been finalised and that day had arrived.

"St John's Wood Underground is within walking distance, Primrose Hill is just over there to the left and look at this." He opened a door which led to a set of stairs down to a basement. "These are quite rare."

"It looks expensive," I added. The parquet floor was beautiful but then everything about the detached five bedroomed house was extraordinary.

"You need to stop thinking about money. When we marry you will be worth half of what I am worth and you will learn to shop."

"You would be really stupid to marry without a prenup. I'm not sure I want to marry someone that stupid."

"That is what I told him." Mr Emerson appeared from a room at the back carrying a toolbox. He laid down his tools and swooped me into a hug. "Luckily he actually found someone too good for him." He smiled and hugged his son. "Don't forget to show her how to set the alarm," Mr Emerson yelled, letting himself out.

Ryan grabbed my hand and led me through the kitchen where a breakfast room had been set up in the conservatory. Two patio doors opened up into the garden where bird tables had been set up. "Dad did a good job, didn't he?" Ryan sounded surprised.

"You are a family of many surprises." I kissed his cheek and walked out into the sunlight. The garden was a good size. Bigger than the garden I had with Scott in Densborough and this one teemed with life. I could hear birds nesting in the tall trees that lined the back wall and a squirrel ran up the oak tree in the far corner and disappeared amongst the branches.

"It is amazing," I remarked. I flicked on the kettle and watched as Ryan filled up the bird feeders with fat balls and Nyger seed. The extra heat from the conservatory made me feel sleepy and for a moment I wondered if this had all been a dream. A perfect house, a perfect fiancé, a perfect life.

"What are you thinking?" Ryan asked as he grabbed his coffee from the table.

"That it doesn't seem real and that it is far too beautiful for people to be in here. Maybe we should cancel our party," I smiled. I had been looking forward to my housewarming / engagement party all month but now the day was here. I wasn't really ready.

"Everything is ready," Ryan contradicted my feelings. "The spare rooms are ready for Josh, Meela, Cassie and Grant. The beer is in the fridge," he walked over to the kitchen worktop and opened a glass door. "Wine is in the designated wine cooler." He raised his eyebrows and waved to the kitchen side where layers and layers of tin serving dishes lay, covered in clingfilm. "I don't fancy eating this lot for the next three weeks if you cancel." He pulled me into a hug which always seemed to rest my nerves. "Let me show you the rest of the house and tell you my amazing ideas."

He led me into a room to the left of the conservatory. "I thought this could be your study slash photography room." He pointed to a catalogue on the white desk that ran the whole length of the room. I flicked through the pages looking at the screens and printers. I could see myself sitting here looking out the the birds on the new bird table while mounting my favourite pictures onto screens which would sit behind me.

"Nice and where is your man cave?" I put the catalogue in the top drawer of the desk and followed him out.

"Behind the garage. Not sure what a man does in a man cave though. I'm not really the messing about with tools kind of man." He grabbed my hand and I followed him around in a trance like state.

Downstairs we had a large hallway, two living rooms, a large kitchen dinner with a pantry and a utility room which was larger than the apartment I had just given up, my office and a swimming pool and gym on the right hand side. Every room made me gasp in awe of its beauty. There was something about the high ceilings and dado rails that emphasised its appeal.

"Are you regretting not looking at it sooner?" Ryan asked as I ran my hand in the warm water of the swimming pool.

"I wanted the surprise, I just wasn't expecting something so large." I walked over to the hot tub that was attached to the pool. "I mean who has a sauna, really?"

"I ran out of ideas for the space, besides I can take Josh and Grant out for lunch tomorrow and you girls can stay here and have a spa day."

I nodded. I had invited Cassie and still wasn't sure if it was a good idea or not. Grant had called and said that Cassie was heartbroken about how things had panned out and after actually speaking to her on the phone, my heart had melted a bit. Amber had no apologies and no remorse but Cassie just got swept away with a lifestyle that Amber represented and I could relate to that. So I had invited her to my party and she had accepted. I had mixed feelings about it but it was too late now. Maybe some of the friendship could be salvaged, only time would tell.

Ryan grabbed my hand again and led me on. "I have no use for the basement as yet but one of the three rooms will be for storage as we have rooms in the attic. We will have a Christmas tree, baby furniture and other stuff." He kissed my cheek and led me up the stairs where there were bedrooms and a family bathroom. Three of the rooms were ensuite and the two bedrooms in the attic shared a shower room. All were larger than any bedroom that I had ever seen.

"It was a good buy." I kicked off my shoes and sat in the sunken bathtub.

"You never asked how much we paid."

He had started using 'we' on a regular basis as if his money was already mine. Several bank cards had arrived but I had not signed them or used them.

"And nor do I want to know. It is perfect as long as you haven't gone into debt or taken loans out in anyone's names then it is all good with me."

"Actually this cost less than I could have sold my penthouse for. Twenty-five years of penthouse rent will cover it. Though I paid cash so the penthouse rent just means we will always stay afloat."

"Are you ready to see our bedroom?" He offered me his hand. "Where some of the magic is going to happen."

"Only some," I pouted out my lower lip in a mock sulk.

"Well, I think we should rule out the swimming pool and hot tub for hygiene reasons, but no other room should be ruled out."

I stopped him and pushed him gently against the hall wall and pressed my body into his. "I do really like this hall." He swung me around so I was the one pinned against the wall and he lifted my leg around his waist. "I think you will really like the bedroom more," he said.

He put his hands over my eyes and guided me to the bedroom. "You ready?" He whispered into my neck causing all the hairs to stand up on end.

"Oh my God, is that my mother's table?" I rushed over and ran my fingers over the joins.

"Yes and wardrobe," Ryan pointed to the corner. "Josh thought you would appreciate it more than Meg would, not that that is an issue anymore." Meg and Josh had split up and Josh had arrived back in London the day after we had.

I gasped looking around the room. Not only did I have my mother's hall table that Ryan had got repaired so that it looked brand-new. I also had the matching wardrobe and several other bits that Ryan had sourced from somewhere. I now had a matching dressing table, two bedside tables and a beautiful gentleman wardrobe with two drawers at the bottom. I ran my fingers over everything and Ryan just watched, amused.

I rushed over and gave him the biggest hug I could manage. "This is the best present that I have ever received."

"Well, I haven't given you children yet." He pushed me onto the four poster bed that I had only just taken notice of.

"Ooh nice bed," I remarked as his slipped off his trousers.

"I knew you liked the one in the Scottish hotel and it matched your mother's furniture." He kissed my neck while unzipping my dress. "I think I'm going to like this one better."

We showered together and then prepared for the party. Ryan had called in a catering company which I had frowned upon at the time but now saw as a Godsend. Time had run out so quickly and Josh had arrived shortly after we had showered and dressed.

"Who are we going to set him up with?" Ryan asked as Josh went upstairs to put his stuff in his room for the night.

"No one." I slapped his bottom as he peeled off the clingfilm at the central kitchen island. "Him and Meg have only been separated for two minutes."

The door bell rang and I closed my eyes to savour the sound. "Do you want me to get it?" Josh yelled bounding down the stairs. He walked back in carrying half of Meela's stuff.

"Blimey Meela, are you moving in?" Ryan joked.

"Well, you said bring swimming stuff so I brought a towel incase you hadn't bought any spares yet and I have an engagement present and house warming gift." She dumped her bags on the kitchen table. "I should have taken a cab." She walked over and hugged us both.

"We said no gifts," I frowned.

"I could have picked you up," Ryan said, pulling her into a hug.

"So could I of," Josh smiled. "I'm Charlotte's brother, Josh. We met briefly at Charlotte's flat." Meela nodded to acknowledge that she remembered him. "I'll show you to your room."

"Don't even think about it." I hit Ryan's bottom again and carried the rubbish to our new pedal bin that was already filling up fast.

"I never said a word." Ryan's smile hadn't lost any of its effect on me. Every time he flashed his pearly whites my heart rate soared and my body ached to be near him. I thought back to our love making earlier. It felt different somehow, more magical and not just because it was our first time in our new house, in our new bed, but also because it was the first time without me on the pill. We had agreed that even though the wedding was two months away we would start trying for a family before hand. If it happened straight away, two months wasn't going to affect the dress fitting at all.

Everything had fallen into place. Okay so everything had fallen apart beforehand but perhaps that had to happen to help me really appreciate the things that I had now. I didn't care about the money, though it certainly brought a lifestyle I could never have dreamed of, it wasn't about the money it was about the type of man I had chosen to spend the rest of my life with. He had thought about me at every turn. The bird table and the photography room had been for me, the bedroom furniture he had sourced to match my hall table, had been for me and I smiled about it every time I showed someone around our bedroom.

"Oh is this the table Scott broke?" Cassie asked running her hand over the top. "Looks brand new," She said doubtfully.

"Ryan had it restored," I beamed.

"It's lovely," Grant smiled. "You really fell on your feet." He circled his eyes around the room drinking it all in.

I nearly defended the fact that I was marrying a rich man but stopped myself. I didn't owe him or anyone else an explanation as to why I was marrying Ryan. I loved him and nothing more needed to be said. I bit my tongue and continued the tour.

"I'm glad you found someone to take care of you," Cassie said, running over my clothes that Ryan had transferred into my new wardrobe.

"That is what people say when you marry an older, ugly guy who is rich," I laughed. "Ryan is gorgeous and younger than me, maybe you should question what he sees in me."

"I didn't mean it like that." Cassie shook her head in defence. "It is obvious that you two are very much in love. I just meant that you seemed happy with Scott and I can see now that it wasn't the real deal. When we met for lunch I really didn't understand why you hadn't taken him back but I get it now." She blushed slightly and glanced at Grant. "I see the way you two move together and its like it is choreographed. He brushed your fingers as he walked past and you looked at him and the chemistry is clear for the whole room to see."

"It's true." Meela and Josh appeared on the landing and Meela placed a wine into my hands. "They are so hot they make the devil jealous." Everyone burst into laughter and I noticed Josh looking at Meela as she looked at me.

"Speech." A voice erupted from downstairs and we all followed the sound of the clinking glass downstairs into the kitchen that was filled with familiar faces from the magazine and a few from the hospital. Buddy and Kylie had their beers raised and Aiden and Emma had coupled up at some point unlike Ben and Freya who were avoiding each other at all costs.

Ryan stood on a chair and raised his beer bottle. "I would like to thank you all for coming and hope you use this opportunity to get to know each other as you all will be guests at our wedding in a couple of months. Josh and Meela, as best man and maid of honour, it is your jobs to look after us so tonight is a trial run of what you can expect." He grimaced as if we were both going to be a drunken mess. "We asked for no gifts yet most of you ignored that request but we thank you anyway. And I would like everyone to raise a glass to my beautiful Charlotte who has foolishly agreed to share the rest of her life with me."

"No one understands what I see in you." I shrugged and the room erupted with laughter.

"It is because *they* haven't seen me naked," Ryan laughed.

"I have," Josh interrupted, "can't be that." The room erupted again.

"Funny, anyway, thank you, not Josh, for coming. Eat, drink and be merry and hopefully this is the first party of many."

By midnight only the overnighters remained. Josh made Cassie and Meela tea while the boys continued with their beer, while I washed the work tops and loaded the dishwasher for what seemed like the hundredth time.

"How was Amber's birthday?" I asked Cassie as we all gathered with our beverages around the kitchen table.

"Oh my God, it was such a scandal," Cassie perked up. "She got this silver dress with matching shoes, it had Gucci in the label. She said she thinks Scott gave them to her but he vows he didn't, anyway, she adores this outfit. It is designer and must have cost whoever sent it to her a packet. It was all she could talk about the week leading up to her big night out. She even had one of those body wrap things to make her lose inches off her body so she could look amazing, which, of course she did." Cassie put down her tea to make full use of her hands. "We arrived at the Soho club and she was having selfies taken with everyone and uploading them to Facebook. She is telling everyone about her designer gift and how special she was and just as we were leaving the club all hell breaks lose. Her cousins were standing there with baseball bats and her aunt had receipts saying the dress is hers and that Amber stole it!" Cassie opened her eyes as large as they could go and looked around the room as if to say, 'can you believe it?'

"Her cousins were there to beat her up!" Meela exclaimed in disbelief. "Glad it is not just my family that has issues."

"Well, they didn't beat her up," Cassie added. "The police were called and Amber was taken to the station for questioning. Scott had to go give a statement because apparently he and Amber were in the house together."

Her eyes shot to mine as if realising what she had said. I saw her shoulders drop back in disappointment with herself. She hadn't wanted to mention the Amber and Scott thing, it was part of our agreement of her coming to our party. The past had to be left in the past.

I could have put her out of her misery and admit that I had seen them together at the cousins house but then that would incriminate me for a crime that I was guilty of and I was turning over a new leaf. It seemed to Cassie and Grant and perhaps, most of Densborough, that I had been the bigger person and even though I felt a stab of guilt for not being truly honest with Cassie it was a secret I was keen to keep.

"Then what?" Meela was eager to learn more about this scandal.

"He denied the whole thing, said he never set foot in the house. She claimed the dress was sent through the post but there is no record of it ever being posted through any courier companies so she had to do community service and pay damages."

"There would be a trail if it was sent to her address, these things are easily traceable," Grant added, getting up to go to bed. "She was not who we thought she was anyway."

"I think we will be together forever," Ryan whispered into my ear as we slipped into the brand new crisp sheets.

"What makes you say that?" I asked, turning to face him and waiting while my eyes adjusted to the darkness.

"I would be too frightened to leave. I dread to think of all the horrors you would line up for me," he laughed and pulled me into his arms.

"I don't think it would work on you, I have lost my element of surprise. No one in Densborough would ever think of me doing something like that, it just wouldn't enter their heads."

"Josh has been following Amber's text messages. She messaged Scott and put you forward as a suspect."

Really! Josh had not mentioned this to me. My heart sank, if I was investigated I still had the Louis Vuitton bag along with other items that might incriminate me.

"Don't look so surprised," Ryan smiled. "She is upset that you bought her plot of land and she would have heard by now that you are building the homeless shelter there. She wanted that for her dream house and she now blames you for everything."

"Do you think the homeless shelter will work?" I voiced my fears. The project was costing a lot of money with no guarantees of success.

"Yes, I think it has been well thought out and with Gerald and the magazine are out there raising awareness, I don't see how it can fail."

I turned around so Ryan was hugging my back and thought about the design that we had come up with. The idea had been on my mind since leaving Gerald's house. If there were no jobs in London then it made sense for some of the homeless people to move somewhere where there were better opportunities. Densborough had been the perfect choice after seeing all the 'Help Wanted' signs. I knew that I couldn't save everyone. Not everyone had a family waiting to welcome them with open arms like Gerald had, but if fifteen at a time could be moved into warm apartments and given the opportunity to better themselves, then somewhere down the line it would make a difference, even if it was just three people permanently off the streets. There had been a little outcry with a few people saying the scheme was just moving people off of the streets onto benefits but Ryan had made a speech weighing up the cost of training English speaking, homeless people to do our jobs against the cost of pulling workers over from abroad. It had been well thought out and finally a grant was issued to okay the project to go ahead.

"It was a really good speech, by the way." I pulled Ryan's arms tighter around my waist and savoured the warmth of his breath on my neck.

"Well, the room haven't all seen me naked."

"I meant the speech for the shelter. Thank you. I think it made all the difference."

"I think it was Gerald's speech that made the real difference and the fact that Emerson's has put over a million pounds into the charity already shows how much my dad believes in you."

"I am really happy." I turned around and pulled his face to my own.

"I'm glad to hear it Charlotte Temple and I hope to hell that I never have to face the wrath of you."

"Ha ha, I doubt you will," I pulled him to me. "I have your credit card and I'm not afraid to use it."

"That's my girl. Did you notice that Meela's bedroom door is open?"

"No, why would I notice that?" I laughed.

"Because she is in your brother's room and I thought girls didn't miss these things."

"No way." I jumped out and opened the bedroom door. Meela's bedroom was ajar and giggling could be heard from Josh's room.

"At least he has found someone a little less challenging," I whispered, sneaking back into bed like a naughty school girl who was breaking curfew.

"I think they are cute." Ryan pulled me back towards him and I relished the warmth radiating from his skin.

Every night was going to be like this one. Perhaps with a lot less people and lot less mess, but ending like this, with me warm in Ryan's arms.

It seemed hard to believe that this time last year I was living a lie surrounded by people who were supposed to have had my best interests at heart, and what was even harder to believe was how little I felt about it now. Scott and Amber seemed like a distant memory and though I missed Amber's constant life updates, Meela had proved to be an excellent best friend replacement. It was like she had spent her life in a cage and now she was free she wanted to experience everything. Every second weekend seemed to be filled with jet skiing, tubing and rollercoaster rides. Something made me think that Josh would now be a new member of that club.

Either way I had a lot to look forward to and couldn't wait for the next chapter of my life to begin.

Acknowledgements

I would like to thank my husband and daughter for supporting me while I wrote this book and for generally being quiet around the house. I would like to thank my mother for promoting it like crazy in the hope that she can retire on the earnings, good luck with that.
I would like to thank studioseast for my amazing cover design, I love it, it's perfect.
I would also like to thank Maria for the proofreading and the wine. I'm not sure which of those I appreciated more. X
To Karen for the print outs, you saved me a fortune. X
And a final thank you to everyone that has bought the book, I hope you enjoyed it.

Printed in Great Britain
by Amazon